Twilight Covenant

Whitney Hill

This is a work of fiction. Any references to real events, people, or places are used fictitiously. Other names, characters, places, and events are products of the author's imagination. Any resemblance to actual persons, living or dead, or to actual events is purely coincidental.

TWILIGHT COVENANT

Benu Media

6409 Fayetteville Rd

Ste 120 #155

Durham, NC 27713

(984) 244-0250

benumedia.com

ISBN (ebook): 979-8-9906781-0-1

ISBN (pbook): 979-8-9906781-1-8

Library of Congress Control Number: 2024910759

Cover Designer: Pintado (99Designs)

Editor: Jeni Chappelle (Jeni Chappelle Editorial)

Content Warnings

This book contains military attacks by and against a government, severe environmental and home destruction, simulated interrogation, medical experimentation, strong physical violence and gore, on-page death, discussions of mental health crises, family estrangement, swearing, slurs (not toward any real racial or ethnic group/identity), alcohol use, knife and gun violence including death by suicide, threat of sexual violence, mention of past abuse by a guardian, blood-drinking, and consensual on-page sex scenes.

For everyone who has followed this journey to the end, and for everyone who is willing to fight for the underdog.

Chapter 1

I tried to remember what it felt like for my soul not to hurt.

Troy's arm tightened around my shoulder as we glared at the laptop on my coffee table, open to a conservative news channel where Sixtus Ead had just landed a job as a commentator. We both knew we had better things to do than watch it.

Both of us also knew we didn't dare rely on second- or third-hand information for this. Not when Troy and Sixtus had nearly come to blood at the elven summit in Chesapeake over Sixtus's part in an assassination attempt on both of us.

Definitely not when we'd severed the asshole from Aether for that same action. Or when the topic he was spewing hateful anti-Otherside comments on was the mundane protests, which were escalating into violence in cities worldwide after a month of simmering, despite coordinated elven efforts to suppress or misdirect them. There had been all-out battles with the Sons of Seth or the police in several cities, with the National Guard deployed in a few cases here in the US—only to pro-Otherside counter-protests, of course—and property damage. My getting magic back had either proven to Othersiders that I was fit to lead and listen to or given Otherside enough of a distraction that they didn't care about the situation with the mundanes except as easy prey in the chaos.

Somehow, blessedly, nobody was dead. Yet.

"What you need to understand about Otherside," Sixtus was saying, "is that most of them are backward cowards adhering to an agreement that's centuries old. It gives them an excuse not to integrate fully with humanity, and that's dangerous for all of us."

Troy growled, the sound coming from low enough in his chest that I could tell he was genuinely pissed even with the control he was exerting over himself. "Tread carefully, Sixtus. The American mundanes like their centuries-old governing documents. Especially the one that lets them shoot people. Even I know that."

The part that irritated me was the suggestion that we didn't want to integrate with humanity. It was a direct contradiction of both fact and one of my talking points. We were already woven into the fabric of their societies.

Regardless of how important this was, I didn't have the energy to do more than snuggle closer to Troy on the new, much bigger couch we'd gotten for his birthday, trying to ground both him and myself. A month after restoring the spark of magic to Otherside in a grueling set of trials, I was still recovering from the mental, emotional, physical, and magical toll. The vitriol that'd come out just in the last couple weeks worsened it, making me sick, tired, and down at a time when I needed good spirits. That was the point—an infowar move by the Bureau for Supernatural Investigation—and I was annoyed that it was getting to me.

We might have gotten magic back, but that'd only accomplished a hard reset and an uncertain truce in Otherside as multiple parties in territories and demesnes across the country, and even a few around the world, considered my proposal to expand the alliance currently governing the factions within the Triangle and uniting the Carolinas and Dominion demesnes. They were moving faster than usual with the current mundane situation but still not fast enough. At least with the water fae Mami Wata on board and the new queens of the Charleston Conclave too scared to rebel, I finally had full control of the

Carolinas for the first time since I'd ascended. Otherside was just one piece in my messy puzzle though.

A still-healing Harqil was shuttling between the Solari mansion and the bar, their exposed wings a potential problem that they refused to have their movement limited by. Cyrus, now back in captivity, was more of an enigma than ever even as the Sight told me there was a big secret yet to be revealed with him. I also still had to deal with a series of criminal charges—and threats—leveled by various powers in the US federal government. Powers that were undoubtedly being supported by the severed Eads now.

All magical action had a price.

Troy glanced down, the tilt of his head bumping his chin against my temple. "This isn't your fault. Any of it."

"If I hadn't severed Sixtus—"

"He still would have been collaborating with the Bureau for Supernatural Investigation, only with magic to make himself more convincing. The Eads lean toward auratic Aether." Troy shifted to kiss my forehead. "You didn't have a better option. Besides, this is a good thing, my love."

Startled, I pulled away. "Excuse me? He's getting on national fucking TV as a—a professional asshole!"

A smile flickered as Troy brushed a curl off my face. "Exactly. Where we can all hear what he's saying publicly. Which lets us extrapolate what he's saying and doing privately, as well as craft and refine our own talking points."

I hated it. I didn't want to play the political game Troy engaged in so naturally. I wanted people to see that Othersiders were people too and to stop fucking with us so I could get enough breathing room to feel safe.

I wanted a family with Troy, and for that, I needed my stress hormones to drop long enough for me to cycle into fertility. That only happened every few years in the best of times, and I hadn't cycled in over a decade.

Troy's expression turned serious as he caught the direction of my thoughts. "You don't owe me a family. Now or on any timeline."

"I know that. Stop reading my mind." I slouched and crossed my arms, feeling sullen and annoyed even if it wasn't his fault.

"Bond's wide open."

With a huff, I threw myself across his lap and buried my face against his belly, not bothering to close the bond if only so he'd know my irritation wasn't his fault. He just rubbed my back and loosened his grip on his passive power, the one that made everyone but the fae feel at ease in his presence. In the background, Sixtus continued disparaging Otherside like he hadn't been captain of the guard for a High House just over two months ago. Or maybe *because* he had been captain of a High House and was now a magicless pariah.

Despite my mood and the seriousness of the broadcast, I dozed. With the increase in mundane threats, we'd started practicing what to do if I was bronze-cuffed. Last night had been a long, heavy session, but that wasn't the only reason I was tired.

I'd been feeling strange lately, especially since the last eclipse a couple of weeks ago. Like the threshold Troy had said Harqil claimed I'd crossed wanted to put me in a cocoon. It worried me. I was used to pushing hard and recovering quickly, but now I kept going down harder and sleeping much longer than I usually did. I was hungrier than usual too, like the magic needed fuel from me to grow or stabilize. We were at a critical juncture with both Otherside and the mundanes, and it was frustrating me to need to pay so much attention to myself.

Troy just said to listen to my body and held me when I crashed or sat next to me while he worked. Probably as much to monitor my physical state as to keep me company.

All magic had a price, and I was paying big time for yet another leap in my power.

My state should have worried Troy though.

That thought roused me. "Why aren't you more bothered by me being like this?"

Confusion filtered through the bond. "Like what?"

"Tired. Hungry. Grumpy."

"Oh. Well...I was old enough to remember what it was like for my mom when she fell pregnant with Evangeline, but I assume we'd both know if you'd cycled. So you're not pregnant. Which means this just looks like elven magical puberty."

My brain blanked and I forced myself to sit up so I wasn't continuing to address his stomach. "Excuse me?"

Troy's expression was as confused as the bond. "You lean elven on most physical reactions. Did you not go through this when you were younger?"

"No." I frowned, thinking back. "Maybe? I just...was always tired. But one day I didn't have magic, and then not long after Duke found me, I did." That had been a hell of a surprise. I'd been sitting outside the bar watching a wind chime, sad that there wasn't enough of a breeze for it to tinkle. Wishing...wishing...and then with a wrench, a small gale had blown from me and knocked it off its hook. Callista had been livid that I'd done it without permission and where someone could see, as if it was somehow my fault when I hadn't even known I was capable of such a thing.

"You were what, seven years old when he took you to Callista?" Troy asked.

I nodded.

"Earlier than elves then. But I imagine the shit diet she had you on contributed to the tiredness. You were technically severely malnourished until recently. That'd impact magical development as well."

"Malnourished and hiding my power," I murmured as pieces came together. "With nobody to compare to, and Callista constantly calling me lazy. Pushing me to do more physically no matter how tired I was."

Fury flashed in the bond, as it always did when I mentioned something new about my upbringing under Callista, even as Troy's caress on my cheek was gentle. "We see this same process with half-elves born to human women, when they're unaware the father is an elf and we don't track down the child in time. It's unfortunate but normal."

"So how do I *fix* it?"

"You rest," Troy said firmly. "You eat a lot of red meat, as rare as you can stomach it. And you do a little magic every day, even if it makes you more tired for a bit." He shrugged. "Like you have been."

I gritted my teeth to stop from arguing with him. He was saying all I needed was time and if there was something I never seemed to have enough of, it was time.

"If it makes you feel any better, it's usually only intense for a few weeks. And you seem to have done it backwards. Power jump and then crash into adjustment, rather than adjustment to prepare for the power jump." He shrugged again. "Or maybe that's normal for trueborn elementals. Or for primordials in particular. Regardless, I'm not sensing anything off in you like I do when you're hurt. Ride it out, cariñamí."

None of that answered why I hadn't experienced this when I grew into my primordial powers. Or maybe I had, and had just pushed through. I remembered being exhausted the whole time leading up to the Wild Hunt, and even more so after, but had assumed it was everything else going on. I also hadn't had Troy around as a live-in partner to keep me grounded and focused on taking care of myself. If it wasn't that, then maybe it was that growing into my maenad magic and Dreamwalking at the same time were a step beyond even primordial magic. Harqil kept hinting that I'd eventually become more, maybe even a celestial.

Cyrus kept taunting that I'd destroy everything, at least according to the updates Etain sent over. Updates that had Troy increasingly riled. We'd have to deal with the man sooner rather than later, if only so Troy could focus, but I needed the whole mess to wait until I'd handled the Goddess-damned mundanes.

Before I could say that I didn't have time for magical adjustments, my phone rang to make the point for me.

"Hi, Maria," I answered, trying to keep my current frustration from my voice.

"Hello, poppet. I trust you're keeping well?"

I frowned. Maria wasn't much of one for pleasantries unless she was flirting—or needed something but was trying honey before vinegar.

She had Allegra to flirt with these days.

"What's happened now?" I asked flatly.

"Who said—"

"Maria." I paused and did my best to wrangle my mood and my tone. "Sorry. What can I do for you?"

The vampire sighed, a clue that she was truly agitated, given she didn't really need to breathe except to speak. "Could you help me understand why there is a triad of unauthorized out-of-state elves in my bar?"

From the background, Allegra's voice hollered, "Tell her they smell West Coast."

Troy went rigid then reached to shut the laptop, cutting off the guest response to Sixtus's tirade.

I raised my eyebrows and tapped to put the phone on speaker.

"Which West Coast, Alli?" he asked.

"I don't know. Cilantro and basil, maybe? Actually, come to think of it they smell like—" she hesitated. "Um. Kind of like that guy from the thing last summer. Haroun was here so I sent him to see if he can figure out what's going on."

"Pull him back," Troy snapped. "That's Northwest Mountains realm, likely the Rainier demesne. You approach as princess and order them to the Solari house. *Order* them, and now, Allegra. Firmly, with my full authority as King."

I stiffened as much for the snap in his tone as for placing the reason he'd be so concerned about that particular region.

Seattle. And the shit he'd done there.

I scrubbed a hand over my face, praying I hadn't gotten magic back only for it to be used against us. That, and I was tired all over again.

Right when I needed a minute to breathe before plunging back into mundane politics, the US West Coast Othersiders were deciding to enter the chat—and trying to test me, Troy, or both of us, for them to sneak in unannounced and turn up at my vampire ally's nest.

I mean, after sending assassins that is. We'd gotten lucky that Cade and Lya were more inclined to join us and then lay low at one of the conclave safehouses in Chapel Hill while Cade caught up on missed feeds and took advantage of an opportunity to rebuild local connections.

We were gonna have to crack down. Hard.

"Maria," Troy continued, "You have my formal apology for the lapse. I would ask you to withhold collecting the forfeit for trespassing until I've had a chance to assess the situation."

"Since you're being diplomatic and taking action, all's forgiven, sugarpuff." Her tone hardened. "This time, at least. We have a lot of through-traffic from other coteries right now. It's not a good look if elves are off-limits for a feed when they should be fair game."

"Understood." Troy shifted, and I scooted off his lap so he could rise. "Allegra?"

"She's gone," Maria said.

"Doing as she's told for once," Troy grumbled. "Good. Do I have your permission to send an escort of high-bloods to Raleigh?"

Maria hummed. "This once. In the interest of keeping all our plans running smoothly."

"Thank you. I'll be in touch with updates."

"See that you are. Bye now."

I ended the call and blew out a breath, trying to find the energy for this.

"I can handle it," Troy said, eyeing me.

I started to answer with a reflexive insistence that I be involved then sat a minute. "What message does that send? You going alone."

He grinned, pleased with me for thinking politically or listening to the tiredness still dragging at me or both, then sobered. "Depends on their inclination. Technically it simply means I'm directly in charge of the Chapel Hill territory. It could be received as anything from an insult to 'proof' that you're afraid to face them though. Or don't trust me to protect you properly."

I grimaced, thinking that through. "And how does your...past history play into this?"

That shot his mood to hell. "Depends on who's in the party and why they're here. We were still in negotiations for the observers to come. Could be anyone."

The mood drop worried me. This could have just been Troy letting his walls down, A) because it was just me and B) because he was trying to ensure he still had my trust after confessing the circumstances of his Darkwatch initiation mission in Seattle. Those were the good options anyway. I needed to tread carefully here because everything to do with that period was a raw nerve for him.

"And if I joined you?" I asked.

He crossed his arms and looked away. His expression shifted, a crack in the mask he'd pulled up, just for an instant. "If you joined me, it would help with some of the rumors."

"Rumors?"

"About me being a queenkiller. Treacherous." The bond twisted with disgust. "Even if they're true."

My heart lurched.

He glanced at me as the sensation hit him in the bond, worry flickering now.

"Troy." I pushed up and went to him, throwing my arms around his neck. "We talked about this. You don't need to keep beating yourself up over it."

It occurred to me as I hugged him that these rumors or truths or whatever we wanted to call them were likely part of the reason why we'd had so much trouble getting the Richmond and Charleston elves to the table two months ago, and probably why he was still kicking himself. If the local elves had balked based on rumors...I tried to follow that thought as an undercurrent so it wouldn't whisper its way through to Troy. Rumors were one thing. Being family or vassals to two dead queens, as House Lestari observers would be, was another entirely.

I'd threatened to take the whole country as mine if that was what it took to feel safe. Maybe pulling myself together for this would be a way of nipping future problems off before they could start. That, and I needed to take up some of the responsibilities that were technically mine even though Troy had been shouldering them. Stepping back and letting him handle the Ebon Guard and Maria on House matters was one thing. Dealing with encroachments on the territory I'd claimed as mine was my job, even if it did involve elves.

Troy's arms came around me as he finally let go of some of his guilt and gave in to his innate desire for physical reassurance.

"I'll come," I said, trying to keep my tone easy before making it wry. "Not because you can't handle it though. We saw what happened the last time I tried stepping back. It's been a minute since anybody's seen me out and about."

"You're sure you're up for it?"

The undercurrent of relief he was trying to hide—and the fact that he wasn't trying to order me to stay home—made me certain. "Yeah. I can't let anyone think that I'll let trespassing slide. Or sending assassins, for that matter. I'll just pack a snack and take a nap in the car if I need it."

His embrace tightened. "I wish we could buy you more time to rest. The bigger the power jump, the rougher the adjustment is."

"Careful what you wish for," I said as lightly as I could, even if I couldn't hide the jolt of fear that shot through me.

The way things were going now, I might find that time in a mundane jail—or worse.

Chapter 2

We left at nearly ten p.m., later than originally planned. Not because I needed another nap—which I did—but because our Darkwatch agent at the airport flagged an incoming flight with an unauthorized passenger: Rio Lestari, prince of that House, flying under an alias Troy had added to a watchlist.

We ordered the teams we had watching the Lestari handlers and the backup assassination team sent with Lya and Cade to move in and secure all of them. Whatever the hell was going on, I wanted it dealt with all at once. If the West Coast wanted to join Santiago and the Miami vampire coterie in making life a pain in my ass, I was just gonna have to beat theirs and shut down the threat so I could turn my full attention to the feds and the mundane riots. I was over being patient with the elves, population decline or not. At some point, they needed to take responsibility for themselves and their death cult culture. Me—an elemental, still subject to elven bounty hunt laws in most of the world—owning it for them was absurd to the point of insanity.

On the drive over to the airport, my phone dinged with an email update from my Chancellor and lead lawyer about the murder and kidnapping charges against me.

"Iago says they got the charges thrown out," I read aloud to Troy, who was in the back seat with me while Thana drove. Pascale and Haroun were in the second row of back seats behind me and Troy. We were in full entourage mode with the heightened threat situation, which meant neither sovereign drove and we had a full triad in the car supporting us. Even the two of us in the same car sent Etain into a snit, until we convinced her it was good to cut down on the number of resources she needed to allocate to defending vehicles. "The prosecution was unable to provide any evidence that would conclusively tie me to any of the alleged crimes, and our team was, quote, extremely persuasive in their arguments."

Reading between the lines, Iago meant he'd had his people take full advantage of the return of magic to use some elven charm.

My grin slipped as I kept reading. "The subpoena stands though, with an amendment. They want to know what I did to the Verve building and how." The slip turned into a full-on scowl. "They want a *demonstration*. Like I'm some kind of circus animal. They want me to put myself on their registry *voluntarily*." I scoffed, outraged.

Troy squeezed my thigh. "We anticipated this."

I made my best approximation of his growl, which made him chuckle. Thana cracked a smile in the rearview mirror before she forced her expression back to neutral.

"The fucking *audacity* of these people! I refuse to perform on command," I snapped. "And I refuse to be forced to *register* myself."

"Nor should you, in either case," Troy said lightly. "You're a high queen. It's an insult."

My moods had rolled off him easily this last month, like this was familiar territory for him. It made me feel bad that I was apparently falling into some place that reminded him of his upbringing, but the bond didn't carry any hint of fear or disgruntlement. Just patience.

I folded forward and buried my face against my knees, trying to drag myself together. When I sat up, Troy was extending a punnet of ripe strawberries from the cooler between our feet in my direction. I snatched the fruits and started devouring them, feeling more settled with each one.

I froze when it was half gone, belatedly catching my bad manners. "Um. Did anyone else want some strawberries?"

"No ma'am," Thana said from the front. She seemed almost as indulgent as Troy, which was weird for me. Better than her being afraid of me though. Pascale and Haroun echoed her from behind us in the same tone.

"All yours," Troy said.

I perked up at that and his small smile and finished my snack. "Thank you for a break from meat."

"A little sweetness in life is a good thing," he replied.

My mood swung from cranky to sentimental, and I let him catch it in the bond as we pulled up to the airport.

He took my hand and kissed it. *You good?*

Better now. I love you.

I adore you.

That had me downright peppy as we parked and then got out, heading for Terminal 2 under a light "don't see me" spell. Not so much that it'd be suspicious when we were picked up later by a review of electronic security without being noticed by human guards but enough that nobody looked twice at a now-notable me and Troy. It felt kind of badass to walk into the airport with Troy at my side and a triad of elves spaced around us, even if mundanes wouldn't really see us. Maybe especially since they wouldn't.

We got to the greeting area right as a crowd exited from the gates.

After barely two minutes, Troy murmured, "There. Six-one, black hair, green coat."

I spotted him almost immediately, as much from Troy's description as the telltale elven smoothness of motion despite a large black duffel bag slung over his shoulder.

Prince Rio was, I guessed, supposed to be Arden candy.

Roughly Troy's height. The same lean muscle and broad shoulders. Thinner lips, higher cheekbones. Same raven-black hair. Lighter brown skin, darker eyes, but stamped from a similar mold.

Sure, he was hot. Very hot. Most of the more powerful queens bred for it. But as he approached and stopped in front of us with a cocky smile, the air movement brought his scent to me. It was...wrong. Not bad, by any means, just—he wasn't *mine*, like Troy and the Carolina and Dominion elves were mine, and I couldn't for the life of me explain why it was suddenly noticeable when elven scents hadn't particularly stood out to me before. Maybe it was the cilantro-and-basil scent, compared to the rosemary-and-sage or thyme-and-oregano scents I was more accustomed to from the local Houses.

"I wondered if you'd remember the name I used," Rio said to Troy when he stopped in front of us. His tone was light and his smile dazzled, but there was something cutting under both that put me on my guard.

"I'd say welcome to the Triangle, but you weren't invited, Rio," Troy said in dangerously quiet tones.

"Desperate times." The prince shifted his attention to me. "Your queen, I presume? What an honor that you came to meet me. Rio, princ' dom Lestari, at your service, High Queen."

I couldn't help wrinkling my nose when he leaned in for the cheek kisses some elves seemed to favor with a familiarity that further put my back up, and I immediately flushed at the flicker of doubt chased by outrage on our guest's face as he pulled away. I didn't know if Troy caught my reaction or Rio's, but smug satisfaction flooded the bond.

Troy tilted his head and smiled at our guest. "You didn't consider the possibility that she'd bonded to me, did you?"

"Why would I care what perversions an oyëori like you indulges in?" Rio said. The harsh bite to the words suggested real hurt or insult on his side.

Troy leaned forward to speak in a stage whisper. "Because you're bait. Just like I was once upon a time. But you're two years too late. And negging only pisses her off. Even if it's against me."

He rocked back to my right side, his attention not leaving the prince.

"What he said," I snapped, finally getting control of my reactions to a whole new range of scents and hormones. "Getting all judgy and calling my king a pervert is definitely not the way to go."

Amusement bubbled through the bond at the flash of frustration on Rio's face, and Troy turned slightly to gesture toward the exit. "With us, if you please. Your people will be collected as well."

"So you can dispose of us?" Rio muttered.

"No," I said. "Although there will be a reckoning for House Lestari sending multiple individuals without prior authorization."

With a stiff nod, Rio strode toward the exit, clearly trying to catch us off guard, only for his gait to stiffen when he realized that put me and Troy at his back.

Is he not Darkwatch trained? I sent to Troy. *Even I know that was a miscalculation.*

He got the basics and at least one mission. I think he got more of the bedroom, where I got more combat and strategy.

I forgot myself enough to look at Troy with wide eyes, unable to imagine what more bedroom training would look like given how thoroughly he reduced me to base need and enthusiastic begging when he wanted to.

The queens have...expectations, Troy sent. *Regardless of what Keithia wanted, securing a satisfactory marriage contract for me was iffy, given the oyëoro. Which is why she leveraged my Aetheric strength for assassinations.*

Ishtar above.

As we reached the car, the implications of that crashed through me. *Wait, are you saying that, rather than kill me, they're going to try to seduce me?*

I killed the first assassin, Cade and Lya threw in with us, and their other team hasn't had an opening in over a month. Three failures means a strategy change. It's not uncommon for a queen to take a claimed consort plus lovers, especially if she's without an heir.

I let him read my automatic disgust and refusal in the bond as we climbed into the far back seat this time, leaving Pascale to sit in the middle row with Rio and Haroun beside Thana up front.

Troy squeezed my thigh. *At least it's a change of pace from fighting for your life, no?*

How are you so okay with this?

Cariñamí, even without the bond, your scent and reactions are practically screaming your preferences right now.

Which meant everyone in the car knew it, even if he was too polite to say that and they were too polite to be obvious about noticing.

I reached for my seatbelt only to realize that I'd sat in the middle seat, practically on top of Troy, and gritted my teeth. *I don't want anybody but you. Just so we're very fucking clear.*

He leaned to kiss my cheek. *Good. Same.*

At the quiet sound of Troy's lips against my skin, Rio stiffened again, like he could already see the disaster his mission was now that he was on the ground. He wasn't the only one. Right when I most needed to play human, this mess threw my already whacky physical and emotional state for another loop.

Things didn't get any better when we arrived at the refurbished Luna mansion that was now the seat of House Solari a short and silent drive later. We marched Rio in ahead of us like a prisoner now that we were on private property, sweeping through a wide hallway and into what I supposed had been a living room or family room. The blinds were drawn for privacy, but ceiling lighting made the space bright.

Troy and I made our way around kneeling West Coast elves under a heavy guard to a low platform set up against one wall, where two ornate chairs sat that I supposed were technically thrones.

Seriously? I sent.

Expectations, Troy sent back. *A performance to misdirect others.*

I held in a sigh, reminding myself that this was better than having to sever someone, and mounted the dais to take the chair to the right. That'd put Troy in the one on my right when seated, which I assumed would be like entering with him on my right.

His affirmative tap in the bond reassured me. When I was seated, he addressed the assembled elves. "Long live High Queen Arden Finch Solari, the Eternal Huntress and Arbiter of the Carolinas and Dominion demesnes."

"Long live the queen!" my people shouted back, thumping fists to hearts in a salute as they stomped.

Okay, that was kind of cool, especially because some of our new captive "guests" furtively made the salute despite their bound hands and mouthed the words while keeping their heads down.

If it was subterfuge, it was well done.

Hmm. I needed to stay alert. Even if they weren't inclined to kill me, this was still a power play. They were just trying to force an alliance based on assumptions about my hormones and sexual preferences rather than approaching me in a direct and above-board kind of way.

Not cool.

Troy was looking at me. I nodded and waved for him to sit.

"You all know why you're here," I said after letting them stew for a minute. "But perhaps you, Prince Rio, would like to explain in your own words."

Rio lifted his head. "Admittedly, my cousin—the current queen of House Lestari—underestimated you. I was sent to make amends for our House's previous trespass and negotiate the safe return of our people."

My mouth twisted before I could help myself, even before Troy sent, *His aura says he's lying about at least half of that.*

"You, personally, wanted to make amends for trespass by arriving unannounced? No. Try again," I said. "You don't send unauthorized elves to the vampires in my territory to make amends after sending multiple assassination teams after *me*." I smiled, making it cutting. "Unless the people sent to Raleigh were intended as a gift? I'm sure Maria would accept, with pleasure. It would buy enough goodwill for me that I could accept the action as amends."

Rio paled. "Another...error, my queen. The power structure in this territory is unusual. Our information was dated. As for myself, I only follow my queen's orders."

Truth, Troy sent. *But the comment was vague enough to mean anything.*

I shifted to look at Troy. "What would you do about this, cariñomí?"

"You know I take threats to your safety with the utmost seriousness, my queen." He scanned the group then stared at Rio. "I could always run a Thread of Thorns."

The prince flushed. "That won't be necessary. I have no problem saying that my cousin hoped you would consider me for a courting contract. My early arrival was only intended to demonstrate eagerness for the match."

"What?" My brain stuttered to a halt as the bond suggested Troy was restraining himself from throttling Rio.

Rio tilted his head, almost looking demure. "This alliance between you and Monteague has served its purpose, I'll acknowledge that. But with House Monteague destroyed, the elven population here depleted, and you ascendant, my queen, what benefit is there in continuing to tie your star to a feral parasite? Why not make a stronger alliance with Lestari?"

The outrage reverberating between me and Troy had me acting before I was conscious of it.

I grabbed Air, snaked a chord around Rio's ankle, and flipped him upside down. I would have thought he looked like the hanged man on the tarot card as he dangled by one leg, but he had none of the serenity.

Nor did the other eight West Coast elves still kneeling but now stiff as boards.

"Guest courtesy is extended to *courteous* guests," I said coldly when I'd gotten myself slightly under control. "I'm going to say this once and once only for our newcomers. Troy *Solari* is my claimed, oathed, and *bonded* king. We are engaged and due to be wed this year. There will be no lovers or side pieces. So, whatever the fuck y'all think you're doing, sending first assassins and now *this*, you are gonna need to dramatically reassess. I might be a queen, but I am not an elfess and I refuse to play these Goddess-damned games."

While Rio spluttered and flushed, Troy looked and felt like he was seriously talking himself down from eliminating a threat. To anyone else, he probably looked as icy as his power signature, but I knew this vibe. This was the cold of barely contained violence—and if he slipped even the slightest toward outward violence, I had a feeling it would only confirm Rio's assertion of ferality. Especially if any of these people knew the old, afraid, locked-down Troy from a few years ago and not the more emotionally engaged and expressive person he was with me.

To keep Troy safe, I needed to get my mood swing under control and break the tension in a way that would underscore my point, not Rio's.

I leaned back in my chair, skimmed my hand up the back of Troy's neck, and threaded my fingers through his hair, tightening them just enough to get him to tilt his head and break the death glare he was giving our visiting prince.

"Shall I let him down?" I murmured, giving his head a playful little shake.

That had more than the desired effect. A pleased half-purr rumbled from Troy before he caught himself. He flushed but relaxed into an arrogant slouch. The bond warmed with his pleasure at being demonstrably mine even as eyebrows shot up and faces went blank around the room.

"You may as well," he said in a bored-sounding tone. "Before he passes out."

"That'd be inconvenient." I turned my attention back to Rio but kept my fingers teasing through Troy's hair. Affection from a queen was practically unheard of, and I knew he liked that I broke that cultural expectation by displaying my desire—and, in the eyes of those observing, his high value as my mate. "Prince Rio, if you're done being an ass, I'd like to discuss where we go from here. Spoiler alert, it won't be more of *this* dynamic."

"Yes, my queen," he said breathily. "You have my apologies."

I was tempted to simply drop him, but that wouldn't be very diplomatic.

When I'd gently set Rio back on his feet, I said, "You will all remain here, under guard, until I've decided whether to accept Prince Rio's apologies. I strongly recommend you think about your approach, both to making amends for the insults to me and my king, as well as to any alliance."

Troy, hearing the finality in my tone, stood. "All rise."

As they did, I took the bent arm he offered and let him escort me out, still utterly confused and annoyed by this latest turn in the elven political game.

Chapter 3

With everyone at the Solari mansion keeping our guests under guard, Troy drove the two of us home. Which was good because I had capital-T Thoughts and was also exhausted again. I wanted to be Arden for a few minutes at least, not the High Queen.

We sat in silence for the first few miles. Troy felt like he was thinking hard on something, but I couldn't tell what. For myself, I was ruminating on the expressions of the other elves at various points in the meeting. Subtle hints of body language and reaction that I'd started noticing after two years in close relationship with elves. Not just how they reacted but to what—especially since not worrying about being attacked meant I had a new context in which to observe unfamiliar elves.

"Troy?"

"Mm?"

"Is it okay that I handled you like that? With your hair?"

His sideways glance and the curl of his smile held banked heat. "Yes, my love."

"Okay." I slumped in relief. "I only wanted them to see that I value you, but it just occurred to me that it might be too much like...like I thought I owned you, I guess. Some of them paid a lot of attention to Rio's reaction to that."

He shrugged, unbothered. "By elven law, technically you do own me, so to speak. That was in the paperwork I filed and Alli validated when I abdicated as prince of House Monteague. Part of it was my agreement to your formal claim and the title that came with it. That's why Keithia was so angry that you'd taken me. I had a legal option to consent to another queen's rule—one that would give me the security she'd always denied me—and I took it without getting her permission. So legally, she had no further rights to use me or loan me out for whatever plots she had going."

The more he said, the harder my insides clenched. I *owned him* on paper? *That's* what the formal claim meant? What the ever-loving fuck? He hadn't described it like that at the time; he'd just said it was changing Houses to mine...shit. He'd also said I had his life. I'd thought he meant it in the context of a fight or his love for me, not like this.

I shook my head, trying to stay focused on the current question because we'd definitely be revisiting that. The very idea made me sick. "No but—"

"Maybe that phrasing was a little strong. Think of it as more like having first rights to my services. In any capacity."

I stared at him, not sure how that made it any better. The low, level tone he was saying all of this in, like he was describing changing a tire, somehow made it worse. This was something he'd sat with long enough to accept, and I'd had no idea.

Guilt swamped me.

He shook his head when it reached him in the bond. "Stop, Arden. There's an out clause for both of us. Don't worry. I'm here very willingly and always have been. Yes, the whole practice is outdated and barbaric. It's one of the things I've been strategizing on how to reform, and none of the incoming elves have been put on similar contracts. But for now...just like at the summit, it's good when it's you."

He paused and I got the sense that his thoughts were spinning, like he was trying to articulate it to himself as much as me. "From anyone else it would feel like a violation. From you, it's safety. A confirmation." He glanced at me again. "Which is why I need you to leave the paperwork alone. At least until we can reform the whole system. For now, with you, the formal claim keeps me safe from some parties. Not all, but enough. Basically, the ones that are traditional enough to want to kill an oyëori are also traditional enough that they're bound by the claim paperwork. I suspect that's part of why Rio is here. We've proven ourselves too strong to assassinate, but if I'm replaced as your consort with no House to fall back on, I'm fair game. It gives someone else an excellent opportunity to eliminate me as a political threat and influence you or your agenda."

I still couldn't quite find my words.

Troy sighed. "If nothing else, it's a sign that we're winning, at least with the elves. Both politically and in terms of military, cyber, and operational security. This is a last-ditch effort."

"Thanks, I hate it," I muttered. My arms were tight around my belly, like that would help keep the acid roiling in my stomach from spilling out.

"That's why I didn't tell you before now. I didn't want you feeling shitty for something that is just business as usual in the Houses and happens to work out well for me. I knew what I was doing when I filed the papers."

I didn't respond, too busy reflecting on all of our public appearances among the elves. Seeing them in a new light—and wondering how this reflected on me.

Then something else clicked. I was focused on *my* feelings, but it wasn't about me. "This doesn't just protect you and buy you time for reform. It advances your whole reform agenda."

He offered the little smile that said he was proud of me, the one I got when I finally managed a difficult move in Darkwatch training. "Keep going."

I frowned, trying to figure out how it worked with the little information I had. "If I...*own you*" —I choked on the words— "or however you want to phrase it, I'm responsible for you. For *controlling* you. You have freedom to move however is best to accomplish your aims, because in their mind it's sanctioned by me while at the same time we both know we're equals. Shit like today just reinforces to them that I'm ultimately in charge and you don't need to be considered a threat. Which also increases the attractiveness of using a new consort as a backup plan to assassination, which I'm assuming y'all just consider normal."

"Very good. What else?"

I thought harder. "If I'm almost entirely hands off, or officially delegating to you...it's all on paper only and there may as well not even be a paper. Which the clever will see, and use as a base to start questioning. Leaving you to simply share your experiences with anyone who wants to subvert the matriarchy via the legal system."

"Perfectly reasoned," Troy said warmly. "And yes. That's exactly it. All of it."

I sat with that as the developed parts of South Durham gradually became more heavily wooded as we got closer to home. "I still don't like it. But I'm not gonna make reform harder for you, if I can help it."

"And that, cariñamí, is another part of why I feel safe with you. Your trust in me to do things my way. And your faith that even if you personally dislike it or disagree with my method, I will make the best choice for myself." He reached for my hand and kissed my knuckles. "That, and you haven't run when everything falls apart. I know you'll put me back together if I fail. Do you have any idea how freeing that is?"

"Maybe. Because I know that with all my leadership fuck-ups, you're there behind the scenes fixing the board. Giving *me* room to fail, even if I don't see the error right away."

"See?" He smiled. "It all works out. So stop worrying about whether you're good enough to do all this. You've got me. And I've got you. Always."

"Okay. Love you." I didn't like elf politics, and I wasn't good with this situation. But if my bondmate and partner was asking me to accept a choice that didn't hurt either of us, I needed to shut up and support his autonomy. This wasn't an "I can fix him" relationship. It was a mutual growth and support relationship. And sometimes that meant letting him make his own choices about his healing, his actions, and his goals.

He read all that in the bond and squeezed my thigh. "I love you too. Now. As pissed-off as that whole audience made me, we have an opportunity."

"Negotiations?"

"Yes. We know about the assassins, so we have leverage to insist on redress." He grimaced, and his mood flipped. "There's also personal leverage between me and Rio, but I want to use that strategically. Please don't ask me about it now though."

Given what he'd already shared about his time in House Lestari, that gave me the icks. But it was his story. "All right," I said. "I seriously dislike how this has played out so far, but I'm thinking if we can swing an alliance somehow, that gives me more room to step to the Bureau and the Senate with this subpoena. Me negotiating for my demesnes alone carries less weight than me negotiating for two or more whole realms."

"Exactly. Plus, with the elves of the Eastern Seaboard and the Northwest Mountains behind you—"

"Behind *us*," I corrected.

Troy smiled. "Behind *us*, I think we'll pull in the handful of Houses in the Great Lakes, the Southwest Desert, and the Gulf realms."

"There's none in the Central Plains?"

"No. Not enough direct influence over human politics beyond the symbolic events in their election season. Most of us are concentrated in the Eastern Seaboard and Northwest Mountains. Lestari is the primary House there now." He wrinkled his nose. "The plains are also not our preferred habitat, to be honest. Not enough trees or shadow cover."

So, getting House Lestari really would be a solid win, one that would make it worth spending time and energy on this when I really needed to be focused on the subpoena. The private investigator in me still wanted to focus on the one main problem, but I was a queen and an Arbiter now.

I had to think bigger to be bigger.

When we made it home, my body seemed to recognize we were on safe ground and suddenly decided it was time to crash. The night had taken a lot out of me, with the driving and the audience and the magic.

Troy caught me when I wobbled. "I'm sorry. I shouldn't have—"

I read where that was going and shook my head. "I needed to be there. Lestari's plan is bullshit, but we wouldn't have gotten that much without me there as the prize. Or, worse, they may have taken the opportunity to move on you."

He stayed silent as we got our shoes off then followed me to the couch, sitting down first and gathering me in when I dropped.

"I hate that you see yourself as a prize," he said as I got comfortable.

"It's not your fault. There's no competition in my mind, only his, apparently."

Troy started massaging my scalp and neck. "It's just so petty with everything else going on."

"Mm," I agreed, laying down and losing my train of thought in the motion of his fingers.

Pleased amusement teased through the bond as he shifted to keep up the massage. "We should tell the queens that all it takes to subdue an elemental is a neck rub."

I snorted a laugh and let myself be lulled. Not all the way under but a light doze. My body needed the rest.

After a little while longer, Troy shifted again. A dial tone said he was making a call.

"Well?" Maria's voice said from the other end.

"We're dealing with it," Troy said, even quieter than usual. "There shouldn't be any more incursions. From this group anyway. If there are, call me directly."

"I should just eat them."

"I might let you."

"Tease. No wonder Arden adores you." Maria hesitated. "How is she, by the by?"

I stirred, trying to wake up enough to answer for myself, until Troy squeezed the back of my neck in just the right spot.

Nah. He could do it.

"She's got this." Troy sounded completely confident in me.

"Hmm. I worry," Maria's distant voice replied. "I'm glad to have magic back, but at what cost?"

"What was necessary. She accepts it, so I will as well. You ought to do the same." Troy's fingers coiled one of my curls then uncoiled it. "In any case, I just wanted to keep you apprised of the situation and thank you again for your collaboration."

"What are friends for, sugarpuff?"

The call ended, and Troy launched straight into the next one, checking on Terrence's new cub and Lola's mate, Darnell. Then calling Helia and Keeya in turn. Then Janae, Zanna and Mami Wata, and even Vikki and Doc Mike. Quick calls for each of them but the work of a politician strengthening his base and confirming his allies ahead of a long battle. If Duke and Iaret hadn't been back on their spy mission and reachable only by my callstone, he probably would have called them too.

"I should do that," I mumbled when a clatter said he'd tossed his phone on the coffee table.

"You do, when it's for the territory or the demesne," he said. "This is different. Keithia always kept the Chapel Hill Conclave separate and superior. It broke a lot of trust and cost the elves goodwill. This is my work as an elven king, not yours as queen or Arbiter."

I let it go and drifted, even though I should have been preparing for the Senate hearing. Iago's team were good at lodging objections and negotiating the conditions of my and Troy's appearance, but even the usually slow-moving federal court was moving fast on this and the date for the secret hearing was coming up.

That just made me frustrated with this magical whatever-it-was all over again.

"How much longer am I gonna be like this?" I grumbled.

"Likely not much longer. It's already been almost four weeks, and you're not crashing out completely anymore. Probably helps that you're getting real rest and not being dragged into the Crossroads or the In-Between or wherever in your dreams these days."

At least there was that. With the gods leaving me alone, the comfort of having my mate close to me, and the exhaustion of the adjustment, I was sleeping better than I had in years. I didn't trust it—the Court of Nightmares was still out there—but I needed it.

I sighed. I needed it, but now I was thinking about the hearing. We only had nine days left to prepare.

Troy sensed the direction of my thoughts and didn't argue when I pushed to sit up. That little doze would have to be enough.

"Grill me again, please," I said. "Make it mean. I need to make sure I can respond well if I'm still tired like this in a week and a half."

After a quick ripple of Aether to check my current state Troy's expression hardened.

Oh yeah. I was in for a test.

Chapter 4

S trange elves in town didn't sit well with me, Troy, or Etain, in general, but especially not with Cyrus as hostile as he was. With so much on the Ebon Guard's plate, Troy decided it was finally time to confront his father and try reducing that threat while we left the West Coast elves to cool their heels a bit.

Noon the next day found us at Ebon Guard HQ, where Cyrus was being held under close watch. He'd woken up from whatever magical coma his experience with Sutekh had put him in a couple of weeks ago, which was why he'd been transferred to this more secure location from a safehouse, but he was still minorly physically and auratically drained by the ordeal. Felip said it was the latter effect that was causing the most difficulty, especially given the Veisi elf's inclination toward auratic Aether. Apparently being first influenced then ridden by a god for at least a few weeks was wreaking havoc on Cyrus's aura. We didn't know about his magic; he was back to being cuffed in lead and silver.

Part of me was sick and sad about that. He'd already spent twenty years in imprisonment. The other part of me wondered how many of his threats had been Sutekh and how many had been him. Wondering if the father of the love of my life was out to kill me was a real downer on multiple levels. According to Harqil though, we needed to bring Cyrus back around to help stave off the apocalyptic dream-prophecy the Court of Nightmares had sent me as a test, so I'd come along.

It was the first time Troy had seen his father since I'd severed Sutekh from him a month ago. The acrid scent of betrayal turned Troy's usual rosemary-and-sage scent bitter even to my nose, but he kept his mouth shut tight and his expression hard.

"Sure about this?" Darius asked when he met us outside the house.

"You know things are coming to a head with the West Coast now on top of the feds," Troy replied. "And you know what he did. This is a loose end."

Darius grimaced and glanced away. This was hard on all of us.

I couldn't help a wince when we were let into the main bedroom where Cyrus was being held. The entire thing was Aetherically soundproofed to keep him from hearing anything sensitive or drawing attention in any way. Half of it had been fenced off, the whole way round and over the ceiling, in silver-coated steel, leaving Cyrus with a bed, an ensuite bathroom with no door, and a chair. I had a feeling the fencing extended under the carpet as well, just to be sure nobody and nothing could get in or out from underground. As soon as we'd recovered from celebrating the return of magic, Troy, the djinn, and I had cast overlapping wards and spells on the property to get people driving past on the main road to ignore this place, just as an extra protective measure.

My chest tightened and my stomach clenched, nauseated by the idea that we had to do this to our own people—to family, no matter what threats they'd made—to maintain safety and control. I hated this.

"Troy," Cyrus said. Emotion roughened his voice, under the tiredness. "She let you—" He cut off as I stepped around Troy, then scowled at me. "I should have known it was you in the room, not just your scent on him. Of course you wouldn't let him out of your sight."

"I wanted her here," Troy said.

"Why?"

"Because I need you to understand that I will always choose her. Not because she's forcing me to." Troy glared at his dad. "You're not in this cage on her order. You were freed from imprisonment in Lyon because she encouraged me to do it. Now you're imprisoned on *my* order." The chill of his power signature flared and he took a breath to get himself under control before lowering his voice. "She fucking hates this—despite your threats against her—mostly because it hurts me. Partly because this isn't how either of us wants to do things. But *you* forced this. You don't get to blame her."

"I don't believe that for a second," Cyrus said coldly. "You didn't hear what she said about you. You couldn't have, or you wouldn't be here. Unless she's gotten someone to spell you." His lip twisted and he glared at me. "I was willing to bet that Sutekh was twisting the situation, until she said all of that about trapping you in ways Keithia never could."

"I was standing right in front of her when she said it, looking into her eyes and heart and seeing that the only lie was in her words to you."

"Bullshit," Cyrus said.

"For the love of the Goddess," Troy snarled. "You trusted she would take care of me. I know you did. But now you're willing to take the word of a trickster god who wanted her dead or worse when I'm standing right here telling you, man to man, that what she said was an act to force your hand." When Cyrus just looked stubborn Troy shook his head. "You read my fucking aura when you got here. You know I'm telling the truth."

He seemed to be doing everything he could not to call Cyrus "Dad", which just made everything worse in my mind. I'd started to notice how much elves acknowledged family bonds between each other—brother, sister, cousin. Even Lya Desmarais had done it, and she was an exiled half-elf. That Troy refused to acknowledge Cyrus as family now seemed intentional.

"I know you're telling me what you think is the truth," Cyrus said.

In the bond, something seemed to snap. Troy turned to Darius. "Key."

Hesitantly, Darius gave him a single key.

With sharp movements, Troy opened the door to the cell and passed the key back to Darius.

Troy turned to me next. "Hand."

I dropped my left into his without question, noting Cyrus's observation of that fact. He hadn't expected it.

Next, Troy extended a hand to his father. "You want to know what she's feeling right now?"

Oooh shit. Troy had a talent for adapting Aetheric tricks, honed and practiced on a very willing me. He had a passive power for making people feel at ease in his presence, but I had no idea what he was about to try now.

Trust me, Troy sent.

I always do. Even if my stomach was now doing flip flops.

After a few calculating glances, obviously trying to determine whether he could escape, Cyrus gingerly put his hand in Troy's.

A weird muffling sensation buffered me from Troy. Then the scent of burnt marshmallow flared.

Cyrus dropped to a knee, gasping and clutching his stomach like he was going to be sick. He breathed in panting gasps, and his expression twisted.

Was Troy amplifying my feelings? Or was I suppressing my awareness of them that much just to get through this meeting?

"I told you," Troy said. When his father jerked his hand out of his clasp, Troy shut the door again, stepping to the side to let a grim-looking Darius lock it. "You want to know what else your little queenkilling tour achieved? Raising suspicions on *me.* Right as I'm trying to unite elvendom so that we can fight off the Goddess-burning mundanes."

"On you?" Cyrus gathered himself with an effort and used the bars of the cage to drag himself upright, sparing a strangely blank look for me before refocusing on Troy. "It was nothing—"

"Even aside from your being listed as my fucking sire on the bloodline rolls, it was *everything* to do with me. But you wouldn't know that, because you wouldn't know that Keithia sent me on queenkilling missions, the repercussions of which could cost me my life in a magical trespass trial."

Cyrus paled.

Troy shook his head, looking disgusted. "You never asked me what happened to me after you were exiled. You just decided that you were going to fix it, whatever 'it' was in your addled head. And when you didn't get your way, you threw the mother of all shitfits and started killing whichever queens you could reach or had a personal grudge against. You do not get to pretend this is about saving me, from Arden or anyone else. This is about *your* vengeance and yours alone." The chill in Troy's voice grew even sharper. "I should execute you."

I was now keeping the wall up on my side because Troy was beyond pissed and it looked like seeing his father was pulling up some deeply buried feelings. When I glanced at Darius, his posture was stiffly at attention and his expression was the conspicuously blank one the Darkwatch elves tended to wear when they were hiding something.

Cyrus dropped his eyes and swallowed hard.

A pained silence stretched, and it took everything in me not to fidget or so much as breathe too hard. This was Troy's conversation.

I was starting to get a sick, sneaking feeling that this wasn't just driven by vengeance either. There was a sense of despair hanging over Cyrus so thickly that it was palpable. What if Sutekh wasn't the only one influencing him? Crows, as far as I knew, weren't a typical Ancient Egyptian bird, and his sigil had been a mockingbird before he'd been stripped of his royal title. So why was he the crow from my dream?

A chill crept over me as the Sight tried to steer me toward a picture I was having trouble putting together pieces for. Something to do with Cyrus. We'd brought him home, but that wasn't enough.

"How do I make things right between you and me?" Cyrus finally asked.

My phone and Troy's both buzzed. I checked mine while Troy was busy glaring at his dad.

"Troy, we need to get to the bar," I said softly, as much from surprise at the message from Terrence as from trying to stay calm for him. "Soon."

He checked his phone, and the same surprise I'd felt rippled from him before he put his phone away. "You want to fix this, Cyrus? You start with asking yourself what family means to you. You ask yourself if you can, first, be the father I need. If nothing else, that is someone who loves and accepts me and my choices when they hurt nobody. And second, stop thinking the worst of my bondmate and fiancée simply because she's a queen and give her a chance on her own merits. No more games. When you have your honest answer, send word. I won't be back until then."

Gripping my hand, he led us out of the room.

I shuddered as the miasma of despair thickened, wondering why nobody else seemed to sense it.

Etain waited with Felip and Lachlan in the hallway.

"Etain, with us," Troy said. "Dari, Felip, Lachlan, stay here."

"Sir," all four of them said.

Thank you, I sent as we got in the car, humbled by the extent to which he was willing to demand respect on my behalf. Family was everything to him. It haunted him. But he'd just put me before his own father.

Nobody ever fought for me other than you and my mother. And nobody has ever fought for you at all. He squeezed my hand. *It's a little selfish. I'm hoping that it helps you feel safer. To know that I'm here for you.*

So I'd maybe be a little closer to cycling and then becoming fertile.

Before I could answer, Troy continued. *I will always fight for you, Arden. And fight for us. Our family together, even if it's just the two of us.*

I damn near started crying at that. I was less tired today than I had been lately, but some of the emotional swings were still live. It did make me feel safer, in that I wasn't alone in the world. The wish I'd always had, that someone would choose me first, put me first, had come true. It was shocking to look back on the years and see how lucky I was now.

Troy gathered me to him in the back seat while Etain drove, doing what he could to soothe both me and himself with physical touch and wordless reassurance in the bond after the upset of that visit.

It worked. By the time we arrived at the bar, I had my balance back, although the itch that'd started in my mind about Cyrus continued. Just in time too because that text had been a bombshell.

We were meeting with Terrence and Ximena to hash out the details of a surprise offer for an alliance with the wereclans in the Southwest Desert realm.

The whole. Damn. *Realm.* Wanted to join with the Eastern Seaboard in what we were doing to stand up to the US federal government.

Not just with me as Arbiter of the Carolinas and Dominion demesne. Troy was specifically invited to the table as well to negotiate as the King of Solari for what was effectively to be a double alliance. The drive over had him shaking his head in disbelief as he reread Terrence's text, like he'd never imagined this much good fortune coming all at once.

You earned this, I sent as we got out of the car and headed into the bar. *You have been busting your ass for everyone and made serious sacrifices along the way.*

That's what I'm supposed *to do,* he sent back, bewilderment heavy in the tone of his thoughts. *It's not supposed to be this easy. You keep saying it could be, but...*

Yeah. Shocking as hell to me too.

He held the back door open for me and followed me in. *Things can be like that for you. You're...you. The Eternal Huntress. Savior of Magic.*

Oh for fuck's sake, they've given me another title?

Troy snorted. *You knew they would.*

I shook my head.

"All good, majesties?" Etain asked.

I looked over my shoulder, kicking myself as I realized why she was asking. "You know, don't you."

Her blank expression said everything. "Know what?"

"That we talk to each other. Telepathically."

"Um. I can neither confirm nor deny—"

"It's fine, Etain," Troy said, his voice tighter than usual with annoyance at himself. "We haven't exactly been careful about it lately."

She blew a breath out. "Well, that's a relief to have it confirmed, at least. There's been speculation."

From Troy's sharp look and what I thought I remembered overhearing of an argument between him and Omar, the speculation was about more than whether we could speak to each other telepathically and probably leaned into questions about my sanity.

She raised her hands and shrugged apologetically. "Just reporting the facts."

I paused before going through the door to the main room. "How many people are wondering?"

"Those of us who spend the most time around you. Me, Haroun, Allegra, Darius, Thana, Pascale, Lachlan, Felip. Iago had theories based on his research. I think Ophelia suspects, after last month." She grimaced. "It's not unreasonable to assume Maria knows or suspects as well, which means so does Noah and probably Dr. Miller."

The people we'd been comfortable enough to let our guards down with. I could deal with that, although who knew what Doc Mike would think of telepathy if he knew. Troy was getting the grumpy demeanor that said he was berating himself again, and we'd had enough of that today.

"Cyrus and Harqil know too," I admitted. "Factor it into strategic considerations going forward. Limited to the group you named only. The fewer people that know, the better, but if some people have figured it out, we might as well use it."

Both elves relaxed at the firm order and the permission to treat the whole thing as not just normal but also strategically valuable. We probably should have said something before now, but it was our special thing, between us, and I'd already had so much of myself exposed to the world when I'd wanted to have more privacy.

That bird had flown though. Like Harqil had said, if I wanted to be left alone, I shouldn't have stepped up to lead the Triangle, let alone everything I'd done since then.

And speaking of the celestial...

I stuck my head into my office, not at all surprised to find the angel sitting in my chair at my desk.

"Boundaries, Harqil," I reminded them. I was precious about my chairs, whether this one or my armchair at home.

They rolled their eyes and slid over the desk to another chair, rotated my laptop to face them, then scratched at the regrowing tips of their four wings in turn. They were forcibly corporeal and largely magicless for the time being, although the ability to be unseen had come back in small bursts. Helpful for getting them moved from Ebon Guard HQ once they'd generally recovered from whatever beating a Sutekh-ridden Cyrus had dealt them, and not much else.

That said, having a messenger angel around had been doing wonders for my management of incoming and outgoing communications while I'd been down. I wouldn't dare to call them a secretary, but their nosy, boundary-violating foray into my email inbox had turned into a full-time job by their unvoiced insistence and general talent. They needed something to do. Comms were their strength. I was exhausted and hated triaging emails. It was a good fit.

"Thank you," I said. "Anything interesting?"

They started to answer, then their attention sharpened. "You've been to see Cyrus."

I exchanged a concerned look with Troy. "What of it?"

"How is our little carrion crow these days?" The dangerous glint in their eyes matched their tone, making that itch stronger.

"Crow isn't just a metaphor, is it?" I blurted. "It's a title."

Harqil nodded as Troy nudged me further into the room and shut the door behind us.

"Title for what?" he asked. "Given by who?"

The angel studied him, a weighing look, before answering. "Sutekh owned your father for a long time. Long enough that Despair—one of the Court—took an interest, given he was already an agent and there was so damn much of it swirling after he was caught. Your dreams changed then, didn't they?"

"Of course they did," Troy said gruffly.

"But they're clearer now, yes? Since you moved in with Arden. They don't whisper to you to find a bottle. Or an end."

Troy swallowed hard. "Yes," he whispered roughly.

"There you have it," Harqil said, as though that answered everything.

At first it didn't, but the Sight finally unfolded. "Shit. That's why it felt despairing in that room. Beyond anything I've ever sensed or experienced, worse than a haunting. You're saying one of the Nightmares is after Cyrus?"

They just gave me an inscrutably angelic look, like they'd seen more than could be borne to tell.

"That's why it's not enough to bring him home." I rubbed my hands over my face. "That's why you said that he was supposed to stay gone."

Harqil nodded. "You buffer your mate against Despair. But who buffers Cyrus? Bad enough that Rage already has an interest. In any case, I assume you're here because of the wereclans," They arched an eyebrow when I opened my mouth to stay on the subject of the Nightmares, a clear sign that the conversation was over. "So, beyond that...Maria is just about ready to close on negotiations with Charity and Renaud to create a true vampire triumvirate, as part of formally bringing them into the alliance. After all of this" —they waved a hand— "unpleasant business with the mundanes is wrapped up, they're anticipating a boom in Otherside-related tourism. It's an economic opportunity to them."

"And blood, I'm sure," Troy said, sounding frustrated at the change of subject but knowing as well as I did that it was pointless to try to force the celestial into doing anything.

"That goes without saying." Harqil clicked through emails faster than I could have read any of them. "Other than that, the witches are forming a Grand Coven to discuss a nationwide alliance between themselves, and you've got half a dozen new elementals applying for residency in the territory, specifically in Helia's House."

"Have Keeya's people do the usual background checks and approve everyone who passes to speak with Helia," I said, trying to resist the urge to focus on the increasingly tangled mess that was Cyrus and Troy. Not dealing with all this myself right now was definitely a relief though. It freed me up to focus on getting myself right and working with Troy, Iago, Etain, and the local parliament on how we wanted to shift our relationship with the mundanes locally. "You're a lifesaver, Harqil. Keeping all of this in order would have been too much for me right now."

"Oh. Well. It's good to be useful." The stumps of their wings drooped. "We angels need to be useful. Not being of service...it hurts."

"I hadn't known that," I said. "I'm just glad you're here."

They brightened. "Good. Send some snacks back as thanks. And some of that good local mead, whatever the seasonal flavor is. I like the variety."

I shook my head with a smile and left them to it.

When Troy, Etain, and I pushed through to the main bar, only Terrence, Ximena, and their seconds Malik and Joachim were there, seated at one of the square tables in the middle of the room.

Surprised, I turned to Zanna behind the bar.

The kobold shrugged. "They're faction heads."

"And?" I said.

"They paid in maple candy and Chapel Hill toffee." She popped one of the aforementioned maple candies into her mouth, grinning impudently as behind her, Ruprecht the gremlin snickered without looking up from whatever mechanical device he was fiddling with.

Zanna shrugged. "Bar closed. Three hours."

I barely managed not to scrub a hand over my face at learning that my bartender and friend, who was known to turn the whole bar's drinks to piss if any single person rubbed her wrong, could be bribed with enough specialty sweets.

Terrence was grinning ear-to-ear and even the usually intense Ximena was smirking when I looked at them.

"We needed neutral ground ASAP," Terrence said. "Solari here has been edgy enough lately that I didn't think it wise to host at your house."

"I suppose you needed to gain at least one virtue in your old age," Troy grumbled. "Luckily for us it appears to be wisdom."

Terrence just laughed, as did Ximena. Joachim and Malik, standing behind their chairs, looked like they felt in over their heads and were trying not to show it.

I led Troy to the table and sat with him at my side as a partner, not a bodyguard.

"Talk to me," I said. "Terrence's text mentioned an alliance?"

"Yes, Miss Arden." Ximena practically purred. "In exchange for a few minor concessions, we'll bring you the entire Southwest."

Chapter 5

Minor concessions or not, there was still negotiating to do on both my part and Troy's. By the end of the three hours though, we had something I could deal with.

"All right," I said. "Territory and guest housing in one of my demesnes, no more than two hours' drive from Durham, to be allocated for visiting representatives from any wereclan alpha, their mate and children, and up to three of their clan as honor guard. Reciprocal territory for anyone from this demesne in each of the seats of theirs. Information sharing between House Solari and all of the wereclans. My willingness to represent their specific interests in any negotiations with mundanes at the federal level. And a special, weres-only, once yearly gathering to make sure they have access to me and to Troy. That everything?"

Terrence and Ximena looked at each other before Ximena asked, "The hunt is definitely out of consideration?"

"It is," I said firmly. Hunts were a special thing for me and Troy. I'd already pushed him too far by giving my blood to our Dreamwalking squad. That it was for the greater good of restoring magic was beside the point. If he was drawing lines with his own father about what was acceptable with me, I would do the same. He hadn't verbally objected when that was raised as a desired outcome, but the bond had tightened as he forced down his knee-jerk reaction to be diplomatic.

Ximena looked at Troy.

He nodded, blank-faced. "As she says."

"Fine. We'll take this back to the clans and get paperwork finalized." Ximena raised her drink. "To the New Détente."

"The New Détente," the rest of us echoed. We clinked glasses and drank to seal it.

I wrestled down a shiver. We really were making history with this. One that was only binding on a few of the North American realms so far but could expand. Would expand, if Maria's work succeeded and if Troy and I had anything to say about it, so that we had the strength that came with collective purpose.

I couldn't be called a rogue element, or rogue element*al* for that matter, if there was a solid group behind me that wanted assertive action.

As soon as our glasses hit the table again and signaled the end of the negotiation session, Terrence grinned. "Imagine that. Weres and elves coming together under an elemental Arbiter."

"And nobody's blood on the floor," Ximena added with another toast. "I'll admit, I had my concerns about the two of you solidifying as much power between you as you have, but I'll also be the first to say you've used it to benefit all of us."

I flushed at the comment. High praise from anyone but especially from a werecat and more so from Ximena, who'd always been more reserved in her relationship with me and Troy than Terrance was. Raising my glass, I said, "To the greater good."

"The greater good," everyone echoed, drinking deep.

A tap at the door's windowpane made us all turn. A clutch of valkyrie stood outside, their wings half-hidden behind an illusion that I could see through. One peered in, hands cupped around her eyes.

I thought I recognized her. "Is that Mist?"

Troy shook his head. "I don't know. I didn't get to know them at the Wild Hunt."

With a grimace, Terrence glanced at Ximena, whose lips pressed together as her expression lost its mirth. Nobody was keen on seeing valkyrie; they only appeared when there was the prospect of a lot of death.

"Let them in, please," I called to Zanna.

She did without comment, too curious about the arrival of these particular fae to snap at me for giving her orders.

"Arbiter!" the lead valkyrie called brightly, icy blue eyes glinting. "It has been some time since we last drank with thee."

The ripple of the air and the pitch of her voice told me it was indeed the same valkyrie who'd led at the Wild Hunt. I rose and gestured to the bar. "Mist, be welcome. You and your clutch."

"Thou dost honor us." Grinning, she clasped my forearm—only for her expression to blank in shock.

Mine must have as well. The last time I'd greeted her, the grave's chill had raced painfully up my arm and numbed me to my shoulder, enough that Troy had turned around looking for the threat. This time, goosebumps rippled, but not more than that, even when Mist narrowed her eyes to kiss my cheek.

"Sister," she said. "In truth now, not just in name."

"Sister," I confirmed, remembering that in that connection was protection for Troy as well, even if I didn't know what it meant to be sister in truth to a fae who sought out carnage. "It has been a long road and a strange one since your last visit."

"I would say I can imagine, but I suspect I cannot. Thou hast the look of one who has seen what mortals should not." Cautiously, she turned to Troy and offered her hand.

He took it, shivering at the contact but completing the greeting kiss without significant effect. "Sister."

"Brother. Also in truth. Thou hast taken another step into Odin's hall since last we met, it seems." Her serious expression broke into a wide smile. "Thou wouldst be wiser not to make a habit of it lest one day ye may not depart. It is good my clutch and I are here."

"Be welcome," I said again, going behind the bar to pour mead for them myself.

She nodded and waved the other valkyrie in then went to greet Terrence and Ximena.

I was slightly relieved to see that a full thirteen hadn't arrived, but six was more than enough to worry about.

Hedging their bets? Troy sent.

Looks like. Alert the Guard and the Darkwatch. If they're here, there's good odds something is going to go down.

Pressure resolved into Harqil's mental voice. *Who's hedging bets?*

Goddess damn it, Harqil, I sent, with a punishing sting of Chaos. *Stay out of our heads!*

The door to the back swung open, and Harqil came out far enough to lean on the bar. Their brows lifted slightly on seeing the valkyrie, but nobody else seemed to notice them.

Stop giving me away, they sent. *Do you know how much effort it took to hide that door opening?*

Mead splashed as I froze mid-pour at the implications that I could see a celestial and their actions when nobody else in the room appeared to have noticed. At Zanna's growl for the wasted booze, I snapped out of it and finished the last glass, putting everything on a platter with a few bowls of bar nuts and carrying it over to the valkyrie along with the remainder of the bottle to top up Terrence, Ximena, and Troy.

As we drank toasts to welcome the valkyrie back to the Triangle, I couldn't help glancing at Harqil and wondering what the knowing look on their face portended.

△▽△▽

"I wish you'd let me post Ebon Guard on the grounds," Troy said as he followed me into the house a few hours later.

Regardless of everything else going on, we'd had an elf-were alliance to toast and valkyrie to honor—because if a shitstorm was coming, I wanted all of them at my back. That, and as more Othersiders had filtered back into the bar, I found myself holding an impromptu town hall to offer updates and information. The alliance with the Southwest Desert was big. Big enough, maybe, to help Maria close the deal with Renaud and Charity, which would lock down the majority of the southern part of the Eastern Seaboard.

"No. Absolutely not." I turned off the security alarm then started pacing. "Whatever it is that brought the valkyrie, they can't fight."

"You don't know that."

"I do know that. The valkyrie arrive in anticipation of mass death events, Troy. Half a clutch is six too many for this to be anything less than pivotal. The Guard and the Darkwatch are good, but I will not put them at risk without knowing why the valkyrie are here."

Mist had been maddeningly coy about that. To be fair, she didn't know what had drawn her either. She could only say that this part of the world tasted like potential.

That statement hung over me as Troy and I prepped for our upcoming trip to Washington, DC. Today's debate was our wardrobe. Troy's penchant for designer everything was running headlong into my insistence that we keep it simple and off-the-rack. My opinion was that we needed to show we could be anyone, to be people that the average American could identify with. Troy's was that we were royalty and ought to look the part so that we'd be taken seriously as such.

While we debated in circles, a sense of dread grew in me. The revelations about Cyrus were part of it, but there was something else too.

"I can't focus on this right now." I slumped over my arms crossed on the tabletop. "I'm exhausted and I can't think."

"Food and bed," Troy said.

Normally I would have laughed, maybe teased him a little. Food, bed, sex, comfort…those made everything better in his mind. This time I was too tired.

"Please tell me we have leftovers," I said to the table.

"We have leftovers. I'll even reheat them for you."

I huffed a laugh, as he'd intended me to.

"You want to tell me what's really bothering you?" he asked when the food was sizzling on the stove and the scent of rice pilaf, sauteed broccoli, and lamb koftas was making my mouth water.

"No."

"But you're going to." The hint of steel in his tone said he was speaking as King, not as fiancé.

"Fine." I sighed and tried to gather my thoughts. "Something feels off. Something beyond whatever Sutekh and the Nightmares have to do with your dad. I don't know if it's the Sight or what, but I feel like there's really a reason why the valkyrie are here."

"Soon?"

"I can't tell. But they arrived hours before the Wild Hunt, so I have to assume yes."

My assumption was right.

We'd only been in bed for an hour, from the feeling of the air and the sky. I'd drifted off to sleep only to jerk awake enough times that this time, Troy just mumbled, "Shh."

No.

Something was *wrong*.

"Troy, wake up."

The feeling intensified, suddenly and dramatically, the Sight screaming and the ring to see the unseen practically burning on my finger.

"Wake up!" I jolted upright then tumbled over him out of bed, dragging him with me.

Despite the unexpectedness of it, Troy hit the floor on his feet, already reaching for his longknife. "Arden?"

"Out! We need to get out!" I had no idea what I was saying or doing even as I moved to throw the bedroom window open and vault out onto the back deck.

"Arden!" Troy followed and the longknife sang as he pulled it free of its sheath. "What the hell—"

I stopped listening to him because *danger* screamed in every part of me. The trees and vines hissed it, the ground rumbled with it, and all of a sudden howls rang out in the night as the gytrash gave warning. Worst of all, the sky roared with danger—life-ending, catastrophic danger.

A drone.

Not a surveillance toy like the one I'd knocked out of the sky when the Sons of Seth had attacked.

Something capable of dropping a bomb.

Reacting purely on instinct, I threw a shield of Air overhead. Even as I did, the wards pinged. All of them at once.

The gytrash spilled out of the trees, leaping the fence.

The scent of lemon zest preceded Duke and Iaret, both of them shouting something I didn't catch.

And then the sky exploded.

Fire raged against my shield. Deflected heat set treetops on fire for a quarter-mile radius. Smoke rose, kept away from us by my shield and the wind and rain I instinctively called to save the forest.

The gytrash thundered onto the deck and positioned themselves as guards. The djinn melted halfway back across the Veil. Troy was hollering even as he hauled me around to shelter me against the side of the house, just like he had when the lich's lair had collapsed around us.

This time, I didn't hide against him. I struggled free, trying to read the path the missile had taken in the disturbed air molecules. Up, up, up...there. Death on quiet, automated wings, angling away. Metal on metal with nothing organic.

With a growl that could have come from Troy's throat, I pulled on all four elements.

He caught the shape of my thoughts before I could will the drone not to exist.

"Evidence!" he hollered into the wind the explosion and I had whipped up.

A twist of my magic switched me from Chaos to Fire and Air. I called a storm of lightning overhead. A bolt struck the drone. It tilted then plummeted away from my property.

That wouldn't do. I needed it to fall here.

With a few taps of Air, I brought it this way and hastened its fall until it crashed into the shield I'd maintained overhead. With another thought, I ripped the wings off and dropped it in the backyard in pieces.

The bodies in my woods drew closer much faster as they broke cover, shouting to each other.

"Soldiers!" I shouted, belatedly understanding what Duke and Iaret had been shouting and what the wards and my own far-flung senses were telling me. These weren't lightly armed mundanes like the Sons had been. This was a full military platoon, thirty-two bodies, all carrying enough metal to be heavy weapons.

We were under attack.

Like, duh, but from more than just the drone in the sky.

I linked tighter with Troy, showing him my sense of the attackers.

"Let them come," he said. The deep growl of his voice and the deeper draw of his magic said he'd been pushed past a limit.

We waited, filled to the brim with magic, as armed mundanes reached the edge of the forest ringing my yard, hollering for us to get on the ground. Gun barrels pointed at us even as faces twisted in confusion at the smoking wreckage in the yard.

Troy reached to me in the bond. *Give it to me.*

I blended Air and Fire to spark all the electronics on the mundanes—cameras and comms, leaving whoever had sent them blind and deaf—then shunted all the Chaos I could handle to Troy.

He didn't hesitate.

With a snarled word of elvish and a twist of Aether that wrenched my guts even as it made the entire area stink of marshmallow burnt to ash, he struck.

In my field of vision, every hostile mundane gun aimed their gun at their own head and, with an empty-eyed look, pulled the trigger.

The bang of a single shot from almost three dozen rifles and pistols rang out from around my property. A thud that I felt in my bones followed as bodies dropped. The land drank deep of the offering of blood and death, feeding the wards as the semi-sentient plants took their due for warning me.

I stood in the quiet, shaking with adrenaline, tears running down my face as my brain belatedly caught up with what instinct and training had made me do.

No.

I scrubbed the tears from my cheeks.

What the *mundanes* had made me do by attacking me for the second time in two months, this time with enough firepower to level a part of Eno River State Park, to destroy my home and sanctuary and any innocent people in the surrounding area, just to get to me.

I refused to cry over this. Not when my mate was still upright and snarling at my side. Not when my forest was still standing and my river was still flowing.

Not when I'd done nothing to call this hell down upon any of us.

"Now you can call the Guard." I whispered it, because if I spoke any louder, I'd start screaming with rage and never stop.

Chapter 6

Everyone except the djinn, Troy, Darius, and Etain gave me a wide berth when the Ebon Guard arrived to check the bodies in the woods. The tiredness that'd dragged at me for weeks was gone. I felt renewed, refreshed, reinvigorated even, in body, mind, and purpose. Even I could sense how that made my power signature roar, but I refused to tamp it down.

Hence the avoidance from the Guard and Duke's silence where he'd usually make a snippy comment.

Troy had started to order the bodies pulled into the backyard, but I belayed that. A missile explosion overhead and my lightning storm would be investigated.

"It's a crime scene," I said coldly. "Just like we needed evidence that there was a drone, we need evidence that we were attacked. If we disturb the bodies, we contaminate the evidence. Keep the Guard concentrated on the gate and at key points in the woods. When we're questioned, we pin it on the wards. That keeps Troy clean and ups the mystique."

Etain's expression tightened in disapproval. "We're going to submit to a mundane investigation?"

"Yes," I snapped. "If we send them away, it looks like we have something to hide. They know they sent soldiers. They will have checked in." Something else occurred to me. "Send a triad to check for identifiers. Patches or something on the sleeves. Do not touch them. Firepower like this isn't local trash. This is government. My bet is National Guard, which means the governor."

"Fuck," Darius muttered, wincing as the word left his mouth but not apologizing for it. "I need to call Alli."

"Do it," I said. "And make sure she tells Maria to keep her people the hell inside."

With a salute, Darius jogged away.

"Duke? Iaret? What the hell happened?" I asked.

Duke phased in, not bothering with a human shape. "Sinclaire got an urgent call. We didn't catch all of the other end, but her reply was, 'They can't destroy her, I need her alive.' We assumed she meant you, since figuring you out has been her pet project this past month."

Iaret, agitated enough to be djinn fire on her bottom half and human on top, added, "When we came out of the Veil, the wards were screaming. You were already up though. Clever girl."

I turned to the gytrash, who were still staying close in guard positions. "Any chance one of y'all can help us piece together what happened on the ground?"

The fae black dogs exchanged a look. Then, in a shimmer of magic and a fascinatingly sickening twisting of his form, Marú became humanoid for the first time I'd ever seen. His eyes stayed the same, a luminous green, and his hair stayed a long, light-drinking black, but the rest of his appearance was a trip into the uncanny valley. There was something clearly but indescribably *not right* about him and something deeply alien in his movements.

His lip lifted in a dog-like expression of disgust as he regarded his fingers. "Hate this form. Unseemly."

I blinked at the impossible depth of his voice and the odd shape to his words but shook it off as he looked at me unblinkingly. "We'll keep it brief. What happened?"

"They came from across the river. Split in two. Circled the house from a distance. Bás and I saw there were too many. Fell back here."

"Did you hear anything? Smell something?"

"Smelled...fuel. Not like your conveyances. More."

"Diesel, maybe," Troy said. "That's good to know. We're looking for something big."

Etain spoke into a wrist mic in elvish, probably relaying that info.

Before Marú could say anything more, shouts rose at the front of the house. He twisted back into his black dog form and shuddered as Bás offered comforting licks to his face.

"Let's go see who's here," I said. "I appreciate the information, Marú, and grieve the discomfort its delivery caused you."

He bowed his head and yipped. Then both black dogs leapt from the deck and dashed into the woods.

"Duke, Iaret, one of you stay close but on the other side of the Veil. The other needs to get back on Sinclaire."

The two djinn exchanged a look before Duke shrugged and phased out, leaving Iaret half-visible to me.

"Etain, make sure the Guard get photos of that" —I pointed at the crumpled Reaper drone— "and the bodies. Especially any of those identifiers."

"Yes, my queen," she said before switching back to elvish and her wrist mic.

Darius kept having to check his pace as Troy and I circled the house and made our way down the gravel road to the front gate. Red and blue lights danced in the small gaps in the trees. The police were here.

"Be easy, brother," Troy murmured. "Trust in your queen."

"Of course. Apologies, my queen."

"Don't worry about it," I said. "It's kind of a big deal."

Troy huffed a grim almost-laugh, but we kept our mouths shut as we approached the gate and the three squad cars parked in front. Not just police. There was a fire truck and the fire captain's pickup as well. A worried-looking Val stood among the firefighters, and I carefully ignored her. Not just because of her being an elemental in hiding but also because there was a bigger issue.

Police were out of their vehicles in defensive positions, weapons drawn but pointed at the ground, shouting at hard-faced but unresponsive Ebon Guard. Among them, unseen thanks to a strong illusion, were the six valkyrie who'd been at the bar earlier. Jo the reporter was practically bouncing at the edge of the crowd where she was trying to take photos from around the shoulder of a cop trying to keep her back.

Ishtar above.

"Hey!" I shouted. "What is going on here?"

Arden— Troy started.

"Ma'am, is this your property?" one of the police officers said. In the wild lights from the cars, all I could tell was that he was pale-skinned with short, dark hair. He also looked on the edge of making a fatal mistake.

I drew my power signature in to try de-escalating things. "Yes."

"Are you aware of an explosion in the area?"

I studied him, thumbing my ring and leaning on the Sight. A teasing heat from the ring made me say, "You mean the one from the bomb the government just tried to drop on my house?"

Shocked silence let me hear crickets for a bare minute before multiple people started speaking at once. None of them elves, fortunately—they had better discipline—but the police were shouting questions, and Jo was shouting her own almost as loudly. Unheard by anyone but me, Iaret started giggling at the chaos.

I raised a hand, willing them all to silence. I was no elf, but Troy took a cue and quit tamping down his passive power. A beguiling sense of calm rippled outward.

"One at a time," I said.

"We need you to open this gate so we can inspect the property," the first officer said.

"No."

"Excuse me?"

"Do you have a warrant?" I asked. "I'm a licensed private investigator. I know the law. This is private property. Nobody here made a call. We were just getting my security team together to do a perimeter check."

"Security team?" The officer frowned. "Who are you?"

"She looks familiar," another officer called from behind the open door of his car. "I know I've seen her on a video somewhere."

"Othersider," a third officer hissed. "Has to be. Can you smell that stink? Smells like rotten eggs and hellfire."

I ignored the sulfur scent of the gytrash circling in the woods and waited for the cops to be finished talking amongst themselves.

Troy *pushed* with his passive power, and goosebumps rose even on my arms with the weight of the suggestion to show some respect and back the fuck off.

"Ma'am," the lead officer said in a strangled voice. "You made an assertion about a bomb."

"Yes. Not one that I had anything to do with other than being disturbed from my sleep by it detonating over my head." Not swearing was taking far too much of my concentration, but I knew better than to give them any excuse to say I was being aggressive. Being Black and Othersider? They'd assume it anyway. "There's no fire, so there's no need to tie up city resources with the fire department. May I suggest you go run the rest of it up the proper channels? In the meantime, my people have security checks to do." I turned to go, trusting my safety and Troy's to the Ebon Guard at the gate, the gytrash, and Iaret's maliciously mischievous inclinations.

"Who are you?" the officer called.

I turned back around. "Get that warrant, officer." Then I pointed at Jo. "She can come up. The reporter."

Jo wasted no time slipping under the outstretched arm of the officer blocking her and darting forward.

Troy muttered under his breath in elvish at my side, not moving his lips as he shaped Aetheric darts and loosed them at every mundane in the immediate area while we waited for Jo to climb the gate.

What was that? I sent.

A little monarch-level something to make sure nobody gets ambitious or wanders where they shouldn't, given Iaret looks more interested in cursing their vehicles. That was risky, Arden.

Sight and the ring said do it. Besides, I had to buy us time.

For what?

An infowar play. Hence letting Jo come up.

Troy saw where I was going immediately. *You want to leak the drone.*

I want to do more than that. I want to make a statement. If we have a neutral third party, it isn't us creating a deepfake or something.

He blew a breath out. *Also risky. But I agree with it. We can't be seen to be easy meat.*

Jo joined us, breathing a little fast, and trotted to keep up when Troy and I started back up the gravel drive for the house, our rear covered by Darius. "Hi, Ms. Finch," she said. "And Mr...."

"Solari," Troy said after a hard, evaluating look. He'd been in full bodyguard mode and hadn't introduced himself when we'd all encountered each other at The Durham Hotel.

"Monteague," Darius added when I nodded.

"Solari. Monteague. Sure." She bobbed her head, looking not in the least bit intimidated. More like she was trying to remember all the times she'd seen Troy before, and in what capacity. "Thank you for the opportunity to ask some questions."

"It's a bit more than that," I said. "You remember that conversation we had about the government attempting to kidnap me? And the one about them using werewolf blood to try creating supersoldiers?"

"Yes, ma'am, of course I do," Jo said. "Those are enormous allegations, which you have only partially substantiated up to now."

"How would you like proof that the government is running a covert war on Otherside, on US soil, putting human civilians at risk?"

Shock made Jo miss a step. "You've got to be shitting me. I mean— Sorry, yes. If you've got proof, I want to see it."

We walked in silence, Jo between me and Troy, until we reached the gate that would let us into the passage to the backyard. Etain stood in front of it, arms crossed.

"Ma'am," she said in a voice so light I knew she was pissed. "Why is the journalist here?"

"I offered Jo proof of my prior claims against the government," I said in the same tone.

Etain swallowed hard and stepped aside, recognizing my mood. "Of course, ma'am."

The five of us made our way to the wider yard. I turned when Jo gasped at the wreckage.

"Oh my God," she breathed. "What is that?"

"A drone. You're welcome to inspect it and take pictures," I said.

She was moving as soon as the words left my mouth, camera hefted. It flashed in the night, each burst of light illuminating something that could identify the damn thing.

I retract my objections, Troy sent on seeing her enthusiasm and hearing her excited dictation into a handheld recorder. *Using a reporter to do our investigative and infowar work and keeping the Guard and Darkwatch free for security? Good plan, my love.*

That assumes it gets past her editors and any government attempts to shut her down. I think she's hungry enough for that Pulitzer now that she'll find a way though. And I still want our people to leak photos as a backup if we don't see anything published from Jo in a day or two.

I'll see to it.

Jo finished her quick but thorough circle and approached us. "May I ask some questions about this, Ms. Finch? On the record?"

"Yes," I said. To Troy, I sent, *Have someone record it. Video.*

He gestured to Darius as I stepped closer to the wreckage, standing in front of it to force Jo's attention my way.

"Ask away," I said.

"First, what is this?"

"I'm no military woman, but I think it's a Reaper drone. An armed Predator."

"What makes you say that?"

"As you're aware, an explosion detonated above my property. Shortly thereafter, this crashed in my yard." Partial truth, but it was a truth.

"Why would someone send a weaponized drone to your property?"

I smiled, feeling the rage in the tight curl of my lips even as I was pleased Jo gave me this opening. "Because I'm a known Othersider and the federal government has tried and failed to recruit me for weeks."

Jo's eyes got big. "Are you saying this was a hit?"

I tilted my head, trying to go for thoughtful and not arrogant. "While I slept, a drone was sent to my house to destroy it and me in an act of warfare against a civilian. I fail to see how it could be taken any other way."

"In a previous conversation, you took responsibility for the destruction of Verve Health in Chapel Hill," she said, going for the juicy story. "That seems to be a pretty aggressive and threatening move, especially for a self-described civilian."

Fortunately, Troy had grilled me on this. "I can see how it would look that way from the outside, and I regret that

that nonlethal, no-casualty action was necessary. However, the Bureau for Supernatural Investigation was working with Verve to reverse-engineer the turning of mundanes—of non-magical humans—into werewolves. This is after they, again, tried and failed to recruit me to be some kind of government supersoldier. Do the American people really want to be experimented on in that way? I know Othersiders want no part of it." I bit my tongue before I could say that I wanted to be let alone, mindful of Harqil's pointed comments on that topic. "I simply want Othersiders to be allowed to live in peace and without interference, under a New Détente, a new legally binding framework for Othersiders who choose to continue living among mundane humans—as we always have."

"That sounds like a lot of excuses," Jo said, scenting blood and pushing harder. "Casualty-free or not, destroying a building and a business is a serious matter."

"Absolutely," I agreed. "But unlike tonight's attempt to blow up my house, the action to protect my people from medical experimentation and yours from the results of that experiment was contained—by me. If the bomb dropped on my home tonight had been poorly aimed, it would have struck innocent people in a populated area. We've seen it over and over again in US military action in other countries, weddings and schools hit instead of military targets. Do you consent to being collateral damage in a war your government hasn't declared it is fighting, on American soil? The Pentagon keeps failing audits, so is this the truth of your tax dollars at work? Destroying your communities rather than working with me to find the peaceful, safe way forward I have been advocating for?"

"You truly want peace?" Jo asked. "Even if the federal government did send this drone, as you claim?"

"Yes. Absolutely. None of us benefit from the state of things now. All of this happened generally because of unwarranted fear of Othersiders and particularly because I refused to be used as a weapon by the US government." Time to make the play that would set the tone for my and Troy's upcoming appearance in Washington, DC—if we made it. "I have to say this: I am an Arbiter of Otherside. That means I negotiate peace and I deliver justice. I do not negotiate with terrorists, and that is what this government has unambiguously proven itself to be. For talks to continue, enforcement of state and federal anti-Otherside legislation must be put on hold." I stared into the camera Darius had trained on me. "I look forward to working with reasonable and peaceful elements of local, state, and federal government toward fair and equal treatment for Othersiders under the law."

I left unsaid that there would be consequences otherwise.

Chapter 7

On Troy's order, Darius sent the video to the Darkwatch for integration into our infowar campaigns. Even if we waited to put it on social media, it would go out to Othersiders. They needed to know what we were up against—that this was no longer just a political game for federal or state governments but also a military one.

Jo was packing up her things when Haroun trotted out of the woods. He shot a grim look at Etain.

I was already on my way over, leaving Troy to distract Jo, when she waved. "What is it?"

"North Carolina National Guard, I think," Haroun said quietly. He tipped his phone my way to swipe through a series of photos showing the same patch. "That means the governor ordered this action or had a hand in it."

"Shit." Rage flared in me again. I'd protected the Goddess-damned governor's residence when Darius had taken the former governor and his wife captive while ensorcelled. Now I was wishing I'd burnt the ugly-ass building down. "This adds a front. Alert Maria in case they try for her coterie. Then get the info to the Darkwatch and Keeya. War footing, all defensive measures authorized."

"Yes, ma'am." Haroun exchanged a look with Etain then wandered a short distance away.

Etain eased closer, glancing over her shoulder at Jo and Troy. "How do you want to play this?"

"The wards, like I said," I said without hesitation. "We have to call it in given how I've played things up to now. But I want Jo on the sidelines as an observer."

"Embedded journalist?" she asked.

"That's actually not a bad idea." I gave it a few seconds of thought. "Run it past her, and if she agrees, get Iago to draw up a contract with a waiver."

"On it." She moved toward the reporter while Troy took her place at my side.

"What is it?" he asked.

I filled him in, adding, "I need to make the call. You're certain nothing can be traced back to you?"

"You killed the recording and comms gear. Unless they have someone like Alli to read residue or maybe a human necromancer or blood witch of some kind, they won't be able to tell it was my active magic. With the video we just sent out, I would hope nobody would be stupid enough to try working for them."

"Last call for objections then."

He searched my face, a hint of worry pinching his brows. "Just be careful."

I nodded and, with a quick check that Etain still had Jo occupied, headed back to the front gate. I paused in the front yard to call Iago and ask him to get here as soon as possible.

"I'm already here," he said. "Darius sent a message."

"Good." I rocked into motion again, waving Troy to follow. "Be there in a minute."

As I'd expected, a squad car had remained behind under the watchful eye of the Ebon Guard. The lead officer stood, legs spread and hand on the butt of his pistol, in front of the gate like he was going to take on the Ebon Guard single-handed and completely unaware of Iaret sitting in the driver's seat of his squad car doing Ishtar knew what with a wide grin on her face. Iago was parked behind him on the narrow road and standing a short distance away, which probably pissed off the cop on both counts.

"Iago," I shouted as I approached. "Good to see you. Come on in."

"Ma'am." He slipped through the gate, ignoring the glare of the officer.

We moved out of human earshot, but Iago still wove a soundproofing spell before asking, "How much trouble are we looking at?"

"A downed Reaper drone and thirty-two National Guard," Troy said flatly. "Dead ones."

Iago's brows shot up. "Come again?"

"I took down the drone, but there was an explosion from the bomb it dropped, which is why the police are here," I said. "Troy wove…"

"A monarch-level mass casualty spell," he said. "For all intents and purposes, it looks like suicide."

"Caused by the wards," I added.

"I see." Iago pulled out his phone after a deep breath and a heavy exhale. "I'm assuming you're going to alert the authorities rather than destroy the evidence? Evolve the infowar?"

"Exactly," I said. "They covered up the attempted kidnapping of me and their part in the Verve fuckery, and they used the Sons in their last attempt to try keeping their hands clean. This is how we show everyday people that their government isn't just targeting Otherside. Anyone could be acceptable collateral damage in an onshore suburban war. It's also how we justify my attack on Verve or at least show why it was necessary."

Iago's expression tightened. "You know this opens Otherside to attack from these right-wing zealots? Not just the Sons of Seth but whatever other idiots are playing militia these days?"

"I know," I said. My stomach turned at the idea. Anyone caught would not see an easy death. Any death, but especially a brutal one, weighed heavy on me. But we didn't choose this war.

It was already coming. This just gave us options to fight with all our strength and all our magic—hopefully while retaining some public sympathy—rather than dying by attrition in the dark.

"We don't have a choice," Troy added, echoing my thoughts. "They're already attacking us. You both know I questioned Arden on coming out of the shadows, but they sent a fucking drone, Iago. While we were sleeping. If Arden didn't have the Sight? Or if the djinn hadn't happened to be watching Sinclaire? We'd be dead."

Iago looked between us. "Let me make the call then. I know someone in the governor's office. If this goes to local PD, they'll send SWAT, regardless of how long that one has been standing at your gate in a staring match with Vern, Uri, and Sinéad."

"Thank you," I said, squeezing his arm.

He grinned. "You do give me interesting legal challenges, ma'am. Good to stay sharp."

△▽△▽

Two hours later, I was sat on my porch steps as the sun came up, taking a backchannel call from the right-wing asshole governor of the state himself. Jo had signed Iago's hastily drawn-up contract waiving her right to sue me, the House, or Otherside in general for any harm, and a grim excitement had her trembling as she held her recording device.

"Governor," I said in answer when Troy and Jo nodded to confirm they were recording, speaking through gritted teeth as I tried to inject an appropriately solemn note into my voice. "My condolences on your loss."

The governor, one Blaine Matthewson, was not nearly so polite as his voice came through on speakerphone. "How dare you, you Otherside scum."

I ignored that with an effort. "I have powerful wards on my property. They seem to have interesting effects on mundanes who wish me harm. Like the thirty-two National Guardsmen and women now laying dead in my woods. Would you like them back?"

Furious silence punctuated by heavy breathing was all I got.

I pushed. "Seems to me like the correct gesture would be to reclaim the bodies and ensure they have a proper burial, no?"

"It would," Governor Matthewson finally said in hard-bitten tones.

"Then I'm going to need assurances." I couldn't keep a hint of the schadenfreude from my voice on that one.

"Of all the uncouth, disgusting—"

"I dunno. I think attacking women with bombs while they sleep at home in a suburban area is pretty uncouth and disgusting," I said harshly. "You made a gamble, sending your military against me, and you lost."

"This time."

"So you don't deny it?"

"I neither confirm nor deny a single damn thing."

"But they are National Guard, and the only person who can order the Guard here is you. Unless, of course, you've turned over command to the federal government?"

"Are you trying to say you didn't have it coming after you destroyed a building?" he said nastily.

"I'll own what I did," I said. "I destroyed an empty building to shut down an experimental supersoldier program run by the Bureau for Supernatural Investigation, one which threatened both Othersiders and mundane humans. I did it without casualties. Your method—nice drone, by the way—would have caused destruction not only to a state park and the private properties adjoining it but also to lives. *Human* lives. We are not the same." I took a breath and spoke over his spluttering. "But you know what else you did, Governor?"

"I'm sure you'll enlighten me, you arrogant bitch."

Again, I leashed my rage with an effort. "I surely will. You brought the little war you and the Bureau were fighting against me out in the open. That means I now have options that were off the table before. What do you think I could do to that silly little mansion of yours, if I was so inclined?"

This time the silence was shock. "You wouldn't dare."

"You attacked what I hold most sacred. You showed me beyond a doubt that there is no honor to be found in your administration and that I need to take extreme measures to protect myself. Think again."

"So now you're making threats."

This was outrageously ridiculous. "I am reminding you that we can have a peaceable solution—or not. But I am done turning the other cheek. This attack crossed a line."

Chatter in the background interrupted before it cut off—the phone being put on mute.

I muted my own and took a breath, rubbing my forehead. "I didn't want it to be like this."

"I know," Troy replied quietly. "None of us did."

Then the phone crackled back to life and the governor cleared his throat. "You mentioned assurances."

Time to go big. "I want you to take responsibility for the attack on me and my home. I want you to acknowledge that it was a misstep—"

"It wasn't even my damned idea!"

"Even better, then." I'd known the drone could only be from the feds, and now he'd handed me the proof. "Point the finger and apportion blame where it belongs."

"I can't do that."

"Can't? Or won't?"

Silence.

I sneered. Coward. "I know you have constituents to answer to, Governor, and that a lot of them don't like Othersiders. But now you've allowed the federal government to use deadly force when you're prepping a re-election campaign in part featuring states' rights, and you've also got *me* here. For the last time: we can find a peaceable way to move forward or another way. What benefits North Carolinians?"

"Wiping your kind from the face of the Earth," he said without hesitation.

Closing my eyes, I gave myself a moment to take a breath then opened them and looked at Troy. His expression was grim as he nodded.

If we went to war, he'd stand by me.

More urgent chatter in the background led to the phone being muted again before I could respond.

I just tried to keep breathing as my vision narrowed to a tunnel. Some people wanted to see others burn more than they wanted anything else, and I was afraid this governor was one of them. North Carolina used to be a purple state. It'd swung fully red in the last election, including Wake County, where Raleigh and its affluent suburbs sat. Durham County and a few others were still left-leaning but by smaller margins. If I couldn't get this asshole to work with me—if I had an active threat in my own home territory...

We were on a precipice.

I'd made a threat. I'd have to carry it out. I was an Arbiter of Otherside, and I wasn't just negotiating within Otherside now. Empty threats made for weak territories, and one way or another, weak territories—and their leaders—were destroyed.

The phone crackled. "Ms. Finch?"

"Governor."

"For the record, I am making this offer under protest," he said, the words slow and heavy with bitter reluctance.

I made myself breathe. "Noted."

"My office will not do as you've asked. We will not take responsibility for this clusterfuck. However, we will bury it."

Hatred made his voice tight and hard. "In exchange for the bodies of the thirty-two fallen men and women; your assurances that you will not use your magic to attack buildings, people, or legal entities in the state of North Carolina; and your oath not to implicate the state or my office in what happened tonight."

I muted the phone and looked at Iago. "With caveats that the peace holds but anything else?"

"Immunity," he said.

Unmuting the phone, I said, "Was the drone yours?"

"No. That was federal."

Perfect. Jo's earlier reporting only covered the drone; we'd kept her ignorant of the National Guard until the call was arranged. We could still run that story while keeping to the letter of this agreement.

"I want protections," I said. "I will continue not to use my magic against buildings, people, or legal entities in the state of North Carolina until and unless I or my people—any Othersiders—are directly threatened or attacked. I also want immunity from prosecution for this event and any and all accusations or lawsuits, whether criminal or civil, in the state of North Carolina. Including anything to do with Verve. If the Sons of Seth or whatever local militia or hate group rises up, I and any Othersiders in the state have the right to defend ourselves by any means necessary, up to and including lethal force. We won't be caged by a bad bargain, only to have you stand up in a press conference and incite something."

He tried backing me down, but I stood fast and just kept repeating myself—no concessions. I had the greater power, and I knew it. If they thought they could do anything, they would have sent another contingent of the National Guard, more drones, something, but they were on the phone cussing me out and trying to bully me into a corner. If I hadn't been through everything I had in the last two years and if I hadn't had that apocalyptic fucking dream or faced every fear, trauma, and literal dead-end in the Duat, I might have buckled.

Not now. Not this version of me.

I would stand up for myself, my people, and our rights.

Finally, Governor Matthewson cracked. I passed the phone to Iago to arrange the fine details, crossed my arms on my knees, and dropped my head.

Troy settled next to me after a quick murmured word to Darius to take the recording device and slung an arm over my shoulders, pulling me in tight against him to kiss my temple. *You did well, cariñamí. You did very well.*

I couldn't answer him. I was too busy shaking with a blend of fear, exhaustion, spent adrenaline, and rage.

Scuffing feet reminded me that we had a mundane present, and I lifted my head, reaching for the tattered remnants of a queenly demeanor.

Jo watched solemnly, still recording. "You really don't want violence with humans, do you, Ms. Finch?"

"No," I said, my body still shaking even as my voice was mostly steady. "I truly don't. But I know what's worth fighting for, and the lives and security of all my people is it. We're people too, even if not everyone wants to accept that."

Chapter 8

Order from the governor or not, Troy had to use an Aether sting to get the policeman at my gate to leave. Iago had insisted on including police harassment in the definition of a threat, but tell that to the asshole who'd been standing outside all night trying to make a point. I finally lost my temper and hollered at him to go investigate the government, Troy used the distraction to work his magic, and my gate was clear by the time the military coroner came for the bodies.

I wished it was Doc Mike who'd come, but he dealt with the civilian cases.

At Troy's insistence, I stayed on the porch, under guard, rather than doing what I wanted and following the mundanes tramping through my woods. Even when Troy and I were on a hunt, we disturbed the forest less than these assholes were. Anger boiled in me as I saw one of them pause to stamp on a trout lily purely out of spite, but Troy's grip on my wrist kept me from saying anything or doing more than glaring and letting my power signature out some more.

Don't give them a reason, he sent. *That was intentional.*

I didn't reply. He could read my mood just fine without me saying anything. The mundanes read it too, from the way they scratched at themselves. Part of it might have been poison ivy, but I was certain that most of it was my bad fucking mood. We'd sent Iaret back to her spying at the Bureau, or I would have had her curse every last one of these assholes.

Each minute they were on my land heated me further. Worse, I half got the sense someone was watching me stew and enjoying it, but every time I reached out with elemental senses, I found nothing other than mundanes trampling my land and elves standing guard.

An ethereal chuckle on my third seeking attempt told me there was no point in looking. Celestials, being nosy. It almost seemed like they were drawn by my rage at the offenses against my land, but they weren't revealing themselves. Damn them too if they wouldn't tell me what they wanted. I'd faced down Sutekh and the tricksters. I'd deal with whoever this was, whether a god, an angel, a Nightmare, or whatever else.

I was out of patience for games.

The mundanes started hurrying as the weight of my signature and Troy's combined to hang heavy the longer they were here and the trees themselves seemed to threaten the humans—especially after a second lily was willfully crushed, likely to get another rise out of me, given the sneering, taunting look I got after.

That look vanished when a bramble inexplicably stretched across his path, tripping him with a thorned cane not just once but until his shins bled through his pants. Even I could smell the blood on him, and with the almost-new moon heightening their senses, the attention of all the elves sharpened at its tang in the air.

Then it was my turn to sneer.

It took two hours for them to finish. Jo sat on the top porch step with her laptop the whole time, oblivious to the potential threat of blood-piqued elves, the keyboard clattering as she drafted her pitch to her editor. With no further drama by the time the military had wrapped up and left, she packed everything in a big backpack and rose.

"I'll be going now, ma'am." She tentatively extended a hand. "Let me know if there's another big move coming, and I'll be there."

I took a breath, pulled my power signature all the way in, and shook her hand. "Will do, Jo. Thanks for your work today."

"Oh no, thank *you*." She grinned. "This is going to make my career."

I summoned a smile, both for her seeing what Troy and I had intended in this being a ladder-climbing opportunity for her and because she seemed to have gotten used to the sig, given she was no longer hunching instinctively or scratching at herself like other mundanes did. I hoped that was a good thing.

"Until next time then," I said.

With a last wave, she trotted down the steps and headed for the main gate.

Troy made a hand signal to the three Ebon Guard still on duty, adding to the weight of it with a vocalized order. "Go with her. Then head home or to HQ, wherever Etain has you scheduled. Thank you for being here."

"Sir. My queen," the three of them said in an overlapping jumble.

The feeling of a watching presence faded with their departure, although I'd have sworn it wasn't any of them who'd been watching me.

Then I was finally alone with Troy again for the first time in hours.

I pulled up my walls in the bond, spun, and threw the front door open, too mad and heartsick at the desecration of my home, land, and privacy to see straight, let alone think. I'd held it together through the long fucking night. Now came the crash, and heaven help Director Sinclaire if she got it into her head to finally pick up the phone and take responsibility for tonight. There'd been nothing, no contact, no news stories or press conferences beyond local news reporting on the explosion and hedging interviews with mindmazed law enforcement.

That just meant Sinclaire and the feds were plotting, and I was going to have to wait for Duke to report back to find out what.

I leaned against the wall separating the kitchen from the bathroom and slid down to sit huddled with knees up and head down. The shakes were back, and I didn't know if they were fear or more rage.

The resonant splash of water in metal said Troy was filling the tea kettle.

I needed to get up, pull myself together, and update Maria and the rest of the parliament on what had happened. Then figure out how this impacted the alliance negotiations with the West Coast elves, which had been the last thing on my mind up to now. Then decide what to do about this radio silence from Sinclaire.

And then and then and then.

There was always something more. When would it end?

It finally crashed down on me that it wouldn't. I could bust my ass trying to fix everything and make it safe for me and everyone like me, but there would always be more danger. How long was I going to put my life—put a family with Troy—on hold for these constant threats?

The tea kettle started whistling and an idea hit me so hard I gasped.

"Cariñamí?"

I lifted my head to stare at Troy as he poured hot water over what smelled like Tulsi and rose tea.

"What is it?" he asked as he set the mug on the table before sitting next to me on the floor, a careful hand's width of space between us. "You're walled up. But you smell agitated."

It was another minute before I could figure out how to say what I'd been thinking. Finally, I just said it. "I keep waiting for the world to be safer so I can feel safe. But that's not the nature of the world, is it?"

He sat very still, scarcely breathing, like he didn't know what the best way to answer was.

"No, I get it now," I said, rushing on. "There will always be some danger or threat. So, it's not for me to try to make the world safe. That's a never-ending quest that someone else will always fuck up for me. That's putting my life and my fate in someone else's hands and hoping they don't shatter me."

Troy listened, posture tense, as he waited for me to finish explaining my thoughts.

"It's not about making the world safe. It's using my strength to protect myself and what's mine and having the courage to claim what I want in spite of everything. And then just leaving the rest. Or rather, accepting that I can only control myself." I pressed the heels of my palms to my eyes, trying to pull the threads together into something coherent. "I've survived everything this far. You're still here. They sent a fucking missile, and you, me, the house...all still here."

My heart thundered with the realization, and hot triumph surged through me as I dropped my hands and shifted to face him.

"*We're still here,*" I repeated.

"Yes," Troy whispered, "We are."

"And we will be until we're not, but if I keep waiting for some imaginary, impossible benchmark to say, 'okay, now I'm safe,' we'll never have our family. I'll never feel safe because I'm always looking for the next threat from the world and always choking on the anxiety of it. But I'm bigger than this. This is where too much is just enough. If I have faith in me—in *us*, because you're here too—*that's* how I feel safe. By trusting that shit *will* work out, even if it gets rocky. Trusting in my ability to make it so."

My words came faster as I reached my conclusion, the one that had been staring at me since I'd told Troy that I wanted to make sure it was too dangerous and expensive for the Bureau for Supernatural Investigation to come for us, and since I'd asked him what I had to do to feel safe.

"I have to claim this," I said. "You said once that I'm used to being the victim, and you're right. I have to shift my mindset and build the life I want in spite of everything. Not wait to be accepted or until I feel like I've done enough to make the world safer. I have to take it and fight for it. For us. Every day, not until some undefined and always shifting finish line."

He was the one trembling now, his knuckles white from their grip on his knees as he held himself back.

"Troy...I choose us. I'll fight for us. Fully and faithfully. Out of hope for what we'll have, not defensive fear of what might come for us. My parents didn't let the risk of what happened to them stop them. I won't either."

He hissed a breath in and looked at the ceiling.

"Thank you." When he looked at me, tears glistened in his eyes, although he blinked them back so they wouldn't fall. "After two years...I was starting to doubt if I could make you feel safe enough. I didn't realize until just now how much—"

He cut off, and tears sprang to my own eyes as I realized he'd been blaming himself for my not cycling yet. He'd been carrying the burden of thinking he was failing somehow, at being an elf or a man or a king, maybe all three, and in all that time he'd only made more of an effort. He'd never put any of the blame or pressure for having kids—the heirs that would establish a new dynasty, or simply fulfill one of his quiet dreams—on me.

"Oh no. Troy, it was never your fault." I slid closer.

He reached for me so quickly it was more like a strike, dragging me to sit astride his lap and then cupping my face in his hands. "I need to be honest."

"Okay." My heart raced. He never lied, but he evaded or obscured. His honesty was usually painful.

"I was afraid this attack on the house, the police being here, Jo taking photos, exposing yourself, all of it—I was afraid it would prove to you that you could never be safe. And I didn't know what to do or how I could fix it. I couldn't figure out how to give you safety. But I'm too selfish to step aside and let someone else try. I love you and our life too much. So, you saying this and meaning it...I feel like I can breathe again. Like I haven't failed at the one thing I was raised to do and be. Like there's still a chance to have the family I want with the woman I choose and love." He pulled me closer to kiss away the tears I couldn't stop from falling. "We have a long and hard road ahead, cariñamí. But I am here with you every step of the way, however you need me."

I kissed him, equal parts gratitude and apology. Glad I had him, my partner in everything up to and including crime.

As that thought crossed my mind, another came right behind it like a lightning bolt. "Oh fuck."

Troy stiffened. "What?"

"We have to get married. The legal thing, not the ceremony. As soon as possible."

He stared at me.

"Spousal privilege," I said, grimacing at my abrupt change in subject right when he was being vulnerable. "We were the only two here for what happened earlier. They can compel us to testify against each other in a hearing."

Troy sneered. "They can try. They're not Monteagues. And I don't see why we'd oblige ourselves to follow mundane law."

"Because I've been saying this whole time that we *do* follow their laws. That's the whole point, that this new legislation is unjustified because we're already integrated and following the law." I eyed him and cocked an eyebrow. "Even if I doubt you've ever willingly obeyed a speed limit in your life."

"Those are inconvenient suggestions intended for people with slower reflexes." He leaned back against the wall though, considering the angles. "You know that one way or another they are going to find a way to pin us with that. Following their laws."

"I know."

"That means arrest, Arden. They know about bronze."

"I *know*." I softened my tone. "We're working on it. We will figure out what to do about that but right now can we focus on the thing we can fix? Please?"

His gaze was hard when he brought it back down to mine. "I want a full elven wedding when the hearing is over. The whole three-night affair. The new moon hunt. The gala. All of it."

I hadn't known any of that was a thing. Didn't matter. "I told you. Your dream wedding. That doesn't change. We'll have it."

"Fine." He nudged me to get off him then got up and headed for the kitchen table, where his laptop sat. "We've got a couple hangups. First, it'll probably be at least a week until we can get an appointment for the marriage license. That puts us dangerously close to the hearing, especially after today. And you know that they'll have flags in the system. As soon as the appointment request goes in, the Bureau will be on it. Second, we need an officiant. We don't have anyone in the magistrate's office."

I got over the mental stumble of Troy being so keen on this that he'd already known what we needed—of course he did—and followed him. "We have to try it. If they're watching us, fine. We gain intel on that front."

"And if they come for us?"

"I won't be taken. Not in my own city."

Troy studied me. "You'd attack."

"I'd *defend*. I have immunity in North Carolina so they'd have to come up with a federal crime. If they could do that, they wouldn't be having us go to Washington, DC. You and I both know that's their real trap."

"Attacking federal agents, even in defense, gives them that federal crime and allows them to accelerate their timeline. Hell, if they figure out you took down the drone, that gives them a reason. That's assuming being a dangerous Othersider of unknown type isn't enough."

The finger quotes he put around that last part and the mocking voice he said it in made me snort a laugh, even if none of this was funny.

"We could have the Darkwatch run interference though," he added.

"Will Omar do it?"

"He can do it or he can reckon with me." The steel in Troy's tone said he'd follow through, regardless of the upset it would cause. Then he sighed. "It's a long shot. We can't use lethal force and we can't do anything that would obviously expose elves. Not right before this hearing. They don't need more to question us on."

"Yeah." I slouched in my chair, frustrated that I'd had this idea so late. Just like with the feeling safe thing, I'd put off thinking about the happiness of the wedding for when things felt calmer. "Well...let's try it. Maybe they'll be too busy explaining a missing drone and a recalcitrant state governor to some appropriations committee. Or, you know, putting together a case they can use to arrest us the minute we're on federal property."

Troy grimaced but nodded. "Okay."

A minute's thought with my cooled tea gave me a possibility for the second part. "We can check with the witches for an officiant. Janae will know someone."

"Will they be willing to be outed?"

"Only way to find out is to ask." There was the additional consideration that the witches were concerned about my power growth, but getting magic back had to be worth something.

"You sort that out. I'll get the paperwork and appointments. Who do you want for witnesses?"

"Darius and Allegra for sure," I said. "Which means Maria and Noah will probably be there, and probably Doc Mike."

Troy smiled, a genuine one this time. "I love that the first people who come to mind are my blood. That means a lot."

"They accepted me." I shrugged, then stifled a yawn as the last of my energy high from using so much magic finally wore off. "More than the elementals did, for sure."

He glanced up at me when I didn't quite manage to stifle the second yawn.

"I know," I said to the warning look. "We can't get married right this minute and nobody is attacking us for the time being, so we need to sleep."

Satisfied, he turned his attention back to the computer. "There. Marriage license appointment booked. We got lucky. Monday."

"All we have to do is hold off the mundanes for five days."

From the flicker of Troy's secondary teeth, he'd get us there even if it meant the second coming of the Wild Hunt and another trip through the Duat.

Chapter 9

The drone attack accelerated our timeline on everything.

As tempted as I was to let the Lestari elves stew, we needed to either get an alliance sealed or get them the hell outta my territory. Plus, truth be told, I was anxious to expand my influence after the win with the Southwest Desert weres. I only wanted to deal with the federal government the once because it wasn't just the US government that was making itself a problem, and the more of Otherside I had aligned with me, the more resources I could bring to bear. If I could get the feds in line, it would have a domino effect on mundane leadership in other countries.

Yes, it was entirely unrealistic and far too much pressure to put on myself, but I was coming to accept that this was how I did things.

High pressure, high risk, high reward.

With the elves and the rest of my demesnes, I'd smashed through every single obstacle, shattered every objection, and overturned any unjust laws that blocked the future I wanted to build. I'd started as I meant to go on without even realizing it—and now that I did realize it, new opportunities sprouted in the cracks I was making in "how we've always done things." I might have still felt like I was too much sometimes, but the more I stepped into my full power, the more life and events either aligned with me or fell away to expose what wasn't going to work.

Best of all, my embracing those facts was making Troy relax. He'd been picking up my personal anxieties for so long in the bond that they'd amplified his own. Growing into my own inner badass gave us both a break, and with the usual feedback loop, the effects multiplied.

These out-of-state elves would be my allies, on my terms.

I wouldn't have it any other way, so I needed to set the example for larger, federated Otherside alliances that stretched beyond contiguous territories.

After a restless few hours of sleep, Troy and I showered, dressed in what I'd taken to calling royal casual, and headed over to the Solari mansion just after noon. The mood had shifted when we arrived, maybe because both Allegra and Etain were present for this audience. Or because this time of day generally had elves at their worst, especially this close to a new moon. Or it might be because Rio was starting to see that his plan really wasn't going to work.

Regardless, it was all points in my favor.

This time, I swept in like I owned the place in spirit and not just on paper. Allegra stood to the side of Troy's chair, playing knight, princess, and majordomo all in one.

"All rise." Her quiet, firm voice said she was not fucking around.

I paused to give her a quick hug and cheek kisses as I passed, startling her enough to tense as she returned them before she grinned.

"Thank you for being here, sister," I said.

"Wouldn't miss it." Amusement bubbled under her tone now that she'd caught on to my playing politics.

Troy echoed my gestures with a similar amusement filtering through the bond. *So you really were listening to our court etiquette lessons.*

Sometimes.

We sat perfectly in unison, which threw some of our guests, exactly as I'd wanted.

I rested my hand on Troy's. "Now, Prince Rio and friends, y'all have had some time to think through your options. Talk to me about making better choices."

If he was feeling the jetlag, the hour, or the captivity, Rio seemed determined not to show it. He lifted his chin. "I wish I could. But other than accepting House Solari's offer to pay off the debt owed by the vampire Cade and his solidaire, all I can offer is a word of warning to show good faith."

I barely managed not to roll my eyes. Of course. More games. "And that warning is..."

He shot Troy a nasty look. "In our House, Troy Monteague has another moniker: Queenkiller."

At my side, Troy made no physical reaction. The bond though...that dropped into the pits of hell before locking down so hard it dizzied me. Troy had already confessed to queenkilling, so his reaction couldn't be for the name. Or not entirely anyway. It had to be that personal leverage Troy was planning to use strategically.

Whatever this was about, there was danger in it.

Rio's attention flicked back to me. "How much longer will you stay safe with him at your side, *Queen* Arden? He killed my mother first, after a year in our House, then spent two more years getting close to my sister before making his move. You only claimed him what, a year or two ago?"

Time to make another point. I arched an eyebrow as I rose, drawing Troy up as well. I stepped in front of him and leaned back against his chest, sending a nudge in the bond. *My throat.*

Troy did more than obey. He put on a show.

His right hand skimmed up my body and between my breasts to encircle my neck and squeeze. His left played along the waistband of my jeans and tweaked the button. A light kiss to the crown of my head preceded his chin settling on it.

"I know who and what Troy is. He's even killed me once, technically." I pushed past Troy's mental flinch. "And yet my life has been in his hands so many times since then that, if he truly wanted me dead, he could have done it any day in the last two years. He could do it now, fast enough that none of my Ebon Guard could stop him. And even surrounded by my Ebon Guard, he's powerful enough that he could escape."

To make my point, Troy squeezed my throat hard enough to make my breath come in a rasp before easing up and shifting his grip to my chin, tilting my head aside. A faint *snick* warned me the sharp teeth had come out before the light pinch to the side of my neck, followed by a kiss to the same spot.

Allegra and the Ebon Guard tensed but stayed where they were at my hand signal.

"Actions speak louder than words, Prince Rio," I said as I scrambled to push aside the flare of heat shooting from my core to between my thighs. Goddess but Troy could work a situation. "As you can see, he's quite thoroughly mine. And I won't tolerate threats against him, in case that's where you're going next. If you and your queen have any interest in an alliance, you need to offer me something else. I don't trade people like livestock, and replacing Troy is a nonstarter."

Tentative relief whispered through the bond as Troy settled, his embrace slipping to a loose clasp around my waist.

Rio watched with open hunger despite what he'd said about perversions. Jealousy tinged his words with heat as he said, "I see you've managed to thaw him out."

I smiled. "Or maybe the people your House threw at him simply weren't worthy of him. He does have standards."

Bitter amusement from Troy in the bond. *I said exactly that once.*

The tension in the room stretched so tight that my guards were getting twitchy, and even I could smell the dangerous combination of anger, sexual desire, and pain—from both men.

I needed to end this before it exploded.

"I can see you need a little more time to consider the situation. Maybe this new information will help," I said. "We're done here. Etain?"

She took my cue to round up our guests and take them back to the reinforced dining room where they were being held.

When we were alone, Allegra stepped closer. "You two wanna fill me in?"

I stayed where I was in Troy's arms, giving myself a moment to anchor, and shrugged. "I want an alliance now, or I want them gone. There was a news alert on the way over about more riots in Cincinnati and a vampire was staked in Paris. We don't have time for this."

Her glance jumped over my head to Troy. "And the queenkilling?"

"Opened the opportunity for the current queen," he said flatly. "If she complains, it's saving face."

Allegra grimaced. "You're not going to deny it?"

"What's the point? You already knew about it."

She glanced at me then back up to him, and her eyebrows lifted in surprise. "You told her."

"Yes," he said. "And like I told you, my reputation was never mine to shape back then."

There must have been a bigger conversation I'd missed because I couldn't figure out why Allegra scented the air quickly then relaxed.

"Good," she said. "I'll just go and see if I can't nudge things along then. This could impact our Senate hearing play."

"Exactly," I said. "Thank you."

With a fist-to-heart salute that actually looked genuine, she hopped down from the dais and headed in the direction Etain had taken the other elves.

You okay? I asked Troy.

I could be better. But that show was a good play for the point I need to make. His embrace tightened. *If you're up for it...*

What?

There's one more thing we could do.

Whatever will help.

Troy kissed my neck then released me, took my hand, and pulled me behind him with fingers laced in mine. *The main suite in this house is reserved for us, in case we ever needed another place to stay.*

The massive bedroom he led us to was tastefully decorated in blues and greens, just like I had at home. Things matched better here in shade and pattern, but between the colors, the small water fountain tinkling away in the corner, the plants, and the incense burner resting on the dresser, it was clear this space had been created to welcome an elemental.

To welcome *me*.

Just like the updates to his safehouse.

Troy was watching my reaction. "You like it?"

"It's perfect," I whispered. Then I caught on to why this room and how it tied into what we'd demonstrated a few minutes ago. "Fucking here will help your agenda?"

"It'll drive home the point to Rio and any others in the group with similar ambitions." He approached and stood in front of me, looking at the hardwood floor. "First though, I should have told you about the assassin sooner. I don't know if it would have helped with this situation. But maybe there would be fewer games. Rio and the man they sent last summer were close."

"You were doing what you thought best. And you did allude to it, when you insisted we go to the beach." I kissed him, relieved when he opened his mouth for my tongue.

His hands stayed behind his back though. I'd be dominant today, then.

Good. Hearing about how he'd practically been sold to another House for their fucking breeding program and then having representatives of that House show up here and try to knock him from his place with me to carry out the same ugly practice...suddenly I understood why claimings—the bites—were such a big fucking deal for him.

This was his choice, freely exercised and validated. A reminder that he controlled his destiny now. He wanted people to know it.

"You. Are. Mine," I said against his lips.

This time, his shudder was definitely relief and, from his scent, desire. "Yes, my queen. I am."

We stripped with the quickness of a need for reassurance. I pushed him back toward the bed and straddled him. We had shit to do today so this would have to be quick, but we both needed it, even aside from the political game. My tiredness meant that we hadn't been enjoying each other as frequently as we usually did, and we were both hungry for it.

When I sank onto his cock, I couldn't help a groan that echoed in the big room. I slapped a hand over my mouth, eyes wide at the unexpected amplification. This room had much higher ceilings than my bedroom at home, but I'd been too distracted to pay attention to the air movements.

"Let them hear," Troy whispered. "Please."

The aching vulnerability in that request stoked the fire in me even higher. I rode him hard, my hips pressed against his as I rocked, his grip on my thighs. I let all the pleasure building inside me spill from my lips in cries and gasps of his name. My movements grew shaky and uncoordinated as I jerked to stay in that spot...right there...

My climax hit me so hard I collapsed forward, catching myself on Troy's chest.

"May I?" he whispered against my ear.

"Yes. And make it hard."

The thrill in the bond at being ordered to do something he deeply wanted to do anyway sent another jolt of pleasure through me. Then he rolled us and started fucking me in a smooth, continuous movement.

I pushed my hips up to meet every thrust, wanting to take him deep. He was *mine*, and these fucking West Coast elves would know it—and that he couldn't be replaced.

A second orgasm hit unexpectedly and hard.

No Aether, just built-up hormones further spiked by what had happened earlier.

Impulse ran away with my tongue. "Breed me."

Those words flipped a switch. Troy unraveled faster than I'd ever seen, plunging from intense desire to unchained passion in a breath. The light focus he always kept on me spun straight down to his balls as he fucked me even harder.

As I sobbed his name, Troy took my mouth with a savage kiss, throbbing where we were joined as he came.

When our motion slowed and then stopped, he rested his forehead against mine. I got the sense he was trying to remember his own name as he panted.

I wiggled, enjoying his body pressed full-length against and in mine. "Those are the magic words, huh?"

"Arden." He lifted his head to fix me with a look of smoldering need that pierced my soul. "You have no idea of the fantasy you've just fulfilled."

"Only part of it, I think." I knew how much he wanted a child. "I suspect for the fullness of it, we'll need to work some more on the hormones."

The look he gave me then was so full of hunger and longing that I wasn't sure if he was going to fuck me again or eat me alive.

"I love you more than there are words to express," he finally said.

"Good. It'd be a shame if I did all this out of loving possessiveness and political capital, and you were just doing your duty."

He laughed then kept laughing as he buried his face in the pillow. Like a dam of emotional pressure had broken. I rubbed his back and kissed his neck and shoulder, pushing away thoughts of what else needed doing today to just be with him.

When we finally cleaned up and got dressed, the tension that'd been riding him all day was gone. He was loose and easy, almost cocky, as we emerged from the bedroom.

Good. I liked him like that. Not beaten down or hiding. Not repressed or wrathful. Not faking or putting on a mask. A king fully at his ease.

Allegra waited in the kitchen, leaning against the island in the center.

"Nice touch," she said.

I flushed hot, still not used to how casually elves took the use of sex in politics. PDA was gauche, but loud sex behind closed doors was just another chess move. Worth it to rebalance Troy and advance his goals, even as it reminded me our guests had almost certainly heard everything, given the quietness in the house.

What specific message did we just send? I asked Troy.

He smirked. *Aside from your preference for me despite another good option? That you're well-pleased with my actions and conduct and rewarded me accordingly. And are further pleased by my performance.*

Fair enough.

That just sent Troy's confidence the last rung up to cocky in the bond, but he kept his voice controlled as he said, "We should get back."

I sighed, really not wanting to go back to figuring out the federal government, even if it would give me a break from Otherside politics. But that was the job I'd taken on, so I'd get it done.

Chapter 10

As we passed the dining room where Etain was now interrogating Rio, the prince gave Troy another ugly look. Insight flashed.

This was about more than Troy ruining his mission to seduce me. The key here was this personal grievance Troy had hinted at but hadn't wanted to talk about. I hoped I was wrong. But from the tightness of Etain's shoulders and her terse questions, Rio had just been flirting rather than answering anything. We weren't going to get anywhere like this.

I paused and eyed Rio. "This isn't just about your queen. This is personal."

His bare attempt at a pleasant expression for me slipped as he glared at Troy again. "Not at all. But seeing as you're obviously completely uninterested in me, I am authorized to offer an alliance with the Northwest Mountains demesne even without a marriage pact." His slow smile dripped poison. "In exchange for your king's heart, that is."

It was too ridiculous to get mad, even with Troy's fury coursing through the bond.

"So, you'll treat with an elemental queen but demand *his* heart? Like hell it's not personal." I approached, ignoring Troy's low warning growl to circle behind Rio and lean forward to speak low in his ear. "Did you know Troy is a truthreader?"

The young prince's expression was blank and his face pale when I came back around.

"Apparently not," I said as I returned to Troy and tucked myself under his arm. I hadn't missed the hungry way half of Rio's entourage had watched us earlier or the way Troy's blood ran hot now. Not even figuratively—as I ran a hand up his back and over his shoulder to play with the hair at the nape of his neck, his skin radiated heat.

This was weird. It looked like Troy was right that the West Coast queens had figured out I couldn't be beaten head-on, so they'd sent options for bedroom diplomacy instead. Only they must have missed something in Rio's background—or maybe they were counting on the chip on his shoulder to push him to succeed against Troy?

"Nothing to say for yourself now?" I prodded the still-quiet Rio.

He started to speak but shut his mouth again, considering before saying, "I do have a personal grievance, my queen."

"Truth," Troy said softly. Then, to my surprise, he added, "With cause."

Rio's eyes widened, and his face flushed. "So you admit it."

"Admit...?"

"You know what you did."

Concerned, I started to step in but subsided when Troy squeezed my hip.

"I know," he said. "But do you? Really?"

All of Rio's composure shattered, and he started to rise, stopping as a grim-faced Etain forced him to sit again with a hand on his shoulder and Allegra slid from behind us to intercept.

"You mazed me," Rio snarled, stabbing an accusatory finger at Troy before shifting his attention to me. "I want justice for magical trespass, with witnesses. Witnesses from *my* House. I'm no human to be manipulated like that!"

Well shit. This had escalated quickly. Magical trespass was a capital offense, a protective loophole in the might-makes-right way things were often done between Othersiders—assuming, of course, that the aggrieved party survived and could prove the crime had occurred.

I moved to stand to the side, settling in a parade rest where I could see both Rio and Troy. "You're asking me as Arbiter or as High Queen?"

"Arbiter," he snarled.

That was annoying. I had more leeway with elven matters as High Queen, although that might have been why Rio hadn't led with this accusation.

I took in the mood of the room. Everyone was dead still, glancing between the three of us.

Troy hadn't moved, but he had a resigned air. In the same quiet tone as before, he said, "As King, I submit to the Arbiter's judgment."

I assume you have an out? I sent.

Sort of.

"Very well," I said aloud, proud of myself for keeping my fear for Troy locked in my heart and away from my voice. "Allegra, Etain, get everyone back together please."

We headed back to the throne room. Troy seemed resigned and more tired than I'd seen him in weeks.

I'm sorry, I sent.

It's fine. I had a feeling it would come out. I just hope I can get them to understand.

I squeezed his hand. I hadn't even considered that magical trespass would be on the table for something other than the occasion that'd resulted in our original bond. Now I was worried I'd been outmaneuvered.

They couldn't have Troy. Even if it meant stepping down as Arbiter and taking drastic action.

When everyone was assembled and Troy was seated, I stood in front of my throne and said, "Make your case, Prince Rio."

"Daud told me everything before he came here and disappeared," Rio snarled at Troy. "He said you mindmazed me repeatedly. That you enjoyed playing puppet master."

Troy sat forward, leaning his elbows on his knees. "First, let the record show that Daud, Lestari House Guard Captain, was captured in the process of attempting to assassinate Arbiter Arden Finch Solari. He didn't disappear. I killed him. Which I admit to openly so you'll know what I say next is also true." He raised his voice over the shocked and outraged whispers. "I didn't enjoy a single moment of my mission to Seattle. Over the course of three years, I was sexually assaulted, coerced into various criminal acts including murder, made to fight gladiator battles, and also forced to commit magical trespass against you, Rio. First by your mother, Queen Yuliana, and then by her daughter and your sister, Queen Vina."

Rio had turned an odd shade of green. It was all I could do to bite my tongue and let Troy speak.

"Shall I undo the maze, Rio?" he asked. "Do you want to know why they ordered me to commit that particular crime?"

Troy, what—

He cut off the rest of my sending by slamming a wall up.

Fuck. This was bad. Or worse than bad. To my knowledge, he'd never publicly spoken about the shit that had either been done to him or that he'd been forced to participate in. He'd barely spoken about it to me. That he was doing so now, with an audience—this had to be an effort to fast-track an alliance that we needed, even at the cost of his secrets and his pain and the risk to his life.

Rage warred with fear in Rio's expression. "You clearly think it will absolve you."

"Not at all. Orders or not, I did what I did."

"Then what game are you playing?"

Troy rose with the slow grace of a stalking lion and stepped close enough that, if Rio was fast, he might get Troy with a fist if nothing else.

"It's not a game. None of this is or ever was. What the queens did, to both of us" —he looked around the room, meeting the eyes of several people on both our side and theirs— "to all of us, was abuse. We stay quiet in our shame. Look away as it's done again to someone else. Help to cover it up. Because that's our culture, right? That's how it's always been. That's what the queens always said was best for the overall management of our faction. But I'm standing here to say that it's not for our good, and it never was. It was for their sick entertainment and thirst for power."

I was trying my damnedest not to shake. The emotions in the room were palpable. The normally blank, stoic, or mocking masks and neutral stances the elves tended to maintain had crumbled. Some were looking into the far distance like they were remembering something awful. Some looked ashamed. Others were crying or looking pissed.

But none of the elves in the room were okay. Oddly, I was the only one not acting like I was reliving the sins of the past, whether they were mine or committed against me.

Which was when I figured out that Troy's passive power had evolved from encouraging others to feel at ease in his presence to feeling what he was feeling. The wall he'd put up combined with my own shields were protecting me, but the rest of the room was falling apart. Even Darius and Thana, now among the Ebon Guard ringing the room, were trembling and fighting back tears. I couldn't even tell if Troy knew he was doing it.

Oh holy hell.

I gritted my teeth and clenched my fists with the effort to keep myself from moving or speaking as Troy continued.

"This isn't a game," he repeated. "I am offering restitution in the form of your unmazed memories."

"Impossible," Rio whispered.

Troy shook his head. "Not for me. I restored my queen's memories once, in much more difficult conditions. I can restore yours as easily as I breathe."

Rio's fists clenched, and he dropped the sharp teeth with a growl. "Then do it. And when I learn what you've hidden from me, I'll take my justice for it in blood."

The scent of burnt marshmallow flared. Then Troy hesitated and looked to me. "Arbiter? By your leave."

I nodded, unable to speak past the lump in my throat.

With walls and shields up, I hadn't realized Troy had done anything until Rio choked. Anguish contorted his features as he dropped to a knee. The Ebon Guard moved to stop West Coast elves from surging forward.

"Nobody move," I ordered, adding a crackle of lightning to make the point as the scent of magic and the weight of Troy's power signature lessened. "Prince Rio?"

"But they told me—" His expression was lost as he looked at Troy. "I *hated* you!"

"I know," Troy said. I wondered if anyone else could hear the note of sadness in his voice.

Rio's other knee and both hands hit the ground as a sob ripped from him. "And they laughed."

"Every single time." Troy stepped closer and knelt. "At you. And at me. They enjoyed our pain."

The younger man growled and recoiled. "How do I know you didn't create these memories just now?"

"Not one of my talents," Troy said. "I can obscure and make people forget. I can modify existing memories or restore what was lost. I can read auras for truth. But I can't take a memory entirely or create a completely new one from something that never happened."

Darius flinched. Apparently, he could do some of those, not just steal them. Good to know.

Shaking, Rio lifted his head. His gaze searched Troy's face before he turned to me. "I withdraw my accusation. And I beg a boon. From both the Arbiter and the King of Solari."

Troy rose and backed away slowly, until he was standing at my side again.

"Ask," we said together.

"Sanctuary. For me and any here who want to stay. I will help you get my cousin to agree to an alliance. But I never want to go back."

I looked at Troy and poked him with Chaos so he'd let his wall down a little. *It was that bad?*

Worse than bad. He glanced around the room, startling mentally to see the shape everyone was in. *What—*

Your passive power. I'll explain what I saw later. Do you want him here?

Better here than there.

I turned back to Rio. "Granted, as Arbiter. Sanctuary for you and any who wish to stay, as long as they follow the rules of my territory. That includes actively defending elementals, by the way."

"Granted, as King," Troy said. "But only if those who stay renounce their House oaths and re-swear to a House here in the Triangle. Their choice, based on their area of community interest, not their Aetheric foci."

Rio frowned. "What does that mean?"

I lifted Troy's hand to kiss it. "My King had an excellent idea: that we should reorganize the House system according to how it would benefit the faction and the broader community." Another thing he'd taken care of while I slept off the effects of the heist that restored magic. "House Solari has leadership in political matters and advocacy. House Mahan, headed by Queen Keeya and King Mansa, steward local defensive efforts. House Azer, headed by Queen Helia and King Ninos, steward local economic and social development. Oh, and there are no more breeding programs."

An elf on the edge of the group stepped forward and tentatively raised a bound hand. "Sovereigns?"

"Yes?" I said. "What's your name?"

He ducked his head. "Taman, my queen. Apologies but...you said your king had this idea. Did that mean you allow males to be actively involved in setting policy, not just offering advice? And that those choosing to stay could choose their own partners?" He blushed. "Even if that partner was...not physically compatible for procreation."

I held in a sigh. Fucking queens. "Let me be very clear. People of all genders and sexual orientations are welcomed to join a House of their choosing; contribute according to their strengths and abilities; to live with, love, and marry who they wish; to make their own reproductive choices—including not to have children at all—and to leave my service for any reason. Troy and I want people to want to be here. We want everyone to have a reason to believe in and fight for what we're all doing here together. And we want to reduce the reasons for power struggles between Houses, within the faction, and with other Otherside factions. We must be unified in the face of the mundane threat. Beyond that, I simply don't have the time to police people's personal lives. As long as it's all consenting, there are bigger damn issues to focus on."

Troy nodded. "You, Rio, I would have swear to Arden, simply based on the history between Houses Monteague and Lestari. Your people have options." He evaluated the room. "Take the night to think about it. You may ask the people here about their experiences. If they want to talk, they are free to do so. If they don't, they won't be forced. We'll open this House tonight for a gathering, and royals will absent themselves so that all can speak freely about the good and the bad without pressure or fear of repercussion."

I didn't love having strangers wandering through what was technically my second home, but if it meant we had even just the Northwest Mountains elves on our side? Then it was another step toward a national alliance. One that would give me the political weight I needed to go toe-to-toe with the mundanes with more legitimacy and an important step toward my goal to set an example internationally.

So, I nodded and wove my fingers between Troy's to squeeze his hand. "If there's nothing else, we'll go make those arrangements."

Rio knelt. "I want it done now please. The oaths. I won't go back. And I want you to be able to trust my word when I negotiate with my cousin to secure the alliance."

I frowned but let Troy answer when he squeezed my hand.

"Are you okay with me administering it?" Troy asked. "We need a workaround with elementals."

Rio swallowed hard and shuddered but nodded.

"Rio." Troy's voice was firm. "I will not force this on you. You choose it of your own will."

The younger elf looked up. "I am sure. I— This isn't how I saw this mission going. But you and your queen—*my* queen now—are the first people to have offered truth. Not only offered it but put yourselves and your reputations on the line to follow through. I want to swear now."

Troy looked at me, expressionless.

If it creates an opportunity to bring us the West Coast, yes, I sent.

As Rio knelt and Troy administered the oath, facilitating the magic that would transfer the existing Lestari oath to me and make it nearly impossible for Rio to betray me, I scanned the group of elves who'd initially come to kill or overthrow me. How many of them would side with me? How many would join one of the other Houses in the Chapel Hill Conclave as a deep cover, only to strike later? Swearing to another queen would still allow them to attack me.

I couldn't know how this would play out. I could only do my best to prove that I meant what I said.

When Rio rose, I took his hands and—to his surprise—exchanged cheek kisses, a queen welcoming a foreign royal. One of the endless court etiquette lessons Troy had drilled into me in the last couple of years. One I'd never thought I'd need to remember because I'd never welcomed a visiting royal to my home at all, let alone in peace, and had figured it'd stay that way, given past history.

Rio's fingers trembled in mine, but when he pulled away, he bowed more deeply than was necessary, first to me then to Troy. "My queen. My king. I will honor this chance to make things right and to unify East Coast and West."

"That's all we ask," I said. "Unity, among and between Othersiders. We have bigger battles to fight with the mundanes than the ones we've fought between each other. Let's build a new world together."

As Troy and I left, the room was silent. A weight hung over everyone in it, like the West Coast elves couldn't believe what'd just happened.

Good. Because neither could I.

Chapter 11

T he drive home was silent. I was glad I'd insisted on driving because Troy was not in a headspace to focus on the road.

He burst out of the car as soon as I parked. For a moment, I thought he was going to try running it off, but he just leaned against the car, hugging himself as he stared at the sky.

"What did I do to them?" he asked roughly.

I shut my door gently and came around to his side, leaning against a tree, out of arm's reach in case he wanted space. "I think your passive power has evolved or grown somehow."

"So, instead of making people feel at ease, I traumatize them."

"No—"

"Or retraumatize them. Goddess damn me to—"

"Hey! Stop that." I pushed off my tree and moved in front of him, crossing my arms to stop myself from trying to comfort him physically. "You didn't know it was happening. As far as I can tell, it was sympathetic. They felt their version of what I imagine you were feeling."

Troy stared at me, bleaker than I'd ever seen from him. "And now you won't even touch me."

Exasperated, I poked with Chaos. "Walls."

He dropped his with a scowl that melted as my deep concern for him came through. "Oh."

"Yeah. Oh. I'm trying not to push into your space because I don't know what you need from me right now. There was too much going on earlier with a whole Goddess-fucked *trial*." I took a breath and tried to temper my voice. This was not his fault. He was dealing with shit, publicly, and it hurt. It hurt him and everyone around him, and it wasn't even his fault. "I'm sorry. I just— Usually I can figure out what you need most, but there were a lot of triggers today. So, cariñomí, I am *asking you* to please tell me what hurts. Tell me what you need and how I can give it to you without making you think about...about what was done to you in Seattle."

With a miserable look, he hesitated then slowly opened his arms.

I checked the bond, finding an ache for touch that he wanted to ignore but was too stressed to, and threw myself into an embrace. "What you did was incredibly brave."

Disgust slithered through the bond. "I manipulated them. Because I didn't want you to have to execute me."

I gave that the consideration I thought he needed from me right now rather than the reflexive denial he'd think was me being a love-addled fool in his current self-destructive mindset. "Did you lie?"

"No. I almost wish I had."

"Did you intend for your passive power to do what it did?"

"Goddess, no."

"Was there any other way that you could have preserved your life against a capital accusation, with mine in the balance?"

Troy's arms tightened around me as he thought about that. "No."

"Then yes, you may have manipulated the situation. But you did it toward multiple good aims. You protected yourself and your queen. You secured an ally using the truth rather than threats, deception, torture, or murder, and you did it in record time. And honestly, Troy? From what I saw, you probably did more to advance reform in fifteen minutes than in the last fifteen months."

He was quiet for a good minute. I waited, using his chest as a pillow and letting the breeze calm me. Keeping my side of the bond wide open so he could absorb some of that calm, if he wanted.

"It was still wrong to hurt them. Even if I didn't mean to," Troy finally said.

"I don't disagree. But now you know, and you can be more mindful of your passive power next time. Yeah, that was a lot to put on people. But everyone's been dancing around it for the entire time since we came to power. You set an example, as a faction head, of coming out in the open with it. Maybe next time warn people or something. But I mean, it was a trial that we didn't know was coming, and you only spoke the barest details of the facts. The hardest parts are stuck in your head and Rio's. Let the dead queens own the burden of what was done. You keep the burden of doing better. Okay?"

Troy shifted, peeling me away from him so he could see my face. "You're not embarrassed of me? Ashamed to be with me?"

Confusion pulled me from the breeze's calm. "Huh?"

"I couldn't— I wasn't strong enough to stop them. The queens. And the way I just—" He scoffed, and the bond twisted and roiled even as his hands tightened on my shoulders, like he was afraid I'd try to escape him. "Just poured everything out like 'poor me' or something. It was pathetic. Weak."

Oh, this man.

He'd come a long way from his self-protective snapping and snarling last summer, when he was initially figuring out that I wasn't playing any games with him and that, when I said something to him, all I wanted or intended was what I said on the surface. When he was still learning that there was no trap in my invitation to move in with me or have free access to our home and land. That he had options and could push back and say no or even shout and be angry if he needed to be. That he was safe.

Coming a long way didn't mean the journey was over though.

Bond or no bond, I had to keep reminding myself that he had more than thirty years of deep, abiding fuck-up-edness to work through. Decades of abuse. Assassination attempts on him; torture by members of his family; his mother and aunt murdered; his father tortured, exiled, and now being held by us for his role in the loss of magic and credible threats against me. That was just what'd happened or been done to him, not even considering what he'd been pushed to do against his will. It was a lot. And no matter how strong he could be for me or how much patience and grace he could offer me as I figured out who I was now that I was free of Callista and head of a growing portion of Otherside, he didn't always offer that same strength or patience or grace to himself.

I gave myself a few moments more to choose my words carefully. "No. I'm not ashamed or embarrassed to be with you. I don't think you're pathetic." I searched the shadowed labradorite of his gaze, willing him to know that I was speaking the honest truth now. "I'm proud of you for leading with vulnerability. I'm honored that you trust me and feel safe enough to talk this through with me now. I don't blame you for the things other people did to you or forced you to do or to be. You're what we need right now. People who can lead with heart, not more tyrants."

Troy studied me then probed with the bond. "You mean that. All of it."

"Yes."

He narrowed his eyes, riffling through my mind in the semi-instinctive way he did, as a born Monteague, when he was dangerously uncertain. It was a slight overstep on our agreed boundaries but one I let pass for situations like this. My continued love and affection were the one real insecurity he still had and only really when he was in this headspace. He wouldn't have asked me to fuck him where people could hear if he wasn't in a bad place; he knew how weird I found that aspect of elven culture.

I relaxed, closed my eyes, and drew him in. Pulled up some of my favorite memories of us together, times when I saw him as his best self.

Whatever he found made him relax, both in his grip on me and his mood. "Thank you, cariñamí. For your faith in me." He rested his forehead against mine. "I think I need to sit with this."

"Take your time. I'm not going anywhere."

Troy cupped my jaw and tilted my head up for a kiss then said, "First, I want to hunt you. Now."

Not surprising that he'd be looking to regain some sense of control. That, I could help with.

"Then let's change."

△▽△▽

After our hunt and its enthusiastic end, Troy withdrew again. He was still physically present. Cooked an extra nice dinner of beef Wellington with wild mushrooms and an exquisite red wine sauce, served with a side salad and a rich Shiraz that got me a little tipsy. But there was something on his mind despite the post-hunt clarity.

I pulled my walls up as subtly as I could and flipped through the various things that'd been going on. His birthday had just passed, but at his insistence, we'd kept the celebration small—just us, Allegra, and Darius here at home to avoid drawing the attention of the mundanes or make a show of extravagance when we were still technically on war footing. Before that had been the massively fucked-up effort to get magic back for Otherside, which had left him with new nightmares and exacerbated old ones. Today was revelations about his time in Seattle, and tonight, our conclave was trying to win over the remaining West Coast elves with us intentionally absent.

Something told me none of that was it.

Troy was...fidgety. In a way that I'd never seen. His presence used to make me paranoid in the early days, just from his mood coming through the bond, but this was straight-up anxiety.

"You wanna talk about it?" I finally asked.

He looked up from his food and stared at me. "What?"

"What's wrong?"

"Nothing."

I blinked at what one might term a lie. From Troy. Who had, as far as I knew, never lied to me in our entire acquaintance.

Squeezing his eyes shut with a wince, he put his silverware down. "I mean, nothing is *bad* wrong. I— Shit. I'm fucking this up."

Okay, it had to be something, given that language from him.

"Stay here." He got up and stomped—stomped! An elf!—to the bedroom.

It was a good thing I'd already cleaned my plate because I wasn't sure I'd be able to finish eating with all this. More secrets? After the deluge that'd come from him in the last couple of months? The excellent dinner sat badly in my stomach, and I tried not to extrapolate what the hell was going on from his weird behavior.

When he got back, Troy extended a small, black box.

"I had this made," he said gruffly. "For you."

Frowning at his odd attitude on top of all of the other weirdness today, I stood, took the box, and cracked it open. Inside was nestled a gold ring exquisitely worked with swirling scrolls that resembled stylized zephyrs. Set almost flush into it was a flawless diamond, flanked on either side by two small, black stones I'd be willing to bet were onyx. My jaw dropped at how beautiful it was and how uniquely it drew together both my origins as a sylph and my heritage as a Solari.

"It's an engagement ring," he added roughly as I stared at it. "You said after the last Duat mission that you wanted to get married this year, and now we've got an appointment for the license. I know it's not how things are done, but you already proposed and with a possible alliance between the Eastern Seaboard and the Northwest Mountains and especially with the mundane hearing coming up..."

He trailed off, looking uncomfortable as hell.

"You wanted both elves and humans to see there's a tie between us," I said, figuring it out. "One the humans in particular would recognize and interpret correctly," I finished as he looked at the floor, hands on his hips.

The bond was closed, but the poor man was flushed and tongue-tied as he nodded, keeping his eyes lowered. He was a romantic in his own way, but unless it was weapons, his usual way was more service than gifts—hence, the special dinner—and this was probably dangerously forward for a male royal. Hell, I was willing to bet it would have cost him dearly in House Monteague or any other traditional elven House.

That he'd done it anyway, especially after the way things had fallen out today, made me want to burst with pride at how far he'd come.

"It's stunning." I put it on, turned around to tuck my back against his front, and held my hand out for us both to see how it sparkled in the setting sun.

His arms slid around me, slow and hesitant, and he tucked his chin over my shoulder. "It's okay?"

"The ring is perfect, and it's absolutely okay that you want to avoid the same stupid games we had to play at the summit and earlier today." I twisted to kiss his jaw. "Thank you. I love it. The ring and the reason."

"Okay." Tension ebbed out of him, and his voice roughened with a combination of relief and soaring delight. "Good. That's good. Dari and Alli said you'd understand. And after what you said earlier about leading with my heart, it seemed like now was right. I just... Sometimes I still get wrapped up in what I was taught."

I was glad that, for once, Allegra in particular hadn't picked at him for wanting to do this. Then again, it probably fell under protecting him—ensuring he was tied as tightly as legally possible to a powerful queen who actually loved and valued him, rather than just wanting him for his genetic contribution or fighting skills. I turned in his arms and wrapped mine around his neck, burying my nose against the corner of his jaw and inhaling so he'd know I wanted to connect with him and his scent. "Thank you for this. I have no idea how to go about a wedding, or what it looks like for you. I'm glad you made a move."

"Yeah?"

"Yeah." I pulled away enough to kiss him. "I thought I'd be in hiding my whole life. A wedding was never on my agenda. I never thought about what it would be like." I hesitated, but I needed to know this. "Did you?"

Troy caressed my cheek with a thumb. "When I was a kid, seeing what my parents had, before—before everything. Then I avoided thinking about it until you proposed." He flushed again and looked away. "A lot since then."

"Then let's do your dream wedding," I said. "Whatever will make your heart happy."

That got me another solid kiss, one that deepened until we were back in the bedroom for the third time in a day.

Worked for me. The deadline to answer the subpoena was coming up, and with all the uncertainty around that, I wanted all the certainty I could always find in Troy's arms.

Chapter 12

The next afternoon, the Darkwatch and Keeya came for the remnants of the drone in my backyard. It was a golden opportunity to gain intel, even if the electronics were fried and it was in pieces. Omar came, but from the wary eye he kept on me while I watched the collection effort, he was more here to evaluate me than supervise his agents.

I did my best to ignore him. The old bastard was following Troy's orders, and Troy himself was watching Omar with an intensity that promised blood if he made the wrong move. Whatever argument they'd had during the Duat trials was festering. Something to deal with sooner or later but not right now.

After that, we headed to the bar, closed it to use as a planning headquarters, and threw ourselves into negotiations with various Otherside factions across the country. The video Darius had recorded was making its way to faction heads, as was news of the alliance with the Southwest Desert. More calls and emails poured in as people saw both what we were up against and what I was marshalling to fight it. When Noah turned up to confirm a successful agreement with Charity of Atlanta and Renaud of Charlotte, we put him to work on the new inquiries from other vampire coteries.

That whole time, nothing came from Sinclaire. No police showed up at the bar. No federal agents. No word from Duke or Iaret about another attempt on me and Troy.

Nothing.

The silence put me on edge more than an attack would have. An attack or an attempt to arrest me, I could do something about. This waiting gave me too much space to worry. We knew they'd have to react to losing the drone and the failed missile strike. They'd have to do something about whatever the governor was throwing back at them, refusing further involvement. Somebody would have to explain why thirty-two National Guards had apparently shot themselves on the same night, or they'd have to figure out a cover-up. Maybe they were arguing over how visible they were willing to be in this shadow war they were waging on Otherside using me as a proxy. There was probably all kind of hustle and hurry in rooms I wasn't in.

The one I was in was stifling. The main room of the bar was bigger than my office but still enclosed, and I was still having trouble with enclosed spaces that weren't my home after the events at Jordan Lake.

"I need air," I said, bouncing to my feet.

"Finally," Harqil muttered. "You're giving me a headache."

Troy shot them a dirty look but only said, "Take one of the Guard with you."

Thana rose from where she was chatting in quiet tones with Zanna at the bar and stretched. "I'll go, if my lady Zanna will excuse me."

The kobold waved her off with a queenly air, turning to continue the conversation with Ruprecht.

"Wait," Thana said as I started to open the door. Then she spoke into a wrist mic in rapid elvish. I caught the word "clear," and then she nodded.

Exasperated but grateful, I got the hell out of the enclosed space and into fresh air, leaning against the window so Troy could see me. The hormonal upset from my trip to Asheville had finally settled, but with things as high tension as they were I knew he'd want at least one of his physical senses on me.

Thana took up a position between me and the parking lot, facing outward to watch for threats and leaving me to a few minutes of peace rather than trying to make small talk, for which I was grateful. I needed to get to the root of what was really bothering me: that if the mundanes did come, I was fucked without some way to get around bronze. Troy and I had been practicing weekly in the time between the Duat trials and now. It was doing wonders to ground his need for reassurance and control and my need to reframe past trauma, given we used sex or combat sparring as our neutral ground.

The problem was that I hadn't yet managed to reach my magic past the bronze. Every time, the elements remained closed to me, completely out of my grasp. We were out of time though. If I couldn't figure out how to get around bronze, we were absolutely fucked when—not if—the mundanes caught me.

I might be a primordial elemental, but even I had weaknesses.

△▽△▽

We wrapped up at midnight and headed home. Still nothing from the feds. No threats. No warnings. They might strike again, but the only anxiety I felt was from my own lack of intel. Nobody had seen the valkyrie or the djinn today, so I was betting we were safe. Iaret, at least, seemed keen to prove her worth these days and would have checked in if there was danger coming our way.

Still, I picked at my dinner, a seafood pasta dish with tomatoes that was probably very good but that I was too distracted to taste.

"Arden."

I looked up to find Troy looking at me with concern. "Huh?"

"What's wrong?"

I put down my fork, finally admitting I had no appetite. "Bronze. We both know that whatever the mundanes do next, it'll involve neutralizing my magic."

"Like you said. We're working on that."

"Unsuccessfully. Troy, you know as well as I do that they need to prove I can be controlled. They've all but declared me—us, even—a national security concern. They know their drug cocktail failed during the kidnapping attempt. They failed to blow up the house and get us from a distance. This is their only next option."

"So, you want to practice now? When they might send another strike?"

"I'm not getting the same nudges from the Sight tonight, and there've been no valkyrie around all day. We've heard nothing from Duke or Iaret either. I think we're okay for now." When he still looked doubtful, I added, "We definitely can't wait to see if they try something between now and getting the marriage license."

He finished his food then leaned back in his chair and crossed his arms. "I'd be lying if I said it wasn't worrying me as well. But we've tried a few different things. I don't see how we circumvent the rules of magic. Bronze negates elemental magic. That's that."

"You only tied me up the first time we tried it."

Troy's attention sharpened and his pupils dilated. He'd enjoyed that a hell of a lot, even if he'd spent the next week mentally flogging himself—unnecessarily—for overstepping with his queen. "What are you saying?"

"Tie me up again. You went easy on me the first time, I know you did. And I appreciate it because I was getting accustomed to the bronze and didn't know what to expect. But this time..." I trailed off, hesitating as his attention got even more focused and I really weighed what I was about to ask him to do. Troy unleashed was, in a word, dangerous. He'd never consciously or intentionally hurt me, but when I was bronze-shackled, there was no bond and I was fuckable prey. Which was to say, completely irresistible on every level, given the training had been my idea and I'd consented to letting him have his way. He ran on instinct, scent, and his extensive experience with me and my reactions—and we'd discovered that if I was both helpless and under his power, wires crossed in both of us. What should scare me aroused me, and what should give him pause made him more ferocious.

And yet...he'd never hurt me. Not beyond what I wanted or had consented to.

I trusted him. That would have to be enough. The Sight and my ring had indicated that there was some way around bronze, and Harqil wouldn't have hinted that I could become a celestial for no reason. Maybe the reason I hadn't succeeded yet was because we were making it a game rather than real training. I hadn't been desperate enough.

With an attack on my home and imminent threats incoming, I was certainly feeling a hell of a lot more desperate.

Troy could push me over and pull me back together afterward if I cracked under the pressure. As long as he could control his hunting instincts—the prey drive that would see me as an irresistible target—he could combine restraining me with the many interrogational techniques Omar Monteague had taught him to push me into desperation without killing me.

If I trusted him completely.

I took a steadying breath and met his gaze, like the queen I was. "This time, treat me like a captive. Like you think the mundanes would if they caught me. And don't hold back. Like Darkwatch training. The stress test."

I'd knocked down a ring of trees in my yard because he'd pushed me to my limits while sparring and caught me in a chokehold. In trying to break free, I'd loosed my elemental magic and also sent the first of our mental communications.

"You trust me that much?" he asked in a rough whisper.

"Yes. Not blindly. I've thought about it." I reached across the table and took his hand. "I know I'm asking a lot. I know it probably taps into parts of yourself you don't like, and I hate asking it of you. But Troy, I have to try this. I know you won't kill me, regardless of who and what we are."

"But I might scare you enough to find a way around the bronze."

I grimaced. "You can be pretty scary when you want to be. Sorry."

A smile slowly curled his lips. "Don't be sorry. You know I love it when I can get away with scaring you, just a little. And you know why that is."

Because it was a way to work through another chunk of pain from the queens who'd hurt and dismissed him. The last few days were probably raising all kinds of hell with his personal demons, hell he'd be working out on me.

I was okay with that. If he found healing and I could figure out how to work past bronze? It was well worth it. We'd be more level for all the shit coming our way.

Troy leaned back in his chair and crossed his arms, the smile vanishing. "You say you know what this is going to require from me. You don't." He held up a hand when I opened my mouth to reassure him. "No. You don't, Arden. Whatever hints you think you've seen of the monster I can be, they're just that. Hints."

I swallowed hard and nodded. "Okay. If you don't want to do it this way..."

He studied me for so long that I thought he was going to refuse. "I swore an oath to keep you alive and safe, no matter what. I just hope neither of us regrets this."

The bond carried a blend of reluctance and resolution. This had to work, or I might not forgive myself.

"I trust you," I said again. "And I know there's a way around bronze. We can do this."

"You done eating?"

Shit. He was going to start now.

I raised my shields and pushed away from the table to stand. "Yes."

"Same signal word?"

"Bramble."

"Limits?"

I started backing away from the table and him, forcing my words out through a mouth dried by anticipation as I pulled on Air. Encouraging him to see me as prey. "None except the signal. I need you to push me."

Troy's expression hardened as his pupils dilated. He shifted his jaw and gave me a sharp-toothed snarl as he shut the window we always had cracked for airflow. "As you command, my queen."

The scent of burnt marshmallow seared my nostrils as he drew as much Aether as he could hold.

I struck with Air, aiming a punch at his head.

He sprang from his chair, ducked, and spun, dancing away from my physical attack and letting it topple both chairs on his side of the table as he struck back.

My shields did fuck-all against a born Monteague with his training, magical strength, natural talent for shieldbreaking and, most importantly, established channels into my mind. Rather than the subtle slip of magic he'd used to get past my shields and tag me unnoticed years ago, he crashed through them like the bull his sigil named him.

They shattered, much like they'd once done in training with Grimm.

And just like then, I was completely thrown off.

Reeling with shock—nobody had managed that in ages—I dropped to a knee, barely swallowing a pained shout as I caught myself on both hands and fought off the all-over stabbing, pins-and-needles feeling. It didn't hurt as bad as it used to, but it still left me breathless and distracted.

Troy's follow-up Aether strike sank hooks into my mind. "Stay like that while I fetch the bronze."

I'd gotten much better and faster at unhooking Aether, but it still took me a minute or two. Troy knew exactly how long and took his time grabbing the bronze cuff I'd fashioned out of Lya Desmarais's abandoned knife and the rope he'd used to tie me up before, if the ominous hissing of it snaking out of his gear bag in the bedroom closet was any indication.

I was fighting off the last of his command when he emerged from the bedroom, lazily spinning the end of the rope, already tied in a wrist-sized loop.

His grin when I staggered to my feet was cold and menacing, nothing like any expression I'd seen on him before. "Now, where do you think you're going?"

Snarling, I put up a wall of Air between us.

Troy shook his head as he stopped short of walking into it. "Clearly, we need to do this more often."

Before I could figure out what he meant by that, he slipped past my tattered shields and stung me with Aether. Ordinarily, I'd be able to slice through it with Chaos. But whenever shields were broken like he'd just done mine, it took time to be able to pull them back and wrangle Chaos again.

I tried.

Troy, the bastard, let me struggle for a couple of heartbeats before tugging on the Aetheric threads now sunk into my mind and saying, "Kneel. And drop this wall. I know you put one up. I can sense it."

I went down in a burst of burnt marshmallow. My wall followed.

He pounced with a ferocious growl, pushing me to the floor and pinning me on my belly as he wrenched my hand between my shoulder blades and cuffed me.

My magic fled like it'd never existed.

Enraged at how quickly I'd lost, I fought him.

Or rather, I tried.

"Enough of that. Get up and strip."

With the Aetheric hooks in my mind, I had no choice but to obey.

Once I was naked he pushed me backward. I yelped as the backs of my legs hit a chair I hadn't heard him move and dropped into it.

Troy wrenched my arms around the back of the chair and secured me with rough, efficient motions, then bound an ankle to each chair leg so my knees were slightly open.

Between my nakedness, the position, and the unusual lack of airflow I felt terrifyingly vulnerable—and that was before he dropped one of the black hoods I hated so much over my head.

Adrenaline raced through me, but before I could move to fight another lash of Aether hit my mind.

"Be still," Troy said coldly from behind me.

Physically, I obeyed. Mentally, I was scrambling. He was right; I'd had only the barest clue that he could make me feel so out of control and so helpless this quickly.

He inhaled, and a hungry growl rippled under his next words. "You have no idea how much of a temptation you are right now, Arden. The things I could do..."

Okay, I had to get free. The longer I let this go on, the wider I was opening the lid of a box I wasn't certain we could close again. Fuck.

"Freedom is one way to stop this," Troy agreed, reading my unshielded thought as easily as he would a mundane's. "Reach for your magic, little elemental. Or give up. Admit this is folly and say your safe word."

No. I would not be giving up. As I tried and failed to find the spark of elemental magic within myself, desperation rose. Real desperation, more than in our past sessions. But just like every other time I'd been bronze-cuffed, it was like there'd never been so much as an ember.

"You say you can reach magic past bronze, but it doesn't look like it to me. You look like prey," Troy taunted in the same empty voice. "Shall I add some incentive? I don't even have to touch you for this. Your mind will do all the work."

My heart raced and I panted under the hood, keenly feeling the lack of air. Sweat made my skin hot and clammy.

"Well? Let's see this magic," Troy whispered threateningly. "Or is it that you know this is beyond you?"

That added fury to the mix. As I had every time we'd practiced before, I tried finding the sparks of the magic within me. I tried forcing through the bronze and envisioning an Air punch.

Nothing worked.

"Remember, you can stop this with a word."

His reminder was my only warning before more Aether lanced through me, like the Thread of Thorns he'd done to restore my memory before the Wild Hunt but lighter—and yet more terrifying, because it went straight for all the fears that had been dredged up in the Duat.

Desperation surged higher, twisting with a stomach-turning blend of dread and frustration as fears of being trapped and powerless swamped me.

It all seared into rage at my inability to break free, compounded by the ease with which Troy was controlling me.

I had to figure this out. I was out of time. I had to be able to protect myself and Troy and our home because if I had to live the fears he was dragging forward or the pain that came with them...I couldn't even think of it without panic ratcheting higher.

I stopped trying to reach for the elements, tired of battering against the wall the bronze cuff made, and twisted, looking for Chaos.

Troy pulled his magic back as I did, and the unexpected stop in mental stimulation startled me as much as Chaos sparking between us.

We both froze.

"Do it again," he ordered.

"I don't know how—"

"Figure it out." The scent of Aether redoubled, an imminent threat. "Quickly."

How had I done that?

I reached again for Chaos and caught nothing. Then again when Troy's breath caught next to my ear, like he was holding himself back from biting.

I yelped as he pinched my inner thigh, both at the surprise of light pain and at Chaos sparking again along with it. Not just sparking, riding my frustration with the ropes to make one of the knots twist.

I pushed harder, reaching wildly for freedom in a way I hadn't since being captured by Leith's Redcaps. Chaos slithered—and so did the ropes as they loosened around my wrists and ankles.

I tugged free and stumbled as I scrambled away, ripping the bronze from my wrist then yanking the hood off and hurling them both from me as I fell into a defensive crouch, full to bursting with all of the elements.

Troy never took his gaze from me as he raised one forestalling hand and slowly reached to open the window again with the other, then fluidly slid over the half wall to stand in a ready stance at the front door. Everything about him screamed predator, from the wide pupils to the sharp teeth to the ashy-sweet scent of Aether. Thin shadows clung to him, making it hard to keep my eye on him, and his hard, blank expression said he was just waiting for my next move.

Fear for myself switched dizzyingly to fear for him. I'd never seen him like this, not even when he was fighting or when we hunted, or during our previous practice sessions with bronze.

I swallowed hard and tried to work spit back into my mouth. "Troy."

He didn't react to my whisper. Just kept an emotionless gaze on me.

The bond was closed when I reached for him, but when I inhaled to try calming myself I caught the faintest hint of rotted herbs.

I wasn't the only one who was afraid. But what was *he* afraid of?

"Troy," I whispered again, steeling my nerve and taking a step closer to him. "I— It's okay. It worked. We did it."

No reaction. Fuck. How did I get through?

Trust. I'd told him I trusted him, then pushed him into this headspace. That it was for the greater good was beside the point. The greater good didn't matter if I'd broken him as badly as Keithia or Omar ever had.

I forced myself to drop the elements and continued my slow steps closer. "It's okay, cariñomí."

This time I got a response: a deep warning growl. One that any idiot would know meant to stay away.

I stepped closer again, because despite the aggression in the growl, his posture had shifted and was now entirely defensive.

"I love you. You did nothing wrong," I said. He'd once told me he'd been punished regardless of how well he served. I needed him to remember I wouldn't do that.

The growl cut off and the shadows around him fled as the first hint of confusion flickered across his face.

I closed the last gap between us and, before I could tell myself it was a bad idea, threw my arms around him in a hug.

He stiffened, crashing backward into the door. The wall in the bond dropped and I gasped as an uncontrolled torrent of fear swamped me, combined with images.

Memories, all heart-wrenching, and none more so than the vision of a woman who looked like Evangeline would have in fifty years turning away from Troy in dismay when he showed her bloodied, trembling hands.

His mother. Had to be. She'd been his protector, the only adult to show him love, and something he'd done had made her turn her back on him. She'd died when he was sixteen, so he was no older than that in this memory.

Ishtar save me, it wasn't just that he was afraid of unleashing his monster on me. He was afraid that I would turn from him as well. And he'd still done as I asked because he believed me when I said I could reach my magic past bronze and saw it as the best way to do what mattered most to him: keep me safe.

"Oh, Troy. I will *never* turn my back on you." I squeezed him hard, willing him to know that what we'd just done was training, where all harms were learning experiences to be forgiven. "*Never*. I'm so sorry."

Chapter 13

Troy's arms came around me so hard and fast I squeaked, but he didn't let go or do anything other than press his face to my neck and inhale deeply. Then the scent of Aether and the pressure of his power signature faded as he shook, his breathing ragged.

I never wanted you to see that side of me, he sent after what felt like forever.

"I love all of you. Even the side you call a monster." I pulled us a step away from the door and rubbed his back, letting him feel the sense of triumph bursting through me now that he was coming back to himself. "And that side helped us today, cariñomí. We did it. We had our first breakthrough and we know it's possible now. We can beat them, even if they get me with bronze."

Troy leaned away and slowly, carefully, like he thought I might still run, cupped my face. His gaze searched mine. *You forgive me?*

"There's nothing to forgive, but yes." When I started to pull away, his expression tightened until I added, "Come on. Let's get cleaned up and go to bed."

He relaxed and let me lead him into the bathroom, staying quiet and keeping his thoughts behind a wall until we'd showered and gotten ready for bed.

"What's wrong?" I asked when he hesitated to join me.

"I want to be close to you."

Translation: he was still worried I'd react badly, the way his family had in those flashes of memory I'd seen.

"Do you want blood?"

That brought hunger to his expression and confidence to the bond. "Yes."

"Come and take it." I slid closer to the middle, relieved that all the effort we'd put into working through our shit was really paying off now.

He joined me with the grace of a hunting cat, pausing to gauge my reaction to his nearness before gathering me close when I reached for him. The Aether that rippled through me then was different than usual—not intended to draw an orgasm, but something softer yet no less pleasurable. Another new adaptation of an old trick, one that still took the pain from his bite but offered a gentler, more affectionate sensation.

I gave myself over to it, hoping my faith and pleasure would help heal a few more bad memories. It wasn't just me who shouldn't have to do things alone. Troy deserved someone to stand at his side too.

"That smelled like Chaos when you broke free, not elemental magic," he said when he'd taken enough blood to settle himself. "Unpredictability seems to be the key."

Then he eased off me and crashed into a deep sleep, his nose tucked against my neck and his hand resting over my heart.

△▽△▽

To my shock, we woke the next day with no harassment from the Bureau for Supernatural Investigation. Neither the Sight nor the djinn had roused me. No intruders had triggered the wards or set off the gytrash. As I reached with my magic, stretching to the limits of my newly expanded range, I found no drones, no people, nothing. Maybe they had a satellite trained on the house from space; that was beyond my abilities. I didn't have so much as a nasty text message, and all of my parliament heads checked in with good progress when I texted the group chat.

Either losing a drone and a bunch of soldiers had caused the mundanes more trouble than I'd expected, or they were planning something really fucking big to punish me for it.

We had to move faster. Sinclaire had talked a big game on TV. Sixtus Ead was still spouting his bullshit on conservative channels. The governor hadn't gone on air with something hateful yet, but given how he'd spoken to me on the phone, he would eventually.

I needed my nationwide alliance. And I needed it now.

I don't like this, Arden, Troy sent as we pulled up to the Solari mansion for a check-in with the West Coast elves. *All that with the attack and now nothing?*

They could still be holding off for when we go to pick up the marriage license, I sent back. *It's downtown, public, high-profile. And to your point, it traps us in different mundane legalities.*

But still nothing from the Sight?

No. I squeezed his thigh as Darius pulled up the long driveway. *You know I'd tell you.*

Probably by dragging me out of bed again.

My mood was still running high from last night's success with Chaos and Troy's big step forward in healing the wounds of his past. A snicker escaped me before I could stop it at the drily amused tone of his sending.

"It is the weirdest thing to watch you two do that," Darius said, looking in the rearview mirror. "The telepathy thing."

I grimaced as Troy shot his brother a look.

"What?" Darius said as Thana and Pascale shifted uncomfortably in their seats. "You told Etain everyone here knows. I'm just glad there's a reason you keep giving each other such meaningful looks or laughing when nobody said anything. It's kind of cute now."

"Darius," Troy said sternly.

The use of his full name when Troy nearly always used a brotherly nickname only got a grin from the younger elf.

"Fine," Darius said. "I'll keep pretending not to notice."

Better than them thinking you're feral or I'm crazy, I pointed out.

True. Troy leaned over and kissed my cheek then opened his door as Darius parked. "We need to close this deal with Lestari. Arden and I have plans for Monday, and I don't want them screwed by anything."

With varied agreements, we all spilled out of Troy's car.

Rio presented himself at the door when we entered, escorted by a wary Allegra. The prince's appearance flipped Troy's mood in the bond from that of a general planning a war to a consort who'd won out over a rival.

"Maria kick you out?" I asked Allegra teasingly. Usually, we had to have an argument to get her to focus on the elven side of her responsibilities as princess, rather than the part that involved her spending the vast majority of her time in Raleigh as House Solari's special envoy to the coterie and Maria's girlfriend.

She wrinkled her nose. "Sort of. Apparently a high-blood like me is too much of a temptation to have around when there are so many new vampires in the nest. You're looking awfully pleased with yourself, brother," she added with a suspicious look at Troy. Then she got a whiff of me when we exchanged cheek kisses, and said, "Ah," her expression blanking.

Rio caught our scents in the wind from the closing door, flushed, and said, "You take her blood?" He immediately flushed deeper and bowed. "Apologies, sovereigns. I didn't mean—"

"We follow the old covenants, as bondmates," I said, my face heating as well. Not that I fully knew what that meant, but both Iaret and Harqil had said it, and Troy had taken blood last night. "More to the point, I've already said I don't believe in forcing my people to suppress their natural instincts, as long as all parties consent to the actions and outcomes."

Troy just gave a predator's smile that made the blood drain from Rio's face.

The younger elf swallowed and nodded, trying to find a neutral attitude. "That must be why everyone at the gathering last night was so...easy. The lack of tension was noticeable, compared to gatherings in the Seattle Conclave."

Despite my pleasure at hearing that, I couldn't help a small sneer. "It's almost like the queens want to keep everyone at each other's throats so they don't actually have to govern."

Rio nodded, looking like he was re-evaluating his situation all over again. "I look forward to exploring my potential here, my queen." He darted a glance at Troy. "There was only ever one path for me before."

"I know what that's like." Troy eased down, seeing that Rio wasn't going to continue making plays for me. He waved toward the hallway leading deeper into the house. "Shall we?"

We settled in around the dining table, which had already been laid out with a smorgasbord of nibbles and beverages both alcoholic and non. For the sake of ceremony, I poured some mead and toasted everyone, reaffirming that we were here in peace.

Before we could get started with an update on what'd happened in the last day, my phone went off with the blaring trumpets of the march I used as a ringtone for the Bureau.

"Damn it," I muttered. "Excuse me, I need to take this."

Soundproofed office across from our bedroom, Troy sent. *Scrambler in the drawer.*

Thank you. I walked at a fast clip in the direction he'd indicated, annoyed with myself for not bothering to have come to my own property before this. A ripple of air molecules behind me said one of the elves had shadowed me, so I wasn't surprised when Pascale posted up outside the office door when I shut it. I hustled to get a scrambler out and on, and then a recorder, before putting my phone on the desk and putting it on speaker.

"Sinclaire," I said on answering the call. "I thought I'd be hearing from you before now."

"It was incredibly stupid of you to overplay your hand like that," she said without preamble.

"Which hand?" I asked, for the sake of the recording.

"You know exactly what I'm talking about."

"The Reaper drone you sent to drop a bomb on my house."

"That wasn't me," she said.

I smiled grimly, glad that her response confirmed it for the recording. "You sound irritated enough that I almost believe you."

"I want you alive, Finch." Menace dripped from her words. "I can't work with ash."

"Right, the part where you want me to come work for you." I let all my derision out on that one, despite being glad she'd confirmed what Duke had said. "You can't think that'll happen now that someone tried to bomb what I hold dear out of existence."

"So Monteague does live with you."

I kicked myself for phrasing it like that and made my tone mocking. "Oh bless your heart, sugar, he's on the deed to the house. Don't act like that was a big discovery."

"You two always play it so cool in public, like he's just a bodyguard. Someone disposable." She paused. "Or is he this thrall Sixtus and Onora Ead keep going on about?"

"What he is, is none of your business." I didn't know what "thrall" meant in this context, but I had a feeling it was nothing good. Whatever it was, Sinclaire was dropping gems in my lap in her effort to piss me off. Maybe it would have worked if I hadn't already been tapped into a simmering rage since the attack. Now? It cost me nothing to let that rage simmer a little longer, a little deeper.

"Come on, Finch. He must be something to you. You want to marry him."

So they had indeed put a flag on the Durham County records office.

Satisfaction slithered through her next words. "You know, I almost forgive the Joint Chiefs for making the call to take military action. You are remarkably difficult to get information on, but shortly after you're nearly killed you file for a marriage license. Now I know I can threaten Monteague and probably get further than hoping you'll see sense."

Despite the kick to my gut, I stayed quiet, as much to avoid incriminating myself on the recording as hoping silence would get her to spill more information. We'd suspected the military had been involved and that they'd pressured the governor to send in the National Guard—probably for election optics on bringing down a dangerous Othersider. But the Joint Chiefs? They were the most senior leaders of the Department of Defense. They advised the president and a few other offices on matters of national security.

And apparently I was at the top of their list. Maybe more so now that I'd come away from a drone strike without a scratch.

"Nothing to say?" she taunted.

"Just waiting for you to get to the point so I can continue planning my wedding."

"You don't really play well with others, do you, Finch."

"I do just fine when the rules are fair. Otherwise, playing well means rolling over, and I will not roll over for you or anyone else."

In Sinclaire's hesitation, I knew she heard the High Queen in my voice. It'd taken me a long time to cultivate that confidence, but the flip side of listening to Harqil's ass-kicking on wanting to be let alone was recognizing that insisting on it was cutting off a source of my power. Only people who stayed in the shadows would be let alone. That wasn't my fate. Mine was to stand strong and shine bright, one foot in the shadows, the other in the sun, like the shadowfire that wreathed me when the gods paid a visit.

"You do know what I mean by fair, don't you Sinclaire?" I asked.

"I know you don't have the sense to know when you're outnumbered. Whatever the hell you are, Finch, you can be beaten."

I sighed and rolled my eyes. "This is getting tiresome. What do you want? Or do you get off on these pathetic attempts at psychological warfare?"

The bitch had the audacity to laugh down the phone at me. "You know, I think I'd like you if you weren't an Othersider. You've got balls."

"Wish I could say the same," I said with faux-sweet poison.

She snorted. "This is your last chance to work with me willingly. Say no now, and you will be forced to comply."

"That sounds like you're gonna try coming for me."

"Not you. We've already seen that for various reasons, that doesn't work." The vicious glee in her voice set every small hair on my body on edge as the Sight keened. "Claret will be destroyed in an unfortunate gas main leak. Properties under the names Onora Ead gave us will have similar problems, or the people named on those properties or their holding entities will turn up in conditions you won't like. I'm feeling generous though, so I'll give you twenty-four hours to think about it."

My world stopped at the threat.

This was why we hadn't heard anything; they'd been moving pieces for a follow-through. We'd known it was a likely possibility, and there were precautions in place. But this was the most present the threat had ever been, with the most resources behind it. My stomach plummeted, and a cold, clammy sweat broke out over me. This was what I'd been afraid of. That they would stop trying for me and pick off my people. The family I'd built up around myself, fractious as we were. The family I was afraid to lose.

Like I'd lost my parents.

Like I was terrified I'd lose Troy, after seeing it over and over and over again in the last trial in the Duat, before we could have the wedding and the children and the *life* he—and now I—wanted so damn much.

A body could only be that scared for so long before it either died...or did something about it.

The fear blended with the rage, cooling it into a hard knot of hate. There was no high road to take here. This woman and her people wanted me and mine dead for no good reason other than that we were different and we had something they didn't—magic. Nothing we offered would save us because they didn't want what was offered.

They wanted subjugation, control, destruction. They wanted to take what should be given freely as part of an equitable trade or negotiation. And if they couldn't get it, then they wanted destruction and death. My death, Troy's, that of anyone who simply wanted to keep living the way we had done for centuries, abiding by the Détente.

No. Oh fuck no. I was the Eternal Huntress and on my way to becoming some sort of High Arbiter. And this, I would not tolerate.

Arden? Troy sent. His tense worry prickled over me. *What's going on?*

War. I walled him out as a tremor of Earth shook the house, then pulled in my magic. We didn't need earthquakes giving us away again.

To Sinclaire, I said, "Now you're the one who's overplayed your hand, *sugar.*"

As Troy skidded to a stop in front of the glass of the office's French doors, I ended the call and the recording and bowed my head.

He burst in. "What happened?"

Usually, him speaking in those icy tones would make me shiver from the danger he was always wrapped in when he stopped making the effort to appear more mundane. Now, I tipped my head back and breathed.

"We're leaving for DC," I said. "Today."

"What? But what about—"

"Sinclaire knows about the marriage license. She also made threats."

Troy's expression shuttered as he mentally zeroed in on defense of the House and me. "Such as?"

"Destroying Claret and everyone inside in a staged gas leak. Detaining or murdering the other faction heads and destroying their properties." I lowered my head to meet his gaze, gold sparkling in shadowed labradorite. "Targeting you."

The rage burning in my heart lashed me in the bond from his side as that damned ethereal laughter started again.

"I know you didn't capitulate," Troy said. "You wouldn't work for her."

This time, it was me who laughed so I wouldn't cry. "No, cariñomí. Never. And I'm smart enough to know that if we tell the faction heads to scatter, the Sinners will pick them off one by one and destroy what they leave behind. That's what they've been doing in the last few days. Setting up their next play, now that the military's failure has demonstrated we can't be bombed out of existence. They're hoping to trap us all so they can trap me. A bomb couldn't get us, so maybe the hearts and souls of our people will."

Behind Troy, Pascale looked stricken by what she could now overhear from the open door, although she blanked her expression when she realized I'd seen her.

I closed my eyes and breathed. I didn't want to harden my heart. I'd promised my people a chance at better lives. But Troy had warned me. He'd *warned me,* said that everything we were doing to establish ourselves—establish *me* in my role as Arbiter, everything I had thought would keep me safe and give us options—would make things worse. That I had to be prepared for some of our people to get hit, and that I might not be able to save all of them.

My mind flickered over them. Maria and Noah and Doc Mike, holding Raleigh in the face of constant protests. Allegra and Darius, who were my family because they were Troy's, and Iago, Thana, Etain, Haroun—all the Ebon Guard who'd been the first to follow me or those like Pascale, who believed so strongly that she'd adopted into the House. Val, Sofia, Laurel, and the other elementals. Duke and Iaret, now back on their mission in DC. Terrence and Ximena, the newly turned Darnell trying to get a better lot in life. Janae and Hope, whose shop kept getting targeted, and Sarah, who had become my lead bartender when being a witch had gotten her fired from her job as a nanny. Vikki, trying to establish a new kind of werewolf pack with a same-sex mate in Ana. Zanna, the gytrash, and Ruprecht and their daring in staying on this side of the Veil to fight for this plane in their own ways. Cade and Lya—the people Troy and I might have been had things gone differently—and Mami Wata and Mason, who'd left their people to join me in getting magic back. Helia, Flint, Keeya, Mansa, and Ninos, who'd had the courage to join me in setting up new Houses. All of them and everyone looking to them as their faction heads.

So many lives in my hands, eyes looking to me, futures in my grasp. All of them now at risk for daring to dream of more for themselves and their people and trusting me to carry the torch.

For change to come, some people would have to die. That was on me in part, for not handling this better.

Mostly, it was on Sinclaire, the human governments, the people who were so afraid of the not-like-them that they would rather have us rounded up and killed. The elven death cult was bad enough. This was assuredly worse.

"You're not going without me this time," Troy said, a low growl underlying the words. "Not like Asheville."

"No, I'm not. The Eternal Huntress has a Hunter for a reason."

The bond carried his deep satisfaction and focused hunger. "Orders?"

"There can be no peace with people who want us dead simply for existing outside of their framework of the world," I said, looking Troy squarely in the eye. "We—you and I—hold power we haven't used yet. So, we will go to Washington, DC. We will play the game we need to play to secure the intel we need to bring the mundanes to their knees. And then you and I will make sure that any sacrifice required by our people is repaid in kind. We might mean no harm, but we will also take no shit. If the mundanes think we're monsters now and they refuse to back off, I will show them what that really means."

Savage certainly firmed Troy's stance and lifted his chin as he saw that I finally, truly understood what he'd been saying in my office after we'd lost magic. "Yes, my queen," he whispered in his icily dangerous assassin's voice. "And long may you reign."

Chapter 14

Troy and I stormed back into the dining room with so much presence that both Allegra and Rio jumped. Allegra recovered quickly, but Rio held very still in the way I'd started noticing elves did when they felt threatened. It looked like Troy wasn't the only one who'd learned it was better to be unnoticed when queens were pissed, but I was so wrathful over Sinclaire that I couldn't rein myself in.

"What happened?" Allegra said. Her expression flickered between Darkwatch blank and the smallest hint of fear. The room smelled like herbs just going off.

"We need the Northwest Mountains," I said. I needed her focused on what came next, not worried about Maria, as much as that broke my heart and made me feel like a hypocrite, given how I kept Troy first and foremost in my considerations. "Right now, or we move without them. Rio? What's the roadblock?"

"My cousin wanted to speak with you directly, my queen," he said, eyes lowered. "That and a...well, it'd be a minor concession in an elven House. I won't presume to think I know your mind."

Smart of him, whether it was genuine or not.

"Get her on the line. Now." Spending so much time on calls was not how I'd envisioned spending my time as Arbiter, given I'd rarely seen Callista on any, but I had to bring people together. I seated myself at the head of the table and took Troy's hand when he sat at my right, lifting it to my lips to kiss his knuckles. *You're definitely with me on this?*

To the ninth circle of hell and back. You don't even have to ask.

I do. And I always will. Your path is your own, and I'm grateful you walk it alongside me.

That got me a curl of loving affirmation in the bond, even as Rio spoke into the phone he'd just dialed.

"Queen Dia. High Queen Arden has made herself available." After listening a moment, he passed the phone over.

"This is Arden Finch Solari," I said.

"Queen Arden. This is Queen Dia Lestari. A pleasure to make your acquaintance at last."

"I wish I could say the same, but my king tells me you sent assassins last summer."

She sighed. "That was the conclave's wish. Daud was in council and jumped at the opportunity."

"Is that supposed to make me more inclined to forgive it? Especially given you then sent a pair of bounty hunters?"

"Another push from the conclave, this time playing on Rio's grievance with your king. I had hoped that sending my cousin now would be a way of mending that."

Rio grimaced when I looked at him, remembering Lya naming him as the source of the bounty.

"What's this about wanting my king's heart?" I said.

"Another demand from the conclave. The assassination attempts failed but you're rumored to be surrounded by elven males despite being a trueborn elemental. The assumption being that there's a reason for that. One that Rio could exploit if Troy was removed," Dia said baldly. "I went along with it on the gamble that you are as attached to your king as all reports say you are and that you mean what you say about ending the culture of death. That you wouldn't kill my cousin out of hand, even if it was him who briefed the bounty hunters. And if by some miracle you accepted Rio over Troy, I still won."

If I'd thought Rio was still before, this time he was stone. His shoulders hunched, and he looked at the table, staring like the last year of his life was being rearranged. I supposed it was, in a way. He'd come here looking for vengeance but had been maneuvered into place by the cousin he'd written off as another selfish queen.

Still though...

"This is all very convenient for you to blame literally everyone else with decision-making power in your territory. You're High Queen for your conclave. Responsibility stops with you," I said.

"I understand this makes it hard to trust me, but I swear on the Goddess and my House that I speak the truth. You've been on my radar since the Wild Hunt, Queen Arden. Your infowar campaigns have everyone not of royal blood in an uproar. Letting people marry who they want, start families with who they want. Telling the Darkwatch they're no longer indentured and paying for their service beyond maintenance." A quick, low growl came from her. "It's too much change too fast, but if I kill everyone who whispers of it, I'll be queen of nothing but dust and bone. I intend to see the Seattle Conclave survive this next turn, whatever it takes."

That oath is binding. Goddess and House. Troy's sending was tinged with reluctance, like he was finding all of this hard to accept but didn't see a way around it.

I was too stuck on "dust and bone"—an echo from my prophetic dream.

Dia pushed forward into my silence. "Has Rio sworn to you yet?"

I glanced at Troy, who gave a nudge in the bond. "He has. I was not pleased with his arrival, but my king can be highly persuasive."

This time, the sigh was more like a heavy relief. "Then in the interest of peace, please accept him as my sincere effort to build a bridge. I don't agree with what my aunt and cousin did to him when they held my title, and I don't agree with what was done to Troy."

Again, I looked at Troy, finding him stone-faced.

"Is that so?" I asked.

"He may not remember, but I—" She hesitated and cleared her throat. "There's no way to say this but to say it. Vina enjoyed using her court to rile him."

"You mean to sexually harass and assault him," I interrupted. We might need this alliance, but I needed to know where she stood. Seattle haunted Troy to this day.

"Yes. An adult male oyëori on an open courting contract? He was an exotic temptation that neither Vina nor her mother Yuliana could resist trying to provoke. I did what I could to avoid being involved." Her no-nonsense tone made it sound like she accepted the shittiness of her role in things. "The conclave here...a year ago, some of them were still stinging from your king's rejection, hence the assassination attempts. Hurting or killing you would hurt him and remove his protector. I've been working to bring them around. Each failure helped make my points."

I said nothing, trying to shift my mindset enough to understand where Dia was coming from.

"Troy's mission here gave me opportunities, Queen Arden," she said. "I owe him. And I owed Rio, for not being able to do what you and your king are achieving now. Sending him with a courting contract was the only way I could try to bridge the gap without undermining my own rule and the work I've been doing here."

"Give me a moment," I said before muting the phone and turning to Troy.

Pain flickered through the bond, but his expression stayed blank. "Dia wasn't good by any means, but she wasn't the worst," he said. "And she did seem to have a soft spot for Rio."

The prince had lost his composure at the overheard conversation and looked absolutely sick. He nodded, unable to look at anyone.

I unmuted the phone. "I dislike that you think trading your cousin like livestock will fix anything, but let's say I accept this. Rio mentioned concessions. What are they?"

"I need you to not only accept Rio's oath but make him part of your court."

"You need me to," I said flatly. "You need me to add a security risk to my inner circle? Keep him close enough to put a knife in my back."

Rio flinched and started shaking his head, eyes wide.

"After how Keithia used Troy, I know how it looks," Dia said. "It looks exactly like an effort to repay in kind. But that's precisely why I need to be able to say that I've placed Rio close to you, even if not as a consort. It will let the conclave here think that we still have a chance to sway you from Troy. That will make them pliable."

"And that benefits me how?" I could guess, but I wanted her to spell it out.

"If Rio is sworn into your court, looking like that security risk, then I have the backing of the other two queens to formalize an alliance between the elves of the Seattle Conclave and those of Chapel Hill, Richmond, and Charleston." When I didn't answer, she pushed on, sounding almost desperate. "High Queen, you are changing the world. I need my conclave to be part of that. I need us to lead the Rainier demesne and Northwest Mountains realm into that, and I need to be the one setting policy so that I can break the cycle of what happened to Rio and Troy." She hesitated, then added, "It's the only way I head off open rebellion and keep my throne."

I put the phone on the table and tapped to put it on speaker. "In that case, I give my king the final decision. He was the one wronged, so he decides what is justice."

Everyone at the table held their breath as Troy looked at Rio, seeing him without really seeing as the bond told me the past was rampaging through his mind.

"Dia," Troy finally said.

"My king?"

Troy's eyebrows shot up. "You acknowledge me as such?"

"You resisted without violence, despite our legends of the oyëori. You stand at the right hand of a primordial elemental and clearly share equally in her power. You both are responsible for bringing magic back to Otherside. For reasons only the Goddess knows, your queen is fighting for all of us against the mundanes. Yes, I acknowledge you both as High Sovereigns. Even if it wasn't the right thing to do for our people, it's certainly the strategically correct thing."

The bond rocked with Troy's shock, and his cheek twitched like I hadn't seen in a while.

"That sounds like you're declaring fealty," he said softly.

"If it means keeping my throne and achieving the kind of change that stops getting the people I'm sworn to lead killed or experimented on by mundanes, then so be it." Her voice was hard and flat, like that'd been a long and hard decision but one she was committed to now. "Seattle leans progressive—for now. But what happens when the bad old days return and the hunts on Othersiders begin again? We have magic, but we're badly outnumbered. I have no plan that can save us, and no contacts to lean on. You do."

Rio's stoic expression had shattered, and he scarcely seemed to breathe. Even Allegra was wide-eyed, like she'd never imagined hearing anything like this.

"What are your demands in negotiations with the mundanes?" Troy asked.

"Legal rights and integration with the humans. But I also want specific hunting rights for elves, even if it means making new laws. Some of mine..." She blew out a breath, and when she spoke next, it was lower, shaky, and hesitant. "Some of my people, the stronger ones, are more stable if they're allowed to run in a hunt at the new moon. Running down prey on foot.

Deer or elk, even a damn turkey, not humans or elementals. We've had fewer fights and suicides since I made a ceremony of it. They're not oyëori, but it's like they feel moonbite all the same, especially since magic came back. And if any of that gets back to my conclave, I will completely deny it."

Troy looked at me, and I nodded.

"We can work with that," he said. "As long as you include the Seattle Conclave's tech research labs and swear to share developments."

"Agreed," Dia said without hesitation, like she'd expected that to be part of the price. "And Rio?"

"He swore to my queen of his own free will, after I restored his memories of what was done to him," Troy said. "If you send over the paperwork relinquishing all claims to him, I'll give it to him. He can choose his own path, as long as it doesn't involve harming Arden. I won't force him to join a court."

"I want to," Rio blurted out. "If it's my choice, I want to stand in your court."

I nodded again when Troy looked at me. We could handle one young elf and his entourage if it meant gaining the support of an entire conclave, along with their research capabilities, and possibly a demesne.

"Done," Troy said. "If and when we have the opportunity to present a case to mundane courts and legislatures, we will advance your demands on behalf of all elves. But I want your oath that you will work to bring the entire Northwest Mountains realm into alliance. Our local werecats have brought the Southwest Desert. There's precedence."

"Done," Dia said. "I, Dia Lestari, High Queen, agree to the terms and enter the Seattle Conclave into alliance with Chapel Hill, with Richmond, and with Charleston. I swear by the Goddess. I swear by my House. I swear on my own honor. Three times sworn, three times bound."

"I, Troy Solari, as king and on behalf of my queen Arden Finch Solari, swear House Solari and the Chapel Hill Conclave into alliance," Troy said. "By the Goddess, by my queen, and on my own honor. Three times sworn, three times bound."

Dia swore in elvish. "Goddess be praised. High Queen, High King, thank you for giving me the leverage to protect my people. May you have good hunting in the courts of the mundanes."

I squeezed Troy's hand, having kept it throughout the conversation. "Welcome to the New Détente, Queen Dia. Good hunting in your quest."

When I ended the call, Allegra smiled, looking as predatory as Troy did sometimes for maybe the first time since I'd known her. "Well hot damn. Look at you two achieving what Keithia always wanted but never could gain the influence for."

"Look at Arden," Troy said, lifting my hand to kiss it this time, "creating space for it."

"All I want is unity ahead of what we have to do next," I said. It was hard to keep my voice even. My heart was soaring and I wanted to celebrate, but part of this win had been bought with Troy's past pain and the knowledge of pain to come.

"Take the win, sister," Allegra said. "Open the House and celebrate this, the alliance with the weres, and the one between the vampires. Maria was on the verge of a deal with Santiago when I left. She has to have made progress now."

"She's right," Rio said in a voice barely above a whisper. He lifted his dark-eyed gaze to mine for a moment before dropping it again then raising it defiantly. "When I left Seattle, I thought to remove Troy and win you as a prize, my queen. I hadn't even imagined that there might be something bigger. If I may be so bold as to speak as a prospective member of your court...claim it as yours and solidify your rule."

I barely stopped myself from looking at Troy. "I wanted to leave for DC today."

"We have no plan and no security for that," Troy said. "It'll take at least a few hours to arrange. Opening the House again lets us manage that while still advancing our agenda." He cocked an eyebrow at me. "And at least trying for our other commitment, threat or not."

Allegra perked up. "What commitment?"

Troy stared at me.

I cleared my throat. "I told Troy we're getting married. As soon as possible, at least in mundane law. Which means we need to go downtown to get a marriage license."

"Spousal privilege," Allegra said, brightening considerably.

"*Thank* you." I flashed back to her quickness at picking up on why I'd needed her to stay with Troy while I went to Asheville. If it touched on her brother-cousin's security, she knew the angle—Otherside law or mundane. I still had another concern. "Opening the House again puts all of us in the same place though, right after Sinclaire threatened us directly."

Allegra snorted. "The arrogant bitch will think you're calling everyone in to warn them. She'll probably get off on the idea that you're scared. At a stretch, she'd orchestrate another attack, but something tells me she didn't orchestrate the first one."

I studied Rio, trying to get a sense for whether we could trust him.

Say it, Troy sent. *His scent and posture say he's accepted I'm both king and bondmate here. He could fake posture but not scent. Prince of the Court still opens opportunities for him and trust secures his loyalties.*

"She didn't," I said, trusting Troy and letting my lip twist in disgust. "Sinclaire says it was the Joint Chiefs. According to her, she can't do shit if I'm ash."

Allegra's expression hardened. "She said that?"

"Mm hmm." I snagged a slice of pastrami and ate it, which pleased Troy. The man never failed to be pleased by my eating some kind of meat. "The call earlier was a demand to work for them."

"And the stick?" she asked. "Because Goddess knows there's never been a carrot."

The hypocrisy I'd felt earlier boiled to the surface again. "The lives of the faction heads and their people."

"Is that so?" In Allegra's soft tone, I finally saw the shadow side of the Darkwatch agent she'd been trained to be. Troy's near-equal in deadliness, for all she played at being the fun one in the family. "Maria?"

I nodded. "Claret would be a primary target."

She studied me, gaze hard. "And you'd allow it."

Meeting her eyes, I leaned forward and let my rage show in my own. "Why the fuck do you think I was so keen to leave for DC right now?"

Allegra's love for Maria ran deep, for it to take two full heartbeats for her to back down. Even then, her cocky smile was tinged with razors. "I see. Permission to undertake diplomatic endeavors?"

"Granted. I'll be doing the same. Apparently, we're opening the House," I said, looking at Troy.

He nodded solemnly. *Trust me on this.*

I sighed and slumped in my chair, giving up on any semblance of a queenly attitude. I needed to act to protect my people. But the bigger a group got, the slower it moved. Me and Troy by ourselves, as two rogue agents, could have gone to DC today. As royals, newly acknowledged beyond territory we personally held? Looked like that was off the table.

I just prayed it wouldn't cost lives.

Chapter 15

As night fell, I was increasingly on edge. The Sight didn't give warning of another drone, but the Darkwatch confirmed the presence of multiple federal vehicles and agents on assignment in the area. That made my bad mood worse; they'd evaded Duke and Iaret somehow. Or there were just that many of them, which annoyed me all over again for my lack of resources to watch them.

Troy was on the phone with other elven conclaves in the soundproofed office for a good two and a half hours, giving orders and getting intel, playing politics, and getting the word out about our win with the Seattle Conclave. I did the same in the bedroom with other factions and checked with Iaret on a source she'd been cultivating in the Bureau for Supernatural Investigation. Apparently, that was what had kept her attention, with Duke watching the military angle in case there was a follow-up attack.

By the time I needed to get ready, I was infuriated by the need to delay. Every passing minute gave Sinclaire more room to maneuver, and we were hosting a party.

"We're leading them straight here. This is egregiously stupid," I griped as Troy zipped me into one of the admittedly gorgeous black-and-gold dresses hanging in the closet in our bedroom. This one was in the slinky, tight-bodiced but loose-hipped style I liked and one-shouldered, covering the one with the most bite scarring while exposing my right shoulder, the one with the

Lichtenberg lightning scar on the front and my kestrel tattoo on the blade.

He kissed the bare one. "I know. It's part of the plan."

"What fucking plan?" I pulled free and whirled. "We're reacting again. I refuse—"

"Arden."

I stood toe-to-toe with him, piqued by his firm tone. Both our power signatures crackled. Anyone coming into the room would think we were ready to kill each other.

"What," I said when he didn't back down.

"We're not reacting if this was always part of a protocol."

When I started to snap at him, he laid a finger on my lips, his expression hard.

"After the vampire Reveal, Omar laid out a strategy to divert attention and allow a special team to deal with a mundane threat," he said. "We're executing it now. That's half of what I was doing on the phone earlier. The only change to the plan is that you and I are both diversion and special team. It adds time to our leaving but also force. We can do more on our own than a triple triad. And if we keep the focus on ourselves, we might manage to spare our people."

"But we put the focus on all of us by making it look like we're plotting!"

"Which makes it that much more urgent when you and I arrive in Washington, DC tonight, unannounced and well before we're due. Then they react to us, having to assume we've got a plan."

I glared up at him then realized I was still getting what I'd wanted at the cost of what Troy wanted—the marriage license. He had just arranged it so that, with all the newcomers and guests both in town and staying at this location, our plan wouldn't be known in advance or in public. I closed my eyes. "I'm sorry. I should have trusted you to know better. I definitely shouldn't go off on you."

He gathered me in, sending sparky little shivers over me as our auras and magic blended. "After our training last night, I think I'm finally past the point where I'm afraid you'll punish me when you do. And honestly? I like our debates. It forces me to do and be better. Or at least make sure I've thought through all the angles." With a kiss to my forehead, he leaned away. "I should have said something to you before issuing orders, but I figured it was what you'd want to do anyway and the sooner I got to it, the sooner we could be ready to leave. Some of the Ebon Guard and the Darkwatch are already scouting ahead, and House Bedoe is making arrangements for us."

"You trust Sonia that much?"

"I trust that your choice to alert her about the threat of my father showed her we don't want her dead. Between that, having DC in her backyard, and having Sixtus on TV, she knows she can't lose us as allies."

With a sigh, I delayed answering by focusing on suppressing the crackle of energy between us. We might be fine with it, but it would amplify the feeling of our already considerable power signatures and make the Othersiders around us uncomfortable. If we had strangers coming, we needed to act right.

"Thank you for handling this," I said. Something about this plan was still bugging me, but it was the best we had right now. Until I could figure out what I was missing, I had to go with it.

I had my attitude under control by the time we emerged, both of us dressed up. We weren't as formal as we had been for the elven summit ball, but it was definitely more than my usual or even Troy's.

Allegra intercepted us before we could reach the main gathering.

"Everything's in motion," she said in a low voice. "Including our personal shopper for dress options, in case you two need to get married in a hurry."

"And you're good with this?" I asked. I wasn't a fool. Allegra loved me as a sister, but if she had any objections, she had the political clout to make life difficult for me. Her agreement was important.

"It will be good for mundane PR, at least," Allegra said. "I don't like the speed—it's a bad look—but given it's to protect Troy, I'll get over the elven optics."

I nodded, studying them both. I had a feeling that and our mundanely accelerated schedule weren't the only reasons why we needed to lock in this wedding. Even if we didn't manage to get the license as planned, they both clearly wanted to be ready to go at any time.

Time to test a theory. "So. Dresses. What do I need to know? Because we all know formalwear is my nemesis."

Troy's small smile told me he agreed before he sobered. "The shopper will get a few options together. It'll need to be custom, but there are some choices that make certain statements."

I thought so. I tilted my head slightly and ran my fingers over the shoulder he usually bit, which was starting to show faint scars from sharp teeth. "Make sure there's an option where these are visible, please."

Both elves went still, the way small predators did when they realized a larger one was hunting them. It was subtle enough that it'd taken me a while to notice the tendency of most elves to do it when the political waters were uncertain. I wondered if they realized it was a tell, given it seemed to be a species thing.

Allegra's gaze darted between the two of us while Troy's stayed on me. Interesting. Looked like I was right.

"That sends a particular message, to be sure," Troy said carefully. Both the bond and his scent were oddly neutral, almost static, in the unusual depth of control I'd only seen him manage out of all the Othersiders.

I smiled, springing my trap, and spoke in a voice low enough that only they would hear me. "Exactly. That there's an elf close enough to the dangerous primordial elemental that he could literally tear her throat out and she's so head-over-heels that she'd just think it was another love bite. Love conquers all, right? Even one's enemies."

If I'd thought they were still before, they were frozen now. Allegra paled, keeping her attention on me this time.

Troy swallowed hard and guilt slashed through the bond before he closed it. "My queen, I—"

"It's okay," I said gently before he could get too anxious. I was not going to turn into Keithia on him, even if I was disappointed. "You're not in trouble."

He still didn't move beyond the old tell of the jump of a muscle in his cheek. Neither did Allegra.

I sighed and stepped closer to him. "May I touch you?"

Troy nodded, eyes wide and pupils dilated.

I went up on my toes to kiss him, a quick brush of my lips. "I'm not mad. You're not in trouble. I wish you'd have told me that was a consideration, but honestly I'm kind of proud of myself for figuring out that particular political angle before you had to run interference again. Okay?"

He shuddered, finally relaxing. "Okay."

Allegra blew out a breath. "Fuck."

"I won't hurt him. I won't hurt either of you. I'm annoyed at the maneuvering that goes on behind my back, but that means I need to look at what I've done—or not done—for y'all to feel like I can't handle being part of the discussion." I took a breath and consciously smoothed the cranky note out of my tone. "Can we have an honest conversation about that? Please?"

"We just didn't want you to have more of a reason to mistrust elves," Allegra said. Now that the sense of danger had passed, she sounded sullen at being caught.

"Not just that." The deadened tone of Troy's voice made me shiver. "There are legends. About primordials."

I flashed back to a half-heard argument between him and the Captain. "Is that what Omar was talking about?"

"Yes," Troy said. "But—"

"Oh fuck's sake, what bullshit is Dad on this time?" Allegra interrupted in a hiss that brought a few people's attention our way.

With an annoyed look at his sister, Troy put an arm around me and guided us over to a corner. "He wants her leashed." Fury rumbled in a low growl under the words. "Which means the rest of the old guard will be thinking that or worse. I told him I have everything under control. But if others are thinking it, I need to at least keep up the appearance of playing the role."

I went cold as my stomach clenched. "You're putting yourself between me and an assassination attempt. Again." When he didn't answer, I twisted, trying to look at him.

He resisted me and kept me pinned where I was. "It's my job, Arden. One I'm happy to do. Let it go. We need to mingle."

I was annoyed, but he was right. The royals of House Solari couldn't spend the night whispering in corners at our own party.

The house was already full, and somehow, we'd gotten catering in. We had at least a couple of representatives from most of the factions, including all the seconds or reps from the main ones: Noah and Giuliano, Joachim and Malik, and Mason. I spotted Flint in one corner, in deep conversation with...

"Val?" I said, breaking decorum to make my way over. "You're the last person I expected to see tonight."

"Hey, Arden. Um. Arbiter." She flushed and wouldn't meet my eyes. "I had to leave my job."

"What?" All of our recent arguments slipped away, and I embraced her. Being a firefighter was her life, and leaving it had to hurt. I wouldn't wish that on a friend, no matter how strained our relationship had gotten. "Why?"

"They introduced a new blood test requirement, something that would look for 'unusual proteins.' The police introduced the same one. Obviously looking for someone non-human, right? There's no way it should be legal, and Durham is the last place I thought—" Her voice broke, and Flint rubbed her arm. "Anyway. I couldn't do it. Not just because of the risk of exposure. It's a matter of principle. Going along with it would be saying that I think it's right. And it's not."

A lick of flame ran over her clenched fists as her voice deepened toward anger, the first time I could remember seeing her lose composure like that. Before I could say anything though, the pressure of someone's focused attention made me look to the side.

Rio stood watching, clearly fascinated.

Not with me. With Val.

I frowned at him, trying to figure out if this was prey drive or something else, and he shook himself, inclining his head before moving away to speak to Samarre.

"What can I do?" I asked, refocusing on Val.

She crossed her arms. "I guess I'm here because I hoped you'd ask that. I want justice. I want to be able to do my job without bullshit tests and scrutiny for not being human." When she met my gaze at last, hers practically sparked, and her eyes glowed gold. "I'm formally joining Helia's House. I'm running out of options to protect Sofi, and Granddad...he's stuck in the past. He thinks hiding will save us, like it always has, but there is nowhere left to hide. I thought destroying Verve the way you did was a stupid risk, but now I get it. I just hope my showing support means Laurel and a few more of the others in our generation can move to follow Helia rather than the Collective in this. So yeah. Fight for us, Arden. That's what I want you to do. Even if we don't deserve it and I'm an asshole for making the demand."

This alone made it worth delaying my and Troy's departure to DC and taking the time to share victories. The elementals were finally coming around fully, of their own accord. And hell, maybe I had one of my friends back.

"You have my word, Val. I will make them accept us."

"Good. Thank you." With a burst of energy, she hugged me, her naturally elevated warmth almost enough to make me sweat in the already warm room. "I'm sorry for what happened between us. I hope we can still be friends."

"We are," I said, squeezing her back. I might not like the huggy stuff, but Val was a dea to match my inborn sylph. We were naturally complimentary, and it felt good to have her back. "I need to circulate, but I'm glad you're here."

As I moved away, Rio edged in. "My queen…is the dea a friend of yours?"

"Yes," I said suspiciously. "What do you want with her?"

"Just your permission to introduce myself to a beautiful woman." He dropped his eyes and cleared his throat as he flushed. "That is, if your earlier statement in that regard extends to your court."

My eyebrows shot up so fast they just about took flight. "If you fuck with her in any way, you answer to me."

"Understood, my queen. By your leave."

I nodded, not surprised to find Troy at my shoulder when Rio moved off.

"What's that about?" Troy murmured.

"Val being here or Rio wanting to flirt with her?"

"Both."

I filled him in on what Val had said, adding, "I don't know that I've seen an elf get that comfortable with an elemental that quickly."

"He knows she's one?"

"He was watching when she got a little…heated."

"Ah."

Harqil wandered over, wings hidden. That was a surprise; I hadn't realized they were that close to being fully healed.

They dropped their arms over my shoulders and Troy's, chuckling. "And that, my friends, is why the queens broke away from the elementals and founded Atlantis to begin with."

"What?" Troy and I said together.

Harqil nodded. "You didn't know? Little King here has the trait as well."

I turned toward them, feeling my face crack in confusion.

Troy's expression blanked. "Explain."

They sighed, like this was old news and boring at that. "Some elves find elementals irresistible. Almost all of you used to have what you now call the oyëoro, but a few without it seemed better able to resist the pull of an elemental. So, the queens started selecting for it, even interbreeding with humans in some cases, and tying the attraction to elementals to the oyëori's natural prey drive to create the perfect bounty hunters." They tilted their head side to side. "Well. That and to prevent this very outcome, just in case a strong enough oyëori was born: the re-establishment of the original order of things with your Houses." Suddenly, mischief was in their eyes. "I bet you didn't even consider that the gods were looking at you as much as Arden, little king. Why do you think they allowed a Hunter?"

Troy frowned, shaking his head. "But I'm only attracted to Arden, not all elementals. And Rio isn't an oyëori."

"*Rio* isn't. His brother was. Looks like that trait was on their mother's side. Shame what happened to the boy." As Troy and I processed the implications in that statement, Harqil kept talking, aiming their commentary at Troy. "As for you—you saved an elemental's life when you should have killed her and made up reasons for yourself to disobey your grandmother. Your land has the touch of an oread all over it. Tell me you didn't find immediate comfort in working it with her, after being told your whole life that oreads would open the earth beneath your feet and send you straight to the ninth circle of hell."

Troy stiffened.

Harqil grinned, looking a little mean, and lowered their voice even further. "Tell me there's anything more satisfying in life than hunting your mate. That moment when she's finally in your grasp after you've run her down, her blood pumping under her skin, her scent hot in your nose. Only you don't want her dead, you just want her as close as possible. In all ways."

"How could you possibly know all that?" Troy asked hoarsely after a moment. Guilt flashed hot in the bond.

"Celestial messenger, remember? Older than dirt and nosy as fuck. Oh, is that ginger mead?" Harqil darted off, making a supernaturally fast beeline for the drinks table and leaving me and Troy to stare at each other.

I felt like I should apologize, but I didn't know what I'd be apologizing for.

Troy clasped my cheek, running his thumb over it in a caress. "It's nothing you did. And of all the things I've done, tying myself to you is the best one."

I should have left it at that, but my mind was spinning too hard. "You don't resent it? Not having a choice?"

He shrugged and stole a kiss. "Being fated to be yours is better than the alternatives I saw for myself a few years ago. Besides, I did have a choice—in how to be yours and when. You gave me that." When I started to give him an out, he said, "Don't you dare tell me I can leave you. I don't want to. I accept my fate. I'm happy, I'm loved, and I have purpose. *We* have purpose, together, as a unit."

All this fatalism was making my head spin even more. It was to my benefit, but still.

And yet...as I thought about it, if our fates were entwined, then he was right. I liked mine with him. He was mine and I was his, and that was just the way of the world. Not only that, but the world was better for it. From what the Duat had shown me, I was alive because of it.

"Now you see it," Troy said.

"I guess I do." I went up on my toes to give him a longer kiss. As frustrated as I'd been with him earlier, he'd been my pocket ace for years now.

Ace.

Cards.

Wild card.

The part of the plan that'd been bugging me thundered to the fore. *Troy.*

What's wrong?

It's not wrong. It's just…we need a wild card. Preferably two. I smiled at Giuliano and Noah as they approached then exchanged pleasantries and congratulations on yet another completed vampire agreement.

Obstacles were falling like dominoes now that I'd shown my power in a way Othersiders could understand and appreciate—violence. Not against my own people but against a power that threatened all of us. In addition to convincing Renaud and Charity to throw in both with Maria and with me, Matthias had called with a recommitment of friendship and alliance between the New York Coterie and the Triangle. Apparently, even Santiago had not only agreed to a ceasefire but opened talks to cede Jacksonville to Matthias's people in exchange for Matthias's good word with me.

When Giuliano and Noah moved on, Troy sent, *It sounds like you have someone in mind for this wild card.*

Pressure on my mind: *Oh, pick me!*

Actually, Harqil, I was hoping you'd volunteer. I barely managed not to smirk at the nosy celestial's mental eavesdropping playing to my favor.

You were? both Troy and Harqil sent.

Are your wings fully healed?

Harqil's mental sending was tinged with derision. *Do you see wings right now? How else do you think I managed to make it here from the bar unseen?*

Perfect. The other card is Cyrus.

That got me dumbfounded silence before Harqil started chuckling again.

Then Troy sighed heavily, having figured out where I was going. *His passive power.*

Yep.

I'll tell Etain to expect us tonight. With a quick kiss to my cheek, he added, "Try to stay out of trouble for five minutes?"

I grinned like he'd said something funny, hoping I wasn't going to regret this.

Chapter 16

The fortunate part of Troy's plan turned out to be that having so many Othersiders leaving a location at the same time meant the feds tracking us all were hard-pressed to follow. We'd warned everyone present before they'd arrived, and I'd authorized the use of any and all non-lethal magic to get people home safely. I even sent a triad of elves with the weres, who went back to a location they could afford to burn if they had to.

Troy and I changed our clothes and pretended to go to bed at the Solari mansion then, with Harqil's help, traveled the planes to Ebon Guard HQ in a way we hadn't since I'd convinced Eshu-Elegba to carry us out of Keithia's torture chamber.

What used to feel like a sharp wrench in my guts was more like a twinge now. Not exactly comfortable but nowhere near as disorienting as when Grimm had carried me through my first trip to the Crossroads. Maybe Troy had been right, back when he pointed out that dealing with the gods was more normal for me.

It'd gotten better for him as well—even if it was still shitty.

When we popped back into reality in one of the spare bedrooms, Troy immediately twisted away from Harqil and bent over in dry heaves that, from the state of the bond, pained him to keep silent. They kept going until he dropped to his hands and knees, although he held up a hand to keep me back.

"Fuck," Troy muttered, breathing hard and bracing himself against the wall to climb to his feet after recovering. "I fucking *hate* interplanar jumps."

"You're in one piece, aren't you?" Harqil said testily. "Mind, body, and soul all as one. It's only thanks to your mate you can make the jump at all. That should have killed you, or at least driven you mad. You're both mad anyway to attempt it, so maybe that's what preserved you because gods know I couldn't manage it alone. Beings of shadow have no business traveling the planes unless they're demons, and your soul isn't *that* degraded."

I kept my mouth shut in the face of Harqil's nervous rambling. The last two times we'd jumped planes carried by celestials like that, Troy's mind or soul—I wasn't sure which—had shattered. I'd had to use the bond and Chaos to convince him to re-anchor himself in his body. I didn't know whether this relative improvement was down to his growth in power, mine, or Harqil's being a messenger smoothing the passage. Either way, this was a much better result than I could have hoped for when I'd proposed it.

"I'm not going to DC like that," Troy said. Grouchiness made a sour prickle in my mind, although he let me approach once he caught his breath.

Rubbing his back, I said, "We can take a car. I want to practice with bronze some more."

That brought Troy upright real quick. "And you think a moving vehicle is the place to try experiments with Chaos?"

I just looked at him. It wasn't like we had more time or other options.

He bent back over with a last dry heave before a mental wrench in the bond indicated he was forcing himself into a more functional state. "Fine. Let's get this plan finalized and get going."

I opened the door of the bedroom we'd jumped into to find a wide-eyed Etain standing outside, backed by Thana, both of them with longknives drawn.

"Surprise!" I said.

Etain shook herself. "How, by the Goddess, did you get in there? When you said to expect you, I thought you meant by the front door."

"Celestial help." I turned to find Harqil doing their indistinct thing and decided to let it be for now. I was kind of interested to see if Cyrus would notice them.

Thana swung around in the hallway. "Front door."

"Probably Alli and Dari," Troy said. "We gave them a head start."

Allegra and Darius were in the main room, the living room converted into an operations center, when we all emerged.

"What the fuck?" Allegra reached for a hidden weapon before catching herself. Then she saw Troy. "You traveled the planes again?"

He nodded.

"We can do that?" Darius asked.

"No," Troy snarled.

Allegra frowned as she took in Troy's state. "Then how—"

"Later," I said, raising a hand and turning for the bedroom that was Cyrus's cell. "We need to move."

"Wait," Troy said. "Were you two followed?"

Allegra's sudden smile was chilling. "We spotted them before they saw us. I wiped them."

"Good," Troy said grimly.

"Wiped them?" I hadn't heard that phrasing before.

"Aside from reading Aetheric residue, Alli's mental talent is complete and total memory erasure," Troy said. "The entire life, including all education and learned skills. Unrecoverable. Otherside influence will be obvious, but we have to assume the Eads sold that information a long time ago."

Allegra's smile widened when I stared at her.

"I'm the family's nuclear weapon," she said cheerfully.

"Got it." I tried to sound like I hadn't just learned my soon-to-be sister-in-law could simply erase my life if she decided it was in Troy's best interest. Darius could steal or implant memories, and Troy could suppress, alter, or restore them, as well as forcibly influence people and truthread.

Goddess, it was amazing I'd survived against House Monteague long enough to kill Keithia.

"Don't worry, sis," Allegra said. "We love you."

"And I would kill you slowly for hurting her," Troy called mildly over his shoulder as he headed for the room where we were holding his father. "Wait there."

Allegra just laughed, and I got the sense that she was riding some kind of Aetheric high on top of enjoying the familial banter. Darius sighed, like he slightly disapproved of the teasingly antagonistic dynamic but was used to it.

We all took chairs as we waited for Troy to return with Cyrus. For all that this was my idea, I didn't agree with letting him out of his cage yet, especially with this additional wrinkle about Despair, but Troy had pointed out that we needed to know what he'd do if he scented freedom before we tried this mission. Better to do it here where we had some of our best security, rather than on the road.

Of course, Cyrus was clever enough that he might sit tight here and make his attempt en route. We couldn't know. I just kept thinking back to the conversation I'd had with Harqil at Jordan Lake, where they'd said Cyrus was the crow in the prophecy I'd spoken while Dreaming and the revelations in my office the other day. Given that Sutekh was gone, Despair might have a greater influence now. I didn't know how much Cyrus knew about the Court of Nightmares, and I couldn't ask without giving him too much information. All I could do was gamble that giving him some hope might counterbalance the influence of Despair. I wouldn't take the risk of bringing him with us otherwise.

Allegra's good mood twisted as Troy marched Cyrus back out and shoved him into a chair next to Etain, but all she said was, "We're all here, so what's this about?"

"Arden and I are leaving for Washington, DC," Troy said. "Tonight."

She straightened from her slouch. "Excuse me? After all this, you're going to fold on that fucking threat from Sinclaire? You're going to walk straight into an obvious trap?"

"The mundanes win a war of attrition," Troy said. "There are more of them, and they have the three severed Eads. Likely more. All that aside, what better way to infiltrate the enemy than to accept their invitation into the heart of their power?"

Etain swore under her breath.

Allegra and Darius exchanged looks that spoke volumes before Darius said, "So this isn't a surrender. It's an op."

Troy nodded. "One with parameters I've already succeeded with previously. We fully expect to be arrested. Rather than waiting for them to pick us off here at home, we force it to happen on our terms."

"Anansi said being trapped is being free." I crossed my arms and shrugged. "If we have no options, we have every option. We know they must have a secure facility somewhere. What better way to get them to reveal it, then be in place to destroy it, than to get them to take us there?"

Allegra looked at me then Troy. "And you're going to let them put a bronze-shackled primordial elemental in a cage? Because we all know they know about bronze. And we've all seen how Arden reacts to being caged."

I grimaced. "I hate the idea of it. But we've been practicing."

"Practicing what," she asked flatly.

"Accessing my magic while I'm cuffed with bronze." I needed to give them something to be confident about, but I didn't want to give away too many details in front of Cyrus. He needed to hear the stakes up front and think we were either stupid enough or desperate enough to trust him, he needed a reason to hope, and he needed to know there was no beating me, but I didn't want him to know everything.

Every elf in the room stared before Etain said, "That's possible?"

"It is for Arden." Troy curled a protective arm over my shoulder. "It's uncomfortable for both of us if it stays on too long, and we lose the bond. But whatever power threshold she punched through in the Duat combined with our unique situation to open up a new strategic possibility."

Cyrus chuckled malevolently. "Chaos incarnate."

"You hush," Allegra snapped, whirling to glare at him. "You've made enough trouble. I don't even know why you're here. Why are we talking about this in front of him, T? He threatened Arden."

Cyrus's grey gaze sparkled. "That's an excellent question, given I'm clearly persona non grata and you, boy, swore you wouldn't be back until I acceded to your demands. Why am I here?"

Troy ground his teeth, looking at me with eyebrows lifted. *Last chance to change your mind.*

He wants to stay in your life. This is his ticket. I shrugged, not bothering to pretend like we weren't talking to each other telepathically when everyone here knew we were capable of it. *And Harqil said he's the crow from my dream. His role isn't done yet.*

"We need a third for a triad." Troy gave his father a hard look. "Someone they won't be looking for."

Another shocked silence was punctuated by Cyrus busting out laughing. "You want me to come with you into this trap?"

I lifted my chin and spoke the truth. "I want to use you, Cyrus. You influenced Keithia for over a decade. You make everyone around you want to spill their secrets. So, I'm giving you a chance to do two things. First, watch over your son, the way you claim you want to. Second, do what you do best: cause chaos and mischief in politically charged environments. You join the audience or the crowd wherever we go. You influence the mundanes to react positively to me, Troy, and any of our allies also nearby. And you make damn sure that, when they arrest us, the public or anyone else witnessing is vocally disapproving and will say so where our reporter can hear them."

He narrowed his eyes at me. "What do I get out of it?"

Troy's voice was cold. "Aside from the information you just overheard? We don't hand you over to whichever House offers the best price for a queenkiller. Minus your tongue, of course."

Cyrus stilled except for his gaze, darting between me and Troy. "You wouldn't."

"Yes. I would." Troy shook his head, looking years older and more like a disappointed father than Cyrus ever had. "You went rogue. You disobeyed a direct order from me and the terms of my queen's resettlement deal with you. You threatened her life. A debt is owed, and I call it in by threes. You can do this to pay off a third of the debt. Or I will have it out of your hide. Nobody, not even family, crosses me as King or Arden as High Queen and Arbiter."

Cyrus's jaw dropped. "But I was being ridden by Sutekh."

"That was an arrangement you made for yourself," Troy said coldly. "We exiled Dari for attacking us while under celestial influence as well. With everything we're trying to do to unify Otherside, we cannot be seen to play favorites."

I glanced at Darius to find him stone-faced and nodding. There had to be justice for what Cyrus had done, one way or another. But as I stood here surrounded by people who were, for all intents and purposes, family, I couldn't help asking a question.

"How much of your threats were you, and how much were Sutekh?"

Troy stiffened. "It doesn't matter. The threats were made. I'm only agreeing to this because—"

Gently, I put a hand on his arm. *Please.*

"Cyrus, you're a truthreader and you can see the unseen," I said. "When you arrived, you said, as a father and an Ebon Guardsman, you were rooting for me. What did you see that made you turn against me?" I knew he resented my relationship with Troy, but I had been pretty sure we could work through it until the Duat mission.

"You hurt him. You, yourself, after swearing to me that you love him. I saw it, but I let my love for my boy stop me from acting until Sutekh showed me the truth." Despairing anger burned in Cyrus's hard gaze on me. "You don't deserve Troy. Not his power, not his loyalty, his skills, or his seed. Primordials destroy everything they touch, and you'll destroy him. I won't have it. I'll destroy you first or die trying."

My stomach bottomed out.

Before I could organize a thought, Troy said, "If we're casting judgments, do you want to hear about how I drowned her? Following Omar's orders of course. I could have found a different way. But that was the way I was supposed to do things, so I did it."

Cyrus froze and Etain swore again. Allegra rubbed her forehead and sighed tiredly. Darius paled, his expression carefully blank. Unseen by everyone but me, Harqil watched from the corner, eyes narrowed as they studied everyone.

I couldn't help grimacing, but I also didn't dare stop Troy. I hated hearing him incriminate himself but was not going to get between these two, not on this, not yet anyway.

"There's also the magical trespass, the kidnapping and forced seclusion, and the time I kissed her without her consent," he added in the deceptively quiet tone that said he was pissed.

"Troy—" Allegra started.

He held up a hand. "No, I want to hear which of my many crimes against the woman I'd happily die for will be enough to cancel out whatever he thinks Arden's done to hurt me. How many, Cyrus? How much of the pain that I've heaped on her is enough to cancel out whatever bullshit a trickster god whispered into your head? Because Goddess knows, neither of us is perfect. But we're working on doing better. Both of us. Together. As a bonded pair, for ourselves and everyone else. For *you,* even."

I felt sick. Not at what Troy had said or at how he called his father by his name rather than acknowledging their relationship. Not even at remembering the incidents themselves, given that Troy had made up for them in effort and blood. What made me sick with fear was the systematic destruction Troy was undertaking. If we had to follow through on Troy's threat to turn Cyrus over to one of the Houses of the queens he'd killed, Cyrus would be able to use this information against us.

But that would require him to open the son he claimed he cared about more than anything up to a death sentence.

Maybe it was actually a brilliant play, even if I had to swallow hard against the green-gill feeling of nausea bubbling in my stomach and throat. Everyone else in the room looked as uncomfortable as I felt, and I prayed this was not going to be the tone of future family gatherings.

"Well, Cyrus?" Troy pushed. "How does all this fit in your perfect picture of me? Can you reconcile it? Because if you can, then you'll also need to reconcile that Arden is the one who got me through hormonal readjustment and a mental health crisis and, having claimed me formally, is my shield against several active threats. Everything I have ever thrown at her, she has turned into something good. Isn't that what you said Mom did for you?"

Cyrus folded forward and buried his face in his hands. "Don't you dare bring your mother into this."

"She was the one who defended my existence as an oyëori to Keithia." Troy's nasty tone accompanied the lash of his passive power, twisting again into shared pain. "She was *there* and you were *gone*. I've got more right to invoke her than you do."

As everyone flinched, I reached for Troy, both with a hand on his shoulder and in the bond, with as much soothing as I could manage. *Hey. Breathe.*

He started to pull away then noticed the uncomfortably still way the other elves were holding themselves. Allegra and Darius were mirrors of discomfort, arms crossed and shoulders hunched as they leaned on each other and kept their eyes on the floor.

"Goddess burn it," Troy muttered, tamping down his power. "We can't go on like this. You can be my father, come with us, and help us outmaneuver the mundanes for the good of everyone. Or you can choose to let Sutekh stay lodged in your skull like a shitty version of the bond Arden and I have, and I'll say goodbye now for the last time. If you won't even try to get over this grudge you have against Arden, I refuse to spare further resources keeping you here. Or alive, for that matter."

Silence stretched in the room, as heavy as the air right before a thunderstorm broke.

Harqil stirred.

I shook my head sharply then pretended not to notice when Etain caught the gesture and frowned, trying to see what or who I was looking at.

Cyrus caught it as well. "Harqil's here, aren't they?"

"Answer your son, please," I said quietly to keep my voice from betraying the depth of my feelings. "We have places to be and we need to leave very soon."

It wasn't Troy that Cyrus studied in the long minute that followed. It was me.

Troy shifted, irritation spiking in the bond.

I squeezed his shoulder. *Wait.*

Cyrus's expression tightened at that before he shifted his attention to his son, then back to me. "If Harqil is walking, if they're here, it's not just the gods in play. It's the Court of Nightmares as well."

It took everything in me not to react as everyone else exchanged confused looks.

Cyrus nodded, probably at my lack of reaction given he was cuffed and couldn't read my aura. "And the Court plus Harqil means there's been a prophecy. You have Ninlil's gift?"

"Not quite," I said.

"But enough." With a heavy sigh, he slumped. "I'll join you. If the world's ending, I want to be with my boy for the time we have left."

Chapter 17

"Hold the fuck up," Allegra burst out. "Before I even ask what the Court of Nightmares is, the world is ending? Again? Is this about her being a primordial or—"

"Allegra," Troy snapped, a growl underlying his tone.

She didn't back down. "I thought we did this shit already with the Wild Hunt! And if the Captain finds out a primordial—"

Troy slid to stand between me and the other elves, probably without realizing what he was doing. "There was a prophecy. Losing magic was part of it. Cyrus was part of it. It is *not* about Arden."

I wasn't sure that was entirely true—especially when Harqil tipped their head from side to side—but this was turning into the never-ending family squabble, and we had shit to do. Working on the hope part of countering this damn prophecy would have to wait for the time being.

"Enough." I slipped around Troy to stand at his shoulder. "Cyrus, if you're coming, you swear to me. Nothing special, just the same oath everyone else here has sworn. You'll drive up to Washington, DC with a triad of Lyon elves and meet us there." I turned to a still-charged Allegra, who was now practically sparking with the effort to hold her tongue and her magic. "Allegra, you're staying in the Triangle as heir and to coordinate intel and offensive ops for the team going to DC. Etain, you're coming with us to manage the team supporting me and Troy. Extend an invitation to Jo to meet us there. Aside from those orders, this is a volunteer-only mission. It's too dangerous for me to order any of the Ebon Guard or the Darkwatch to go."

"You're going to risk both of you?" Allegra asked dubiously.

Troy pulled himself to his full height. "I am going in at Arden's side. As her king. Not her bodyguard."

"Troy—" Allegra started.

"No. We're both going," he said. "But we're not going to the hearing. We're both planning to get arrested before it starts to flush out what the BSI is doing. I won't hide behind my queen any longer."

He would if I ordered him to. Looking up at him though, I couldn't give that order. As much as I wanted to protect him, keeping him behind me would undermine him among the elven Houses. More than that, it would undercut the personal autonomy he'd fought so hard to claim for himself.

"At my side. As my king. Introduced as such," I agreed for the benefit of everyone present.

As Troy nodded firmly and the bond carried me his relieved pride, Darius jumped to his feet.

"That's it!" he said.

We all turned to him, and I asked, "What's what?"

"Americans may have fought a war against England, but they love the British royal family. Right?"

I frowned. "Some, I guess?"

Troy got it faster. "Me and Arden aren't the same thing. They're not going to join a fan club just because we're royals. They don't know the history or the—"

"Exactly," Darius said. "You can craft whatever it needs to be. Make it the fairytale. Goddess, Troy, you're an elven king with a face that breaks hearts. That alone would get you followers. But add your story with the queen? Your obvious and obviously genuine devotion to her?" He spread his hands wide. "People want good stories right now. They have been through two years of shit, finding out the supernatural is real and being told that we're all demons from hell. The riots. The political bullshit. Give them something to build a fantasy around. Play up your charm."

"It would be a PR coup," Etain said from the side. "We all know that. Throw in some Darkwatch info ops to influence the conversation, plus your pet journalist writing supportive pieces, and boom."

Troy looked at me and, in a heartbeat, read my hesitation to make our life so public. "We'll consider it. Is that everything?"

"I'm going." Harqil finally shifted to full visibility. "In case that helps anyone decide to volunteer."

Even with Cyrus having guessed they were present, Etain and Thana swore, hands dropping to their weapons.

"What's in it for you?" Cyrus asked.

Murderous satisfaction curled Harqil's lips. "I get to fuck you up if you step wrong. Do you know how painful it is to grow back wings, you bastard?"

"Given what you pulled in '92, you had it coming, you meddling, up-jumped firefly."

"Firefly?" Something twisted, an illusion or a glamour, and Harqil seemed to shimmer. To my eyes, a glimpse of something terrifyingly, almost incomprehensibly otherworldly peeked out before they caught me looking and resumed their more usual form.

Cyrus started to clap back.

I dropped my shields to let my power signature spill free, pulled on Air, and made a thunderclap. "E-fucking-nough!"

This time, it was Troy nudging me in the bond as panic frayed the edges of Etain, Darius, Allegra, and Thana's composure at the combined weight of whatever Harqil had let slip and both my sig and my fury with the bickering and the delay.

I closed my eyes and took a breath then another and a third before opening them again. I'd thought that, with the deals between the Southwest Desert, the Seattle Conclave, and the vampires, we were finally finding some unity. We'd been getting somewhere! But there was one step back for the two steps forward we'd taken today. That didn't mean we were doomed for the trip to DC or my and Troy's play there, even if we'd lost a good hour on hashing all this out.

When I was calmer, I said, "Etain, pull together an honor guard of volunteers and coordinate with the Lyon elves on a triad to accompany Cyrus. As soon as Cyrus swears his oath, Troy and I are swinging home to get bags. I want everyone ready within an hour. Got it?"

"Yes, ma'am," Etain said.

Even Troy didn't argue, despite his hope that we'd be able to pick up the marriage license before being thrown into everything. That made my heart clench. I'd wanted it for us. Not just for the security of spousal privilege but because it meant so much to Troy.

Not even the Eternal Huntress got everything she wanted.

After Cyrus grudgingly swore his oath, a quiet Darius offered to drop us off at home. We'd left Troy's car at the Solari mansion to add to the appearance of our staying there after the party.

When we arrived and I thanked Darius for the ride, he squeezed the steering wheel before saying, "I volunteer."

"Dari—" Troy started.

"No. I'm your knight, T. Always will be. I get why you have to leave Alli here, but you're not leaving me. We're family." He swallowed hard. "But after this, I want to talk about options. And I want to decline Sonia Bedoe's marriage offer."

"You can do that anyway," Troy said. "You don't have to put yourself at risk or bargain with us for it."

Darius looked at me.

"Like I said in Asheville." I offered what I hoped was a reassuring smile. "It's your choice. Nobody here will be forced into a relationship they don't want. Not even royals."

Darius exhaled and slumped. "Okay. Thank you. I needed to hear that."

On impulse, I leaned over the seat and hugged him as much as I could, given the awkward position. "You're already my brother, Darius. I won't use you to secure my advantage with Richmond or any other conclave. You're safe here, just like Troy is."

I was close enough to catch the twist in Darius's scent as he squeezed my arms quickly, the sweet-rotten of crushed, slightly off herbs. Bitter sadness was usually what I got from Troy in the bond with that scent.

"Thank you," Darius whispered again. He cleared his throat. "I need to pack up a few things, then I'll be back here to pick you up for the drive north. Okay?"

"Okay, Dari," Troy said quietly. He squeezed his brother's shoulder as he got out of the car.

I followed him into the house as Darius pulled back down the driveway, my heart heavy at the hard choices forcing shifts in Troy's family just in the last few hours and the dark weight of sadness I was getting from the crack in the walls of Troy's side of the bond.

As dysfunctional as his birth family was, it was still a family—at least for Troy. These dynamics had been in place for years: the roles, the disagreements, all of it. The dysfunction was normal to him. And while it wasn't my job to provide an alternative, I wanted to. Just now, I wanted to give him a family, a flesh-and-blood family that we created together, more than anything. I wanted to do as I'd said I would and claim the safety I needed to cycle. I wanted him to father the heirs to my House and for us to establish a new dynasty that would be the change we were both trying to kick the world's ass into accepting.

Otherside was finally coming around.

Damn Sinclaire and the mundanes to the lowest circle of hell for making it so hard.

I'd go to DC, and I'd carve out space for us—for Otherside but especially for Troy and for *myself*—if it was the last damn thing

I did, no matter who or what I had to burn to the ground to get it.

And as that thought crossed my mind, so did the ethereal laughter I kept fucking hearing.

△▽△▽

Between the security concerns, his disappointment about the marriage license situation, and being not only deprived of his usual new moon hunt but also forced to sit in the tight confines of the car, Troy spent the drive north moody and jittery as hell. Enough so that, rather than practice with bronze like I'd planned, I spent most of it letting him hold me and brood, his thigh jostling against me with the rapid bouncing of his foot. Darius seemed to pick up the vibe, ricocheting between speeding and falling under the speed limit, so I had to keep an eye on him as well.

A four-hour drive brought us to the DC area just after sunrise.

I was relieved when Darius pulled up to a large building tucked away down a private drive in a heavily wooded area. All the trees would help both me and Troy settle before we had to go into DC proper.

I stretched and glanced at the map on the car's HUD as Darius turned the car off. "Where are we, exactly?"

"A camp just outside Quantico." Darius got out and stretched, circling the car to grab his bags from the passenger seat.

"Um." I looked at Troy. "Like...FBI Quantico? That Quantico?"

"Yes. The East Coast Darkwatch owns this property." He moved to get out too, still talking. "Combination of a training facility and an outpost."

The outpost bit presumably being in place to watch the FBI. Shit. It was one thing to walk into a trap and kind of another to sleep right next to the enemy. The FBI had largely stayed hands off on Otherside matters, leaving that to the jurisdiction of the BSI, but for me that was part of the problem. They could have been investigating the human supremacy terrorist groups—the Sons of Seth and others like them. That they hadn't even added them to any kind of list told me all I needed to know.

I took a breath to stop myself from asking if we could really afford to burn this location and followed the elves out, slinging the backpack with the magical artifacts I didn't dare leave at home for an extended period over my shoulder before joining Troy at the trunk to get my two bags. It wasn't whether we could afford to lose the facility here; it was a question of what would happen if we didn't go big and use our resources now, while we were still able to move freely enough to do so.

The land had a similar feel to the warehouse we'd stayed in closer to the North Carolina border, after I escaped the human kidnappers. Mixed hardwoods and ferns interspersed with pine grew from moist soil of clay and sand, silt from the nearby river, and a little bit of swampland. A tall, shrubby plant with bright red flowers grew in clumps along a small stream running alongside the building we'd parked in front of, and a woodpecker called from somewhere deeper in the woods. I couldn't help reaching with the elements to get a better sense of the place, which got me a nudge in the bond from Troy.

"Later," he said, already heading into the building.

I reached for that as I followed, not really surprised to find the wood facing making it look like an oversized log cabin was just that—facing. The rest of it was heavily reinforced concrete with powerful monitoring equipment tucked away in the roof.

"Barracks are this way," Troy said, leading me down a hallway toward the back. "There are cabins farther out, but I want us in here for security."

We passed an open door where Darius was already unpacking with brisk efficiency, starting with hanging his weapons neatly on the wall with hooks jutting out for that purpose. The room Troy turned into was smaller with a single bigger bed and an ensuite bathroom. A large window looked out to an inner courtyard, all grass in the center and pavers interspersed with training dummies along the edges.

"Captain's quarters," Troy explained as he stowed his bags. "Cyrus, the Lyon elves, and any volunteers will stay in the common barracks. Some in the cabins farther out as guards."

"This is all part of the Darkwatch plan you're adapting?" I asked.

"Yes. The Darkwatch picked up some threats after the vampire Reveal, so Omar wanted us to be prepared to strike if necessary." He started unpacking his weapons, as Darius had, and I blinked to see the range of what he'd brought with him. I hadn't even known he had this many knives, let alone—

"Is that a *grenade?*" I asked.

"Yes."

When he kept going without adding anything further, like this was a completely normal thing to be carrying around, I said, "That was in our *house?*"

"Of course not. It was at HQ." He glanced at me. "It's not good safety protocol to keep munitions this close to someone who sparks fire and lightning. I wanted to be sure we had options though."

Troy as conclave general was kind of a new level of scary.

He paused and straightened, turning to frown at me. "Do I need to store these in a different room?"

"I can keep control of my magic for a day," I said drily.

After a quick evaluating ripple in the bond, he nodded and started hanging up the dress clothes he'd packed for the hearing. We'd compromised in the end—brand names but well tailored, all in black and gold.

"Hey. Leave this stuff to me. Go run off the moonbite," I said.

We were on a tight deadline to catch Sinclaire before the twenty-four hours she'd given me to respond expired, but there was no way I was going to bring Troy like this. The bond hummed with barely restrained energy that had a fiercer edge to it than usual. One that could very easily turn violent if I was threatened. He always did an excellent job controlling himself, but the more energy he had to spend doing that, the shorter and growlier he got. We both knew he needed to be the charming king today, not the silently glowering bodyguard.

Troy grimaced.

"No, it's not that obvious, but yes, you need to go. I'll finish up here, make a quick land tie, and get a nap and a snack in before we need to leave. I'll be here the whole time." That should give him the reassurance he needed to focus on himself for half an hour. I hugged him. "Okay?"

He debated that for a moment then gave me a quick squeeze back and bent to dig in his other bag for something he could run in. "Okay. Thanks, my love."

Once he'd changed and headed out with a terse order to Darius to stay here and keep watch, I walled the bond up to a crack, shut the door, and sat on the bed.

I needed a minute to process the fact that we were really doing this. After everything I'd said about wanting to be let alone, not being a killer, working within the law, and trying to find a peaceable way forward, I was sitting in the room of an elven combat outpost staring at a wall full of knives, guns, and grenades as my fiancé and almost brother-in-law prepared for an op. One that I was leading.

Okay, I needed more than a minute.

Because one way or another, shit was about to get blown wide open.

When that happened, somebody could—probably would—die. Someone I cared about because I knew the volunteers would be more of those most loyal to me. They wouldn't let their High Queen and Arbiter walk into a trap and face the full might of the mundanes alone.

But I'd authorized war.

Now I had to find a way to live with that...and with myself.

After today, there was definitely no going back to being a nobody hiding in the woods ever again. And that might scare me more than the idea of going head-to-head against the federal government.

Chapter 18

Once I got all of our stuff unpacked and had a quick nap, I showered and dressed so I'd be ready when Troy got back. When he stalked in, still radiating a vague menace but in better control of it, I found Darius and got some practice with bronze in the courtyard while Troy showered. The playfulness I'd seen hinted at in Darius's comments about my and Troy's telepathic communications came out as soon as I said I needed him to surprise me with things, especially when Harqil made an appearance and insisted a blindfold would make everything more surprising. I didn't love being blindfolded, but I'd found my way to trusting Darius and needed to try new situations to reach Chaos past Aether.

Now that I knew it was Chaos I needed to reach for, I had slightly more success. I didn't manage to impact anything, but sparks of magic came faster with each attempt. It was nowhere near enough to free me if I was captured, but it was much more consistent and a hell of a lot better than nothing.

The rest of our team filtered in bit by bit over the next two hours, nearly the same three triple triads that had come for me in Virginia. Cyrus was accompanied by Samarre, Jacinthe, and a hard-eyed Luc. To my surprise, Rio had joined a triad. Apparently, House Lestari leaned toward mental Aether but wasn't as strong in it—or the bloodline as tightly controlled—as House Monteague had been. Troy took it as a matter of fact, so I let it be. The grim air of anticipation in the main building was doing enough to spike the tension without me adding to it with objections when the new prince had already sworn an oath to me.

It was a big group and would leave a lot of the elven holdings in the Triangle undefended, but Troy had considered the risk of losing properties, or even other elves, to be worth the need to defend me. I reminded myself that that was part of living with the war I'd authorized as we drove into DC under heavy magical workings and with falsified Virginia and Maryland license plates.

Downtown Washington, DC was another hour's drive away. We spent it refining our plan to make a big media storm in front of the White House. Jo would meet us there, having booked lodgings somewhere between the White House and Capitol Hill.

My pulse raced as we drew closer.

Magic and technology had gotten us to the heart of our enemy's territory, and we were already considered terrorists by some here. DC was a neutral zone in Otherside—no permanent holdings allowed. The only support we'd have was from the team we'd brought in and any Othersiders who'd infiltrated the government and military, assuming they were on our side. I hoped they were, but I'd had too much experience getting screwed over by the elves to trust in it.

We found parking on New York Ave and waited in the car for the triple triad that'd accompanied us to find their own, spaced out so that we wouldn't all be scooped up together. The other two triples were being held in reserve, one at the camp, one halfway between the camp and here, in case an extraction was needed.

When all our people had checked in and Jo's livestream—a series of interviews about Otherside with people outside the White House—had started, it was time to face the people who'd been behind so much pain and division.

I took a breath to settle my nerves. "Ready?"

Troy caught my arm. "Wait. I need to cast a spell before we get out."

"Just to walk around?"

"Yes. Trust me."

Darius twisted to smirk at us from the driver's seat. "Charm spell?"

"Yes," Troy said.

"Has she experienced it yet?"

"No. That's why I'm warning her." Troy looked at me. "It shouldn't affect you too much, Arden. But it's a monarch-level spell and you're only half-elven. There might be spillover. Sorry, that didn't occur to me until just now."

"Okay then," I said. "Whatever gets us to the fence without a SWAT team being called."

With a nod, Troy reached for Aether, filling the car with the smell of toasting marshmallows. The spell he spoke in elvish was more of a song than the usual firm chant, and it twined through my heart, lifting it.

When he finished with the invocation word, all I could do was stare.

He grinned roguishly at my suddenly blank expression and flushed cheeks. "I guess it's working."

"Mm hmm!" I squeaked. "Yep. Working."

Troy was unreasonably hot on a good day, or even a bad one. This...this was dangerous. I couldn't even say why. It wasn't just that the spell amplified his natural physical attractiveness. A layer of goodwill and, well, charm smoothed out the menacing rough edges that'd clung to him despite his effort to relax. Rather than feeling threatening, his power signature felt like an invitation.

I shook myself and adjusted my shielding until I could perceive that he was running a spell but not be affected by it.

"Good," he said when I had it. "I prefer obfuscation to charm, but now you know how Keithia managed to go to the hairdresser without setting off every human in the salon."

Because the old bitch had had a power signature too, and none of Troy's practice at tamping herself down and being less. That and she'd oozed menace. Of course she would have needed a spell to leave the house.

With a last self-satisfied grin, Troy darted in to nip my neck, drawing another squeak from me as he smoothly pulled away and got out of the car.

"You good, sister?" Darius's attention was on me in the rearview mirror. "Or do I need to rein my brother in?"

"Good." I took a breath, shook myself, and gave him a smile. Usually, Darius kept me at more of a distance, but maybe telling him he really didn't have to marry Sonia Bedoe had shifted something. "Thank you."

He offered a similar affirmative grunt to what Troy often did, and Thana nodded from the passenger seat.

Troy was still smirking when we got out of the car, but he smoothed it into a politician's smile when I arched an eyebrow at him.

"Jerk," I muttered, adding a teasing curl to the bond so he'd know I wasn't really mad.

"You love it."

I pinched his ass as I slid my arm around his waist. Not that he reacted externally but it made me feel better. At least until I remembered all the surveillance cameras that would be on us in this part of town. Darius and Thana had accepted being outed—Thana already had been, when the Sinners made their first kidnapping attempt—but I still didn't like having more of my people exposed.

Nothing for it.

They drifted away from us as we hit the street, staying at a safe distance. Elsewhere in the throng of sightseers would be Cyrus and his guard triad, adding to the effect of Troy's spell with Cyrus's passive power. Pascale would be waiting with a getaway car just in case our plan to be arrested went awry and they tried killing us instead.

We'd agreed not to bother with a "don't see me" spell because the entire point was to be seen and draw Sinclaire's attention, although Troy layered a light "stay back" spell over it. I still wasn't prepared for the reaction to his charm spell though.

A few people stopped and stared outright. Not everyone. That would have been too obvious. But I was willing to bet the people who did were human sensitives, people like Haroun's mother, who were more susceptible to elven magic than the general populace for all that some of them were elf-blooded themselves several generations back.

Of course, we were recognized before we'd gone a few steps.

"Is that—" someone said before being shushed.

When I turned to look, a woman was staring, bug-eyed, as she fumbled with her phone. I forced a smile and a small, friendly wave but kept walking. We needed to reach Jo for part two of her livecast.

A growing crowd followed me and Troy. My anxiety kicked up a notch, tightening my chest. I wasn't used to being seen like this. I didn't like it at all. But I was here to stand up for my people. And that meant stepping into a spotlight so that my people could remain safe in the shadows.

Easy, Troy sent. *This is all still according to plan. Including the police trying to push through.*

I barely managed to keep my pleasant smile in place. I'd been so distracted by the sheer number of people with phones that I hadn't even noticed the threats.

You have me and the Ebon Guard for that, Troy responded to my unsent thought. *You focus on you.*

I did as he said, taking a breath and reaching for the same attitude I had when I faced the gods.

There you go. Perfect.

I let my smile widen in genuine delight when we finally reached Jo's position in front of the White House. "Jo! Good to see you again."

She must have spotted us coming before I spoke because she smoothly wrapped up what she was saying and smiled back. "Ms. Finch, welcome to Washington, DC. I'd like to introduce you to a few folks and hold an AMA, if you're open to it. But first, what brings you to the nation's capital?"

In the distance, police sirens screamed. I was surprised it'd taken someone that long to do something, given we were enough of a threat to have merited a Reaper drone, but it looked like Omar's Darkwatch agents—and maybe a few other rogue Othersiders—had come through on the part of the plan that involved hacking, delaying, misdirecting, and generally fucking up the security response Troy and I would have triggered.

I forced myself to ignore the sirens and the inevitable complications the arrival of security forces and law enforcement would bring and focused on being a ray of sunshine for the camera and mic Jo was now pointing at me.

"We were invited. Well. Sort of." I offered a cheeky smile and lowered my voice to a stage whisper. "There's a legislative hearing we're due to attend next week, and Director Sinclaire of the Bureau for Supernatural Investigation also personally invited us to DC."

"She did?" Jo's eyebrows shot up. "That sounds like it's in direct contradiction to public comment."

"She called just last night actually," I said. "With an offer I couldn't ignore. So here I am, ready and willing to work toward peaceful negotiations toward equal rights for Otherside in the United States."

Incoming, Troy sent. *But keep going.*

From Jo's darted glances, she was equally aware of what the ripples and the rising shouts in the crowd portended. She hesitated then plowed forward. "Some have called you a terrorist,

Ms. Finch, yet here you are at what should be one of the most secure locations in the country. How did you manage that?"

The sunny smile I offered was helped along by a flash of internal mirth that we'd managed to get here at all. "It's not illegal to sightsee, Jo. And none of my people intend harm to anyone here. We've always lived alongside humans. I see no reason for that to change."

"Would you be open to taking a few questions?" Jo asked, allowing me to evade her question as her gaze darted back to the growing law enforcement presence. "I've been interviewing people on the Otherside question this afternoon, and some expressed a desire to be heard directly."

"Of course." I looked at the SWAT teams who'd finally pushed their way through the crowd. "Assuming the folks who've now joined us will give us the opportunity."

Jo turned the camera to pan across the now enormous crowd blocking traffic and still growing despite the bullhorn-amplified orders being shouted by Capitol Police and ignored. The energy in the area had shifted dramatically, from curiosity and titillation to anger and fear. Not directed at me and Troy, whose charm spell was still running, but toward the security forces now looking uncertainly at each other as one man front and center held fingers to his ear like he was trying to hear orders.

A ripple of magic pulled my attention, and I glanced in that direction, continuing to look past Cyrus when I spotted him in the crowd. He leaned on his cane, surrounded by his guards, his attention intense on Troy.

"I want to hear what the supernatural has to say!" someone in the crowd hollered.

"I have questions!" a man standing closer shouted.

Troy? I sent.

Keep going, he replied grimly. *Cyrus is playing his part, and with the number of cameras on us, they can't afford to make us martyrs. Be prepared for a rough arrest though.*

I pulled on Air and made a quick wall just in case someone in command didn't agree with that assessment, glad of the colored contacts Troy had produced before we left camp. They were a simple and elegant solution for the golden glow of my eyes when I worked magic, one I'd never considered before.

I raised my hands, both an appeal for silence and a gesture to show I was unarmed—not that it would matter, given my magic. "As I said, I'm happy to take questions. I can't expect my fellow Americans to understand Otherside if we don't engage in dialogue."

A roar from one of the bullhorns cut off Jo's next comment.

"Arden Finch! Stand down and stop talking!"

I glanced up at Troy. *Here we go.*

All going to plan, he sent.

Plan or not, adrenaline flooded me as the SWAT teams closed in, rifles lowered. I hastily pulled my Air wall closer until they stopped advancing twenty feet away.

"Have I done something wrong?" I called.

"You're an unregistered supernatural of unknown type and, as such, subject to the Supernatural Activity Limitation and Tracking Act. Surrender peacefully."

With a kick, the Sight drove me toward an answer that wasn't in our plan. "If I'm under arrest, I can't speak at the hearing the Senate has set up."

The SWAT captain, a beefy white man, frowned as he clicked the bullhorn off and spoke into a microphone. "There is no Senate hearing listed," he finally said. "Comply."

"Funny that it's not listed," I said loudly and clearly over the sudden hush of the crowd. "My fiancé and I were issued a subpoena. Check with Senator Wright. He's who I was working with originally."

Arden, what are you doing? Troy sent. *We are supposed to be arrested.*

Not yet. Sight.

He simmered in the bond even as the charm spell twitched up a notch to compensate, prickling over the back of my neck.

I raised my voice further. "Is this how your government works? How your tax dollars are spent? Secret hearings and information hidden from the American people by their own government? I mean, if they want to accuse me of—"

"Shut her up!" a new voice shouted, one belonging to a man in a military uniform with a lot of shiny shit on the front of it. "Finch, you and Monteague are in violation of the SALT Act and the Patriot Act. You will surrender peacefully and come with us. Now."

"I'll do no such thing," I said calmly, my hands still up.

Troy twitched at my side, on high alert and ready to do whatever it took to extract me from this.

Another nudge of the Sight had me pulling on Chaos.

Boost it, I sent to him.

He took what I funneled him and did as I said but twisted the charm into something more dangerous. The people closest to us in the crowd started rumbling.

Aether prickled and crested as the other elves in the crowd took a cue and did what they did best: influenced and manipulated their enemies. The mental Aether users mazed minds, those with talents for bodies raised heart rates and stress hormones, and the auratically talented put a pressure to act on our behalf over everyone susceptible.

Someone shoved a cop and said, "Fuck the police! I want to hear the Othersider talk!"

Everything exploded like a tinderbox doused in gasoline.

Suddenly it wasn't me, Troy, and Jo that the security forces were worried about. It was the crowd, now grown to hundreds of humans interspersed not only with my guards and Cyrus but with Richmond Conclave elves sent by Sonia Bedoe stirring everything up even further.

Through it all, Jo kept recording. "This peaceful gathering has now shifted to chaos as…"

That was all I heard because Troy gripped my arm and tugged me after him.

I shifted my wall of Air and let him drag me into a run as he cut the charm spell and muttered a "don't see us" spell that rolled out like an attack. We dodged past more SWAT and through a police cordon, running until we made it to the rendezvous with Pascale's backup car. She pulled away as soon as Troy and I tumbled in, taking her time like she was just another commuter caught up in the mess the gathering or riot or whatever it was now had made of the already atrocious traffic in DC.

The whole drive out of town, Troy sat with a face like a thunderhead as he furiously swiped out texts and tried to figure out what had happened to our people.

I only had one person to deal with.

Your little stunt got the attention of every branch of government, Sinclaire texted. *Our deal is off the table.*

I'm in DC, like you wanted. Leave my people alone, I texted back. *Or whatever is done to mine will be answered.*

I didn't even care that it was incriminating. Of all the roles and titles that'd been put on me, the one I'd claimed for myself was protector. If that meant exposing myself to criminal charges from a government that I refused to submit to, then so be it.

They didn't matter anyway.

Nothing did, except for the rage simmering another notch higher in my heart.

Chapter 19

It took hours to get back to our camp. We had to make sure we weren't followed. Then we had to change cars twice before taking a roundabout way back. I was a little surprised when Pascale swapped out with some Bedoe elves, but maybe I shouldn't have been. It did prompt me to call Sonia directly and thank her for the support, which thawed Troy's mood a little but not completely.

The debrief when we got back was tense. Fortunately, it was just me and Troy to start, behind closed doors and a soundproofing barrier. He might have been pissed, but between his training and his respect for me, he wouldn't argue with me in front of everyone else, no matter how angry he was about a good plan changed at the last minute.

"That was *not* what we agreed on, Arden," Troy snarled. "The plan was for us to be arrested and taken to whatever facility the Bureau is working out of so we can protect the people Sinclaire threatened. That last-minute change put three triads of ours and three of Sonia's at risk, even if she's too polite to say so. Not to mention everyone sworn to us—to *you*—in the Triangle."

"I told you, the Sight—"

"The Sight is not a military tactic!"

"Do you want me to explain, or do you want to keep telling me off?" I snapped, temper flaring.

He shut his mouth but glared, entirely the general in a full-on stand-off with his queen and not at all my fiancé right now.

I held my own tongue, taking a moment to breathe, and made sure my walls were tight. The bond would do more harm than good right now, giving us all of each other's emotion with none of the context that would come with words that traveled more slowly between us.

When I was calm enough to speak without shouting at him, I said, "For reasons I don't know, it's not enough for us to be here. We need to be at the hearing specifically. We needed to push today and fall back. A..." I searched for something that would sound like a military term. "A planned retreat. A concession. They see us run this time, and they get more confident."

Troy kept me pinned with his glare and utterly uncompromising expression.

"I know it grates," I said. "Running from mundanes when either of us could have dispelled the crowd entirely or progressed with our original mission. But we had to get all of this in the open, and we had to be seen fleeing instead of being taken. Call it a feint."

"There'll be consequences for this choice, Arden," Harqil said as they phased into the room.

I jumped. They'd been so subtle about it that I'd missed the usual flare of magic. "Goddess damn— What consequences?"

They shrugged, for once not smiling at my discomfort. "You chose the harder path." At my stiffening posture and Troy's growl, Harqil added, "That's not to say it's the worse one. There are no good or easy paths forward, and there haven't been since you committed to stealing magic back. But this choice changes your future more than anyone's. Depending on what you do next, our carrion crow may well tip the balance. Which way is up to you."

Before I could ask what the hell all that meant, Harqil disappeared.

I squeezed my eyes shut and tilted my head back, trying to breathe and trying not to cry as pain lanced through my heart.

I'd signed up for this, for pain and consequences, when I decided to be a protector, to be Arbiter, to be known. That didn't mean I was okay with it. Especially if I'd just cost myself and Troy our family or given whoever was still influencing Cyrus the opening they needed to use him to bring my apocalyptic dream to fruition.

Troy's arms coming around me made me jump, but he held me tighter rather than letting go.

"I'm still pissed," he said in a low rumble. "But you smell like pain. I can't bear you being in pain, Arden."

I snaked my arms around him, taking solace in the darkness created by pressing my face against his chest. *I will see us through this. I want our family. Everything I do is toward that end.*

After a moment, he shifted to grip the hair at the base of my skull and pull my head back to look at him.

"I know," Troy said. "And I'm sorry. Following an elemental queen as she fucks all your carefully laid plans to follow the whisper of the Sight in a high-risk situation was not covered in training, and it threw me."

Shit. This was his debut on the public stage as general and King as much as it was mine as Arbiter and High Queen. That's where this mood was coming from: a need to prove himself as worthy of his titles and as an oyëori while at the same time demonstrating that he could still maintain elven culture and tradition, despite all the changes he was making, in serving a queen. I'd been thinking of it like the showdown in Raleigh, when we escaped the SWAT team sent to Claret, but bigger. He was seeing it as not quite something else entirely but something far more meaningful.

"I can't promise it won't happen again," I said, trying to find a point we could agree on. "But I understand that it creates difficulties."

"I don't need you to promise. I'll adjust orders to factor in the Sight and the need for flexibility. It'll give every elf following us the shits, but rigidly sticking to plans and protocol has failed for every elf sent against you." He smiled tiredly and brushed a kiss on my lips. "Including me. Hell, maybe this is how Quinlan felt trying to keep up with your mother."

I couldn't help a flinch. My father died in that quest, and my mother followed him. I didn't want that to be me and Troy.

"I didn't mean it like that," he said.

"I know. It's just very fresh, having just seen them."

Troy didn't try to comment on that. He'd woken up to find me crying over it enough times in the last month that he knew holding me was all he could really do, so that's what he did until I took a shuddering breath.

"What's our united front?" I asked. No matter how much we disagreed on something related to the House or my management of Otherside, we used that as the lightning rod to ground whatever sparks crackled between us.

"The plan is still the same," he said. "We're just adding a step and actually going to the Senate hearing."

"And you're good with that? For yourself, not just because I'm chasing the Sight?"

He started to answer then paused to think it over. "I disagree—strongly—with us subjecting ourselves to human law and government. Yes, we've more or less abided by their laws up to now. But it has gotten us hurt." His gaze was shadowed labradorite as he studied me and took a breath. "I'm tired of hurting, Arden. Sometimes it feels like it's all I've ever done, except when I'm in your arms. I might not believe ease and safety are my lot in life, but I want..."

Heart pounding, I waited for him to parse out his thoughts.

"I want at least the *possibility* of safety and ease. I want space for it." Troy sighed and leaned to press his forehead against mine. "Which is why I'll back you on this. Your read of the Sight hasn't been wrong yet. I know we'll get hurt again following it. But I'm choosing to hope this is the last time. For long enough for us to start a family, at least."

"Okay." I twisted to kiss him. "Thank you. I know this is hard. I know I do things completely differently to how you were taught and trained, especially when it comes to taking action. But the Sight got me through the Duat trials. I have to have faith in it—in myself—to get us through to the other side of this. Even if there'll be a cost to it."

"Let's go then. We need to brief our people here, and then the rest of our people in the Triangle and the broader alliances."

We emerged from our room with fingers interlaced and heads high. I took the responsibility to explain what had happened and the change of plan, and Troy backed me and issued the orders. I expected our people to protest or even just look worried, but they didn't. They looked tired, sure. But they also looked resolute. They trusted me. They had faith in me. Maybe my way of doing things would give other elves the shits, to use Troy's phrasing, but these ones here had my back.

Somehow, I managed not to cry at that as a piece of the weight that'd hung over me for years lifted. I truly had people. Yeah, it'd been proven over and over again, but this time the hell and the high water were really coming. Everyone except Cyrus looked like they were along for the ride.

Cyrus mostly looked resigned and angry. Waves of despair came off him, enough that there was a space around him and the Lyon elves looked a little sick.

Shit. I had to bring him around. The ring to see the unseen buzzed on my finger at the thought—not just around but *now*, before it was too late. Something pivotal was coming, and we needed Cyrus on the right side of it.

I pulled him aside when we dismissed everyone, holding up a hand so Troy would keep his distance.

"Walk with me, please," I said to Cyrus.

"As my queen commands," he replied, more than a little sarcastically.

I let it go and led him outside. Troy and Cyrus's guards trailed at enough of a distance to give us some privacy, but I didn't miss that Troy now had his longknife out and held not-so-casually at his side.

I pulled my shields up tighter to defend against Cyrus's passive power and stopped next to one of the training dummies in the courtyard. How could I give him enough hope to sway him?

Then it hit me. All of his actions were driven by the loss of his family and the chancre Sutekh had grown in his mind. I had to counter that first. I had to find a way to let him feel like he had Troy back.

I thumbed the ring that was now vibrating on my finger. "I wanted to thank you."

"Thank me." Cyrus's brows drew down hard.

"Yes. You played your part today, with the crowd. I know it was out of fear for Troy. I accept and appreciate that. We both love him, Cyrus. We both want to see him thrive." I put every ounce of sincerity I felt in the words. If he was the crow from my prophetic dream, I needed to bring him back into the fold, regardless of how I felt about his machinations and his deal with Sutekh.

Especially if Harqil's hints about the Court of Nightmares being involved were part of it.

Cyrus studied me, not quite squinting the way Troy did when reading an aura but almost. "You believe what you're saying." He paused, nostrils flaring as he added scent to it. "And you're frustrated, but you accept it."

"I do."

"You're not going to scold me? Insist on absolute loyalty?"

"What would that gain me?" I looked at Troy, saddened as always by the rift between father and son, allowing Cyrus to see it. "This road is going to get harder before it gets easier. I just wanted you to know that, if it comes down to it and you have to choose between your oath to me and your love for your son, I want you to choose your son. Find a way to save him."

Cyrus's lip twitched into a snarl before he could smooth his features. "What has Harqil said now?"

"That there will be consequences and that they will impact me most of all. But an impact to me is an impact to Troy. He's my greater good. I want you to do what you want to do anyway and keep him safe." I smiled wryly. "Consider it part of your House oath to me."

He tilted his head, and a ripple of Aether hit me and had Troy growling and lifting his blade.

I held up a hand to stay Troy's reaction but otherwise didn't move.

"You really want this, down to your soul," Cyrus said. Confusion and suspicion twisted his voice almost into a growl, but some of the despairing mien lifted. "Sutekh said— I was *convinced* you were playing a game with Troy. With both of us."

"I know. But given the turn things took today, I need all of us here to be fully aligned. If the only point of alignment you and I can find is that we want Troy to have some kind of happily ever after? To live his best life? I can work with that." I extended a hand. "Deal?"

Cyrus left me hanging for so long I almost dropped my hand.

"Deal," he finally said as he clasped my hand. As he did, he shuddered and pain rippled over his features. "I hurt him in threatening you. In hurting you. Didn't I?"

"You did. And I understand if you can't trust me or don't want us to be close. Believe me when I say that I know what it is for the gods to twist you when they ride you." I pushed away memories of Neith's gift taking over my mind. "But I want to give Troy the family he so deeply craves. I want him to stay and be a father to his children—*our* children—the way he wants to be. The way you wanted to be to him."

That got me my first real crack in his demeanor, a hard swallow and a look to the side as his eyes shone.

I pressed it. "Cyrus, my parents are gone. You and Duke are all I have left of the people who knew them directly. All I'm asking is that you set aside your dislike for me to be there for your son, and maybe, if you come to it on your own, that you might tell me about them someday. I'm hoping you can set down some of this unimaginable pain and find a way back into your son's life."

He looked away then cleared his throat as the snarl of emotion he was projecting grew even more muted. "I still think you are the least queenly queen I've ever met. I've never seen one humble herself like this. I'm not sure what to do with it, to be honest. I don't know how to react to you if you're not punishing me for being an almighty ass. It almost gives me hope for a better future."

"Yeah, well..." I pressed my lips together and shrugged, remembering Troy going through a similar phase a year ago. "The mission is worth it. More than that, *Troy* is worth it. Right?"

"Right." Cyrus inhaled deeply and blew his breath out. "Fine. I'll do my duty here and pay off my debt, as Troy asked. When this is over, I...request...that the three of us sit down and talk about my paying off the other two thirds of it." He glanced at Troy, regret in the slight curl of his shoulders. "It's clear now that I've fucked up with my boy, and he's made it even clearer that's the only way to begin making my way toward being his father again. Give me that chance, and I'll see if I can find my way toward the rest."

"Request granted, assuming we survive this." I managed a smile as the ring flared with one last burst of heat before going cold, and squeezed his arm. "Get some rest, okay?"

"Yes, my queen." This time, he sounded more genuine, maybe for the first time in our acquaintance.

The Lyon elves moved forward as I stepped away from him, and Troy sheathed the longknife.

You're okay? he sent.

I will be. When Troy only turned us toward the doors to the wooded outer area, I huffed a sigh. *He was still holding out after the debrief. We need him on our side. Fully on our side, or who the hell knows what his magic would do at the hearing. Or if that would count as managing the crow from my dream. More than that, I don't want to be the reason you two aren't at least on speaking terms. I know you're pissed, but if we don't give him some hope, something bad is going to happen.*

Alarm flared in the bond. *What did you offer him?*

My truth. That if nothing else, he and I can align on wanting you to thrive. And that I want you to be able to be a father to your children with me, with him in our lives if you both choose that. I know it's not fair to push you on this, but something catastrophic is tied in with his being the crow. I took Troy's hand. *The elementals tried to force me to choose them or the elves, and the djinn wanted it even if they didn't do more than grumble. I refuse to make anyone pick just one piece of themselves to hold dear. It hurts too much, and like you said, we've hurt enough.*

Troy stayed quiet as we walked among the trees, decompressing from the tension of the day with my light connection to nature swirling through both of us. *I still don't trust him,* he said when we were nearly back to the outpost. *But I think you made the best choice here.*

I hoped I had. Harqil had scared me with their talk of consequences.

And everyone here knew that we had to be united as Otherside against the mundanes, no matter what our personal grievances were.

Chapter 20

S inclaire had to know that most Othersiders, including me and Troy, were naturally nocturnal. If nothing else, Onora or Sixtus Ead would have told her. Which was probably why the dark march that was my ringtone for her trumpeted shortly after dawn.

I was tempted not to pick it up, but that wouldn't keep my people safe. After checking with Troy that location tracking scramblers were on and I had a recording device ready, I answered.

"Your little performance backfired, Finch," she said smugly. "The hearing has been moved up. Your appearance is required on Capitol Hill tomorrow. Nine a.m. sharp. You'll even get your wish on being heard. We're making it an open hearing."

"What, so you can be seen to arrest me?" I managed to keep my voice light and mocking with an effort, although Troy grimaced as much from me suppressing the urge to draw on Fire as for the day. Tomorrow was Monday, almost a week earlier than the hearing had originally been planned for and the day Troy and I should have been getting our marriage license. On their side, that would mean an almighty upheaval and scramble to rearrange schedules, prep rooms, and get senators back here if they were elsewhere.

Looked like we were a big deal.

Troy's surprised expression as he checked his phone made me hold back my next words. When he turned the device toward me, a news article was pulled up: "Arden Finch Solari Visits White House – Secret Otherside Hearing Exposed."

"Oh, we'll do that, certainly," Sinclaire said lightly. "The arrest warrants are already drawn up."

"Then what motivation do I have to do a damn thing you say?" I asked.

"If you do as you keep saying you do—follow the law—and set a good example for the rest of Otherside, I will authorize leniency for your people in the Triangle."

Setting an example has to be the real reason for making it an open hearing. She doesn't want a war, but she needs a win to solidify her new title, Troy sent.

I was going along with it anyway because that had been the plan from the beginning. We needed to get arrested so they would take us to whichever secure facility had been built to hold Othersiders. But my people came first.

"What does leniency look like?" I asked.

"Relocation to a secure containment facility rather than eradication," Sinclaire said.

That made me snarl. Yeah, we might be going along with her bullshit for a reason, but I needed my people free in the meantime. I could not be worried about my parliament in particular being rounded up and imprisoned or killed. "Not good enough. My people have done nothing wrong. They deserve to live freely."

"You can take it or leave it," she said. "The United States government does not negotiate with terrorists."

Fuck that. "Troy, have the recording I made of Director Sinclaire threatening a gas leak on Claret released please. Something like that would have collateral damage, and the American people deserve to know who's really waging war on them."

"Recording?" Sinclaire's voice was nearly a screech. "That's illegal."

She was right, at least in the state of North Carolina, but I was done playing by mundane rules. "I like to make sure I have a record of anything I need to arbitrate on. Accountability is the key to justice, after all, and I don't negotiate with terrorists either."

A long silence, during which I could practically hear her seething, stretched.

Troy, with a shit-eating grin, said loudly, "Ready for send, Arbiter."

"Wait," Sinclaire snapped. After another long pause, she asked, "What arrangement are you proposing?"

"I will come alone to the hearing. You leave my people alone for the duration of the hearing plus one week."

I pressed a hand over Troy's lips to stop him speaking when he stiffened, the cocky grin slipping into a snarl.

Trust me, I sent.

"Absolutely not," Sinclaire said. "That gives them time to scatter."

"And go where?" I asked. "You have your Bureau busybodies searching high and low for Othersiders, tailing people, freezing bank accounts. They're not going anywhere. They need to see how things play out as much as your people do."

"I want Monteague there as well."

See? I sent to him. *Now it looks like a negotiation, regardless of what she said before.*

Good. Because you are not *walking into another trap without me. Not this time.*

"He's not on the table for this deal," I said, just to pique Sinclaire. I was starting to think she hadn't been chosen for the role because of her strategic thinking but rather for her doggedness in pursuing us and her clearly anti-Otherside sentiment.

Then again, maybe there was a deeper plan here, one I couldn't see because I had tunnel vision on protecting my people. There was only one way to find out just now.

"He is on the table," she said, "or we carry out a total enforcement action in the Triangle in one hour. Release whatever silly recording you have. We'll call it fake news."

The annoying thing was that they'd get away with it. The same average people who were staunchly anti-Otherside were convinced of all kinds of conspiracy bullshit. The truth was whatever they believed it to be, regardless of fact, and neither media literacy nor critical thinking were among their skills. Worse, most media outlets would run with whatever was most inflammatory, purely for the clicks and the ad revenue, and fact-check later—if ever. Even if they did, the damage would be done.

"Give me a moment," I said.

She'd barely agreed when I muted the phone, double-checking to make sure it was really muted.

I paused the recording as well.

Before I could say anything, Troy said, "Don't you dare tell me I have an out. It's not even a question. Secure safety for our people. You and I can figure out the rest."

Are the Darkwatch and the Ebon Guard ready to foment riots when we're arrested? I sent, trying to be extra careful.

Yes. Not just in DC.

That was news to me. *Where else?*

Conclaves in Richmond, Charleston, Seattle, and San Francisco will kick off. The weres have assured me that they'll get Phoenix, Houston, Portland, and Denver going, and the vampires will cover Atlanta, New York, Philadelphia, Los Angeles, Chicago, and Miami. Ximena has contacts in South America she's reaching out to, and Terrence has some in West Africa. House Desmarais is coordinating hits on political, police, and financial targets across Europe with support from the Zurich vampire coterie. It'll spread globally from there. The minute we're in custody, the mundanes will have their hands full.

Troy had been up to more than I'd realized when he was making those phone calls a few days ago. With all that, it'd be war. There was no way the mundanes would allow open Othersider rebellion against these registration and containment laws, certainly not in the US, at least. We'd have one shot at this, and I could only barely manage Chaos while shackled.

Then again, there would really only be one chance anyway. If Troy and I couldn't break free fast and violently, we'd be fully subdued. Who knew how long it'd be until we'd have another chance, especially once the mundanes got their hands on more of us and managed to synthesize drugs or other solutions that would actually control us.

I made my choice. "I love you."

"I love you too," Troy replied. "And I'll follow you anywhere. Even into death."

I kissed him, hard, because I didn't want it to go that far. But it was going to end that way one way or another. At least this way it'd be going down fighting for the future we believed in and wanted for the future generations of Otherside.

Rage simmered in me again, closer to the surface, as I restarted the recording and unmuted the call. "Sinclaire?"

"Still here. What's it going to be, Finch?"

"Troy and I will both come in, alone. On the condition that all actions against Otherside are suspended for the duration of the hearing. A fair trial and all that. The American way." When she didn't respond, I pushed, letting all the rage I felt into my voice. "Or we can do things the hard way."

"You—" She paused. Maybe she was remembering what I'd done at Verve and the storm I'd dispelled over Durham. Or maybe she was running through her options one more time; she had to be calling because they hadn't been able to track us down overnight. "Very well. Agreed."

"Call your people off. Now. I'll be checking in with my parliament heads in fifteen minutes. If any of them tell me they are still being watched, the deal is off."

"Done. See you at nine tomorrow. Dirksen Building."

When Sinclaire hung up, I turned off all the devices and let a nasty grin curl my lips.

"What?" Troy asked. In the bond, his hunter's anticipation spiked.

"I only said we'd *attend* the hearing."

He laughed and kissed me. "And the humans have forgotten how to bargain with Othersiders."

"Yep. We need to play this carefully but yeah. I'm not inclined to roll over for them."

"Good," he said.

After checking in with our people and confirming Sinclaire had kept up her end of the bargain, we started the work to fill everyone in and make final checks, including more practice with bronze.

I got better, but I still didn't manage a sustained hold on Chaos and went to bed fretting, trying to figure out how I'd succeeded before.

△▽△▽

The next morning, something kept bugging me as Troy and I showered and then dressed in black and gold. "Why haven't they tried arresting us before now?"

"Good question." Troy straightened his tie then adjusted onyx-and-gold cufflinks in the shape of my kestrel sigil. "Lack of resources? They didn't know what they were dealing with for a while. Plus, Duke and Iaret running interference had to slow things down dramatically."

"Maybe," I said.

I hoped that was all it was. Everything about the shadow conflict with the Bureau had been big on talk and low on action. It made me anxious for what we were walking into, but like Harqil had said before the last Duat trial, there was only one thing to do: keep moving forward.

My rage had blown into fury by the time Troy and I were pulling into a private parking lot next to the Dirksen Senate Office Building under a police escort that'd picked us up as we crossed the Potomac. Not hard, given we'd been driving with the windows down so they could see us.

Sinclaire had kept up her end of the deal and pulled her people in the Triangle. But reports had come in on the drive that there'd been attempts on my people last night by the Sons of Seth, held off largely by elven Aether and vampire glamour. The Triangle was holding its own, but it was by a fingernail. On top of that, Jo had been arrested and held overnight after our livestream stunt but released ten minutes before we arrived when they couldn't prove she'd done anything. For better or worse, she was incensed at the overstepping of her First Amendment rights and her job as a journalist and was more committed than ever to reporting on what was happening to Otherside and our supporters. Darkwatch maneuvering had gotten her a press pass, so she'd be present with the rest of the journalists.

Troy sang his charm spell again before we got out of the car—and it was a good thing because camera bulbs started flashing as soon as we were past the street barricade and climbing the steps to the building. He ignored our police escort and pulled me to a pause at the first landing, positioning us to our best and most glamorous advantage with a few nudges in the bond and slight cues with the hand I was holding.

"Ms. Finch! Mr. Monteague!" a reporter called. "Give us a statement!"

I drew on the effects of Troy's spell to offer a dazzling smile despite my rage at being treated like a spectacle and my instinctive fear of being in the spotlight. "We look forward to speaking with the honored officials about how Otherside and mundane humans can have more productive and peaceful relations in future. That's all."

Troy led us forward and the rest of the way up the steps.

Getting inside, security checked, badged, and all the rest passed in a blur.

There was a small confrontation when an aide, backed by a policewoman, extended two cuffs—one bronze, one lead and silver.

"Put these on please." His voice wavered.

"No," I said.

"Ms. Finch—"

"Are we under arrest?" I asked.

The aide glanced at his backup, who said, "No, ma'am, not at this time."

"Then why are you extending those?" I arched an eyebrow and lifted my chin, pulling on every scrap of presence I had.

"I was asked to, for security reasons." He wilted under my and Troy's combined stare, and the hand holding the cuffs started shaking violently.

Clacking heels announced the arrival of Director Lara Sinclaire. Her dark hair was up in a ponytail, and she was in an all-white pantsuit in what was probably a not-so-subtle effort to position herself as the white knight standing against the dark and dangerous Othersiders.

"Come now, Finch," she said. "Stop being difficult."

"We had an agreement," I pointed out. "If you'd like to break it now and force the issue, know that Otherside looks very poorly on oathbreakers. It sets a bad precedent."

She studied me then decided she heard the double meaning I had spoken: I would have to be bound by those same terms. "Very well. Leave them with me, James."

"Yes, ma'am. Thank you, ma'am." James dropped the cuffs in her outstretched hand and beat a hasty retreat.

"Shall we?" Sinclaire tucked the cuffs into a surprisingly functional-looking purse and swept her hand for us to precede her.

When we walked into the public hearing room, a heavy table sat in front of a single row of senators behind a curved desk, fronted by press including a determined-looking Jo. Ugly tan chairs behind the witness table held a small audience. Recessed lights in a high ceiling and dark curtains covering the windows added to the feeling that I was in a wood-paneled cave, and I shuddered as I tried to breathe through a spike of claustrophobia.

From a back corner, unseen by everyone except me, Harqil waved, looking more serious than I could recall seeing them before. As I glanced around the room, I was somehow surprised to find Cyrus seated in the middle but glad that the wily old asshole had gotten in and would, if nothing else, have his son's back.

I hoped.

So much of this trap might be a massive miscalculation and exercise in hubris, but the alternative was a war of attrition Otherside couldn't win, given our lesser numbers. We might have magic back, but all it took was a lucky shot with the right ammo and we'd be down a life that could take years or decades to replace with another body, if it could be replaced at all.

I barely shoved down a shudder at thinking of my people like that.

It's necessary, Troy sent, knowing what'd made the twist in my emotional state. *Focus on the here and now, Arbiter.*

There was more ceremony, oaths, and pompous opening statement nonsense that passed in another blur before questioning began, with Senator Wright acting as chairman of this circus.

"Please state your names for the record," he said, glaring at me. Not surprising, given I'd broken into his house and scared the shit out of him, his aide, and his wife and kids. Well. The one kid anyway. The other seemed like she was a tough little thing.

"Arden Finch, Arbiter of the Carolinas and Dominion demesnes, High Queen of House Solari," I said. I wasn't sure how my voice stayed calm and even, but it did. "Speaker for multiple parties in Otherside."

In a melodious voice that oozed sex appeal, Troy added, "Troy, born Prince of House Monteague, now King of House Solari. Speaker for multiple parties in Otherside."

The humans blinked at all that, although the Eads had to have briefed them. Maybe they hadn't expected us to be honest on that point.

After a long stare, Wright handed off to a Democratic senator from New York.

"What is the nature of your relationship to each other?" the new senator—Bradley, from the name plate—asked.

I offered a modest smile, despite my confusion at this starting point. "Troy is my fiancé."

The senator flipped through some papers. "I have a note here that says he's your thrall. What's that all about?"

Troy's voice dropped a register, and a flicker of outrage came via the bond as he answered. "You may be unaware, Senator, but that term is deeply pejorative and derogatory. Perhaps you could rephrase your question in a way that adds clarity and lessens offense?"

Senator Bradley flushed a deep red, his brows drawing down in anger.

Thrall? I sent, remembering Sinclaire having used the word.

Ugly elven term for a bonded male.

Yikes. My bet was that the Eads had supplied that, either out of their own ass-backwardness or to try piquing the stereotyped oyëori temper and get a rise out of Troy.

The senator shuffled his papers again. "You name yourself king, Mr. Monteague, but our information says that you are completely under the control of Ms. Finch. An unshakeable level of compulsion. Can you shed light on that?"

I couldn't see where they were going with this, and the Sight wasn't giving me any hints. Probably safe to answer. I sent, *Go ahead and answer that.*

"I can, Senator," Troy said. "Arden and I are mated. There's no compulsion in the arrangement."

"Mated." Senator Bradley wrinkled his nose, like it sounded dirty. "So she does control you."

"Absolutely not," Troy said smoothly. "Equality is important to us. Our connection is reciprocal and simply allows us a deeper emotional and physical understanding of each other."

"Physical?"

I let a smirk bloom as I side-eyed Troy appreciatively. Everyone mundane already assumed that I was sleeping with my bodyguard-slash-king, and everyone in Otherside would expect that kind of thing or worse from an elven queen.

Cameras snapped wildly.

"I...see." This time, Senator Bradley's flush looked to be embarrassment. "And the nature of this connection is..."

"Hormonal and magical," Troy said.

"Magical. Which is possible because you're an" —again, the twist of expression that suggested there was something distasteful— "an *elf.*"

Troy sat with a look of pleasant bemusement on his face. "I am, Senator. Which you're aware of because you have at least one working for you in the federal government." He raised his voice to be heard over the small uproar starting in the room, including Senator Bradley trying to speak over him. "Oh, and another working for the right-wing news channel that serves as your conservative party's propaganda arm."

The uproar grew louder.

"I don't know what he's talking about!" a woman in the press section said.

"Order!" said Senator Wright. "Mr. Monteague, please limit yourself to commentary related to the questions."

"He didn't ask a question," Troy pointed out mildly. "And it does have bearing on the current topic. I'm simply trying to make sure we all know where we stand, since he's so interested in my personal life."

"Mr. Monteague, you will be quiet, or you will be held in contempt."

Somehow, Troy doing just that got a flush of anger on Senator Wright's neck. Behind us, the audience muttered amongst themselves, sounding unhappy.

"Not fair to ask a question and then tell him to shut up," someone said under their breath.

Looked like Cyrus's passive power and Troy's charm spell were working.

Perfect.

"Mr. Monteague," Senator Bradley continued when order was restored, "what is the...the *nature* of elves?"

Troy let a confused look flicker across his features. "We're nocturnal."

"I see. Anything else?"

"I'm not sure I understand the question, Senator. But we're omnivores, much like humans," he said, still with the confused look, despite the mischief singing through the bond. "Oh, and we're highly compatible with humans. Genetically, of course."

His smile somehow managed to blend innocence and sex appeal in an impossible—and from the reactions of various humans in the room, irresistible—combination. The cameras clicked and flashed again, capturing the look in all its seductive glory.

I barely managed to keep my own amusement from bubbling up. There were chat rooms and internet groups full of self-declared "monster fuckers," people who were desperate to be the romantic or even just sexual partner to Othersiders. It was part of the touristic aspect that Maria and the other vampires were trying to cultivate with their alliance.

I suspected these monster fuckers had just gained a new poster boy. Maybe Darius had been right about cultivating the royal fairytale.

"Order!" Senator Wright called again. Exasperation warred with anger on his wrinkled features. "Senator Bradley, do you have any final questions?"

The next question was where things started getting difficult.

"Just one," the same senator said. "Ms. Finch, would you confirm that you are an elemental?"

"I will not," I said firmly.

"I see. Senator Wright, I yield my time," Senator Bradley said.

Good. Maybe now we could get to the important shit.

Chapter 21

S enator Wright had to call for order again as other senators rolled their eyes and scoffed, the audience buzzed at this new-to-them term—elemental—and cameras continued to click and flash. Troy sent a steadying curl of Aether when I tensed at the onslaught.

"Now, Ms. Finch," Senator Wright said sternly, "I was given to understand you were going to be cooperative today."

"I agreed to attend this hearing," I responded coolly. Time to set them on their asses and turn the narrative. "So far, we have been asked only offensive and intrusive personal questions that have nothing to do with the real matter of concern."

The senator took my bait. "And what, to you, is the matter of concern?"

"The reasons and justification for the federal government's egregiously unfair and draconian crackdown on people who happen to be Othersiders." I tilted my head and arched my brows a little, daring him to move to the questions I knew they wanted to ask. The ones that could, if I wasn't careful, if I didn't stick to the points Troy had drilled into me, trap me. Trap us both or, rather, us all—all of Otherside.

Senator Wright stared at me. "The floor is open for the honorable Senator Lang from North Carolina."

"Thank you, Senator. Ms. Finch," Senator Lang said in a firm tone, straightening the American flag pin on her lapel, "you claimed responsibility for the complete and utter destruction of a healthtech startup in our home state of North Carolina, Verve

Health Solutions." Behind her, a video screen showed helicopter news footage of the slagged heap of obsidian that remained of the building. "Why are you attacking human businesses when you keep saying you want peaceful relations with us?"

Finally. Questions worth answering. "Thank you for asking, Senator," I said. "First of all, I want it to be clear that the action resulted in no injuries or deaths, nor was it intended to. Second, Verve was known to be conducting research into the use of Otherside genetic material, including participating in a program that used unconsenting humans."

An uncomfortable silence followed.

"We have no record of that here," Senator Lang said after flipping through papers in front of her.

"That's unfortunate, Senator," I said. "Perhaps Director Lara Sinclaire could shed some light on the matter if you requested her testimony."

Lang frowned. "What proof do you have?"

Given that I had immunity for crimes past and current in North Carolina, I said, "I broke into their facility on multiple occasions and personally confirmed the presence of said genetic material. I also spoke with witnesses who implicated a US federal agency based on direct interactions with, and payment from, said agency."

That bombshell put the room in an uproar as elven magic lowered the mundanes' self-control.

Senator Wright had to call for order again, looking furious. Aides were hurrying about with fresh papers and harried expressions, and when I turned to Director Sinclaire, she looked murderous, despite the various elven magics going on. Half the senators looked confused though, like none of this was going the way they'd planned, and I had to smother a grin. Elven magic was on my side this time, and I would use every advantage I could get.

Finally, the room calmed again.

"*You* broke into Verve?" Senator Lang looked confused. "Our records say that you're a private investigator, not some kind of burglar."

I nodded agreeably. "Yes, Senator, I am a licensed PI, and I have experience in penetration testing. In fact, Verve hired me to run such a test for them, to ascertain whether they were up to code on HIPAA and other compliances. They were not." I cast my eyes down, trying for demure and modest—unthreatening—like I'd practiced with Troy, then back up. "While the majority of my work was in support of mundane, that is, non-magical human, cases, Verve was on our radar—on Otherside's radar."

"For what reason?"

"Exactly what I've said. We recognized them as a security risk. Their genetic tests were nearly capable of flagging Otherside samples, although they didn't know what they had yet and at that time Otherside had not been Revealed." A small lie. Verve had managed to flag an elven sample. But I didn't give a shit about lying to these fucks, and my oaths only held in Otherside. Swearing on a Bible did nothing to me, not when the oath was administered by a mundane and I had higher oaths to protect other people.

"So, you took it upon yourself to melt a building?" Senator Lang asked incredulously. "While we're on the topic, how did you manage that?"

"You took it upon yourselves to try bombing my house with me and Troy asleep in it," I said bitterly, dodging the question of how with an incendiary truth of my own. As tempting as it might be to call on Air and blow every single paper in this room into a cyclone to demonstrate my powers, I was a damn queen. I did not perform on demand.

This time, the uproar was too much, especially when every reporter's phone dinged at once with Jo's report from my house, pushed through by the Darkwatch who'd been waiting for me to mention it as a cue.

When Senator Wright finally got control of the room, he called for a recess.

Troy and I were flanked by armed police and led to a small room. We were allowed into it alone, but my elemental senses could track two people—and their guns—standing outside.

I see what they're trying to do, I sent, wary of bugs listening in on us. It had come to me on the walk over, as I turned over why they'd let Troy's comments slide and yet be so quick to jump to Verve despite my being the one to lead them there. *They know they already have elves working for them, and they need that to be okay, for the* right *elves. Ones that are both registered and rendered harmless. So, they position you as the lesser of two evils and me, who has already admitted to destroying a building, as the threat. Divide and conquer at the very least.*

Good read, he replied. *What do you think the odds are that we don't finish out the day in the hearing?*

Solid. There's no way they can let us keep talking. Or let you keep charming and me keep obstructing. In fact, that's probably why Sinclaire allowed us in without cuffs. They had to know one or both of us would be using some kind of magic, so they'll get one of the Eads in as an expert witness and spin it as a manipulation of the democratic process.

A flare of energy resolved into Harqil, hazy and indistinct as they stayed invisible to any cameras in the room.

The two of you are playing a very dangerous game, they sent.

I barely stopped myself from shrugging. *It's the plan.*

And you're determined to be arrested? they asked.

Yes. Troy looked like a thundercloud. *What did you overhear?*

Harqil sighed. *There will be no reconvening.* They looked at Troy. *Between you and your father, you overplayed the Aether. They're all confused and upset by how far out of their control this hearing has gone and are convinced it's magic. Which, frankly, duh. You were too clever for your own good.*

I grimaced. We hadn't considered that. Usually, mundanes didn't notice a damn thing when Othersiders used magic, whether it was elf or djinn Aether, vampire glamour, fae illusion, the witches' life magic, or a quick spark of were dominance. We were so used to that and so secure in the knowledge that the Eads had been severed—and therefore would be unable to read any Aetheric spells going on—that I at least hadn't considered the Eads would still be able to recognize the effects.

This is it then, I sent to Troy, peering up into his eyes.

My heart seemed to turn over in my chest. For all that we'd agreed the plan was to get arrested, I'd nearly lost him too many times. I didn't know how many more I could bear watching or how many more I could pull him back from. We both knew the feds would be brutal with any captives. With what we'd learned at the hearing, they'd separate us eventually. Maybe hurt or even kill him in an effort to get control of me.

Tears welled in my eyes.

No, he replied. *None of that.*

The force of his thoughts made my breath catch. *I know. But know that if* anything *happens to you, my greater good is burning everything to the ground. So stay. The fuck. Alive.*

I half expected Harqil to jump in with a snappy comment, but they just looked on solemnly, a celestial witness to the turning of great events.

That just made my heart rate kick up another notch.

I closed my eyes, took a breath, and forced it all down. I was a High Queen and an Arbiter of Otherside, not only of my own territory or demesnes but speaking for more. I was the Eternal Huntress.

I would. Not. Yield.

As that certainty settled over me, Troy smiled and flashed his secondary teeth in a predator's grin. *We'll both do what we have to do.*

With startling speed, Harqil surged forward to hug us both.

Luck, they sent. Then they disappeared.

I think they like us, Troy sent, sounding wry.

They do. I knew it, down to my core. I might only have known a couple handfuls of celestials, but they'd all either been out for themselves or in service to someone else. Harqil was different. Maddening sometimes, elusive as all the tricksters were, keeping secrets about the Court of Nightmares for sure, but on our side. They'd chosen a side. They'd chosen us.

And so had all the people who'd entered into alliance with me as Arbiter and Troy as King of House Solari from across the country.

We would get this mission done.

As that resolve settled in my soul, the door swung open.

In unison, Troy and I turned to glare at the police officer who stood there as Troy slid in front of me.

"Let's go!" the officer snapped, the bite of a frightened dog in his voice. "You're being summoned."

I barely managed not to say that I was no djinn to be summoned. The expression I was wearing as I stepped to stand at Troy's side must have said everything because the officer quailed, stumbling back.

Troy took a moment to offer his crooked arm. "My queen."

I slid my hand around his forearm. "My king."

In the words were declarations of love nobody would hear but us, and his grin was a little wild. Mine probably was too.

Kill the charm, I sent. *Let's throw them all the way off and make this arrest big.*

He covered his muttering the counterspell by cupping my cheek on the side facing the officer and kissing me even as his lips moved with the word.

A swear echoed in the hallway as the sense of ease fled.

When we emerged, there were a full dozen mundanes in suits or uniforms with hands on weapons of various kinds. Behind them, Jo hovered, looking anxious as hell. Cyrus was farther back, leaning against a wall with eyes full of anguish only for Troy.

I lifted my brows at the assembly of mundanes wavering between hostile and uncertain. "This seems dramatically unfriendly, even for y'all."

A man in a suit swaggered to the front, hand on his unsnapped service pistol. "Arden Finch, you are under arrest."

I kept my gaze on the asshole making the statement as I sent to Troy, *As predicted.*

All I got back was focused hostility as I said, "For what?"

"Unauthorized magic and contempt of court." The man who must have been a BSI agent puffed himself up, like he was getting ready to fight.

Two years ago, it might have worried me, but in that time, I'd bested Troy a few times, passed a round of Darkwatch training, and throttled the gods.

"No," I said.

"No?" the agent repeated.

Troy snickered arrogantly, a calculated reaction, given he could keep himself perfectly silent if the situation called for it.

"Something funny, Monteague?" the agent asked. With a wave, he summoned several more agents and police officers to his side. All of them drew batons and Tasers.

"Who's Monteague?" Troy asked blandly. "I'm Troy Solari. Check your records."

Okay, not only calculated but also both amused and triumphant. Or rather, especially calculated to piss someone off.

"You son of a— You know what, you're both in contempt of court in addition to being dangerous Othersiders."

Seemed like we'd been right. They were going to try for me, maybe using my captivity to secure Troy's good behavior.

"I'm only dangerous to people who make threats," I said, unable to help myself from riding Troy's mood. "If you're threatened by that, that sounds like a you problem. Are you making threats, agent?"

Outwardly, Troy just stared at the man. Inwardly, he was a riot of wild disobedience, arrogant sovereignty, and protective rage.

I adored it, and let Troy feel it in the bond.

"Arrest them both," the agent snapped.

Jo bouncing on her toes caught my attention. "Ma'am? Ms. Finch? A statement?"

At her request, a *push* of Aether announced Cyrus amplifying his passive power.

Bless Jo, and hell, bless Cyrus too. He saw where this was going and was doing everything he could to protect his son, like we'd agreed. Maybe I had given him a ray of hope to cling to.

The room settled into an uneasy pause.

Troy dropped his shields and let his power signature flare, buying us another few precious seconds as the fear of being hunted on a chill, dark-moon night shivered through every mundane present.

I answered while the mundanes hesitated to close on me and Troy. "I came here for a dialogue, which is apparently not of value to this government. I do not consider these charges valid, since they don't consider my personhood valid. But I didn't come here to shed blood."

Like that was a cue, Sinners closed in.

I stretched to kiss Troy as they wrenched my arms behind my back. The bond flared—and then was lost along with the elements as cold bronze slid around my wrist, followed by simple handcuffs.

"I love you," I said, looking Troy in the eyes. "Always and forever."

"And I love you, my queen." His voice wasn't pitched to carry, but somehow it did. And for once, everything he felt was on his face: deep adoration, abiding respect, fierce devotion.

My heart clenched as I blinked away tears again.

If this was it, at least the last time I might see him was like this.

The room fell silent except for the clicking of cameras and the scribbling of pens against paper. The rapt attention of dozens of mundanes was nearly palpable.

Then someone swore and broke the headiness of the moment, like they just realized the PR coup they'd handed us: a pair of lovers, not resisting, just existing, being roughly jerked into cuffs in 4K HD livestreamed to the nation.

"Someone get these journalists out of here and cover their heads," Sinclaire's voice called from behind me as cameras snapped nonstop. "This is going to be a goddamn media circus."

Troy, his gaze still on me, smiled in the lopsided way I was more used to seeing from Allegra and Darius.

"Too late," he murmured.

I tossed my head and twisted away as much as possible when someone tried to put a coat over me. "Back off. I am a High Queen and an Arbiter of Otherside. If this is the bed you choose to make, then lie in it. Or are you ashamed of yourselves? Because I'll stand in what I've done and answer for it."

The background noise rose. More cameras flashed.

Without the connection to the elements, I felt adrift but also less assaulted than I would have with all of the aggressive air movements this much talking and pushing and movement would be generating.

This had been our plan all along. And not only was it working, but the Sight wasn't screaming at me that the path was wrong. Maybe that was because I was cuffed. But I was going to run headlong with the idea that it was because this was what needed doing. I wouldn't have been led to this moment if it wasn't the right one.

"Just get them the fuck out of here, now!" a different male voice said.

Troy and I were marched out, side by side, heads high as befitted the royals we were.

The moment we were outside and visible, I planted my feet at the top of the steps, using my greater-than-human strength to force a stop. Every eye and lens focused on me as the crowd outside roared then quieted with something that felt a little like awe.

I took a deep breath and spoke loudly into the silence. "This is a dark day for Otherside." I forced a cold, arrogant smile. The kind that would pull the most vicious of the Othersiders still holding out to my side with the hope that I'd excuse any excesses. "But we're better in the dark anyway, aren't we?"

"Get them out of here!" the same voice from before roared.

I resisted the hands around my arms to lean toward Troy for a last kiss as the Sinners fought to separate us. Our lips brushed. Then he was pulled toward one car as I was bodily dragged—with a not-so-subtle gut punch—to another.

Chapter 22

As soon as the door slammed behind me, the man in the back seat next to me dragged yet another black hood over my head. I didn't like it, but I let it go, keeping my chin high and acting as unbothered as I could. That'd happened enough times, and I'd escaped enough times, that compliance until we got where we were going was my game. This was part of why I'd pushed Troy into practicing the way we had that last time at home, so I'd have a chance to confront my reactions then and be better able to control them in the real situation. I didn't need to piss these assholes off more than I already had and get dosed with something.

My focus was on reaching Chaos. It sparked a few times, but I still couldn't hold onto it. Desperation spiked as my stomach sank. I had to get this. I *had* to, or this was the worst plan in all of history.

The drive to wherever they were taking us was short enough to suggest these arrogant fucks were keeping us within range of Capitol Hill. Which meant that despite being unable to get a connection to Chaos, when I did, destroying this location would probably force a security shutdown of the Houses of Congress as much for the physical damage as for the danger to the members of Congress.

I'd been afraid that they'd take Troy to a different location, but when I was hauled out and marched forward, a chesty growl just under human hearing range told me he was here. He was playing along for now, like I was, following the plan. But being separated from me with both of us in danger had to be pushing him to the limits of his self-control.

His presence was confirmed when I was yanked to a halt and the bag tugged roughly from my head. Dangerously furious, from the hard blankness of his features and the spark of the gold flecks in his eyes, but still in control. The tension singing through every line of his body heightened as I was grabbed and positioned in front of a camera as one of the men held up what I guessed was a booking card.

I shook my head, needing Troy to let this go. If there were multiple levels to this place, this was only the first one. There'd been no stairs or elevator.

Besides, I was certain they wouldn't keep the good stuff on the first level.

Once my photo was done, they opened the handcuffs to bring my hands around in front and re-cuff them then took my fingerprints, a gun that smelled real and loaded pointed at me and at Troy the whole time. Everything with the handcuffs was ridiculous; they were basic steel. Troy certainly could have snapped them with the right leverage, given the Sinners hadn't followed Darkwatch protocol and double-bound him with rope or zip ties or something as well.

But aside from this many guns loaded with lead being a deadly threat to Troy, it wasn't the right moment to break free yet. I didn't need the Sight to tell me that.

I kept my expression neutral and focused on breathing, trying to slow my racing heart. Troy's better senses would be honed in on my physical reactions, and even if he was controlling himself, he'd be strung tight doing so.

The mundanes repeated the booking process with Troy. Then the same man who'd ordered us removed from the Capitol approached. He was average height and soft around the middle, with thinning, dark hair and dark eyes sitting squished in features that looked like they'd been carved from a potato.

"Get them to Processing," he said. "Sinclaire wants to know what the hell makes an elemental different from an elf. Now."

One of the men with a hand around my bicep said, "We have orders to take them to Holding."

"We don't have time for that," Mr. Potato Head said. "These cases are supposed to be expedited."

"Then get somebody with clearance to get shit moving because Processing is backed up. We can't take any more samples."

That was not fucking good at all. They had more Othersiders here? So many that this Processing stage was backed up?

Hell no. I didn't even need to know if they were from a demesne or realm that had sworn to me. They were Othersiders, so they were mine to protect. This place was going to burn.

If I could reach and hold onto Chaos.

"Hey!" I shouted, not bothering to hide my outrage. "I don't consent to giving samples."

"Neither do I," Troy said. The growl under his words became audible in the human hearing range, and a few hands twitched toward guns.

A snarled curse in elvish pulled everyone's attention.

Onora Ead bore down on the clutch of agents surrounding us with the same queenly air she'd had at the summit. "I told you to keep these two separated and to secure them with more than handcuffs."

"Can it. They're cuffed with whatever magical bullshit you said will shut them down," Potato Head said. "You're a civilian advisor here so get. The fuck. Back."

"The closer they are to each other, the more dangerous they are," Onora said even as she stepped back, hands out to her sides. Outrage flashed across her face at the agents' dismissiveness before she could school her features. "Very well. On your head be it."

Another frog march followed, through a hallway, down a level in an elevator, and into what looked like a waiting room. Troy was shoved into one chair—or rather, allowed himself to be shoved into it—and I was pushed into another as the mundanes moved through a door into the next room, arguing over how to make space for their new priorities.

Troy and I stared at each other, instinctively checking for injuries on the other before our gazes met.

Even without being able to sense him in the bond, I knew what he was asking with his expressions.

A jaw shift, the kind that signaled the desire or intention to drop the secondary teeth, and an arched eyebrow. He wanted to attack now, while they were distracted with procedure.

I gave the smallest shake of my head.

The other eyebrow joined the first, to ask why not.

I glanced up then rolled my eyes. We weren't deep enough into the facility for this to be worth it.

Troy considered that, blank-faced but eyes darting to evaluate the space again, before he gave a slight shrug that would have looked like testing his cuffs. His lips twitched in the suggestion of a pucker. I was right, but he wanted to get me out of here before it got worse.

I gave him another slight head shake. Greater good.

"Are they really engaged?" someone behind me asked. "I mean, they're just staring at each other."

I snorted. "Would you rather I cried for him or something?"

"Don't worry, honey," the man replied menacingly. "You'll cry soon enough. I can't wait to see it."

I flashed my teeth at Troy, a modified threat display, when he met my gaze again after glaring death at whoever I couldn't see. We didn't have time for dominance games, and he was going to give us away.

This time, the flat anger in his gaze said everything: if I didn't take action, he would.

I glared right back. We had a plan.

After a few heartbeats, he tilted his head, accepting his queen's orders. Cheek twitch: under protest. Muscles bunching at the corner of his jaw: if I hurried up, he might even let some of these fuckers live.

That was a good point. Even if we didn't move right away, there wouldn't be a better time than now, with the guards distracted with the procedures for our last-minute arrest, to grab Chaos.

I closed my eyes so I could focus. I'd managed to reach Chaos past bronze and act with it twice before. I'd gotten sparks of it since then. I could manage now. It was harder with all the distractions in the room though, the strange smells, the overt hostility. Like trying to grab a single hair in an ocean. Right when I thought I had it, it kept slipping away.

"Take her first," Onora's voice said from behind me. "If you have her, you control him."

I opened my eyes and twisted to glare at her. *Nobody* would be controlling Troy, via me or any other way.

"Arden," Troy murmured.

Just my name, but I knew his voice better than my own. It carried a warning. A reminder to focus. And it held faith. He knew what I was trying to do.

Movement in my peripheral vision. A man with a Taser. They were getting ready to force us into this Processing place, and from the look of it, we weren't going to like what they did there.

Adrenaline flooded me.

Alongside it came desperate rage. I had walked into this trap for the greater good, but I would not allow myself to be taken. Not again. Not when I'd already been kidnapped so many times already.

I closed my eyes and *twisted* with my reach to my magic—and missed.

A hand wrapped my arm, surprising me.

Troy growled.

Chaos sparked and was gone.

No.

There was no need to reach because Troy had been right. Unpredictability was the key. Just as the elements were woven into everything, so was Chaos. The chance event that sent a dandelion tuft on this breeze rather than that or had a coin land on its edge. It was in people acting against their interests and in life itself, the accident of birth.

Mostly, it was in me. The primordial elemental. The Dreamwalker. The god-speaker. The one who had stopped the Wild Hunt and stolen magic back from the tricksters.

Magic flared.

I gasped, eyes flying open.

Troy's growl cut off, and he stared in shock, even as I was hauled out of my chair.

"Let's go, demon," ordered the man trying to circumvent my will, my dignity, and my consent.

Rage sang in me—and so did Chaos as I finally managed to hold onto it. I stood firm. "No."

The bullets in this room needed addressing first. I wouldn't lose Troy, not here, not now. As more shouting mundanes flooded the space, I flexed Chaos and took three atoms from lead. Gold would hurt, but it wasn't lethal. Not to us.

"Arden!" Troy shouted.

I laughed.

Matter couldn't be created or destroyed, so the three atoms I took from all the lead I shifted to the copper and tin in the bronze cuff on my wrist. That became a brittle, silver-white metal—and my elemental magic returned in a rush as I powered free of the hand around my arm, slammed my wrist against the chair, and shattered the cuff. I shunted the excess atoms into any other copper in the room: pipes and wiring. The pipes burst, and electronics fried.

The room went dark.

I sensed Troy rolling to the floor and covering his head.

With him relatively safe, I pulled Air to me and *pushed* outward.

No chord, just pure power.

When I opened my eyes, dim emergency lighting from the next space showed Troy already springing to his feet, the chain on his handcuffs broken. Mundanes had been thrown against the walls, some knocked unconscious, some dead from the empty feeling I got from their corpses. Onora was one of them, crumpled at an awkward angle that said her neck was broken.

Good. The bitch finally got what was coming to her.

With a thought, I weakened the metal in my handcuffs and Troy's so we could break them open then heated the lead-and-silver cuff with a thread of Fire and flexed it off his wrist with Air. "Nobody controls you. Not me and not using me."

He spun to take in the room as the bond flared to life, sharing his savage joy and deadly focus. "We need to move."

I pulsed with Earth. "There's one more level beneath this one. I think there are beings down there, but it's hard to tell. The structure is reinforced somehow."

Troy stalked toward the door opposite the one we'd come in—the one they had been trying to drag me toward. "Locked."

I paused only long enough to slag the metal down the seam in the elevator doors and the doorframe to the stairs, sealing them shut. I could get us out another way, and I didn't want to be flanked. Then I blasted the door marked Processing off its hinges.

Someone behind it cried out as it hit them with a crunch.

Troy snagged a gun and ammo belt from a dead soldier and moved forward to clear the hallway. Easy, given it was all fishbowl-style labs with their windows open to the corridor. He paused long enough to push the door away with a heel.

"Mundane," he said in a clipped voice. "Military. Dead. Hallway clear."

I followed him, freezing immediately at what the glass rooms contained. My heart broke, then was stitched back together by threads of fire on seeing the beds and the Othersiders held to them by restraints. Tubes and wires sprouted from bodies. Machines beeped and whirred. Monitors bolted higher on the walls showed graphs—and most of the ones I could see were trending downward.

The Bureau were forcibly taking samples from Othersiders to do who-knew-what with them. And they didn't seem to care that vital signs were decreasing while they did. Hell, maybe that was the entire point.

That ended today. At least here.

It looked like a bunch of people had left in a hurry. Spilled coffee cups, scattered papers, and overturned chairs littered the labs. Two doors—one at the other end of the hallway, one perpendicular to it in parallel to the staircase that led down here—said where they might have gone.

The huntress in me rose. I would have blood for this.

It wasn't revenge. It was justice.

And justice could not include tolerance for the hateful, violent, painful actions being carried out here. Tolerance would only encourage more of the same harm, and I would not have it.

I turned to my right. The room closest to the main door was cleared, clean but in a way that looked hurried and untidy.

Then I saw the monitor.

Subject: Arden Finch

Species: Elemental

Horror stole my breath the moment before pure rage flooded me anew. Before I could think about what I was doing, I overloaded every piece of tech in the room in a shower of sparks.

"Arden!" Troy called.

The same ethereal laugh as before echoed, not quite in my head this time.

And this time, the laughing voice spoke. "So much rage."

I whirled, looking wildly for the source of the voice and only finding a worried-looking Troy.

"What happened?" he asked.

"This room was set up for me." My voice came out lower and more guttural than usual. Before Troy could say anything, I pushed past him. "Come on. We need to free everyone here and get the fuck out. They have to be sending reinforcements."

"On it." He hurried to a room that released the oregano-and-thyme scent of an East Coast elf when he shouldered the door open.

I wrenched doors off their hinges with Air, barely seeing the people I freed. Barely hearing their thanks, whether werewolf, elf, or witch.

This had to stop.

I would do anything to make it stop.

Again, the laughter echoed.

"Anything?" the same amused voice from before asked.

I ignored it. Right now, there was only time for the mission.

"Arden! Going to need your help with this one."

I hurried to join Troy, hissing at the desiccated vampire chained down with silver in the last lab. A massive UV light in the ceiling shed a purple-blue light over the space, making her skin blister and peel.

This wasn't just processing.

This was experimentation.

"Please..." the vampire whispered. Her eyes darted even as saliva dripped when our scents hit her. She struggled weakly, starving and taunted by the smell of hot, powerful blood.

With a thought, I slagged the restraints.

Troy reached to pull the woman from the table, only to recoil when she struck, starved and crazed by the scent of elf.

I grabbed her with Air. This wasn't supposed to have been a rescue mission, but we couldn't leave anyone behind.

When I floated her out, one of the werewolves said, "There's blood in the next room. End of the hall. They—" He shuddered. "They took samples."

I melted the lock.

Troy kicked the door in, gun level, and swept in when he confirmed it was clear. His expression was grim when he emerged with four bags.

"There is more than just blood samples in there, Arden," he said. "This is barbaric."

"Please!" the vampire screamed, fighting against my ties of Air, her voice breaking.

I let her go when Troy set down the blood and backed away. She fell on the small bags, hunching over her knees, biting through the plastic and slurping.

I turned to the rest of our group. "Does anyone else need something to be able to walk out of here?"

One by one, they shook their heads. Some straightened, like they found new resolve in my reassurance that we were getting out of here. Others hunched in on themselves, like they couldn't bear the weight of hope.

Part of me wanted to reassure them. I didn't bother. They would make it out, or they wouldn't. Either way, this was the hard part.

"Harqil!" I hollered, leaning hard on Chaos. "We need you!"

It took a moment, but the angel phased in. "This was not— Oh bloody hell. Arden, I can coordinate your people topside or I can get these out, but I can't—"

"Get them out," I snapped. "Or show me how to make a portal. Like you showed me making and unmaking."

"It'll hurt. And there will be no going back."

I had no idea what that last part meant. "I don't care. We don't have time for easy or slow."

Their lips thinned. Then they shrugged. "If you can break free of bronze, then you should be able to manage this."

Everything in me short-circuited as they laid fingertips alongside my temple and *pushed* with Chaos, like Troy did with Aether but worse. Harder, sharper, a torrent of magic and knowledge that scoured through my mind.

When I had my breath again, Troy was on the ground beside me, and the elves we'd freed were standing over us as guards, armed with weapons they must have found in the other room.

I heaved air into my lungs. Then again, a slight whimper escaping. "Ishtar above."

"I warned you," Harqil said. "But you survived it. Your little king did too. Bonus points."

Troy muttered a vile curse in elvish as he pushed himself up to hands and knees. "Please tell me that was worth what I just experienced."

Only one way to find out.

I reached for all four elements plus Chaos and *flexed*—and tore a hole in reality.

Chapter 23

On the other side was the boathouse at Jordan Lake. Haunted, but hopefully safe.

"My queen?" one of the elves asked. "May I?"

"Go." I hauled myself to my feet. If this one wanted to be the first through and would acknowledge me as queen in the process, fantastic.

He leaped through, secondary teeth down and gun up. On the other side, he spun in a circle. "Clear!"

The other two elves followed, joining him in an impromptu triad.

"Secure the area," the first one said to them, sounding surer than he had, before waving the other freed captives through.

They needed no prodding from me or Troy, following the elves through in a rush and collapsing on the ground, like time had done a hiccup on their way through. Some stayed down, looking exhausted. Others rose. Two of the werewolves shifted, cringing with pain, but shook themselves and stood watchfully over those who couldn't rise.

Troy scooped up the two bags of blood the vampire hadn't drained and tossed them through.

She dropped the bag she was just finishing and stumbled after them, falling heavily to the ground then reaching for a new bag, not even bothering to find shade despite the daylight shining on the clearing in front of the boathouse.

"You too," I said to Troy.

"Fuck that," he snapped. "I'm staying with you."

Harqil cleared their throat. "I'd recommend keeping him. You can only do this so many times in a short period before those consequences catch up with you."

"What's a short period?" I asked, even if I didn't have time to worry about consequences either way.

"You know, a year. Maybe more, maybe less." Harqil shrugged. "Especially given one of the Nightmares is already speaking to you directly now. Or two, technically, given the dream your mother interfered with, but only one wants you."

"They *what?*" Troy said.

I didn't answer. Just raised a hand to the elf who'd taken the lead on the other side in the signal to secure the area and hold there for reinforcements.

He made the hand signal for an affirmative response to an order, confirming my charge.

Well shit.

With another flex of Chaos, I closed the portal—and dropped to a knee as dizziness and nausea overtook me.

"Don't! Touch her," Harqil said, intercepting Troy's lunge to me and hauling him back like he was a headstrong child, backing them both away. "Unless you want to be unmade in the time it takes her to wrangle that."

That was a haze of unreality centered on me and creeping outward, warping the cell I was closest to. Glass shattered and hovered in a storm of glittering edges as plastic reverted to crude oil and black sludge that begged for a spark to set it aflame.

I shuddered and swallowed down a wave of nausea. I didn't have time for this. There was another level to clear and more people to rescue.

And I couldn't unmake Troy. That more than anything.

With a wrench, I reset reality with a speed that made me bend over and dry heave.

"*Now* you can touch her," Harqil said.

Troy's hands were on me a heartbeat later, a grounding grip on the back of my neck and a supportive one on my hip as he knelt behind me. "Breathe, cariñamí. I have no idea what just happened, but you feel spacey."

I more than felt spacey. My thoughts swirled like leaves in a windstorm, and my muscles barely felt able to keep me upright.

"Is this normal?" Troy asked.

"For a mortal a hop, skip, and a jump away from crossing the threshold to celestial? Of course." Harqil didn't sound amused though. They sounded, if anything, a little scared. "If she—"

"I could make it go away," the laughing voice from before whispered. "If you agreed to do me a favor."

"No favors!" I shouted.

Confusion flooded the bond as Troy's grip on me tightened. "What—"

I pushed through another wave of dizziness just as sparks and the buzz of power tools announced that mundanes were trying to break through the door I'd slagged in the main room. "I'm fine, Troy. We need to clear the other level. Now."

"Maybe I should stay with you," Harqil said.

"You do you. I'm burning this place down." It was the only way I was going to be able to keep my people safe, and it was justice for the crimes committed against them here.

I suited actions to words and wrenched Fire to me to send an incinerating but contained wave of heat through each fishbowl and the sample room I hadn't been able to bear looking in, utterly destroying any trace of Otherside on this level. The main room, I left on fire. It'd be too hot for fire extinguishers to handle. There might be another way in here, but the fact that they were trying that way first suggested it was the main door.

When all that remained of the Processing spaces was ash and melted glass and plastic, I gathered myself and made my way to the last door. Stairs went up and down.

Gunfire rang out, deafening in the enclosed space.

"They're here! They're coming this way!" a masculine voice said. "They—"

I didn't bother with anything fancy. Just took all the breath from his lungs and everyone else I could sense upstairs then turned their blood to acid—the very thing Val had once warned me might happen by accident if I wasn't careful. They all died, quietly but painfully.

"Clear," I snarled. "We need to move."

Troy moved past me, gun trained on the stairwell, as he made his way down. "We've got cells," he said, peering through the thick glass in the door at the bottom. "And armed guards. Jumpy ones."

A gunshot and the thud of a bullet hitting the wall next to the door on the other side underscored his statement as he slid away from the door.

I made my way to his side, closed my eyes, and reached with elemental magic. I couldn't really distinguish between mundane and Otherside bodies yet if the Othersiders had been stripped of magic, but there was metal and the blankness of plastic concentrated along the walls in neat cubes. The cells, most likely. Other metal—which would include guns with bullets I hadn't stolen atoms from—was in a staggered pattern in the center.

"I've got this." I used Air this time just in case I was wrong and pulled all of it from the lungs I could sense in the center passage.

Bodies dropped, one by one, in my elemental senses. When they were all on the floor, I slagged the keypad and the lock on the door.

"Go," I said.

Troy hauled the door open and burst through without hesitation, gun up and seeking. "All guards down. Clear."

I staggered through the door, hit by another wave of dizziness, leaned on the wall, and shook my head in a sharp negation at Troy's furiously worried expression. We didn't have time for him to play mother bear, and he was the one who kept saying to keep the mission front and center.

Harqil flitted past me. "I'll help free the captives. You'll need your strength if you're going to insist on attempting another portal."

I gave up on trying for the appearance of strength and dropped to a cross-legged seat, head down, focusing on actually *having* strength. Fury simmered in me, and I let it fill me, hoping that would help.

"It doesn't have to be this draining," the joker said, again in my head but not.

"Will you shut up!" I snapped.

Nobody said anything, Troy sent. *What's going on? Are you okay?*

Mental pressure. *One of the Nightmares*, Harqil sent. *Likely Rage, given she's filled to bursting with it. She'll be fine. For now. He's intrigued or amused, not threatening.*

Whoever it was could fuck right off.

A boom from above and an influx of bodies told me we were out of time, but Troy and Harqil were still working on the locks as Othersiders staggered out. Some looked at me warily, a wariness that swiftly became alarm when I melted the door to this space closed.

"Is there any other way out from this level?" I asked.

An emaciated, light-skinned man who looked vaguely like Mason and smelled like musk and cedar shook his head as he kept his feet with a trembling hand on the wall.

Portal it was then, since blowing a path to the surface with Earth would require us to then climb a few stories up and out of it, likely under fire. First though, I was gonna need help.

Clutching my callstone, I hollered, "Duke, I need you or Iaret to my location, now!"

With a shimmer, Duke phased in. "Arden, what—"

"I know this wasn't the plan, but I need a boost."

Duke looked at Troy, who shrugged irritably.

"She's making portals," Troy said.

"Oh, for the love of the lamassu, what— Fine."

Next, freeing everyone.

"All of you, to me," I said.

For once, nobody argued or made a snarky comment. I wrenched Fire to me in a way that had once upon a time given me heat blisters, and then I melted every lock in the place. The dizziness that hit me stopped me from hollering for everybody to get out, but there was no need. Cells burst open as staggering, weakened Othersiders spilled from them. The stench that followed some of them said they'd been here for days or weeks, left with their wounds and filth to rot with the blinding bright lights of the hallway exposing them.

Horrific. Barbaric beyond describing.

I let my rage at what my people had been put through—because they were my people now, all of them—fuel me.

"Harqil," I said. "How do I open a portal to the same place as before?"

"Hold it in your mind," they said.

"And how do I make sure I don't warp a person on the other side of it?"

They grimaced. "I'll just pop over."

"Hurry," I snapped. "And then check the courtyard where we were staying. Please."

"Is that wise?" they asked carefully.

"Just do it!"

The door slammed as something heavy hit it. We were out of time.

With a curse, the angel phased out.

As our freed captives shook and looked spooked, Troy casually placed himself between me and the door and nudged me toward the farther wall. Duke hovered nervously in his djinni form, flames sparking.

I leaned heavily against the wall despite the disgusting smells that got sharper as I got closer to an open door. I focused on gathering my magic, trying to go more slowly this time, just in case it might help me avoid passing out.

Magic buzzed along my skin as Harqil phased back in. "The waterfront is clear. So is the courtyard. Arden, are you—"

"Everybody get ready to go." I couldn't bear to be asked if I was sure or if this was a smart choice. These were my people. Troy was my greater good. I'd dragged him into this trap, and now I would do what it took to get him and everyone else out.

Linking with Duke and Troy was easier than I'd expected, but I was in too much of a hurry to be relieved.

With another flex of unreality, I tore a hole while focusing on the beach at Jordan Lake. I had no idea how the physics or metaphysics of this worked, so if they ended up in the water, so be it. It was better than here.

When the portal ripped jaggedly open, it was indeed facing the lake. Nobody hesitated though. I barely got the word "go" out before the first of them was hauling ass, freaky magic or not.

It was a good thing because Harqil was right.

This was not a thing I could do this frequently, even with an elf and a djinni to stabilize me.

The last person was halfway through when my control buckled. I thought they made it before it slipped, but I didn't know. What I did know was that when I panicked and cut the connection to Troy and Duke, the portal collapsed rather than being closed.

I abruptly lost all sense of my magic.

Arms came around me and Troy with the sound of wings.

Everything went white.

Then there was grass under me.

A body crushed against me smelled like Troy, but I was too spent to move and check on him. I couldn't even open my eyes. Couldn't think. Could barely breathe.

"Darius!" Harqil shouted with a spine-tingling resonance that I'd only heard when they'd summoned Usir.

As footsteps thundered against the earth, I stopped trying to hold on to consciousness.

△▽△▽

The In-Between was as cold and dark and starry as ever. And as ever, I wasn't alone.

"You're stupidly hardheaded," the voice that'd been speaking to me—laughing at me—before said. "Or did you mean to come within a hair's breadth of killing yourself, your mate, your guardian, and your angel, alongside warping reality to the ninth circle of hell and back?"

"I don't know," I whispered, too tired to be evasive. "I have no idea what happened. I was just so *angry*. And I had to get my people out." I had to get *Troy* out, but I'd learned better than to make him the focus of interest for the celestials. "I had to show the mundanes we're not easy meat."

I blinked, and there was someone hovering in front of me. Older, from the laugh lines alongside his eyes, but still boyish somehow. Pale-skinned with dark auburn hair pulled back in a short tail, a wide mouth, and eyes just the green side of brown with a scattering of gold flecks in the irises. He was grinning at me, like I'd done something dangerously hilarious.

"Angry," he said, sounding delighted. "My dear, you seemed downright enraged."

"What they're doing is *wrong!*"

"No need to convince me." His grin widened. "I think you're perfect."

That caught me up fast. "What?"

"You're full of rage, but you're not indiscriminate with it." His eyebrows flashed. "Nowhere near as wild as I was."

"Because I know what I'm fighting for."

"Like I said. Perfect for the job in these times."

I went cold, and it wasn't the chill of the In-Between seeping into me. "The job," I breathed as my brain caught up to what was going on. "What job?"

He just looked at me, shifting his jaw back and forth to make sharp teeth flicker over and over again.

I put the pieces together. He was an elf, with the oyëoro and the teeth, but how could that be? Elves couldn't reach the In-Between, and I couldn't imagine any other than Troy thinking I was perfect for any kind of job.

Unless...

"You're Rage," I said, heart hammering. He wasn't an elf. Not anymore. He was a celestial, or close enough.

A Nightmare.

Harqil had hinted that a strong-enough elf with the oyëoro and auratic Aether could do this, but I hadn't thought that meant there already was one.

Rage saluted me with a fist to his heart then started circling me, moving with an ease I'd never managed in this liminal space. "In the flesh. Or as close to it as I get these days. Easier to keep my temper leashed if there isn't a physical form involved. Nobody likes what happens if I lose my temper." When he came back around in front of me, he nodded. "You just might do. Ironic that it would be an elemental who replaces me, but Harqil didn't lie."

"Harqil?" Confusion swept me then cleared as I remembered them saying they'd been pulling strings. "Were you the one who sent the dream?"

"No. That was Despair. She's a sneaky one. Far more subtle. But she has her eyes on the carrion crow." Rage arched his eyebrows. "Let's see if you pass the next test. And if you actually manage to touch celestial power, of course. That's the important part. Well. That and preventing Despair from continuing to influence your father-in-law. If you like your plane the way it is anyway."

Oh fuck. After the Duat, I was tired of tests. I was tired of trials. I was tired of celestials and the world ending. Fuck all of this. When was it going to be my turn to live my life?

"Good," Rage said. "Stay mad. You'll need it."

And then the In-Between flared bright as a burst of magic pushed me out of it with the feeling of a palm strike to my chest.

I slammed back into myself and gasped awake, staring up at the sky in a courtyard.

It was afternoon, from the sun. Something was wrong though. A piece of me was missing.

"Arden!" Darius was shouting as he held Troy's hand over my heart. "Wake up. Wake up and anchor Troy before we lose him!"

That's what was missing—my sense of Troy.

My head flopped more than turned. Troy lay beside me, eyes closed, breathing shallow, complexion washed out, and my sense of him fragmented like it was most of the previous times I'd dragged him through on an interplanar jump. Panic made my heart skip as I rolled to press my forehead to his, wrestled past exhaustion for Chaos, and closed my eyes.

There. The shattered pieces of his mind or soul or both, hovering at the edges of his aura and on the verge of fleeing to leave Troy a husk.

Come back, I sent, coaxing them back as slowly and gently as I dared. *Come back to me.*

With a shuddering snap, the sparkling fragments arrowed back.

Troy heaved an inhale that sounded like it hurt.

Before I could do more than open my eyes, his hand was around my throat, squeezing as he dropped his sharp teeth and growled.

Multiple voices started shouting.

It's me! I sent, throwing a hand out in the hopes it'd stop someone from going for him. *Troy, it's—*

Arden. His hand sprang open, and he rolled away with an awkward slowness, eyes wide and guilty. *I could have—*

"Of all the *stupid*..." Darius started.

"Mind yourself, nephew." Cyrus sounded rough, like he'd spent the last few minutes afraid to breathe. "I'm sure there's a reasonable explanation." His tone said there had damn well better be for the risk to his son, even if the words were in keeping with the agreement we'd made.

"Of course there is," Harqil said from where they sat at my feet, balanced on the bones of their seat with feet dangling in the air. "One of the Nightmares decided to have a chat. Arden was in the In-Between, and Troy's passage through the planes is linked to hers. She wasn't all the way here, so he didn't come all the way back."

"Oh, bloody hell," Duke muttered. "I *knew* there was a reason you were involved. Of course it's the damn Nightmares."

Horror and guilt choked me. Even when I wasn't trying to put Troy in danger or bring him to the attention of celestials, he was at risk just by virtue—or by curse—of being linked to me. I pushed myself up to my knees, aching to touch him but well aware how much he hated interplanar jumps. Now I'd made him do two in a few days and almost lost him again because I'd been too stubborn and angry to worry about consequences or find another way.

"We didn't dare move you," Darius said. "But then Troy's vitals started slipping."

I bit my lip to stop myself from crying and fisted my hands against the dirt of the courtyard. "I'm sorry."

Troy dragged himself to sit with knees up, head dropped between them. After a few stabilizing breaths, he asked, "Did we get everyone out?"

I looked up, my attention darting between Cyrus, Duke, and Darius.

The latter nodded, looking grim. "Everyone got out, but we assumed something went wrong. The portal collapsed and made a small reality warp at Jordan Lake that'll need to be sorted out sooner rather than later, but for now it's contained. DC though..."

Cyrus's smile was small and dark. "That was a good trick, Arden."

"What trick?" I asked.

"You didn't just find the facility and escape with captives and intel." Mischief danced in Cyrus's gaze. "The entire building was consumed in the reality warp. Then—from what I could see from newscasts—you must have let off a burst of pure elemental magic."

The world seemed to spin. "What did I do?"

"Reset a full square mile to the way it must have been five hundred years ago." Cyrus's grin widened. "Complete refresh. And every drone or robot they send in disappears."

I stared, stomach sinking. I'd planned to collapse the building and make it unsalvageable.

It sounded like I'd accomplished what the gods of the hunt had originally intended for me to do, if on a smaller scale.

Troy lifted his head. "They'll be hunting her. We need to get ahead of this."

"They're hunting you both," Darius snapped. "T, I don't know what we do now. The only forces we have to mobilize are anyone who made it back here. The last few hours have been—"

"Hours?" I interrupted. "We lost *hours*?" I'd only been talking to Rage for a few minutes.

"Sorry about that," Harqil said. "I talk to Rage. I don't interfere with him. Too unpredictable."

Darius raised his voice. "The last few hours have been absolute chaos. Every major city in the US shot straight past riots and into anarchy. Daylight or not, attacks have occurred on mundane targets, well beyond what we planned for. We've completely lost control of the situation."

With a ripple, Duke shifted from his djinn form to the slim Black man that was his favorite and gave me a wide smile. "It gets better. Your little declaration? About us being better in the dark? Othersiders we thought were dead, old ones, are coming out of the woodworks. And they're rallying troops behind them. Utter, delicious chaos."

Cyrus's little smile became a full-on grin of malicious delight to mirror Duke's. "Forget the US. The whole world's on fire. All thanks to the two of you." He studied Troy, then me. "You know, Arden, I'm glad I came back now. This is so much more fun than going after queens one by one. And if my boy shares in the glory? So much the better. I feel hope for the future for the first time in decades."

Chapter 24

The Othersiders were calling it the Twilight War: the time of the shadows eating into the light, reminding the mundanes of the beings and powers their ancestors had allowed to fall into myth and legend.

When Troy and I had been taken, it lit fires not just across the United States but around the world. Literal fires in most cases, given the extensive planning Troy had outlined. The Sons of Seth and other right-wing groups were fighting the Darkwatch, vampire coterie heavies, werewolf militia, and rogue fae in the streets. Witches had followed the example set by my coven in the Triangle and were offering any nonviolent aid they could, although there were apparently some blood witches and sorcerers having a field day as one-person armies, summoning demons and raising hell. Valkyrie and other psychopomps had been spotted in a number of locations, serving not as death-guides to mundanes but as early warning systems for Otherside, since any Othersiders who spotted them would know to clear out before whatever mundane countermeasures exploded.

Mundane souls, they and other fae were taking to Odin's halls or other purgatories, heavens, and hells by the hundreds.

I listened, freshly showered, swinging wildly between horror and rage as I shoveled food in my mouth in a mess hall that'd been closed off for me, Troy, Duke, Darius, Cyrus, Etain, Haroun, Samarre, and, to my slight annoyance, Rio.

I hadn't wanted any of this.

But this was what it was going to take to get the mundanes to back off.

The only good news? Peace was, against all odds, holding in North Carolina. Apparently, the governor was taking our deal, or at least the threat I represented, seriously. My people were respecting the bargain I'd struck, although they were all on war footing, according to reports sent by Allegra. Cyrus seemed downright jolly, the miasma of despair dissipating.

"How long do we think the peace will hold?" Troy asked between bites.

He'd already finished two steaks and was working more slowly on a third. He still hadn't touched me, and the bond said he was shaky as fuck. Hiding it well, but the last six weeks would have pushed anyone to their breaking point. He'd faced nightmares in the Duat as much as I had, but he'd come far closer to dying. His night terrors had come back with a vengeance for a few weeks afterward, but taking care of me seemed to have held him together.

Now it was my fault he was breaking again.

"—deal Arden made is not going to be enough," Cyrus was saying, sounding almost anticipatory.

I scrambled to find the thread of the conversation. North Carolina National Guard deployed to major cities to protect property but not acting otherwise. The governor on TV, appealing for calm. Right.

Troy grunted an affirmative. "Maria's behaving?"

"For now," Darius said. "Alli checked in. Maria's holding the coterie by a fingernail. Noah's faced a few dominance fights and won, but it's getting bad. Something is going to blow."

"And the weres?" I asked.

"Terrence and Ximena are keeping their people under control," Etain said. "Viktoria has had a few rogue hotheads. She's got one in chains with several broken somethings but swears up and down she's going to keep Arden's peace. I think the lesson with her brothers stuck."

My peace.

My head spun. This didn't feel like peace. I'd made these moves knowing what had to be done. Knowing that we'd tried everything diplomatic, all the negotiating, all the legislative and non-violent options.

"I did what I had to do," I whispered. The food sat poorly in my stomach, and I swallowed hard to keep it from coming up. "They were hurting people. Experimenting on them. If they were allowed to keep that facility and those Othersiders, they would have been able to develop countermeasures. Toxins, drugs, something."

Everyone fell silent.

"Give us a minute," Troy said. "Go send word to our people and have them spread it. The Eternal Huntress went into the lair of our prey and brought them a reckoning for their many trespasses."

"Her Hunter as well." I looked at him, praying he could sense in the bond how sorry I was for nearly dragging him too far again. "Otherside can win, but we must work together."

Troy nodded sharply. "We're not done. We will keep fighting until we have justice and a safe and fair path forward with the mundanes."

Backs straightened and heads lifted at that. Etain, Samarre, and Haroun stomped and gave a fist-to-heart salute, belatedly echoed by a worried-looking Rio. Darius just sighed and nodded, hands on hips. Duke looked thoughtful for once, and Cyrus looked like the Cheshire Cat.

"As you will, my queen, my king, so shall it be done," Darius said.

They all went to take care of the business of war communications, with Duke taking news back to the Djinn Council before rejoining Iaret, leaving me alone with Troy in a room that was fortunately big enough not to trigger my claustrophobia.

He scooted his chair back and opened his arms. "Come here."

I blinked fast and my heart sped up. Did he really want me to go to him?

"Come on. I'm sorry I held myself apart. I was scared, cariñamí, and I needed space. But I know you won't ever intentionally hurt me."

The speed with which I scrambled out of my chair and into his lap was unseemly in the extreme.

"I'm so sorry," I said again, hugging him. "Intention isn't impact, and I keep hurting you. Just like Cyrus said."

His arms came tight around me, and he kissed my temple. "You do. And you'll keep doing it."

Shocked, I tried to lean away, only for him to tighten his arms and keep me against his chest.

"Power has a price," he said. "Even with all these old Othersiders making themselves known again, intel says nobody has come close to your power sig or your magical strength. That means you're still the most powerful of us here. I hate what my dad said, but you are sharing your power with me. And like *your* dad said, you shouldn't have to do this alone."

I took a shuddering breath, trying to find acceptance in his acceptance. "You really want this?"

"What I want most is to build a new dynasty with the woman I love." He leaned back to look me in the eye. "Which is you. Still, and always. The stronger you get, the stronger our children will be. That's a good thing. All we have to do is make space for them."

I curled my fingers in his shirt, wanting this but having to be honest. "But you said you were scared."

"I'm terrified, Arden." His lowered voice was tighter than usual with the admission. "You keep taking us into situations I was never trained for and am flat-out not equipped to face. I've died or almost died more times than a mortal should. But like you said at home, I'm still here. *We're* still here. And I will *never* let my fear say you're too much or ask you to be smaller for my sake. I will step up and grow alongside you. I will earn the right to sire my children."

Warmth curled through me, a confusing, dizzying blend of relief, disbelief, and sexual attraction. The leaps and bounds in my power growth—magical and political—still frightened me sometimes. In two years, I'd gone from a nobody in hiding to Arbiter, Eternal Huntress, High Queen, and candidate for the Court of Nightmares. I had it in me to be a celestial. The rapid adjustment those changes forced threw me off continually.

And in that moment, I realized that I'd been holding myself back because I was afraid I'd lose Troy in the process. Goosebumps chilled over me as I stared at him, seeing all the ways he was both my support and my limiting factor.

But only if I let him.

He couldn't support me in the way I needed if I didn't step into all of my true potential and show him where I needed him most. And he'd only limit me if I allowed myself to see it in a negative way. There had to be checks and balances in every system. If mine was love for an elf, so be it.

Troy cupped my cheek with one hand. "I can't promise you won't still scare me sometimes. I'll need space when you do. Like today. Especially if interplanar jumps are involved." He tensed, clearly suppressing a shudder. "But I will do my best to find my way back to you. No matter what."

"I promise the same and that I'll do what I have to do to bring you back. Every time, until you tell me you don't want me to."

He kissed me, skipping past gentle and going straight for feeling like he was trying to consume me. Aether twined through me, stoking the heat of my arousal to make me gasp.

"Sorry not sorry," Troy mumbled against my lips. "All this nearly dying makes me want to remind us that we're still alive."

"And that you can still overpower me sometimes."

"Guilty." He kissed me again.

A clearing throat made me jump, which made Troy smile.

"What, Dari?" he asked, clearly having noted his brother-cousin's presence.

"I'm not going to ask if now is the time for that, but word has been sent, as ordered. And, uh..."

"What," Troy snapped, taking his focus off me to glare at him.

"Dad wants a word. Now."

"Omar doesn't order a king."

"I'll let you be the one to tell him."

Troy sighed. In the bond, the heat of lust was swinging toward something closer to anger. "He's been making himself a problem."

"I understand. And I stand with you," Darius said. "With you both."

I twisted to look at him then back at Troy. "That sounds like a civil war kind of problem. Please don't tell me we have that kind of shit on the backburner right now."

"We shouldn't," Troy said. "But Omar is being difficult these days."

"Troy, are we at risk of losing the Darkwatch? Because—"

"No. I'll make sure of it. One way or another. Omar is just not as flexible as Cyrus when it comes to changes of plan." He kissed my cheek. "That and you scare the moonbite out of him."

"Understatement," Darius muttered. He flushed when I looked at him with a frown, wondering what Monteague family conversations had been had out of my hearing.

"Just the usual fears about primordial elementals," Troy said, answering my unspoken thought. "Dari, tell him I'll be free in a few hours. I have some things to attend to. Tell our people here to rest and be ready for a briefing in two hours."

Darius grimaced and rubbed the back of his head then saluted and left.

"Things to attend to?" I hoped he meant me and what he'd started with his Aether tease, but we were in the middle of a war I'd started.

"My queen, of course." Troy shifted, nudging me off his lap, then finished the last couple bites of his steak. "And myself. We both do better when we're grounded. It'll have to be quick, but I think I can manage."

We cleaned up our plates quickly and then I let him lead me to the room assigned to us. Conversations in rooms with open doors paused as we passed, our power signatures and the faint scuff of my feet giving warning. Troy was a man on a mission though, ignoring all of it. I barely had time to wonder if leakage from his passive power—the evolved empathy—was going to cause problems, given that I knew we had a few couples with us before he pulled me into our room and shut the door behind me with a gentleness that was not evidenced in anything else about him.

As soon as it was closed, he fell on me, trapping me against the door and kissing me hard. Aether shot through me, dragging a whimper from me.

"I will *never* leave you," he growled when we broke for air. "Even when I need space. I will come back. Because you're *mine* and I'm yours. I hate that I made you doubt it earlier."

I couldn't answer because he kissed me again, dragging his hands down my body to grip my hips. I didn't need to answer with words anyway. My hands running up his back and my hips arcing forward to grind against his hard-on were doing the talking for me.

The world was going to hell in a handbasket, but I'd told Rage I knew what I was fighting for: this. A life with Troy where, to use Harqil's words, I could fuck my elf until I was bow-legged with all the kids we could handle. I wasn't going to begrudge myself a little time to restore our connection after nearly losing him first to the mundanes and then to the In-Between.

Losing him. No. Absolutely not. I couldn't.

The fury at the thought that I might spurred me to kiss him back as hard as he was kissing me, to try reaching for him with Chaos like he reached for me with Aether.

Troy pulled away and smiled, looking more predatory than anything else. "Are you trying to take control, little elemental?"

My body reacted, heat spooling down to my pussy as my heart raced. "I could."

"You could. But you won't. Because you like being mine."

Aether shocked through me, drawing a pleasure so intense that I moaned and dropped to my knees.

While I caught my breath, Troy opened his pants. "Show me how much you like being mine, *my queen*."

The possessive tones lit the exquisite blend of arousal spiced with just a little hot shame that both of us knew drove me wild. I dragged my nails up his thighs, trying for at least a little art, then took him in my mouth. His groan of pleasure got me even hotter.

"Don't you dare," he said when I let one hand slip toward my aching clit. "You'll come when I want you to."

Bastard. He was in full king mode and I was fucking loving it. If this was what he needed to prove that he could hold his own with me, after I'd nearly killed him? I'd play his game happily.

"Focus, little elemental." His fingers tangled in my hair and he set a faster pace.

I let him, doing as he'd ordered and using one hand to help my mouth with his shaft and the other to tease his balls.

A low growl was the only warning I had before he pulled me off him, drawing my head back to expose my throat.

"Almost got you." I let a bratty chuckle spill from me, knowing it would set him off when he was in this headspace.

Troy's pupils dilated to hunter black, and he shifted his jaw to drop the sharp teeth then retracted them again. "I won't bite you mid-mission. Not this time. But when this is over, your blood is mine. For now..." He levered me to my feet and directed me to the bed with the grip in my hair, pushing me to bend and press my face against the mattress as he kicked my feet wider. "You take what I give you."

He got my pants down and pushed into me without hesitation, knowing from bond and scent that I was ready for him.

I struggled and fought, needing more.

Troy knew me better than anyone. He knew that after being under someone else's control, cuffed and hooded, I'd need him to give me space to process it safely.

"Be still," he snarled, sending a light dart of Aether through my mind along with the command.

Once upon a time, those words had stolen my will and terrified me.

Now they gave me release. I slumped and didn't try to unhook the Aether from my mind, even though it would have been easy.

With him in control, I could let go of everything that had happened and everything I'd done in the last day. Everything I'd need to be after this was over. I could give myself fully to this moment, drown in his Aether, and take every one of his thrusts as his hips thudded against me and his arm snaked around my throat, squeezing lightly to add the physical effect that mirrored the magical.

I could lose myself in him.

"Come for me now, Arden," Troy breathed against my ear.

My body responded. Wave after wave of clenching around his cock as he kept moving in me. The scent of rosemary and sage, salt and meringue, filled my nose. His low growl rumbling in his chest, his grip on my hip and around my neck, his blunt-toothed bite to my shoulder as his body chased mine into completion.

The last few thrusts drew grunts from me even in my mindmazed state, but I needed his passion as much as he needed my compliance just now.

When he was done, he stayed deep inside me, draped over my back as he kissed my neck.

"One day," he whispered with a last thrust.

I knew exactly what he was thinking. One day, we'd do this to start a family.

We stayed like that until the Aetheric command wore off, a much shorter time than it used to be. Then Troy pulled out and carefully positioned me on my side on the bed before going to the ensuite bathroom. Water ran, and he came back out with a cloth.

I smiled and beckoned him closer. I loved this part as much as the sex, the aftercare where he cleaned me up and said sweet things in elvish I only half understood. It was the tone that soothed me more than anything else, and the faith that whatever he was saying in full, it was something we both needed to hear aloud.

I would take this moment of peace, because when it was over, it was back to the Twilight War.

Chapter 25

The buzz of Troy's phone followed by his heavy sigh brought me out of a post-coital doze.

"What's wrong?" I asked.

"We need to talk about Omar."

"What about him?" My stomach dropped as I remembered the terse conversation between Troy and the Captain at Jordan Lake, when they thought I was asleep. Troy had basically warned Omar to stay away from me.

"He's shown himself to be a problem," Troy replied. "A serious one. He sent a coded message that concerns me. I'm going to need to convince him I have control of you if we're going to avoid complications in the near term."

I inhaled deeply and stretched, feeling better than I had an hour ago even if I didn't like where the topic was going. "You sound like neither of us are going to like what you'll have to say."

"I... Yes." He grimaced. "Like the role you had to play to trap Cyrus at Jordan Lake."

"You're going to try trapping Omar?"

"I have to. He has the military strength and the influence to stage a coup. I can't be watching our backs for that while we push forward with our next move in this war." He looked away then met my gaze. "In all honesty, I should arrest him. I was hoping to bring him around, but now he's too much of a threat to you. Unfortunately, he's also the best military mind we have, and his experience is decades longer than mine. We need him and the loyalty he has with the Darkwatch to get through this."

I studied Troy, wishing that his family dynamics were less...what they were. Wishing the elves would quit doing this to themselves—tearing themselves apart for no good reason when they clearly needed the comfort of tight-knit family groups.

It was a problem for after the Twilight War was won.

"Do what you have to do," I said, letting him hear my sadness for him as much as feel it in the bond.

Troy rolled from the bed and went to the bathroom, turning on the shower only to come back. When I started to ask what that was for, he held a finger against my lips. "Stay quiet for this."

I nodded.

Satisfied, he rejoined me on the bed, sitting propped against the headboard as he dialed.

"Omar," he said in a firm voice—his public king's voice—when the call connected. "I need an update on combat actions and casualties."

"I'll provide it," Omar replied. The phone was barely loud enough for me to hear, but I stayed where I was as he continued. "But first we need to talk about your queen."

"*Our* queen," Troy corrected sharply. "Or are you declaring the Darkwatch for someone else?"

"There is a reality vortex in the nation's capital," Omar said in a hard tone. "You cannot tell me that was part of the plan. She is losing control."

Troy's smile was far more reptilian than I usually saw on him, and his tone was coldly satisfied. "She's a walking weapon of mass destruction. She'll win this for us with minimal elven casualties."

"Are you really telling me you have her under control enough to guarantee that? Because I won't risk further elven lives on your hope-and-faith bullshit, king or not. It was an effective role for reeling her in, but the stakes are too high now to slip." Omar hesitated. "Where is she anyway?"

"In the shower and probably nearly done, so I need this part of the conversation to be over." Troy ran a thumb over my lips, his expression softening for a moment and a curl of apology coming through the bond before he hardened again. "Listen. We cannot keep having this discussion. I mazed her again barely an hour ago. Why do you think I rut with her so much? You read the reports from Seattle. You saw how I was when I got back. So you know how much I resist it when I think I can get away with it. She's tied to me and this little daydream of a family now, even if she's too scared and stressed to cycle. And she only runs as far as I allow."

I went cold and my stomach clenched, not only at the words but also the icily disdainful tones he delivered them in.

I'll explain, Troy sent urgently. *It's a role, remember?*

"Hmm." Omar sat silent for a few more heartbeats, regardless of what Troy had said about the conversation needing to be over. "Fine. But the minute she slips your maze—"

"Enough, Omar. She's mine," Troy hissed. "Body, heart, mind, and soul. I'm doing what you trained me to do. Get close to a queen. Make her mine. End her. I'm doing my job. I'm doing it well. And not for the first time. Now do yours. Report."

Role or not, I felt sick. Me figuring out that this kind of subterfuge was both Troy's training and his long game for protecting me was one thing. Hearing those words...they dragged every fear of elves and every hidden doubt that'd been exposed to me during the final Duat trial and refreshed with that last bronze practice at home to the surface.

I wrestled with them, distracted enough to miss the rest of Omar's report. I knew in my heart that Troy was playing Omar. I knew that Omar's bullshit wasn't even personal to me; it was related to what Troy had said about elven legends about primordials, and what Cyrus had said about us destroying everything we touched. I could even see how Omar must have been playing me since our first meeting at Occoneechee, and that it might be entirely out of a desire to protect his children.

That didn't mean the whole thing didn't hurt.

Troy ended the call then sighed, looking as miserable as he felt in the bond. "I'm sorry. Do you want space?"

I laid there hugging myself, trying to untangle my emotions. I'd done exactly this to him at Jordan Lake, and he'd kept faith with me. I would do the same.

But I still had questions.

"So before the Wild Hunt, when Omar said he figured you were either my captive or my lover...he wasn't trying to confirm your safety. He was trying to confirm that you were in position to take me out if needed?" I asked.

Troy nodded, a single tight jerk of his head.

I refused to ask if he was. We both knew that he was and, as I'd said to Rio just days ago, Troy had had every chance to kill or otherwise break me for years now. Rio and the West Coast elves could throw Troy's three-year queenkilling mission in my face all they wanted. After everything Troy and I had been through, I had to believe that I wasn't some dupe.

"The lunch we had, us and him and Cyrus and Allegra, was that fake?" I'd felt like we were a family, even just for a few hours. It'd felt healing, and now it felt like a sham.

Troy looked away. "Not entirely. Certainly not for me or Alli. This is complicated, Arden. More than usual. I'm both son and tool to both of them. They love me as best they know how, even if it's toxic. They want me to have the best in life, even if our definitions of 'best' are wildly different. And they're constrained by their training and experiences as to what that looks like. Omar can see that I'm happy with you, so he worries that I'm losing myself to the role I let him believe I'm playing."

I sat with that for a minute. Then, with a force of will, decided that I would not punish my love for his family's nonsense.

When I snuggled closer to him, he opened his arms and drew me tight against his body.

"Look," he said.

I didn't know what he meant, but then every wall dropped in the bond, including some I hadn't even been aware were there.

I don't know how, I sent. I wasn't a mental Aether user.

Like this. With light tugs of Aether, he drew me in, welcoming me deeper into his mind and heart in hesitant, halting steps, like he was as scared to let me in as I was to see.

Tentatively, I reached back with Chaos.

Our magic twined, and he drew me even deeper, to the heart of his greatest fear.

That he was unworthy. Not enough. And not to protect others from me, like Omar was demanding, but to be with me at all. It was a small, hardened seed in his soul, one that I had the sense he was trying to stuff roots and sprouts back into the shell. Around it, feeding it, was a layer of fear, that choosing me meant losing everyone and everything else in his life—a choice I sensed he would make without hesitation, but which would still hurt him. Nowhere in evidence was any desire to cut me down, whether my life, my dignity, or my power.

All he wanted was for me to live, be free, and be happy. At any cost to himself and anyone else.

"Troy," I whispered, brokenhearted for him.

"It's why what you said to Cyrus hurt so much," he said. "I knew you were playing a role. But it's what I was raised to believe. That I would only ever be a toy or a prize stud. That I would never be worthy or enough on my own merits as a person. Certainly not for someone like you."

"But you're too damn stubborn to let go," I said.

He nodded, every muscle tense as he fought his personal demons.

"I don't want you to let go," I said. "I want us to plant different seeds together. Generational trauma stops with us. That's our vow to each other. Okay?"

His relief flooded me. "Yes, my love. I want that. I want our children to be free of it so they can spend their time and energy and gifts building something new. Something better. For all our people. And maybe us working on our healing will help my family with theirs." He blew out a breath and gave me a hesitant kiss, like he wasn't sure I'd want him to after what he'd just confessed. "Maybe we can be a real family one day. One that cares about each other instead of throwing these barbs of suspicion and fear all the time."

I'd told Rage that I knew what I was fighting for, but this took it to a new level. The fears that had been drawn up in me during Troy's call with Omar quieted. Resolve hardened in me. "Let's shower again for real and get this shit done."

"Yes, my queen." Troy kissed me again, still uncertain at first, then with more amorousness when I responded.

We'd be okay. It might only be by the grace of this bond and our hard-learned, oft-practiced communication skills, but we'd be okay. Which was perfect, because I couldn't deal with a breakup and a Goddess-damned war at the same time.

Once we'd showered and dressed, we headed back out to the mess hall that also served as a briefing room. Neither of us missed the scent of sex coming from several rooms as we passed, but as long as it was all consenting, it wasn't our business. It did seem like I'd been right to wonder about Troy's passive magic though.

Etain met us in the mess hall, keeping a careful distance from Haroun even if she kept glancing at him with a flush. "Majesties."

"Everything all right?" Troy asked sternly, looking between the two half-elves to make it clear what he was asking about.

"Yes, sir," Etain said.

Haroun nodded enthusiastically, even as he didn't meet anyone's eye.

They got caught up in our game, I sent. *We need to be more careful about that.*

Troy sent an affirmative ripple back but replied to Etain in a low voice. "I have an update from Omar. We've had elven casualties in several cities. Their queens are sending support for the action against the Bureau, but they're demanding to know what comes next. We need to plan a decisive strike."

"We have options," Etain said, still flustered but with her head on straight. She glanced at me, clearly uncomfortable, but continued. "Omar is cooperating on the intel front."

Ah. So she was aware of the complications with the Captain. I offered a wry smile that settled her a little, just glad that she was still on my side.

"You checked it against our own intel?" Troy asked bluntly.

Etain barely suppressed a wince, from the twitch of her lips. "Yes, sir. Some of it, we can't confirm, but we did independently confirm comms and power surges to other locations after the facility you two took down went dark. They're going to try restarting elsewhere. From the looks of it, multiple somewheres."

"Like a hydra." I looked at the ceiling, pissed all over again.

After all that, we'd only managed to rescue a handful of people and kill a few mundanes. Of course they'd have backup or secondary facilities. And after what Troy and I had done, they'd be redoubling their efforts and reinforcing those locations.

Movement in the corner of my eye made me turn my head to find Rio hovering. I waved him over.

He approached with eyes downcast. "May I speak, my queen?"

"Of course," I said. "You're in my court."

That brought his gaze up and straightened the curl in his shoulders, although he looked at Troy and waited for his nod before saying, "Thank you. I've just received word from Queen Dia. A new algorithm from the Rainier R&D labs is available, one that will allow us to decrypt and hack federal, state, and mundane military communications more effectively."

"That's timely," Troy said neutrally.

"We've been working on it since the Reveals two years ago," Rio said. "Top priority, all available and relevant resources, no expenses spared. The East Coast elves have the military might; the West couldn't match it and focused on tech. The councils I was present for assumed that, especially given the rumors and partial footage coming out of Durham after the Wild Hunt, some mundane government or military branch would be coordinating strikes. We wanted to be able to turn them to our advantage." The slight flush to his neck said that advantage could be against the East Coast Houses or me in particular as much as the various mundane government or military entities.

Trustworthy? I asked Troy.

Smells like it. He looked at Etain. "Thoughts as Captain of the Ebon Guard?"

"Worth testing," she said after a long look at Rio. "I can put Z on it. See if she can use it to crack any of these comms we've been tracing."

"Do it," Troy ordered. "Carefully."

"Sir." Etain stepped away and pulled out her phone.

Rio didn't bother protesting his birth conclave's innocence or pushing their good intentions. That might have been a ploy in and of itself, but none of us had time for it. I, in particular, had to get over my fear that elves were going to betray me and count on the need to push the humans back so hard that they'd stop trying to control us as incentive for good elven behavior.

Troy started saying something else, but an intense twist in my gut and heart distracted me.

"Arden?" he asked.

The twist grew stronger, taking on a fiery edge. I closed my eyes, shuddered, and tried to breathe through it. "Something's wrong."

"What?" He squeezed my shoulder when I didn't answer. "Talk to me."

I shook my head and pulled the walls all the way up in the bond, scared of what would happen to him, given how intensely this was coming to me. "I— It's magic-related."

I figured out what it was as it burst into a conflagration in my soul: my tie to the land my home was on.

Trying to keep the scream in was pointless. I dropped to my knees, nails catching against lines in the tiles, and keened as all the semi-sentient plants around my home cried out—and burned.

"Etain!" Troy hollered. "Find out what's happening at HQ. Now!"

In my mind, fire consumed everything. Flame and ash, choking smoke, and the acrid scent of accelerant.

I was so taken over by the sensations that I was barely aware of the words leaving my own mouth. "They're burning it!"

Then the weight of a forest aflame smothered me, and I went all the way down, still partially aware of the room around me but painfully tied to the cruel, visceral, and intentional destruction of my land and home.

Eno River State Park, burning.

My little house and everything in it, my haven for over a decade. Where I'd finally started allowing myself to envision a future with Troy. The big oak that'd shaded the lawn. The small fig tree Troy had planted with Laurel to prove he could grow things, not just destroy them.

All consumed, in their entirety.

It was all I could do to keep the walls up. Troy hated fire. I couldn't expose him to this. He'd already faced a nightmare in the Duat. This might be worse.

"Arden, let me in," he said urgently. "What is happening?"

I couldn't answer him, choked as much by the sensation of asphyxiation and fiery death as I was by unrelenting despair. I didn't know how long it took for the worst of the flames to move on from the spot around my house, but I lived every searing moment of it. When the fire had passed to farther reaches of Eno,

I took a deep, shuddering breath, blinking rapidly to clear the tears from my eyes.

I was still on the floor of the mess hall, throat sore and face damp. Troy had me pillowed on his lap, looking down at me with his heart in his eyes as furious, horrified elves looked on.

"They burned it," I whispered, choking on the words as much as my tears. "It's gone. It's all gone."

"Home?" Troy asked, voice tight with the effort to control it. I jerked a nod.

Rushing, half-heard footsteps made the elves surrounding us part to reveal Etain, paler than usual with what had to be shock.

"I only just got hold of our people." She looked at me, cracked, then pulled herself together. "They had to evacuate HQ. The gytrash came running up, hurt bad with gunshots and burns, smelling like smoke and gasoline. Bás shifted to humanoid long enough to say there was danger before passing out. Everything is secure, all of our people safe thanks to the fae's warning, but..." She shook her head and swallowed hard. "Over a square mile of Eno River State Park is burning, centered on Arden's house. It's spreading fast, in all directions. All of North Durham is under evacuation orders. Terrence and Ximena's pride is in the path of the fires if the winds keep up in that direction, but if they shift, it might go to Chapel Hill or the elementals out toward Hillsborough. I can't reach any of our contacts."

"Who did this?" Troy asked in a hard voice roughened with pain.

"We don't know yet," Etain replied hesitantly. "We assume the Bureau for Supernatural Investigation or the North Carolina National Guard under orders from the governor, but we don't know for sure. We just know that there's no way anything is left of your home."

If I'd thought rage had hardened into hate at Sinclaire threatening my faction heads, it had nothing on what I was feeling at hearing that.

My land, my home, my haven, the place that had sheltered and hidden me for most of my life, the place that was as alive as I was and where I'd wanted to welcome new life in the form of my children with Troy, was gone.

Dead.

Burned to ash.

Chapter 26

The only good thing about losing the thing I held dearest to me—after Troy, of course—was that it was easy to be cold. I dragged myself together with no more fear, doubt, imposter syndrome, or concern for my reputation.

I was an Arbiter of Otherside. A High Queen. The Eternal Huntress.

And someone had just struck at my home, destroying it utterly. Hurting the people sworn to me, whether fae, elf, or the land spirits in the plants and earth who had taken it upon themselves to protect me and what was mine.

Someone had stolen everything I had that wasn't my love or the things I'd deemed precious or dangerous enough to pack and bring with me. They had thrown a gauntlet to the one who had already bested them once—twice, given I'd taken down their drone and then destroyed their torture facility. They'd made me an elemental without the core land that sustained, anchored, and grounded me. They'd cut my deepest ties with my elements and left me adrift, far from home with no home to return to.

This. Could. Not. Stand.

I'd always said—always believed—that elementals were nonviolent by nature, maenad magic notwithstanding. We weren't predators or hunters like the elves, vampires, weres, or most fae. We didn't have the teeth, the claws, the bloodlust, the moonbite. It had been hard for me to imagine what reason or pain would have driven the ancient elementals to take the actions we thought they had at Atlantis, to drown an entire city, burn its ships, turn wind and wave and shore against those fleeing the destruction.

Now, I knew.

Because now, I wanted to do the same. A second Atlantis, against the entire United States. Why stop at an island when I could destroy a continent? When I could make them feel my pain? It was what the mundanes were afraid of, after all. Like the elves. They were all afraid that people like me would make them experience the fear and pain and loss, the torture, that they had inflicted on us.

The impossibly beguiling thing was that I could do it.

I could make them all feel my pain.

My home was in ashes. Why should theirs stand?

A heavy silence weighed on the base as we reconvened in a smaller conference room for planning. My core team—Troy, Etain, Darius, Haroun—only, all of us seated around a heavy wooden table. Rio was in my court and Cyrus was allied with me for his son's sake; Pascale and Thana, Felip and Lachlan, Samarre, Jacinthe, and Luc, all of them had proven themselves. But I needed my inner circle. The people who had always kept faith with me and never required me to prove myself or be anything other than what I was. Odd for me to include Darius in that number, given what he'd done to sever me from Troy before the Wild Hunt, but like Troy, he'd worked to make amends. In the month between the Duat trials and now, the brother-cousins had deepened their family bond over something, likely their shared experiences, and for all Darius wanted out of elven military service, he was with Troy to the death. I didn't know what it was they'd connected over. I didn't need to know. Only that Darius had become more unstable in the time since he'd come home and more committed than ever as Troy worked to bring him back, and I didn't punish him for going through the same process I'd already helped Troy survive.

We gathered around a table. Haroun, as the lowest-ranked present, poured mead for everyone, and we drank.

"To justice," Troy said grimly.

"Justice," everyone echoed.

Everyone except me. I just drank, too angry to speak.

My hand tightened on my glass as I set it down. I wanted vengeance. I wanted to burn the mundane world to ash as they'd burned my home, so that they could never rise up again. But Harqil had already said that vengeance would be my downfall, and Rage was already sniffing at my heart and soul. Despair had been trying for Cyrus and might try for me if I gave in to the tendrils of it trying to take root in me.

I couldn't afford to lose myself.

I wouldn't be able to claim what was mine if I did. There would be no happily ever after with Troy. No children. No family of my own. No doing better or healing.

So, I had to smother my despair and keep my rage in check for the sake of love and for the sake of the future. I had to numb the fury burning in me, the demand that I tap into the full strength of my magic and warp reality beyond repair.

Arden, Troy sent, a prompt to take control of the meeting after too long a silence.

I looked at him, my chin lifting to an angle that he apparently read as dangerous from the way he quickly dropped his gaze and went very still in body and bond. Everyone else followed his lead, reading all the micro-tensions in our unspoken interaction—maybe reading more into them because everyone here now knew we spoke telepathically and wouldn't know what we'd said.

I sent a curl of apology in the bond and pushed my glass away. The maenad magic fed on death as much as sex, as I'd learned killing Roman. There were no targets here, elves or not. These were mine, by right of power, conquest, and merit. I'd earned the right to lead, and now I would.

"Eno is gone," I said harshly, even as I was unable to bring myself to acknowledge the more personal loss of my haven. "Clearly in an effort to draw me out after losing me." Their time frame was much faster than it had been after the first attempt to destroy my home. That meant mine would need to be faster still. "Strategically, it's small. Morally, symbolically, it can't be allowed to stand."

Troy tipped his glass my way in a silent elven gesture of support, as did the rest.

"We succeeded in our first mission," I continued. "We found and destroyed the facility the BSI was using to torture and detain Othersiders, and we sent a powerful statement that it would not continue. But from reports, it sounds like that message was taken as a minor setback rather than a definitive statement. I know what I want to do."

The scent of rotting herbs filled the room—elven fear—even as their expressions stayed blank.

I looked around the table, meeting everyone's eye. "I would hear your thoughts before I decide on further actions."

"I agree, my queen," Etain said when Troy nodded in response to her glance at him. "They fear us, now more than ever, but they still think they have the upper hand."

"In numbers and outright firepower, they do," Darius said, sounding frustrated. "That's a simple strategic fact. Our strength was always in outmaneuvering them or turning key positions from the shadows."

"Until now," Troy murmured. He looked at me. *How far can I speak?*

As far as you must to get justice for us, I replied. *Omar be damned.*

Troy tilted his glass toward me again and spoke louder. "The developments in Arden's magical strength present opportunities."

"Such as?" Darius asked.

Troy looked at me again. *This is for you to tell.*

I leaned forward and rested my elbows on the table. "The reality warp that brought down the facility was an accident. Harqil showed me a trick with the portals. I tried it."

At the vocalization of their name, the celestial phased into the corner. Nobody else reacted, so I didn't acknowledge them beyond meeting their solemn gaze.

"Bringing down Verve was an intentional effort," I continued. "One that wore me out at the time. But since then, I've done so much more. And I could do it in a way that doesn't warp reality."

"You have a target in mind," Troy said.

"They took our house." I allowed an angry snarl to curl my lips. "I will take theirs. An eye for an eye and blood for blood, three times over. As is just."

Troy's gaze went distant, considering the strategic possibilities. "The White House?"

"Yes," I said. "And Capitol Hill—the houses of Congress. And lastly the Pentagon, because you know that they will organize a military response against us for the previous two targets. That destroys their executive, legislative, and military leadership. Or at least where they stage from. At the same time, we leave other governmental organizations—the ones that pay out benefits and manage social services—untouched."

Again, the room hung silent, although in Troy's case it was anticipatory, the hunger of a predator with prey in sight. The others wore shocked expressions that said they hadn't quite imagined striking so high or so hard.

"You'd destroy them, my queen?" Haroun asked. "These targets?"

I nodded. "A military strike. I don't want to harm innocents. But I cannot allow the attack against me and Troy to go unanswered, and I cannot leave them the capability to hit us again. I'll handle the strikes. I just need a way to minimize casualties. I know people will be hurt who I'm not intending to hurt from the chaos this will cause, aside from accidental casualties. But this system cannot be salvaged. It must be destroyed, starting with the head. As they've tried to do with me."

This will have further consequences, Arden, Harqil sent.

I looked at Troy as I answered them. *Will it cost me my bondmate?*

That's been a possibility since he swore to you.

Troy pushed in. *My life and death are Arden's. Her land and home are mine. This must be answered, and I'll answer it with her.*

"We can use the Sons of Seth," Etain said, oblivious to the silent mental conversation going on in parallel. "We have three remaining that the vampire didn't eat. They can be our fall guys. They call in threats against the government for not doing enough to protect humans against the Otherside threat. We send one to the White House, one to Capitol Hill, and one to Reagan Airport in pickups loaded with explosives. Let public imagination latch onto the stereotypes."

I thought that through. "And while they're focused on that threat, we move in with our own."

"With the buildings as clear as they can be of innocents," Haroun said. "School groups and the like. We don't want to kill kids."

"We do not," I agreed.

This was definitively war, and that meant there would be deaths. But I did not want Otherside to take on the role the United States had in Vietnam or dozens of other conflicts. It was bad enough that there would be unintended consequences. I would not allow myself to conflate the actions of the government with the everyday people.

The plan made sense, but I still didn't see how it could work, not on the timeframe I wanted. "It'll be hours before the reprogrammed Sons get here and more before they're in place. I want to move now."

"They're already nearby, cariñamí," Troy said quietly. "Fully armed and mindmazed. Someone just needs to call with a target and the code word that will trigger them. It was the other reason I had us delay with the House party. A backup plan I hoped we wouldn't need."

I fixed him with a glare as Etain winced.

"I didn't tell you for operational security," Troy said, speaking confidently as my general and unaffected by my temper this time. "If they took you alone, or even if they took us both, you couldn't betray what you didn't know."

His words were firm, the bond was firmer. He believed what he was saying was right, and he'd stand by it.

Fine. I wasn't going to argue with him. Not in front of our people. Not at all given he'd been right to make the call. Besides, he was the one who'd had anti-interrogation training, not me. It made sense, even if it pissed me off.

"Get the West Coast elves' algorithm tested," I said instead. "We'll need a way to evade their countermeasures."

"On it, my queen." Etain swiped out orders on her phone. "How are you getting back into DC? The roads have checkpoints on them, there's a curfew, and between Verve's work and their own they have some kind of test they think is accurate enough to differentiate between human and non. Everyone going that way is being stopped and checked."

That had to be some politician's wet dream—an excuse to exercise control over the population that way. Probably Senator Wright. Especially after Troy and I broke into his house and then all the protests and riots that'd broken out in the last six weeks.

Didn't matter.

"I can clear a path," I said.

Darius scrubbed a hand over his head and leaned back in his chair, looking a little sick. "You want to do a direct assault? Plow through?"

I started to snarl back, then took a breath to bring my rage back down to a simmer. Darius wasn't who I was mad at, and he had a valid point. "I can't open another portal." I glanced at Harqil in the corner. "Right?"

They nodded vigorously.

"Who—" Etain started.

With a ripple, Harqil made themselves visible to everyone else. "You know, I miss the days when I could spy on this plane without being noticed."

That sent the mental equivalent of a red flag up in the bond as Troy let his secondary teeth flicker at the angel.

Harqil raised a hand. "Generally speaking, of course. And this does not count as sneaking, little king." They arched a teasing brow at Troy. "In any case, I would *strongly* recommend against any more portals, assuming you want this plane to retain any semblance of reality. You're lucky the other warp is relatively small. I told you that's a once-per-year trick for someone of your power and experience."

I flushed at being called out publicly and glared at them.

They just shrugged. "I did warn you."

"I had to get my people out."

"And we did," Troy broke in, probably to stop me bickering with Harqil the way I did with the djinn. "No portals, and please for the love of the Goddess no more interplanar jumps."

"Which means plowing through," Darius said.

Haroun fiddled with a pen. "We have the bikes. We could stealth it at least a little, with obfuscation and misdirection spells."

Etain rose and moved to the room's whiteboard, where she sketched out a rough map showing the locations of our targets and us. "Let's work backward." Again she looked to Troy, and again he nodded, giving permission for her to take lead. She looked to me next, and I allowed myself a small smile as I nodded, happy that she was fully stepping into the role of captain as a half-elf who'd been passed over for positions of authority multiple times before.

She straightened with pride and turned back to the board. "We have three targets. Two" —she marked the White House and Capitol Hill with an X each— "are relatively close to each other and sit on lower ground. That said, so does everything else in the area—it's a riverbottom."

Troy leaned forward, studying it. "If we can find a high point between those two, that's two out of three. We have to assume countermeasures will be deployed after the strikes that will make the third target more difficult, if not impossible." He turned to me. "Is two out of three acceptable, my queen?"

I almost said no. I wanted Otherside justice: three for three. But again, I had to remind myself that if either Troy or I didn't escape alive, that was against the whole point of what I was doing.

Still...I wanted all three.

The huntress in me was thirsty for blood in a way I usually only experienced vicariously via Troy and the bond.

Take what you can get, Harqil sent.

I glared at them and pulled on Air to make my eyes flash gold, all threat and no patience.

They raised their hands and leaned back against the wall, curling all their fingers down from pinky inward as they tilted their head and arched an eyebrow mockingly. *Or is it really vengeance you're after?*

That stopped me cold. I'd done the briefest amount of research into Regulus in the month between the Duat and now. Everything was clear: the fixed star brought greatness...but with conditions. It brought a fall if you sought vengeance on your path. I didn't understand Harqil's comment that I had the stamp of that star, nor did I fully understand the concept itself, but at my magical and political power level, that fall could cost me everything, given what I was playing with and how much I was playing for.

Troy's gaze was heavy on me as I considered all that. The bond was still more open than usual on his side from earlier, letting me read the split in him. He'd follow me no matter what, but it'd take some self-reconciliation if I did push toward vengeance.

It wasn't just me and my needs I had to think about now, no matter how hot rage burned in me.

I closed my eyes in a long blink, took a deep breath, let it shudder out, and decided. "Two out of three is acceptable. As long as I take their seat of power, as mine was taken."

The elves relaxed subtly, losing their wary stiffness at my concession to reason.

"I want the White House," I said. "That's symbolic to the mundanes. They think it's untouchable and I want it to burn to the ground. I want the ground itself to be unreclaimable."

That it was probably the most heavily guarded target in the entire country didn't faze my elves. My acceptance of a middle ground and definition of a primary target and objective made all of them settle into the sharpened hunter's headspace Troy had been in since I'd spoken my goal aloud, if scent and posture were any indication.

Oh, this was good. I liked this.

I wasn't running from elven bounty hunts anymore.

Elves were taking *my* bounties. My desires and objectives set them to the hunt.

Etain looked up from her phone and tapped a point between the White House and the Capitol, closer to the White House. "Intel says there's a few possibilities, but I think the tower at the top of a landmark here, the Old Post Office Pavilion, will be best."

Haroun reached for the remote in the middle of the table, turned on the TV behind my head, and tapped on his phone until he had something pulled up.

I twisted to see the building Etain had mentioned up on screen.

"It's a hotel now, but that part of the building is managed by the National Park Service," Haroun said. "Which we could circumvent or overpower easily, if they're even still there given the lockdown. The tower itself has vantage points in four directions, including the primary target. If we can punch through to downtown, we might be able to cloak ourselves enough to reach this point."

I studied it. High tower. Arched windows or lookouts, arranged on all four sides of the structure, as Haroun had said. Not perfectly aligned with the White House or the Capitol, but well enough that I'd be able to see and target my magic tightly enough not to destroy extra locations.

"I like it," I said. "Make that our staging point. If I can reach that, I can take one or both primary targets."

"King Troy," Etain said, "can we count on ties to House Bedoe to supplement our forces? We'll need distractions."

"I'll make it happen," Troy said.

My phone chirped. I glanced at it, ready to dismiss the message, but the preview made me open it. The full text made me smile. "We've got other help incoming. The Farkas Blood Moon wolves. Vikki says they need to know where to meet us."

"What kind of help?" Troy asked.

I texted a reply and got an answer back almost immediately. "Apparently, they're a biker gang. Werewolf militia. Vikki says it was send them to DC or they were going to wreak havoc at home."

"Good news," Darius said. "I'll take it."

"So will I," I said.

The wolves and the elves might not get along on a normal day, but these were not normal days. If Vikki Volkov wanted to send me paramilitary forces, I'd damn well take them.

And with those forces, we'd take the mundane seat of government.

Chapter 27

When we met our new forces at Meadowood Special Recreation Management Area, the werewolf biker militia was a hell of a lot more than I was expecting.

For one thing, there were SUVs in their number. For another thing, those SUVs were modified and packed full of the kind of weaponry that no civilian population should be able to acquire, but which was apparently available on the Appalachian side of Virginia. I didn't even know how they'd gotten across the state with everything going on, and when I asked, I just got wolfish grins that looked more feral than Troy ever had.

That meant somebody had probably died. I couldn't bring myself to care.

The wolves' leader, a grizzled older man named Gus, was missing an eye and didn't bother with a patch, although he kept his greying hair pulled back from his face with a bandana. He tugged on his long beard as I ran through the plan, keeping his remaining eye on the elves in general and Troy in particular.

For his part, Troy pretended to ignore the werewolf leader—not out of fear or disdain, but in an effort to avoid an inter-factional fight when tensions were high and we needed to work together. The bond said he was fully aware of every breath the wolf took though, and was ready to pull his longknife at the slightest hint of a threat.

"So lemme make sure I got this," Gus said when I finished outlining the plan. "You wanna destroy the two buildings the mundanes govern the entire country from."

"Yes," I said firmly. For once, I wasn't even having to try to be the Arbiter. I was so pissed that I just insisted on carrying the authority for myself and others. Virginia was in the Dominion demesne and I was its Arbiter, and while my role would normally only call for conflict resolution and passing judgment I was determined these wolves would follow my direction.

"And you got a plan to reduce casualties on the little guy. Kids and the elderly and folks just trying to scratch out a living."

"Yes," I said again. "I don't deny that the average person will probably find themselves hurting as a result of this action. I know that people need government support for food, healthcare, all kinds of benefits. Some of those people are probably Othersiders, and even among the mundanes, I'm not trying to make life needlessly difficult. It's not how I want to do things, number one. I don't want to crush everyday people for my own benefit. And number two, it's bad politics, bad optics, and bad for business in local communities. I get that. But I also cannot allow even the faintest question that Othersiders are easy meat. I'm hoping that one decisive strike makes them so sour on the idea of hunting us that they don't try again."

"And this ain't about them burning your woods down in North Carolina?" Gus gave me a hard look. "We heard about that."

"Oh, it is," I said honestly. "It's an eye for an eye and blood for blood. But it's bigger than that. Whatever anybody thinks, the mundanes have fixed on me as a leader and a problem. So I'm using the power I have to show them what we're not gonna do going forward. My hope is that it protects others of us from being rounded up like those Troy and I already freed."

Gus stared at me for so long that he pulled Troy's direct attention. Then he said, "I was ready to think you a bitch, Ms. Finch. Some rich, uppity, power-hungry, elf-loving bitch. I was ready to take my men and follow our own plan. But I reckon I can get behind yours." He pursed his lips and turned to the side to spit a stream of tobacco before raising his voice. "What say y'all? We ridin' with the elves and our Arbiter today?"

His people, lounging nearby or checking their bikes and weapons, pumped their fists and howled.

I couldn't tell if they were normally this democratic, or if Gus was making a point.

"There you have it, Ms. Finch. We'll follow you. For now, anyway, even if it's unprecedented for an Arbiter to lead into battle." He glanced between me and Troy, his gaze lingering on Troy like there might be a problem there. "After this, we'll see."

"That's all I ask. Support in hitting hard in this one task." I shrugged, allowing a dark smile to curl my lips. "After this, we'll see."

Gus chuckled and shook his head then extended a hand.

I shook it, meeting his firm grip with one of my own that got me raised brows, before he shook with Troy.

After that it was hashing out details, which was surprisingly easy. The wolves were keen for something to fight. If it was a sanctioned battle, so much the better. They'd take point and hit the roadblocks hard while the spell-cloaked elves followed. The Ebon Guard were already prepping the West Coast elves' algorithm to hack everything from traffic cams to comms, ensuring that any spell slips wouldn't be caught by tech.

Shortly after sunset, we were finally ready. It was probably not the best time to strike, given the mundanes would be expecting us in the dark. At the same time, it was when all Othersiders would be strongest. Even I was finding that I got a little boost to Chaos at night. The wolves and elves would definitely be stronger—especially the elves, with the moon still only a thin waxing crescent.

As we all scattered to vehicles, a thrill ran through me. Troy was taking us in on a motorcycle, to my enormous surprise. We'd driven over in one of the cars, but most of those were staying behind with a rearguard. If wounded needed to be carried out later, we didn't want those vehicles hit in our first run. On top of that, we might need to squeeze through some tight spaces. This gave us options.

How did I not know you can drive a motorcycle? I sent, bounding ahead to the one Troy was angling toward.

You never asked. And I don't own one. He took the helmet I handed him and pulled it on. *I can ride a horse as well if I have to. But I'd rather not.*

The sending had the dark tinge of bad memories, so I let it be as I put my own helmet on. *I've never ridden one of these.*

Amusement rose in the bond. *This should be fun then. Hold on to me. And keep your magic under control.*

After a quick check—for tracking or explosive devices, I imagined—Troy got on and started up the engine. I clambered on behind him, found the footrests, and threw my arms around him, buzzing with excitement.

Around us, the wolves howled as they revved engines and headed for the road, a convoy of heavily armed rebels. The elves formed up in an honor guard around me and Troy.

Here we go, he sent.

My grip on Troy tightened involuntarily as he got us in motion. This was a lot more exposed than I was used to and with a lot more vibration. By the time I got over the unusual air movements, we'd hit the highway.

And then we flew.

I whooped, unable to help myself, as Troy gunned the engine and the air whipped around us. *We're getting one of these!*

Hush now, he sent, affectionate under the stern order. *Remember your training.*

With an effort, I reined myself in. I was a Darkwatch agent for this, or as close to one as Omar would allow me to become.

Fuck that.

I was the Eternal Huntress. And hunters moved swiftly and silently, bringing death in their wake.

On either side of us, a full clutch of valkyrie phased in, all of them mounted on spectral horses that somehow kept up with the motorcycles.

That sobered me. Whatever was about to happen would be a mass casualty event. No avoiding it. I just prayed that the casualties would be more on the mundane side than mine. I'd lost enough in this war already.

With the roads nearly empty and our own speed, we made it to the Capital Beltway in just over ten minutes—and hit the first roadblock.

The few cars on the road in front of us slowed as red taillights gave warning.

"Bull?" Gus's voice crackled over our radio with Troy's sigil and codename.

"Go ahead," Troy said.

"We're engaging."

"Copy. Onyx riders, slow but do not stop."

Tension sang through me, making my heart race and my skin prickle, as the wolves pulled farther ahead. I pushed at the Sight and my ring, looking for danger.

The valkyrie kept riding.

The wolves split wide around the handful of waiting cars, pivoting back toward the road to slam into the six state police cars holding the road.

My turn.

Pulling on Air, I wove a ramp. Earth would have been a more stable choice, but it would have been a dead giveaway that something was happening and we were trying to keep them from knowing I was here. Air was shakier. I'd tried and failed multiple times to make stairs that I could climb into the sky.

We didn't need stairs, though, or to stay in the air. We just needed to get over the obstacles in front of us while everyone was distracted by reinforced werewolf Hummers plowing into police vehicles.

I toggled my radio. "Set. Straight ahead."

"Onyx riders, go," Troy ordered. "Single file in front of my position."

Without hesitation, shadow- and spell-cloaked elves roared forward, hit a ramp nobody but I could see, and took to the sky.

I held my breath until the last one had cleared the pack of now-panicked mundane vehicles trying to turn around and flee the wrong way down the freeway. One managed the turn and glanced off the wall I threw in front of the ramp but kept driving.

"Go!" I said.

Troy went, all trust and no hesitation.

We hit my ramp. And this time we really did fly, landing easily on the other side of the tire spikes and the swiftly ending battle with the police.

They might have decommissioned military gear. They might have been accustomed to terrorizing a human population.

But they weren't Otherside. Tonight, it would be us against those who'd earned our wrath.

I grunted with the force of the landing and unraveled the ramp behind us, relieved that I'd judged the angle correctly.

"Onyx riders, go!" Troy barked. He matched action to words and got us moving.

The other elves fell in around us.

"Moon riders, Onyx is clear," Samarre said from the elven rearguard. "All Wild Hunt advance."

"Copy." Gus's voice held enough growl that I wondered how close to the surface his wolf was. As long as the wolves stayed with us, it wasn't mine to worry about.

They caught up and passed us, barreling off-road to plow through the next roadblock.

And the next.

And the next, four in total.

The defenses grew heavier the closer we got, both because of the proximity to Washington, DC and because news of an attack coming up the road and winning had reached the people who could do something about it.

The wolves lost both of their remaining Hummers in the second to last roadblock and bailed, detonators in wolfish mouths as they fled for the trees lining the freeway. Behind us, orange explosions roared into the night as the vehicles blew, taking what remained of the roadblock with them.

Unfortunately, that meant I had to clear the last one. It wasn't unfortunate because I had to do it but because I could only do so in a way that would finally tip off that this wasn't a rogue werewolf gang at work. We'd held my presence back because we wanted to give the mundanes as little time as possible to raise anti-elemental countermeasures.

But there was no more hiding now.

As we approached, it grew clearer that it was always going to have to be me at this last roadblock before the bridges over the Potomac because two gods-damned tanks sat in the road—and the cannons were angling for us as their instruments picked up by proximity what mundane eyes and hacked defense systems could not.

Troy read the situation the same way and issued the order as general. "Kestrel. You're up."

"Copy," I whispered.

Air and Fire came to me gleefully, and I ripped lightning from the sky, striking first the helicopters hovering overhead and then not only frying the ground electronics but bursting in a line of chain lightning to kill men and blow up smaller vehicles. With another push of Air, I cleared the road. The tanks rolled away slowly, tumbling on their sides. Smaller support trucks went faster, toys thrown by a child having a tantrum.

"Road and sky clear," I said.

Troy gunned the engine and leaned low, pulling me lower with him. "All riders, on me. Push through. Tight formation."

Now came the dangerous part: crossing the river. It was on me to get all of us across, or as many of us as possible. Keeping everyone close was a huge risk; if we took a direct hit, that was all of us gone. But as much as my control had improved over the last couple of years, it was still iffy at greater distances.

So, we kept our forces close to me, where I could keep my elemental defenses strong and focused. Where I could keep everyone who'd made it the twenty-plus miles from our joint staging point protected.

No pressure.

I set the flicker of doubt and worry aside. That wasn't who I was anymore. Or at least not now. Not in the moment. Not with my blood singing with a Wild Hunt of my own devising with me and my Hunter at its head and elves, wolves, and valkyrie riding into battle at my side.

That felt pretty damn badass.

Electronic signatures flared both above and below.

"All riders, be advised," I said. "Hostiles in sky and river. They're mine."

"Copy," Gus growled. "Eyes up and down."

"Copy, eyes front and back," Haroun said from our vanguard as Samarre echoed him from the rear.

Good. They were watching and ready. Everyone who wasn't me or Troy would scatter once we'd made it over the bridge, drawing security forces into a race through the city to distract them from our real target before finding cover or escape routes. Everyone on this mission had committed to dying if it meant achieving our objectives.

I was going to do everything I could to make sure my people made it through this.

Or, in the face of Troy's stern realism, make sure as many of us as possible made it home.

It wasn't just the choke point of the bridge that was a problem now; it was also the military boats on the river itself. Small flotillas of ships bobbed on either side of the bridges crossing the Potomac. As I reached with elemental senses, I found the crackling signatures that said these were armed vessels with active communications, not simply civilians trying to flee.

They must have thought they could beat us because they hadn't pulled the bridges themselves down yet. They were probably waiting for our convoy to dare the crossing, with the intention of blowing the bridge as we crossed and sending us all tumbling down like the Potomac was the Styx.

Their mistake.

As Troy kept a grim focus on gaining us the other shore yard by yard, I pulled bolt after bolt of lightning from the cloudless sky. I put walls of Air on either side of the bridge as we raced across the first half-mile stretch.

Fighter jets screamed in the distance, scrambled from an air base nearby.

Nah. I wasn't letting them have air support. Not that easily.

With a shudder that tightened my grip on Troy, I fell into Water and twisted the area's humidity into a storm. I whipped Air into gusting winds that spawned tornado cells. I poured my broken heart and frustrated rage into building a storm for the ages. Lightning sparked wildly.

Save some for the real target, cariñamí, Troy sent.

I growled at him.

Save. It. He pushed at me in the bond. *You have a primary target. Everyone here knows the stakes. Or do you not want all three targets?*

That snapped me back into focus. *I want all three.*

Then listen to me. Do only enough to get us across. There's still a tower to take and two buildings to crumble.

Troy was right, and that was why he was my general and my Hunter. I knew my strengths: power and vision. But he had the control and focus to balance me.

Like my father had said, I shouldn't have to do this alone.

Tonight, I wouldn't, and it wouldn't be on Troy alone to help me get the job done. We were all stronger together.

As wolves howled defiantly on the radio and elves tapped into their primal sides to growl, I pushed just enough to clear a path to our target.

Nobody was gonna stop me now.

Chapter 28

Everyone made it across in one piece. The elves and weres riding with us scattered the minute a side street presented itself. From there, I had no idea where they went. Part of the plan but unsettling nonetheless. I couldn't protect people who weren't nearby, and they'd come to fight for me. Only Darius, riding solo on his own bike, stayed with us to complete a triad, ever Troy's knight.

Troy slowed the motorcycle, drew shadows close, and muttered a monarch-level obfuscation spell as Darius pulled up alongside us.

"Status," Troy said when the spell had blanketed us.

"We'll have to ditch the bikes and go in on foot." Darius pulled off his helmet. "The patch for the West Coast hack came through a mile back. It sounds like the mazed Sons succeeded at pulling attention closer to the targets. Civilians are clear and all decoys are dead. One succeeded in causing damage to a perimeter fence. Now the mundanes are deploying military to the entire square mile surrounding the White House, down to Constitution Ave on this side, in case there are copycats or follow-up attacks."

Troy asked, "That includes our staging area?"

"Yes, sir," Darius said.

"Fine. We get as close as is reasonable and then go the rest of the way on foot."

We got as far as the Smithsonian before we had to abandon the bikes. The two elves checked their gear and weapons—light body armor on both of them; longknife, handguns, and grenades on Troy; an assault rifle and longknife for Darius—so I did the same with my armor, knives, and Ruger. I felt silly and unskilled in my slower evaluation, but Troy nodded his approval.

Remember, Arden, he sent as we stalked closer to the Old Post Office, *Dari and I are here to cover you. You push forward and up, no matter what happens to us.*

Understood.

He shot me the look that said he heard my lack of complete agreement and didn't like it, but he didn't say anything else, keeping his focus on the buildings around us and the patrolling police and soldiers. His spells should cover us, but I wasn't an elf. I didn't have their silence in movement or their decades of training. Any misstep on my part might draw attention that could make a trained mundane look just close enough to see something off and come investigate.

It took a nerve-wracking ten minutes to make it to the building. It had been redeveloped into a hotel and was, like everything in the area, locked down. That didn't mean much to a pair of Darkwatch elves though, and we got in easily enough via the south entrance conveniently marked Museum & Clock Tower. I hoped using a spark to make the camera blip while they mazed the guards and opened the door would be missed; blowing the whole camera would tip someone off. Another one in the area might see us—the IRS building was across the plaza—but I was hoping the chaos the Ebon Guard and the Darkwatch were introducing to the government systems meant nobody would be watching those too closely.

My heart thundered as we made our way down a hallway with stone flooring, past a gift shop and some educational displays. Troy and Darius took out security guards and service staff in complete silence, leaving unconscious and mazed mundanes secured with their own handcuffs or with zip ties the elves carried and hiding them as well as they could. I followed Troy's instructions and kept moving forward, trying to keep my steps silent and sweeping ahead for more humans with my elemental senses.

We made it to the first elevator without incident.

I ran through breathing exercises as we went up that one then the second, knowing that our activation of them was probably setting off alarms somewhere and too keyed-up to really take in the opulence of the hotel below.

Troy and Darius burst out of the elevator with knives drawn the moment the doors opened.

Clear, Troy sent. *Come out but give us a moment to sweep.*

I did as he said and used Air to block the doors open. They had to know we were here, so holding the elevator couldn't do any more damage, and it might save us from having people come up behind us. If we were lucky it'd be taken as a malfunction.

All clear, Troy sent. *Get it done.*

I hurried to the western side of the tower, glancing at the helpful placard noting all the landmarks. Between the darkness, my storm, and the distorting effect of the flashing red-and-blue lights of law enforcement vehicles, it was difficult to make out my target, but I found it.

"I thought the White House would be bigger," I muttered, having first mistaken the Treasury building for it.

"Get going, Arden," Troy snapped. "We'll hold the stairs."

"Do we have confirmation on the President and VP's location?" I asked.

Darius spoke into his mic in elvish then nodded. "Confirmed in the White House. They just wrapped up a news piece ten minutes ago."

"Is Jo there?"

Another exchange. "No."

Good. This would be a decisive strike. I hated that journalists would be caught up in it, but I had to take this building.

Now that I had a sense of the location and size of my target, I closed my eyes for focus.

The pain I'd felt at the destruction of the Eno and my home, and rage that'd been simmering in me with it, bubbled and roiled to the surface. I drank it in, letting it fill the cracks of doubt and the crevices of fear, and pulled deeper on my magic than I had in the Duat.

Lightning built. I poured Air and Fire into it, pushing it bigger and bigger still, then unleashed it with such force that something exploded and car alarms started going off as streetlights overloaded and blew. When I opened my eyes, a fire burned in the distance, right where I needed it to.

It was a start. I was still too wrathful to feel anything else about it.

With quick steps, I hustled to the east side of the tower. The Capitol stood in plain view down Pennsylvania Ave, an even easier target than the White House. Rage still burned hot in me and, with it, the lightning. I pulled down more strikes, each one accompanied by simultaneous thunder and hitting like a bomb.

With lightning as the match, I poured all my rage into the fires it had sparked until both buildings were engulfed in twin infernos. Those blazes I stoked even higher until the entirety of the structures were ravaged by fire. Even then, I kept going, until the stone itself tumbled in huge, broken pieces and started melting. When the flames were so high they consumed even the sky, I rent the earth, cracking it open like an egg, destroying any underground structures and toppling everything left standing so that nothing could be rebuilt on these spots.

I stood there, still shaking with enraged pain, as I surveyed my work.

This wouldn't bring back Eno as it had been. It wouldn't rebuild my home. It might not even keep me safe.

But it would send a powerful fucking message: Otherside could have struck like this at any time. We could strike again. The fact that we didn't wasn't because we couldn't. It was because I'd meant what I said about wanting to live and let live. I'd meant what I said about wanting to build a new world where Othersiders no longer had to hide or face being hunted.

And for wanting a secure, authentic, honest place in the world, my people had been hurt. Our supporters among the mundanes too. We had lost lives. Homes. Businesses. That was not a world I wanted to live in, let alone one that I was going to bring up my children in or ask anyone else to. I had the power to change it, so I would.

There was more than one way to remake the world. I didn't have to destroy all of it, like the gods of the hunt had wanted. No Great Flood was needed here. I just needed to take care of this little corner. This human government was now shattered. The country's imperialistic, racist, hegemonic, extractive capitalist dominance over the world would be too...with one more strike.

"Let's get out of here. I need you to take me to the Pentagon," I said to Troy.

He didn't answer.

When I turned to look at him, he and Darius had completely turned away from the stairs they were supposed to be guarding and were staring at the ruins I'd made of a government. The fires were spreading even in the rain, the earth rumbled with aftershocks that pulled down more of the surrounding buildings, and first responders were joining law enforcement in a cacophony of sirens. It was complete chaos below, which was probably the only reason nobody had come to check out why an elevator was stalled at a hotel.

"Troy." My heart clenched when he didn't pull his eyes away from the destruction.

Was this finally too much for him? He and other elves had...not quite hinted but definitely given the impression that the elves had some pretty bad stories about primordial elementals. His own father had accused me of essentially being a step away from destroying everything at any given moment. Now I'd pulled down two big, historic buildings, the executive and legislative seats of power for one of the most powerful nations in the world, and effectively crippled the federal government. Even if I hadn't taken out the whole chain of succession, the government had been divided enough along partisan lines that it'd barely been functional as it was.

When Troy dragged his gaze away from the destruction, he took me in from head to toe and back up. Then he smiled, cold and dark, the predator in him brought fully and unapologetically to the surface.

"Arden," he said, "you've just won us the war in a single strike."

"Not quite." I shuddered with relief. He wouldn't reject me. I'd grown enough that I was willing to step into my own fullness, come whatever may, but having him at my side would take it to the next level. "The Pentagon. We have to knock out the seat of their military power. The repercussions will be global. The humans might fear us enough to try dropping a nuclear bomb on Durham, but there will be too much disarray for them to focus on anything but their own populations."

"Especially if the rest of Otherside makes similar moves at the state and local level, and internationally," Troy said. "We've already seen that they'll follow your lead. Make a public statement that we'll negotiate but that it will be done fairly if they don't want more of *this*."

A twitch in reality pulled me around.

Rage stepped from a portal, surveying my work with more solemnity than he'd had the last time I'd seen him.

I glared at him. Now was not the time for games. I had a mission to finish.

Troy and Darius snarled, both with sharp teeth dropped, and took up defensive positions in front of and behind me, ready to fight a celestial if it meant finishing our mission.

"Hold!" I said. "I know him."

Rage gave me the same up-and-down evaluation Troy had but with less sexual interest and more potential for violence. "Welcome to the Court of Nightmares, Arden Finch Solari," he said with a cold smile. "I abdicate my position and bequeath it unto you—along with my immortality."

"What?" I darted backward so fast I bumped into Darius. "No. I don't want it if—"

"Any benefits you receive, your Hunter will as well," Rage said, anticipating my objection. "You've been bonded tightly enough for long enough."

I swallowed hard. Mission or not, this was important. This was my greater good. "Could we still have children?"

That was a big part of why we were doing all this. If we couldn't, there was no point.

Well. There was; it just wouldn't be the point we'd started this war with, and we'd been fighting so hard for it that something in me might break.

"Yes, but only through the natural span in which you would have without the gift." Rage glanced at Troy, who was still standing in a guard position in front of me. "Your Hunter would also be buffered against the effects of crossing the Veil. Convenient that you're so tightly bound."

So many gifts. All it had cost me was my soul and the last vestiges of my ability to think I was a good person. Good people didn't willfully take steps that would harm so many others. They didn't—

Stop that, Arden, Troy sent. *Good people take only the steps necessary to protect the ones they're responsible for. You tried everything not to get to this point. You took steps to avoid collateral casualties. In return, the mundanes burned our home. This is how a leader of Otherside responds to an existential threat from a strong enemy.*

I took a shuddering breath. He was right.

Anything I take on, you take as well, I sent, pivoting to the more immediately impactful issue. *Do you want immortality?*

Warmth curled through the bond, and Troy lowered his longknife then reached back and took my hand while still keeping a watchful eye on Rage. *An eternity with you? Don't threaten me with a good time, cariñamí.*

"Well?" Rage grinned maliciously. "I could force the issue."

I stiffened and pulled a primordial ball to my free hand. Nobody would force me or Troy on anything, gifts or otherwise. Both of us had had more than enough of that in our lives.

"You could try," I said. "Then I could unmake you."

Rage deflated. "I *could*. But I'm tired and want to die. There hasn't been a candidate in far too long, and if I kill you now, it might be another millennia or more before someone else comes along for my role."

"Again," I said. "I could simply unmake you if you want death that badly. I know the secret of it."

That got me a feral grin from the celestial. "Oh you could, most certainly. I know better than most that Harqil has been a busy wretch. I know what they taught you. But you know as well as any of us that Otherside abhors a vacuum. If I'm destroyed before passing on my cursed gift, someone else will be found." His grin shifted from a wild, I-dare-you kind of look to an outright malicious one as he glanced between me and Troy. "Haven't you learned by now, Arden Finch Solari? You can claim what Fate has ordained, or you can suffer the consequences of turning from your path."

I resisted the flinch that rose in me and studied him, seeing my future or what a version of it could be. So consumed by my own rage that after ages I was spent and just wanted everything to end. I believed him. Otherside abhorred a vacuum and always had. But if I was going to claim this power, I needed it to be for more than power's sake.

"What did you fight for?" I asked, reining in my rising sense of impatience. "In the beginning."

"First, a loss. Then the joy of it." Rage shrugged. "The power. That's the nature of nightmares as dreams and Nightmares as entities. Our power stems from its source. The more of it there is in the world, the more powerful we become as celestials." He cocked an eyebrow. "Watch out for Shame. He's gained a foothold since these Christians have taken this land. And Despair, with this economic system, this capitalism. Terror loves social media—so many horrible things spread in an instant. You'll need to find your own source to work with, but with what you've done here, there should be plenty to fuel you."

I set those comments aside. My rage was and always had been fueled by injustice. If there was none, I had no need for the power. I had my core values and my personal mission.

And just like I couldn't wait for someone else to make the world safe enough for me and Troy to start a family, I wouldn't allow someone else's misguided feelings of rage to dictate the world we built from here on out.

"I accept," I said. "On one condition. You portal me and my elves directly to a location of my choosing."

"You accept the burden of a place on the Court of Nightmares for so small a price? A mere portal?" Rage asked.

Troy and Darius were silent and still as I considered that, neither of them hinting by posture, movement or thought that they had a feeling one way or another.

I was High Queen here and I would have final say.

Lifting my chin and chilling my attitude, I said, "That you reckon it small speaks to how out of touch you are. This will have unimaginable consequences. Thousands, maybe millions, will be harmed by what I propose to do in service to Otherside and my own rage at the loss of my home. I accept that burden. I will be their villain. But it's only because I've been cast in that role for so long that I might as well make something of it. I work from the shadows. And sometimes those shadows have to eclipse the light, as is the nature of Otherside."

Rage shuddered. "I feel the truth and the power of your words, and the burden of what you propose to take on rides with them. So be it—and may you be a more worthy representative of the Court than I ever was. Agreed."

"Passage by portal to the place the mundanes call The Pentagon, for myself and these two elves," I said quickly. "Directly and with no harm to body, heart, mind, soul, or magic to any here. Agreed."

That got me a quirky grin that was almost fond from Rage. "You'll be a force one day, Arden Finch Solari."

The fires and emergency lights illuminating Washington, DC flared then blurred and dimmed as a portal opened and we stepped through.

Chapter 29

Rage brought us out in what must have been the air traffic control tower at Reagan National Airport.

"You seem to prefer high vantage points," he said.

The rest of us spun, trying to orient ourselves. The space was empty except for a single unconscious air traffic controller slumped in his chair.

"A parting gift," Rage said when I noticed him.

I looked out the windows, turning until I spotted the Pentagon to the north and slightly west. "The deal is done."

"The deal is done." Rage grinned, as irreverent as ever. "Now a word to the wise: Immortal simply means you will not die of old age. You can still be hurt, lose limbs, all of that. As you killed Callista, so can you be killed. It's not a get out of jail free card. It's just time to grow into the role and the power that comes with it."

Before Troy or I could react, Rage pressed his hand against my sternum. A crushing magical force hit me harder than any blow.

Everything went black.

I woke to Darius patting my cheek.

"—up, Arden," he was saying. "Come on, Troy needs you to wake up."

With a jolt and a gasp that hurt, I came back to myself, feeling more alive than I ever had. "What—"

Beside me, Troy groaned, twitching.

He was laid out flat on his back, taken down by what had to be Rage's transfer of celestial power as much as I had been.

"Cariñomí?" I rasped.

Troy grunted. Forced himself to roll to his stomach and push up to all fours. Shook his head with eyes squeezed shut.

A sensation of discomfort reverberated through the bond, but it was fading fast.

"Arden!" Darius snapped. His Knight of Monteague voice, not the more timid tones he usually took with me. "Get up!"

My lips peeled back in a snarl as I did so, glaring at him.

Darius rose with me but stayed crouched in a defensive posture close to Troy. "Keep your mate safe. Finish this."

I shuddered with the force of the rage that crested in me at that. The idea that anyone would dare threaten my mate had me ready to remake the world in its entirety.

Troy got to his feet with an effort. "Not the whole world, cariñamí. Just that building."

He pointed at the Pentagon.

Oh, hell yeah. The Predator drone that'd made the first attempt at my house would have had its orders from here if the Joint Chiefs had been involved.

I took a breath, steadying and focusing myself. The goal was justice, not indiscriminate carnage. I would not be what the old Rage had become.

With a burst of Air, I blew all the windows in the tower outward in a crystalline shower of glittering glass. Wind whipped in as the glass fell away, caressing me, embracing me, and fueling my rage. It slithered through me now, warming me and twining through my soul in a way it never had before.

It felt *good*.

The broken windows brought new sounds: more damn fighter jets.

I laughed, feeling the wildness in the sound as it left my throat. The jets were toys against the power burning in me now. I was the worst nightmare of every being on this plane come true, immortal and in the flesh.

I'd been more than enough in my existing roles.

As Rage of the Nightmare Court?

I laughed again with the joy of fury.

The storm still boiling over DC was easy enough to pull this way, although doing so with this relative quickness built it into something more akin to a hurricane, slower-moving than a tornado but with sustained winds and lightning that not even a fighter jet could fly through safely. Radios in the tower crackled and screamed with calls from various pilots.

"Tell them to land," I said coldly.

These particular individuals hadn't necessarily been against me, even if they fought for the wrong side. There was a chance they could learn.

If not, they could be unmade. It would be their choice.

Darius moved to the still-unconscious air traffic controller and took his headset. "All aircraft, be advised. Immediate grounding is in effect. I repeat, immediate grounding. All aircraft are under a ground stop."

I kept my focus on the Pentagon, building the storm.

Troy came up behind me, his arms sliding around me in a supportive embrace. *Take them, Arden. An eye for an eye and blood for blood. I'll stand with you against the Grand Conclave. And anyone else.*

I struck.

Bolt after lightning bolt crashed down. The earth rumbled with the tectonic shift that I forced and lava boiled in the cracks. These motherfuckers had advised and actioned the destruction of my mate, my home, myself, and my people—all of Otherside. Everything I held dear. More than any other branch, they had the resources to accomplish it. Always had; the military took a disproportionate amount of this country's budget. There was always money for war and killing, but somehow never enough to help people. Never enough to feed them, house them, educate them, provide opportunity for them—unless they fed their bodies and futures to this machine.

It infuriated me.

I'd show them war. And maybe afterward, we could focus on helping people in ways that didn't involve killing others.

In moments, the Pentagon had been shattered, pulled to the ground and consumed.

For the first time, I wasn't tired when I released my magic.

All magic had a price, always...but this time, the price would be the weight of my own conscience.

I wouldn't lose that. I couldn't, or I wouldn't believe myself fit to lead. With great power came all the responsibility in the world, and I'd be better than my predecessors. I'd be better than the elven legends of the primordials who came before.

For once in my life, this definition of better didn't require me to be less. It required something harder: for me to embrace and embody my fullest, biggest, most powerful self...without trampling those with less power.

I closed my eyes and let Troy take my weight. Not because I needed him to, but because I wouldn't do this alone.

"It's done," I said. "An eye for an eye and blood for blood, by the rule of three. Get us to safety. Then we negotiate."

Even without being able to see him, I sensed Darius relax.

"Yes, my queen." Troy squeezed me and kissed my temple. *And long may you reign.*

Darius called in for transportation as we hurried back down to ground level. "This is Eagle, requesting extraction. I have Bull and Kestrel with me. We're at target three."

I couldn't hear the response, but from the way Darius stiffened, it might have been Sonia who picked up the call.

"Copy, Red Fox," Darius said, confirming it. "Making our way to extraction point."

"How far?" Troy asked.

"Two miles west."

"Arden, are you up for that? We'll need to run hard."

I started running as soon as we hit the tarmac. "I got this."

Troy didn't question me, just fell in behind me as Darius took the lead. The pace they set was faster than the training jogs Troy had me do to keep up my condition, but I was still riding the high of using so much of my magic.

I'd crash later. For now, I had to escape.

"Get us home," I said. "I need to see what they've done to my land."

And then I'd need to do something about it.

△▽△▽

Seeing the desecration of my land was almost as bad as feeling it burn.

Blackened, barren sticks and stumps were all that remained of the forest. My car was a twisted husk that was barely recognizable as having been a vehicle. A scorched foundation marked where my house had stood, and nothing else.

The destruction stretched for miles.

I stood in the ashes and let the tears fall. Any last shred of guilt, shame, or doubt for what I'd done in Washington, DC disappeared, consumed by the rage in my heart. It wasn't just the loss of my home and all the memories made in it. It was that the whole forest and all the beings in it—plant, animal, and otherwise—had been victim to the mundanes.

When I reached for the land with elemental senses, I hissed in pain. Fire might be a natural part of life, but this had been unnatural in occurrence and nature. Set and enhanced by chemical accelerants past what this area would naturally be able to bear. Left on its own, it would grow back...eventually. In a few centuries maybe. For now, the entire area was changed for the worse. Even the river was choked with sludge, ash, and dead animals who hadn't managed to flee.

I dropped to my knees, feeling sick, and dug my fingers past the thick layer of ash to try finding what remained of the scorched soil beneath.

"We'll rebuild it, cariñamí." Troy's pain, both at my own and at the loss of what he'd finally accepted was his home, made his voice tight. "I promise."

"I don't want to rebuild it," I whispered after a few heartbeats.

That house, that *life* was gone. As much as what had happened here had broken my heart, I'd outgrown it. I had to step into what was now mine. That was the only way I could make this hurt less. For that to happen, I'd have to restore the forest first, but that was within my power now.

So much was within my power now.

But only if I embraced it. All of it. And stopped trying to hide or be small in any way.

I looked up at Troy. "I want six bedrooms."

He went very still. "Six?"

"Yes. A big one for us with an ensuite bathroom and two walk-in closets, so you have room for all your gear. A smaller one for guests. And two more in pairs with their own ensuites between them." I fixed him with a look. "For the kids."

"The kids." Troy went to a knee beside me, his expression as intent as mine. *You'd let me sire four with you?*

I know elves usually stop at two, but I figure we can see about getting one of each element. If you're in agreement, I mean.

He kept staring for another moment. Then it was like the sun had come out after a hurricane as pure joy lit him. The sense in the bond said that I'd just made every sacrifice he'd ever made worth it as he dragged me to him in a hug so tight I lost my breath for a moment.

When I got it back, I added, "We're gonna need a bigger kitchen too, whatever you want. More counter space at least, since I know that drove you nuts before. And a library. And a dining room big enough to host the parliament, three from each faction." I squeezed Troy's arms. "House Solari is ascendant. I want us to look the part. Or rather, to live it."

Because playing small and hiding all that I was had never gotten me anywhere but my personal hell, or anything but a war. It was time to try something else—and to reward Troy for his faith in me. In us. We'd come into this with different ideas of what home and family meant, but this year had shown me where they were growing together. Just like we would.

Hell, it was time to reward myself as well.

Not only that, but to provide the same haven I wanted for myself for my people.

Before I could tell someone to get the mayor of Durham on the phone to negotiate what that could look like, another car pulled up what remained of the driveway. Omar's, with a tense-looking Allegra in the passenger seat. Other cars were behind him: Cyrus, Etain with Haroun—hell, half the Ebon Guard and what I assumed were a good number of the Darkwatch.

Troy immediately rose and put himself between me and the approaching vehicles. Darius shifted back a step to my side. I stayed where I was, kneeling in the ash, too tired of death and destruction for whatever showdown was about to happen to do more than sigh heavily.

Omar parked and stepped from his car with the gravity of a royal, staying behind the door of the car like it was a shield. "Enough, son. It's time to end this."

"So, it is a coup, then?" Troy asked coldly. His hand dropped to his longknife.

"Of course not," Omar said as more elves emerged from their cars and Allegra jumped from his to stand next to Etain. "You can still be king. But Arden has proven herself to be what we always knew primordials would become: too dangerous to live. Finish this."

"I wouldn't," Cyrus said lightly as he came closer, halting in place at Troy's warning growl.

Omar glanced at Cyrus. "Is this about the bond? I thought you said it was nonsense."

Cyrus didn't bat an eye as he leaned on his cane and shrugged. "Nonsense or not, there's something bigger in play now."

"I don't have time for this. Troy—"

"Yes. Troy," Cyrus said. "We both failed him. I wasn't here. You gave him the skills he needed to survive. But he had to learn love by himself. With her. I see the truth of it now. You want the elves secured, Omar. Right?"

The Captain nodded tightly. "That's all I've ever wanted. Maybe not with the matriarchy as it was, given that they were driving the faction into the ground. But that does not mean we can risk a primordial elemental."

I took a breath as all my anger at the state of my land found a new target. It would be so easy to unmake Omar and any of the elves that stood with him.

With an effort, I swallowed it down. I'd destroyed enough.

Etain, Haroun, and a few more of the Ebon Guard fanned out in positions that would defend me. Allegra took the opportunity to join Darius on my other side, a clear statement of support that made her father's expression darken. Omar's Darkwatch elves shifted position to oppose mine.

Was this the consequence Harqil had spoken about?

For fuck's sake, we could not have a civil war. Not at all and not in the ashes of my home.

The angel phased in, probably drawn by my focused thought, and nodded sadly when I caught their eye.

Fucking consequences.

Cyrus tilted his head and gave one of his mischievous grins. "I say we can't *not* risk a primordial. Not with what she's just set in motion."

"You Ebon Guard—" Omar clenched his jaw shut, like he was well aware that his people were surrounded by the Guard and it was probably unwise to say something uncomplimentary. He looked around before finally settling on Pascale and making a hand gesture.

One that I recognized: attack.

Pascale sprang into action—but even as Troy was preparing to meet her and I was pulling on Air to grab her, she planted her feet, dropped to her knees, and pressed her forehead into the dirt. "I yield!"

The other Darkwatch froze in their own moves to attack.

Troy's fury lashed me in the bond, feeding my own, as he glared down at her with longknife drawn and ready to kill. "A shadow second?"

"You were clearly determined to be a disappointment." Omar glared daggers at Pascale. "She had promise. Or so I thought."

I blinked fast, stunned as I processed what this meant. Someone in my guard had been a traitor. Not just anyone but Pascale, who'd adopted into House Solari. I thought she'd believed in me and in what we were trying to do, but it'd been a ploy. She might have come around to my side or been playing Omar from the start. I didn't know. But she hadn't confided in me or Troy, so I had to assume that this was for her interests, not mine or the House's.

My head spun and my chest tightened. Whatever this was, it was too much.

I embraced all of the elements, drawing a primordial ball to my hands.

"Back off!" Troy roared at elves now scrambling for weapons. "All of you, stand down."

The clearing stank of burnt marshmallow, but everyone obeyed. Even Omar, who watched with a look that said he knew his death was coming but he'd go feeling vindicated.

Slowly, Troy knelt in front of me, dangerously close to the ball floating between my palms, his hands hovering over my arms but not touching me. "Remember the Wild Hunt? What I said when the godblade took you?"

I flashed back to the gritty street in a wrecked downtown Durham, the fingers of one of my hands threaded through his hair to pull his head back and expose his throat, my fist holding Neith's gift to it as the godblade whispered for his death. Troy had been willing to let me kill him if that was what I'd needed to come back to myself.

He loved me that much.

Love twined with the rage in me. From my own heart, not Troy, but sending tendrils through me all the same. Giving me room to breathe and to see past the reflexive urge to defend myself.

I had no land left. Everything that was mine was gone.

But I still had Troy, and I had hope.

I didn't have to destroy anything more. Not even these threats.

"Oh, now that's clever," Harqil said, phasing in fully. "She's shackled rage with love."

"What does that mean?" Cyrus asked, not sounding surprised in the slightest at the angel's appearance.

"That she might not end the world after all, thanks to your son," they said. "Today, at least."

No. I wouldn't.

Fuck calling the mayor to make a deal. I'd create my own world, on my own, and let those who wanted to live within it peacefully do so. I'd prove to these elves and everyone else that their bullshit propaganda about primordials only being able to destroy was dead wrong.

With a scream of frustration, I slammed my hands on the ground and dug deep, pouring everything I was feeling into fueling my magic.

Into setting things right.

Cries and shouts rang out around me as I not only reset the land but used the raw potential of char and death to enhance it. An old-growth forest rose from the burn-scarred earth, surrounding a clearing large enough to hold the house I'd described earlier. I couldn't bring back the animals or any people who had died. I couldn't bring back houses or structures. There was no going back.

But I could do this. I could create potential and make space for something new.

When a half mile of forest had grown and was still spreading with smaller, younger trees at the edges, I followed the bond back to my sense of self.

By now, it was all quiet.

Even Troy and Harqil stood in stunned silence, staring at the towering pines and hardwoods interspersed with a wild variety of native shrubs, vines, and flowers.

I pushed to my feet and slid past Troy, advancing on Omar while wreathed in shadowfire.

The Captain froze when I pointed a finger in his face.

"You keep your life today, Omar," I snarled. "I'm tired of killing. I'm tired of death and destruction. Once upon a time, the elementals destroyed Atlantis. You've held it against us ever since. In upholding these bullshit stories, you've helped the elementals be hunted almost to extinction—and that means you're equally as culpable as the mundanes in the state of the earth right now."

I threw my hands in the air to make a gesture encompassing what I'd just created.

"We could have *this* instead," I said. "We could raise children and grandchildren with harmony and balance between ourselves, our factions, and the earth itself. But *you* won't see it. Because you'll be imprisoned. For life."

Troy, who'd followed, held out a hand. "Surrender, Omar. And be glad she's giving the orders. We can't risk sending you out on exile, and a betrayal like this is still a death sentence in my book."

Omar glared, letting his teeth flicker in a threat display as he locked eyes with Troy. "*You're* the one betraying everything."

"I'm restoring the balance we once had. The one that lets us keep magic." Troy's voice was as icy as the burst of his power signature as he pulled on Aether and tightened his grip on his longknife. The blade sparked blue with the protective spells my mother had laid on it decades ago, fueled by Troy's rage. "Give up, Omar. Don't make me kill you."

Tension stretched. Neither the Darkwatch nor the Ebon Guard moved. I stayed where I was, not wanting to set either man off.

"This is what has to happen," Troy said. Aether built in him, rising to the level it had when he'd used the mass-suicide spell. "What *will* happen, or so help me I'll unleash hell on every traitor here."

With a shuddering breath, Omar looked at the elves who'd followed him then dropped his eyes, drew his longknife, and handed it to Troy before digging in a pocket for a lead-and-silver cuff to put on his own wrist.

"I accept the judgment," he said in a rough voice. "I only ask that you spare the Darkwatch here. They followed orders. Nothing more."

The bond twisted with a blend of triumph and disappointment as Troy looked at each of the Darkwatch elves who'd come with Omar. "We'll let a trial decide that. *After* this Twilight War is over," he replied harshly. "Until then, all Darkwatch here go into holding. Pascale as well."

I glared at them all as they dropped weapons and allowed the grim-looking Ebon Guard to take them into custody. Pascale tried to catch my eye, but I looked away, too sickened by her betrayal to be sure of my control if I had to look at her.

"Well. That was certainly exciting," Cyrus said.

"Shut up, Cyrus," Troy snapped. "And be glad you still owe us twice more, or you'd be going back to prison with them. If I didn't need you influencing mundane politicians, I'd send you anyway."

As the elves sorted themselves out, I wandered away, trying to get a feel for the land and forest that was now mine more than ever.

"This wasn't quite what I was expecting to happen when I said there'd be consequences," Harqil said from beside me. "You're an exciting one to serve."

"You don't serve me," I said tiredly. "You're free to do what you want."

"On the contrary. An angel must give service. It's in our nature. And you just happen to have reached the tier that allows me to formally do so."

I stopped to look at them. "Is *that* why you've done all of this? The warnings, the intercessions? Picking my side?"

Their grin was more than a little feral. "Of course. I grew tired of being passed from god to god. Rage was the one who suggested this path to begin with, decades ago. I watched how you dealt with your little king and decided service to you would be the closest I'd find to being my own master." They spread their hands. "So, here I am."

"As long as we understand each other." I wasn't in the mood to argue with them. "We need peace now, Harqil. If it pleases you to serve as a messenger, can you help me bring about that minor miracle?"

"That would please me greatly," Harqil said. "Though not half so much as being asked whether it does so to begin with. This is going to be a beautiful partnership, Arden."

I certainly hoped so, because the number of enemies I'd made this week was going to take celestial intervention to manage.

Chapter 30

A forest popping out of nowhere would have made news on its own, if the helicopters overhead were any indication. I wanted to solidify it though. Make sure that people knew who and what they were dealing with. Whether they saw me as friend or foe was out of my control. I could only be myself, do what I thought was right, and say what was in my heart.

Jo had been rescued from DC but hadn't made it home yet, so I stared into the camera Etain pointed at me, Troy at my side, resolved to do just that.

"My enemies sought to destroy me by destroying the land I depend on," I said, still covered in the ash and soot that evidenced that destruction. "But I can create as well as destroy. I *prefer* to create. It's in my essential nature: not only to create but to protect, to nurture potential." Even as I said the words, I knew they were true. I'd never reflected on the inherent nature of elementals before, but Harqil's statement about the nature of angels had sparked the idea in me. "The destruction I caused elsewhere will have far-reaching consequences. It may have been in accordance with Otherside justice—an eye for an eye and blood for blood, by the rule of three—but many others were and will be hurt. I apologize for that and have instructed my people to assist with community efforts in territories that acknowledge me as Arbiter."

I paused, looking up at Troy. *Still with me?*

Always and ever.

Looking back at the camera, I said, "Any and all who seek peace with Otherside—with *my* factions of Otherside—whether mundane or supernatural, may join me and my king in the Triangle for negotiations at the next full moon."

I nodded at Etain and she cut the video. I slumped, feeling more drained by the need to do yet more politicking than anything else. That timeframe was just under two weeks out, but I'd run everyone around me ragged. Hell, *I* needed rest too, before I got as exhausted as I was when we were getting magic back.

I also needed to assess the needs of my people and theirs. If I was going to speak for anyone other than myself, I needed to make myself available to be heard. I'd just carried out the actions of the world's most powerful tyrant. Building a safer future meant showing, not just telling, that I would step back from wholesale destruction and power grabs. The mundanes still might never find a way to trust me, but Othersiders would. Or could.

I hoped.

Aside from all that, I had to at least try to make ties to my own local community, the city of Durham. With Othersiders and mundanes alike. At the very least, I had to open a door. Hopefully a commitment to devote resources to rebuilding the area affected by the fire and donating money and time to people impacted by my attack against the government would show that I meant what I said about creating, protecting, and nurturing potential. I'd partially destroyed and helped rebuild Durham once before, but I'd been much weaker then and nobody had really known what I was capable of—not even me.

Now?

Now it was fear that kept the National Guard or whoever else from being ordered to this spot.

I was a Nightmare now. I supposed I should get used to it.

"Anchor," Troy murmured. He leaned in to kiss me before taking a step toward the waiting elves. "I don't like where your thoughts are going, but I know you need to muddle through that on your own. I'll get orders in motion."

"And then summon the parliament to the Solari mansion or get them prepped for a video call," I said. "I want to know how everyone is doing and make sure we're not going to have local problems."

Probably should have thought of that before issuing invitations but whatever.

Troy nodded and made a quick fist-to-heart salute before turning and hollering for the remaining elves to gather.

I dropped to the ground where I was, despite the dirt and ash, and reached for the elements. They all came easier now than ever, even Water. Like in accepting my full power and everything that came with it, I'd broken down the psychological barriers that were stopping me from engaging fully with my own magic.

Imagine that.

My land felt different now. That much fire had cleansed it in the worst way, stripping it almost as thoroughly as salt would. These new trees and plants had sprung up from the seeds that had escaped destruction somehow, under ash or carried in by the wind afterward. In a rare few cases, the roots of older trees had survived and put up new growth.

I let go of all my shields and walls, trusting Troy to wall himself out, and reached for everything. With Earth, I tasted the nutrient balance and shifted it where necessary. With Water, I traced the roots and found them thirsty, so I summoned a light rain that would make all of the elves miserable but help these plants establish themselves. And with Air, I sought out breezes that would soothe me and bring in more seeds. More potential. Fire had already been overused here, and the land was still wary of it, so all I did was check that there weren't any lingering embers waiting to burst alight.

The land felt...better. Not good, not yet, but soothed. An undercurrent of betrayal I hadn't noticed at first—that I hadn't been present to defend it—crested, bold and angry to match what simmered in my own heart.

I fell deeper into the connection, sharing of myself. Not making excuses but reaching for a sense of something like a migrating bird. I would be here, in seasons. And in some seasons, I would need to be elsewhere. But in all seasons, this was my home. I was nourished and nurtured and offered the same in turn. I was the land, and the land was me. Not only the land but the sky and waters and the heat of the sun that warmed all.

Slowly, the forest settled itself.

I fully intended to build a new house here, but now was not the time to discuss it with this place. The land and its spirits might accept that I would need to be away from time to time, but it still held me responsible for not stopping the pain of burning.

Tears warmed my closed eyes as I accepted that. As with Troy, it had never been my intent to cause hurt or harm. But my presence was a magnet for it in some ways. The strong and the righteous always drew those who were threatened by such.

"Arden?"

At Troy's call, I sent a last pulse of apology and love to the land and spirits before pulling back into myself with an effort.

He was crouched in front of me, walls still up high and tight in the bond so as not to fall into the work I was doing with the land. "Is everything okay, cariñamí?"

I stared at him, taken as ever by the pretty gold flecks in his eyes and the quiet strength of his presence.

Troy brushed tears from my cheeks with a thumb. "It's not okay now. But you're committed to making it so."

Too choked up to speak, I nodded.

"Can I hug you?"

That made the tears fall faster. I threw myself into his arms, a fall more than anything else, and he sat back and pulled me close.

Which, of course, only dragged something like a sob from me, a noise I tried my best to strangle. I was still a High Queen, and there were still elves in the area. Fewer than before with those taken to holding to await trial, but members of my Ebon Guard were here and watching.

"It's okay to mourn," Troy said, holding me tight and rocking. "You can build something new. But it doesn't all have to be silver linings. You're allowed to just be sad for what is gone and will never be again. And it's allowed to be now, in the moment. Not just when you're alone." His hand rubbed along my spine. "Remember what Quinlan said? You *can* do this alone. But you shouldn't have to. And you don't. We're all here. We're all in pain with you. We all mourn with you and honor your loss."

"Her loss and her vulnerability," Darius said from nearby, sounding as choked by grief as I felt. "Long live the High Queen."

"Long live the High Queen," others of the Ebon Guard echoed, in voices as tight and emotional as I felt.

"Long live the High Queen, and long may she reign," Rio said in a quiet voice.

The emotion in them was palpable. Maybe it was Troy's amplified passive power. Maybe it was my newfound strength. Maybe it was both of those and a magic of collective pain.

All I knew was I'd never had this before from anyone other than Troy. I'd never had space to be held in community with my feelings witnessed and validated. I drank it in like parched earth and fed it into the land, balancing the hate that had accompanied its burning with the compassion and hell, even love, that surrounded me now.

Two and a half years ago, I'd been alone. Afraid. Hunted.

But now was not then. And now I could open a new chapter. A better one.

For all of us.

△▽△▽

It took another hour for me to pull myself together and be willing to leave the land that was now at least in a neutral state. I was silent on the whole drive over to the Solari mansion, deep in thoughts that had nothing to do with speaking to the mayor of Durham or the governor of the state about promises or protections, and everything to do with the road that'd brought me here.

When we arrived, I was slightly surprised to find the house bustling with activity. Elves moved and spoke with a level of efficiency that bordered on violence. My newly enhanced senses picked up not only their magic but also whispers of the intent behind it in a way that hadn't happened before. They were furious—but not at me. At how mundanes and other elves had both sought to control me and Troy, if I was correctly reading the waves of energy that momentarily stunned me. Ebon Guard HQ had been relocated and compressed to fit into the dining room and the office Sinclaire had threatened me from before, and however dedicated they'd been in their mission previously, they were fanatical now.

Sinclaire.

The rage flickered in me again.

What is it? Troy sent. His hand drifted to his longknife as his eyes darted, landing on each passing elf in search of a threat.

Darius and Haroun both picked up on Troy's alarm and started doing the same.

"Sinclaire," I said aloud. "Something tells me she survived."

Even as I said it, the Sight kicked me hard in the gut.

"Survived and is plotting." I tilted my head back and closed my eyes, scrambling to do as Harqil had noted and chain rage with love. Going on another rampage would help nothing. I might be the embodiment of Rage now, a member of the Court of Nightmares, but I would not let it lead me to the place it'd taken my predecessor, who didn't even dare take corporeal form. I'd apparently used up all the portals I was allowed at this stage of my development, and I was not about to try that shit again, immortal or not.

Besides, I was only newly immortal and not quite celestial yet. I didn't have an ephemeral form and might never. Certainly not if it meant losing a shot at my own family, not if I had a say in it.

"The Sight?" Troy asked.

"Yes." Still furious in spite of myself, I shook my head, a forceful negation. I would not have Sinclaire waiting in the wings to start a new front in the war. Not after what I'd already done. I'd paid too much to force a peace.

Troy mulled that over, his expression hard, before saying, "Orders?"

Rather than answer him, I grasped my callstone and pushed for a connection. "Duke. I need you and Iaret at my location. Now, please."

The two djinn popped in almost immediately.

"Ishtar fuck me with a spear, Arden," Duke complained, massaging his temples. "You're going to be unbearable to leave a callstone with if you keep growing in power."

Iaret had her eyes squeezed shut and stood stiffly with her fists at her side.

"I'm sorry," I said, immediately swamped with remorse. "I didn't realize it would come through as a compulsion now. Y'all were always free to ignore me before."

"No longer, apparently." Duke reached out to draw Iaret closer and whispered in her ear. Whatever he said must have soothed her because she shuddered and relaxed into his embrace. "Please tell me you've called us here to confirm we can take word to the Council of the immense opportunity now provided by the utter chaos of the situation to the north."

It hadn't even occurred to me to use the djinn in that capacity, which was so gods-damned foolish, given my current rank and power, that I started laughing.

"Has she cracked?" Duke asked, sounding bewildered.

"She's fine." Troy rested a hand on the small of my back.

"I'm good," I said. "Yes, please do tell the Council there's opportunity to be had. But more than that, I need the opportunity of your source in the Bureau. That Nora."

"The vampire?" Duke asked, looking confused.

"*Nora,*" I repeated. "Iaret's human. Not Maria's second. Assuming she's still alive?"

"She lives," Iaret said. Then she grinned wildly. "Does this mean my work mattered?"

"It did indeed," I said, clasping her arm. "Can you influence this Nora to push Sinclaire into the open? Feed the bitch some bad intel? Something?"

Iaret's mood flipped from pained to joyous. "Of course. Whatever you need."

"I need an attack on the negotiations. Or something that's clearly intended to prevent them. Something that can obviously be traced back to Sinclaire," I said. "Something that will show her to be working directly against the goal of peace for everyone else."

Startlement came through the bond the moment before Troy busted out laughing. "Subtle and effective. Making their own blunt instrument twist in their hands when they most need it to obey. I like it."

I couldn't help my own proud grin. "Thank you. In the meantime, we proceed with genuine efforts toward peace and reconciliation. But Sinclaire...her, I will not allow to continue operating."

Living. I wouldn't allow her to continue living. But the elves and the djinn understood both what I was saying and the reason why we couldn't just assassinate her quietly, if their wide, sharp smiles were any indication.

It was damn nice to be understood.

I held on to that thought as I showered and dressed, choosing comfortable leggings and a loose, soft, short-sleeved tunic. There might be loads of people around, but this was my home now, and I'd be comfy in it.

Home.

I rubbed my chest as a pang of loss hit me at the loss of my real home—my *old* home.

Troy, taking his turn in the shower, sent a soothing curl of Aether through the bond but left me to my thoughts and feelings.

A quick dig in the nightstand drawers turned up some incense cones. I grabbed a frankincense-and-myrrh one, set it in the burner on the dresser, and lit it with the fastest hint of Fire before sitting cross-legged on the bed and closing my eyes. I needed to gather myself. We were at an ending but not quite *the end*. What happened next depended on the clarity of my thoughts and intention.

I'd gotten the justice that was mine to have, in full. What remained was to end the Twilight War before it continued spinning out of control—including stopping Sinclaire—and start building the new future.

Including marrying Troy.

That gave me the warm and fuzzies.

A burst of lemon zest pulled my eyes open.

"Iaret," I said, pushing down my irritation about having someone other than Troy in my bedroom. That would be true of me no matter where home happened to be, apparently. "That was fast."

"Something about magic coming back has made it stronger. Like it was refreshed by its absence." She had the distant look that said she was thinking more about magical experiments than the task at hand.

"And Nora?" I prompted gently.

"Oh! Her." Iaret flipped a hand before making it go misty and playing with the rising incense smoke. "She will do as you wish. I even made her think it was her only choice to prevent Sinclaire from seeing that Nora herself is some kind of sensitive."

"What exactly is she going to do?"

Iaret's fire-opal gaze sparked. "Put together a case against Sinclaire on the basis of having worked with the Sons of Seth. The girl has folders upon folders—all handwritten, on paper, since I make every computer assigned to her forget itself—of notes on evidence Sinclaire thought was buried or non-existent."

I blinked. "You...didn't think to mention this earlier?"

"I suppose I forgot." Iaret deflated, looking utterly miserable and half-shifting back to the smokeless fire of her djinn form, before shaking her head aggressively. "In any case, Nora will push Sinclaire into using the Sons again, this time to stop negotiations. Your journalist is in a safehouse covered by Bedoe House Guard, so I suggested Nora set up a meeting in parallel to turn over all the data. It's total chaos up there, nobody will notice."

The mention of chaos brightened Iaret's mood considerably, and she went full djinni.

In the bathroom, the shower stopped.

"Arden, is one of the djinn back already?" Troy called.

"Iaret's here," I replied.

The bathroom door cracked and Troy stuck his head out. "That was unexpectedly fast."

"Turns out she had already been laying extensive groundwork and just needed to confirm the players were in place before getting our go-ahead," I said.

At my positive spin of Iaret's forgetfulness, the fire of her djinni form flared with her pride.

"Just so," she said.

Troy's eyebrows lifted slightly, but he didn't call either of us on the statements, nor did he have any objections when I repeated what Iaret had told me.

"Even better," he said. "Let the mundanes kill their own. Better still would be if we can get Nora installed as the new director, or something almost as senior, and have a plant in the Bureau itself."

I stared at him, somehow not having thought to try that.

He shrugged. "Djinn whispers are more subtle than a mindmaze. A maze only allows for what the caster can imagine. Whispers offer more flexibility. If Iaret has the talent for it and a susceptible mundane, it's a golden opportunity."

At this further acknowledgment of her skills and actions, Iaret flared up again. "I can do it," she said. "Trust me, Arden. And Troy, you too. I—" Her fire contracted again. "I've struggled to rekindle who and what I was before the soul crystal or even to get my mind back. I didn't want to trust elves or anyone other than Duke. But I understand now that I can't be who I was before. Please. Trust me enough to stumble through who I am becoming, and you won't regret it. I swear it."

I looked at Troy, reading his mood in the bond.

"You have our trust, Iaret," Troy said. Then he grinned his shit-eating grin. "You may even have our friendship."

"I don't know about going that far," Iaret said, recoiling. "Next thing you'll want is for me to babysit whatever brats you two are going to whelp."

I laughed at the thread of longing under the disrespectful response. "Let's just start with ending the threat of the Bureau, okay? Babysitting our brats is going to require a whole lot of trust. It's not an honor we'll entrust to just anyone."

"Hmph." Iaret changed planes with a shimmer.

The amusement bubbling in the bond burst from Troy in a chuckle. "Keep that up, and I might have to revise my opinion about your lack of subtlety."

"I've spent long enough with you that I should have learned at least a little," I said. "Get dressed. I want to talk wedding things before the parliament gets here."

Troy rarely let me hurry him into doing anything, but he jumped to obey.

I smiled. There was still a lot of uncertainty. But things would come together.

I wouldn't have it any other way.

Chapter 31

If this was any other situation, we could have simply assassinated Sinclaire and disposed of the Sons of Seth with her, even if I'd been reluctant to take steps like that in the past. Now my home was gone. My reluctance—my efforts to take the high road, turn the other cheek, and be the bigger person—had cost me far too much for me to make any further concessions.

I'd still rein in the desire to simply unmake her, but it was equal parts needing to maneuver the mundanes into getting rid of her and wondering what the effect of unmaking was on the bigger scale of things. Would there be ripples somehow? I had no idea, and if Harqil knew, they weren't saying anything beyond there being consequences to that action.

While we waited for Iaret's trap to spring, there were deals to make and a wedding to plan.

The formal negotiations weren't starting for another week and a half or so, but there were still pre-negotiations on location, security, and attendees. Keeya and House Mahan took point on that while the Darkwatch, temporarily headed by a reluctant but dutiful Darius, kept tabs on Sinclaire and the people she was positioning around the Triangle while the Ebon Guard kept a strong watch on me and Troy. Helia and House Azer took over the management and distribution of the local development funds and volunteer efforts, ensuring that we had good PR and success stories continually flowing.

There was something deeply satisfying in seeing how the new conclave arrangement was working out. Elves, djinn, and elementals working together to secure ourselves and our neighbors, in a way that hadn't been done since my mother was young millennia ago. After having to fight everyone in the territory for my right to be a player at all, and then fighting more to be listened to, I was captain of the team, so to speak. It wasn't ego, it was relief. I'd finally grown into the boots I'd been trying to fill.

In an effort to play nice with others—and set the stage for our plans to end Sinclaire—Darius forwarded a limited amount of information on the Sons and their illegal actions to local law enforcement, mainly focusing on the bombs they were making. To our surprise, Detective Rice not only accepted our help but actually did something with the information, organizing a unit to monitor the movements of the Sons of Seth in Raleigh.

"It was fucked up what you did, Finch," he said when I called to thank him personally for taking this seriously. "And I still don't like you or trust you. I will always think you and Monteague are unnatural sons of bitches. But..."

I waited when he trailed off.

Rice sighed heavily. "What they did here, the firebombing, it was too much like Philadelphia in '85. What *you* did was too much like Hiroshima and Nagasaki. You'll get your results, but I don't want that mess coming here to Raleigh. I have a community to protect and serve. If that means working with you people, so be it."

"I hear you," I said. "And I do want peaceful working relationships. So again, thank you for accepting the hand we extended."

"Just keep your freaky powers in their box," he said, ending the call.

Nearly all of the conversations I had with mundanes in the leadup to negotiations were like that. Grudging, resentful, angry acceptance that a new way of doing things was here. Venom spat at me and mine. Threats that were empty only because

I'd drawn the teeth from them myself. It hurt my heart, but I had to accept that I was effectively a conquering force who was imposing my will on a populace. These people hadn't come around to a change on their own time and merit—they'd been forced to it. That it was the choice that would keep more people, both Otherside and mundane, safe and prosperous in the long run didn't matter to them. They'd "lost" a war they'd started against a minority population, and it stung.

The ongoing skirmishes between mundanes and Othersiders in other demesnes and territories—skirmishes the mundanes kept losing now that I'd suspended the Détente and Othersiders were free to fight with their full magical strength openly and without consequences—only dug the knife in deeper. The United States had been founded on revolution, enslavement, and genocide, and those weren't working anymore for the formerly dominant populations. Not with their leadership in shambles and the reality of how soft most of modern mundane society was now exposed. Not with weres and vampires able to turn mundanes with abandon and bolster our numbers in a way we hadn't been able to ever before. Not with the fae and the djinn given free rein to play tricks, make bad bargains, and entrap any who trespassed. I doubted there was a single safe crossroads, cemetery, abandoned building, bridge, or circle of mushrooms in the country.

This was war. The only limits I set on my people were that the innocent be spared and that we act defensively. No pre-emptive strikes. No attacks on people minding their own businesses and communities. No attacks on hospitals, schools, morgues, essential services, or first responders. No movement against the elderly, the disabled, or children. Only limited action on confirmed anti-Otherside intel or retaliation to completed attacks by rule of three. It only took one rogue sorcerer breaking my edict and being publicly punished to get the rest in line.

Iaret had said magic seemed stronger when it came back into the world, and we all saw it now. This wasn't just the Twilight War; it was the Twilight Renaissance, a rebirth of magic, mystery, and the danger that came with it in the mundane world. Old myths and forgotten legends became frighteningly real in a way the mundanes could never have imagined when Maria's first vampire Reveal aired, and while monster fuckers reveled in it and human sensitives learned to accept themselves, many of the mundanes hated it.

So be it.

If mundane conversations and war status reports were painful, at least the situation in Otherside was better.

We sent Rio as a diplomatic envoy to the West Coast, delighting him with the honor and smoothing the path to full elven acceptance of an elemental High Arbiter. Terrence and Ximena sent their seconds to the Southwest Desert, Oscar went to the Gulf realm, and Giuliano visited coteries in the Northeast and Great Lakes. In the time it took to finalize the negotiation arrangements with the mundanes who would be coming at the full moon, Othersiders on this continent quietly unified and agreed formal treaties that stitched us into a nation stretching from Canada through Central America. Othersiders elsewhere in the world did the same.

Harqil took to their new job with relish, clandestinely informing those who were aware of the Court of Nightmares of my new position on it—and their role as my messenger—which was a major factor in the speed with which Otherside came together.

I left most of the work to the representatives and leaders of each faction, realm, demesne, and territory. Partly so that I could set the tone—that this was an alliance of equals, not a dictatorship, in which I would only do what my job title said: arbitrate.

The other part was so that I could make myself available for dress fittings and everything else necessary for an elven wedding and the various events that surrounded it.

Negotiations and general chaos or not, I refused to make Troy wait any longer for a ceremony and the next new moon was right before the summer solstice. Aside from our personal preferences, there was also the political consideration: if there were more elves who thought like Omar, having Troy formally married to me should go a long way to convincing them that I was "under control." It was bullshit subterfuge in the worst way, but news of the event would prevent any more attempted coups while we got negotiations done.

Troy, Allegra, Darius, and Noah, of all people, worked overtime getting everything planned and ready while Iaret maneuvered the Bureau and Duke negotiated for the spoils of DC with the Djinn Council, sowing chaos of a different sort that gave us the space we needed to get our shit in order. The wedding would be a simple event for a pair of royals with our standing, but Troy was happy with the plans. That was all that really mattered to me.

As he took point on those, I did what was necessary to secure our safety and standing in Durham. Although horrified by the events in Washington, DC, the politicians of Durham were, after some serious work, willing to strike a bargain.

In exchange for my complete restoration of the parts of Eno damaged by fire, a significant financial contribution to the city's economic development, and my promises to both assist with any environmental hazards as climate change worsened and allow continued recreational access to a limited area of Eno, the city and county of Durham, as well as the state government, would allow me to claim a chunk of the state park as private and sovereign Otherside territory and to live there indefinitely. Everyone here was clearly terrified of me, but they seemed to have decided the devil they knew—the one who'd been living within the Durham city limits and paying taxes almost her whole life—was better than risking some of the other big bads who'd surfaced elsewhere and might move in if I vacated my seat of power. That, and being able to stake a claim as the most progressive city in America, I guess.

I mentally wrote off the several millions of dollars that entire deal cost me as an asshole tax and resolved to do better in future. Being able to do so boggled my mind—I'd been worried about keeping my business afloat and my bills paid a few years ago—but elven money and investments were no joke, and the gods knew I'd paid enough and done enough to earn a fairly claimed slice of peace.

A further hefty but quiet financial contribution to the university got us a reservation at the botanical gardens for the wedding and a special dispensation to have a closed ceremony after dark.

I'd told Rage that I knew what I was fighting for. I'd owe any children Troy and I had everything I could give them and more for dragging them into this world. But I'd started this journey facing Leith Sequoyah to gain the strength to stand alone. To stand for myself. Then I'd wanted the strength to reclaim what'd been taken from me.

And now I was going to claim everything that meant to me. It was my turn to thrive.

A combination of elven wiles, djinn whispers, and Otherside vigilance got us to the day before negotiations with the humans were to take place without incident. Sinclaire was in the Triangle, plotting and building up her forces. We hadn't managed to infiltrate her operation directly. Her experiments on the elves in her keeping had allowed her scientists to take Verve's initial work to the next level and refined the working blood test to identify non-human proteins. But we had enough human sympathizers and captured, Aetherically reprogrammed Sons of Seth that we were able to watch from a close periphery even with Raleigh,

Durham, and Chapel Hill law enforcement playing their ends very close to the chest.

We knew Sinclaire was planning to strike the negotiations themselves...and we didn't tell the mundanes.

After so many losses in the Twilight War, they needed to think they'd had a win.

More importantly, I needed to see who stood where in terms of action, not in terms of paper and words.

Which was why I marched into a newly completed office park in Research Triangle Park looking every inch the queen, even if I'd left my crown at home, dressed in the black-and-gold designer everything Troy had selected with my king on my arm. Maria had offered The Umstead, but I didn't want to burn that location as Otherside-owned if anyone went digging. This office park had been on the verge of a grand opening, intended to compete with the one a few miles away, when the Twilight War had started and delayed the opening event. It was close to the airport, close to the Solari mansion, and most importantly not an obvious location for peace talks to occur—which would only make it more obvious that Sinclaire was overreaching and unreasonable when she eventually attacked.

The mundanes in the lobby, similarly dressed their best, quailed at my appearance, despite me and Troy tamping down on our power signatures. Of course, that might have been the triple triad of Ebon Guard shadowing us as bodyguards. Or it might have been seeing me in the flesh and realizing the imminent danger that put all of them in, my promises of peaceful intent notwithstanding. We'd refused to wear magic-nullifying cuffs or to require our people to wear them and had allowed the mundanes to come armed with guns—ostensibly as a concession but really because we knew the Sons and Sinclaire were close. That put the elves especially at risk, but only Troy and I knew that there were djinn watching for betrayal from the other side of the Veil.

Cold prickled over me at the hard looks we got. I'd known from Rice's comments and others that I was viewed as a threat, but knowing a thing intellectually was a different thing entirely to experiencing it after living most of my life playing a harmless null. Mundane security details took defensive postures, hands hovering over their weapons, and a few people crossed themselves.

It was up to me to calm things.

I picked out the most visible spot in the room and made my way there under the watchful eye of everyone who'd arrived first. As I looked around, I spotted not only local government—the North Carolina governor who'd had so much shit to talk a few weeks ago, the Durham authorities with whom I'd negotiated for the new arrangement at Eno, a handful of leaders from surrounding counties—but governors, legislators, and negotiators from other states within my demesnes as well. No one from the US federal government was present, not that that was a surprise. Given the flavor of the upcoming elections, I could work with this.

I passed all that I'd noticed to Troy. *Anything to add?*

I don't know if you caught it, but their scent is odd, he sent back. *Terrified, but laced with…hope? It's like a kicked dog seeing someone with food. They don't want to trust us, and at a base level, they don't. But they're hardwired to look to a hierarchy. We represent the most powerful faction in the room, so we lead that hierarchy even if we're not human.*

Interesting. I hadn't thought of humans that way before—hardwired to look to a hierarchy. Even if they were, Troy's notes about their scent said they'd resent having it shoved in their faces.

The room had fallen silent during our exchange, and Jo had arrived as well, positioning herself out of the way and taking pictures. I went on my toes to kiss Troy's cheek, which got me a curl of affection in the bond and a flick of his gaze my way before he returned to surveying the now-silent space.

"Thank you all for joining us," I said in tones I'd learned from Troy, low and quiet, inviting intimate conversations rather than commanding attention. Tones that forced others to strain to hear us and obliged them to pay attention rather than demanding their compliance. "I know the road here has been paved with intentions both good and bad and actions both helpful and harmful. I hope that in the coming days, we can find a way to end hostilities between mundane and supernatural peoples."

That broke the ice in a way. Nobody died. I wasn't sparking lighting and Troy was the picture of a doting if protective partner rather than a commando on the verge of violence. The mundanes' defensiveness eased, and we all made our way to the main conference room that had been prepared for talks.

I barely managed not to stiffen as it gave me flashbacks to the elven summit.

Troy pulled out my chair for me, every inch the gentleman and somehow managing to perfectly balance service to me as High Queen and Arbiter with his own power as King.

I sat, along with everyone else, with Troy seated to my right. Jo and the handful of other journalists present took their seats at the edge of the room. That had been a condition I insisted on, that these negotiations not occur in hidden rooms. All of this would be done exposed to the world.

The governor of South Carolina scrambled to speak first, invoking some prayer or other. Magic was real and the gods—plural—walked this plane twice in the last few years, but they were bound and determined to continue believing there was only one god and that he would intercede on their behalf.

Fine. No skin off my nose. I'd met a dozen gods or more at this point.

Unseen and unheard by anyone but me, Harqil giggled in the corner.

I didn't bother to rein them in.

The same governor ended his prayer with an attempt to steer the conversation. "These talks are aimed at ending the war between the God-fearing human people of America and the supernaturals. Despite the many injustices and grievous, cowardly attacks perpetrated by the lead Otherside representative, we're here to seek a resolution."

I let my eyebrows lift at that but only said, "Otherside is also seeking a resolution."

The governor's expression pinched in frustration at his failure to get a rise out of me. "Which presumably you'll secure by force if need be."

Calmly but firmly, I said, "That's not my intention, no. Nobody has sole dominion over the beings on this plane, whether human, Othersider, animal, plant, or the land itself. Not even me. That being said, you will all be in right relation with all else, or I will correct you. Preferably gently and verbally, but if all you understand or respect is force, then that's what I'll use. But I would like this to be the end of it. The end of this Twilight War." I paused to let that sink in then softened my voice. "We could let this be a turning point. We have a chance to do better for ourselves, our communities, and our peoples as a whole. I know some of you are asking yourselves, 'What if another bad thing happens?' but could we ask instead what it would look like if good things happened? If we chose to chain hurt and fear with love and build new futures?"

Governor Kerner sneered. "So, you're saying it was love that made you destroy our federal government?"

"No." I shook my head. "That was rage and pain and a feeling of loss so deep that I doubt I'll ever get that piece of myself back. I would never dare claim that was done in love. But it was also not love that moved hearts to attack Midday Moon in Durham for suspected witchcraft, or Claret in Raleigh for harboring vampires. It was not love that moved hearts to burn not only my home, but an entire forest and the lives and homes of other people living there, both supernatural and mundane. It wasn't just me harmed by those actions. It was all of Raleigh and all of Durham and beyond."

Several people reddened, either in anger or in shame, and some looked away.

"This hatred of Otherside hurts mundane humans as much as it does the supernatural members of our communities," I said after letting the uncomfortable silence stretch. "It led to actions that pushed us all past our breaking points. But in that breaking, we have a chance to build something new. Something better. I hope you'll stand with me in doing so."

I sat back and waited for others to speak. I'd said my piece, and I had to be mindful of the optics here, especially given the journalists I'd insisted on being here were from a range of political leanings.

Well said, my love, Troy sent. *Now we just have to hope they listen.*

Chapter 32

I t took a week of arguing, posturing, and deal-making to reach an agreement, a grueling process that I kept the pressure on to complete so that we could end this war...and, of course, be able to celebrate my wedding without the ongoing conflict hanging over our heads.

Through all of it, Troy and I sat mostly silent except to raise objections or put forth counteroffers. The mundanes seemed to think that our magic was in the words we spoke rather than an inherent force in our beings, and passive powers like Troy's expanded empathy were outside their comprehension, so we stuck to facts and simple statements that could be easily fact-checked or were undeniably fair.

And throughout it all, we waited for Sinclaire to make her move.

To my consternation and deep suspicion, she didn't. She just kept attracting Sons of Seth to her cause and bringing them to the Triangle. The conclave, Maria, and the werecat pride all made complaints about the number of combatants we were allowing to remain undisturbed in my territory, but I overruled them all.

This situation had a specific end. I would have faith and see it through.

An agreement was hammered out without a single twitch from Sinclaire or the Sons of Seth in the Triangle. We called it the Twilight Covenant.

Under this agreement, I would limit the combative use of my active powers on non-Otherside territory to actions explicitly requested to avert climate disasters in a hundred-mile radius from my location at the time of the request. Even agreeing to that much gave Troy fits—until I mentally pointed out that given a lack of definition on that point Otherside territory was anywhere I happened to be, given my power and influence, and that for now the mundanes lacked any real way to detect or measure magic if I wasn't turning a storm or mitigating an environmental disaster.

The agreement said nothing about how anyone else used their magic beyond not harming unconsenting mundanes, which fell under the old Détente anyway. The compliant would continue acting in agreement, and those who didn't give a shit would continue evading mundane attention.

The more things changed, the more they stayed the same. I wasn't about to be the kind of helpful that undercut Otherside, not when I represented all of us now. I'd do my best to rein in the most excessive abuses of Otherside power or require my fellow Arbiters to do so in their jurisdictions. But I wasn't going to hamstring my people or force them to go against their natures and needs.

In the end, it wasn't a perfect agreement by any means, and none of us were completely happy with it. For one, it was a patchwork of states and jurisdictions that would be a headache to track and enforce. We stood firm on equal rights for Othersiders under human law, which necessitated the nullification of the requirements laid out by the Bureau for Supernatural Investigation. That those requirements were at the federal level made no difference to me; they were unenforceable and unjust laws weren't worth following anyway.

I got the sense that all the mundanes really wanted was to go back to the way things were before the Reveals. They couldn't have that, so the agreement we hammered out was the closest thing to it. Most importantly, it would preserve peace and offer a starting point for other places to join or adapt.

It wouldn't solve anti-Otherside prejudice or prevent further attacks. Only choosing to do better going forward as individuals and societies could do that. But it established a common text we could all point to as what we were intending to do.

When it was printed up and signed, I forced my expression to stay neutral, even if my heart was soaring at this victory, however small and partial. We'd stood up. We'd fought. And we'd won, at least in a foundational way. Otherside had come together in the process, to an extent that we never had before.

A new day—a new future—was here.

I'd just stepped up onto the hastily erected stage and approached the podium for my turn to make a comment to the crowd of journalists and news crews now packing the parking lot when the Sight screamed.

Not for me.

For Troy.

Without pausing to examine that, I whirled and tackled him, throwing a wall of Air over us—one that twanged to my senses as a bullet lodged in it at the level of Troy's heart.

He rolled us, shielding me with his body.

"They were aiming for you!" My shout was muffled against Troy's shoulder as he tucked me under him. I struggled, trying to get him to let me go and get to cover. "Troy! I'm not the target. You are!"

The platform wobbled as the Ebon Guard poured into it, and I hurriedly expanded my shield, knocking over the podium in the process to make the microphone squeal. Troy let me go when we were surrounded by the Guard, only to haul me upright and propel me in the opposite direction we were supposed to be exiting the stage from to take cover behind a tree.

Another gunshot rang out, thudding against my shield again. Then another and two more, two of them followed by a cry from different throats.

I kept the wall of Air over us and let Troy and the Guard focus on keeping me safe while reaching with elemental senses. "Three bodies down," I said just loud enough for elven hearing to catch. "Mundane."

"Clear!" a male voice called. "Shooters down, one friendly wounded!"

Troy snapped an order in elvish for one of the triads to make a sweep.

"No," I said as the Sight twisted. "Everyone stay close. Something's not right."

The crowd parted enough for me to see Detective Rice was down, looking more shocked at who he'd shot than at having taken a hit himself.

Director Lara Sinclaire was also on the ground, gasping around a shot to the chest. At her side, a man dressed in a suit stared at the sky with dead eyes. They'd infiltrated the crowd to get close and must have been assuming their shared humanity would let them come in as heroes.

Iaret had done good work with her whispers.

While the mundanes panicked or buzzed, calling for an ambulance or praying to their god, I reached with the elements.

"There's more in the trees!" I hollered when I found them in the thin woodland ringing the building. I reset my wall of Air wider, around the politicians and the news crews as well as my people. "We're—"

Before I could say surrounded, automatic rifle fire exploded from the trees.

If I'd thought there was panic before, it was worse now. Screaming mundanes tried to flee, only to hit my wall.

"Troy, get them down!" I said.

The scent of burnt marshmallow flared as he roared, "Be still!"

Mundanes dropped, some more gracefully than others. Not all the way under—he must have pulled some of the strength I knew he was capable of with that spell—but they sat, quivering and staring with eyes wide as bullet after bullet hit my wall.

And still the hail of rifle fire continued.

Jo figured it out first and looked at me, pale but surprisingly steady. "How long can you hold?"

That drew the attention of the other mundanes to me, standing with my arms thrown wide, Troy in front of me, and the Guard arranged around us.

"We'll find out," I said.

I could have stopped this easily. But this had been exactly what we needed the mundanes to see: that the greatest threat to their lives was only me if *they* decided it would be.

Some of them, including both the governors of the Carolinas who'd been so hostile to me, scuttled closer, fighting Troy's maze to seek what they imagined was safety: proximity to the person holding a shield studded with the bullets that should have killed them.

The elves growled and lifted longknives defensively, until Troy barked an order in elvish to hold.

Sirens wailed in the distance, drawing closer rapidly, and a helicopter buzzed overhead—only to swerve as a rocket shot toward it.

Ishtar above, we were lucky they hadn't started with that. Sinclaire must have intended a targeted assassination and expected at least one or two of the people here to help her with it.

Troy, Sinclaire might have had another ally among the people in here. This was even more tightly executed than we were expecting.

Agreed. He spoke rapidly in elvish, and the Ebon Guard stiffened, looking sharply at the people trapped with us.

Jo, bless her, had even more courage than I'd given her credit for—or maybe the recent experiences had hardened her that much—and pulled out her phone. After a few taps, she said, "This is Jo Hernandez, reporting live from the Nexus office park in Research Triangle Park, North Carolina. We're under siege at the formal signing of a historic peace accord between state and local governments and the High Arbiter of Otherside, Arden Finch Solari." She tapped again. "As you can see, Ms. Solari is maintaining some sort of protective barrier, preserving the lives of not only her people but many humans. Director Lara Sinclaire and an unidentified man have been shot by local law enforcement, who is wounded himself. We need urgent support."

The scrape of a foot behind me made me twist to find one of Governor Matthewson's aides with a gun pointed at my head from a distance.

Before I could even think to redirect my attention to splitting a chord off into an Air punch, Vern Monteague threw himself at the man.

The gun went off.

"Shots fired inside the barrier!" Jo said.

Uri and an elfess I thought was named Sinéad leaped to support Vern.

Troy snarled a spell.

I stayed focused on keeping us all safe from the ongoing external onslaught.

The now-unconscious aide was zip-tied and dragged to the side, still breathing from what my magical senses told me.

Good. If they'd killed him, that's what the focus would be on.

Not good was the fluttery way Vern's blood was moving.

"He needs healing. Now," I said. "He has a minute at most."

It risked exposing an elven talent to the mundanes and opened us to a second attack if there were any other infiltrators, but I wouldn't lose a Guardsman if he could be saved.

Troy gave the order, and the scent of burnt marshmallow flared again. As the elves worked to save Vern, Troy said, "We've got vehicles incoming."

The emergency vehicles we'd heard approaching spilled into the parking lot, SWAT vans among them. Ambulances stopped slightly farther away, screeching to halts as police SUVs kept plowing onward toward the woods. Some took fire, but for the most part, the gunfire stopped.

"They're running," I said quietly.

"Maintain the shield," Troy replied.

I did, nowhere near strained yet and now fighting a surge of rage building in me. All I'd wanted was peace. Here was what they offered. I could track every one of the lives fleeing the scene. I could reach them with Water and stop the blood in their veins or Fire and tighten their nerves and tendons so much that their backs broke.

I could unmake them and all their hate.

Stay with me, Arden, Troy sent.

I shuddered, trying to find enough love in me to push the rage down. *I'm here.*

In the next ten minutes, it was over. The Sons were either captured or had fled the scene and were being pursued by law enforcement with K-9 units, a massive manhunt that had to be pulling in teams from around the Triangle.

When I dropped my shield of Air, thousands of bullets dropped with it, falling in a sparkle and hitting with tinkles that seemed too small and cute for how much thwarted death they held.

As EMTs sprinted for Detective Rice and Director Sinclaire, some of the mundanes I'd sheltered turned to stare at me.

"Why didn't you let us die?" Governor Matthewson asked.

I looked at the leader of my state and remembered him calling me scum. Rage flared in me again, and I closed my eyes in a long blink before fixing him with a steady stare and tilting my head.

"This is what it means to be an ally of Otherside," I said. "I don't like you. I don't like your policies or the things you've said and done, to Otherside in general or me in particular. I don't know if you had anything to do with your aide pointing a gun at my head while I was trying to keep us all safe. But we made an agreement that would give Otherside space to exist alongside mundane humanity. I honor my agreements."

I bit my tongue before I could add, "Now honor yours," and restricted myself to arching an eyebrow that I hoped would say it for me.

"Ms. Solari?" one of the EMTs called. "The detective is asking for you."

Troy led me over, keeping himself between me and the still-armed Detective Rice. Jo shadowed us, probably still livestreaming given police hustled over to stop her from getting any closer.

"Did you set this up?" Rice asked.

I shook my head. "No. We passed information on the Sons and Director Sinclaire's whereabouts to all local law enforcement just in case though. I know you want to see me and mine as the bad guys, Detective, but I've been honest with you from the start. I stand between y'all and the bad guys. Even when the bad guys are on y'all's side."

"You could have killed everyone here," he said doggedly.

I shrugged. "You could have let Sinclaire and her buddy take another shot at Troy. Or me."

"Guess we both did things we'd rather not have done today," Rice said after a long look at me and Troy.

I didn't grace that with an answer, completely unwilling to make any acknowledgment that the rage in me would have been happy to end more human lives if it meant protecting Otherside.

I controlled my emotions and directed my actions. Not the rage.

Not going forward.

Gasping paired with the skip-stutter of a failing heart pulled my attention.

I made my way over to where Sinclaire was dying despite the efforts of the EMTs, glaring at the police officer who tried to bar my path until he eased aside enough that I could make eye contact with her.

As though the sight of me living and unharmed was the last thing she needed, a vessel in her brain burst. She died with rage of her own in her eyes.

And I didn't feel a damn thing about it other than relief.

Behind me, Troy sighed. *They're going to make her a martyr. And they're going to say you had a hand in killing her, since you were standing here when she died.*

So be it. At least this way we know who and what they'll be rallying around.

I wandered away while the EMTs were still trying to resuscitate the bitch, going cold as I realized why she would have targeted Troy. *They figured out that they can't attack me head-on, so they went after you to try weakening me.*

More likely that the Eads pointed them that way, Troy sent back.

Either way, this puts you in danger.

And I won't have it any other way. Better I go down than you.

I closed my eyes and focused on my breathing to stop myself from glaring at him.

That was how he thought. How he'd always thought. Troy had been ready to die for me for years.

Besides, I felt the same way about him, and he knew it—even if he hated the idea.

As the chaos around us intensified with law enforcement, security details, and first responders all going into overdrive, I sat in the grass under one of the trees close to the building, waiting for the full import of the day to come crashing down on me.

The Twilight Covenant was signed. Its signatories had all survived the attack, thanks to me. Sinclaire, my greatest known enemy, was dead, and we had a plant in the hateful agency she'd headed. Jo's reporting might just have me coming out of this as a hero, which might at the very least add some nuance to the admittedly complicated picture I presented to the mundanes.

But most importantly, the future I'd fought so fucking hard for was in my grasp—and under my leadership.

Duke phased in just enough to catch my attention. When I clutched our callstone, he spoke through it in my head. "A bloodless victory, little bird."

"Not quite," I replied in a whisper. "But near enough."

"A new chapter either way. A different one to what Ninlil saw."

I couldn't help looking at him, even if it would look like I'd suddenly looked off into the distance to anyone else. "What?"

"The reason Ninlil was in Durham to begin with was visions of the future. A difficult and bloody one. An ending. The Wild Hunt was just the beginning of that end."

And so it had been. I'd thought that was all I needed to do—avert the Wild Hunt. But that had only led to a brief peace that was more the peace of denial rather than anything real. This time, I'd faced what I'd thought I could run from before. I'd taken the lead role center stage rather than playing understudy or crew. And I'd finally embraced all that I was, all that I could be, and all that could be done collectively.

My heart twisted and I blinked back tears.

Troy knelt beside me and rested a hand on the back of my neck. "What is it?"

I pressed my lips together and shook my head. *Duke's on the other side of the Veil. He said my mother saw an ending but not this one.*

Aloud, I said, "Did we change the course of the future?"

"You did. Both of you," Duke said. "For the better, I think, given this doesn't appear to be leading toward fire and blood. For now."

"All of us." I dropped my head into my hands as the weight of it all finally hit me. "We did it together."

Chapter 33

After all the stress and pain and death, it was finally time to claim my happy ending.

I stared at myself in the mirror in the prep room as Noah adjusted the spray of freesia nestled around my crown, still thunderstruck that it was finally the day of the wedding ceremony. The ceremony I was now dressed to within an inch of—or maybe an inch past—my life for, in a fitted gold gown that left both shoulders bare to show not just the Lichtenberg line scars and kestrel tattoo on my right shoulder but also Troy's bite marks, heavier on the left and including the mostly healed one he'd given me during the customary new moon hunt last night. I'd left the selection of the dress to one of Troy's personal shoppers with firm instructions and turned up for the fittings that were done at the Solari mansion, squeezed in between Triangle parliament meetings, calls with politicians both local and national about legislation or rebuilding work, discussions with Arbiters in other demesnes, and briefings with my legal team about various things I or Otherside as a whole had been accused of.

Somehow, I looked damn good.

The dress, which probably cost another small fortune that I refused to think about, hugged me close in the bodice and fell sinfully smooth from the hips down, the gold accented with black swirls that were almost dizzying when I moved. The circlet I'd worn for the elven summit in Virginia had been upgraded to a full crown, gold shaped into swirling zephyrs and studded with onyx orbs in various sizes. It matched the engagement ring Troy had given me.

I might have been a primordial Nightmare of an elemental now, but I'd always be a sylph in my heart.

"Stop fidgeting," Noah scolded as he twitched fabric here and there. "I just got the drape of the train perfect."

I did my best to stand still, too keyed up to be contrary for once.

I was getting *married*.

To Troy.

We'd both been cranky as fuck in the last few days. Didn't matter. The hunt last night had been wild and vicious and good for both of us, and we were finally *here.* Butterflies leapt in my stomach and nerves prickled. A small cramp twinged in my lower belly and was gone.

"Hekate save me." With another twitch of fabric, the vampire stepped back. "So?"

Allegra and Maria bracketed me, their attention critical in the mirror. The former grinned even as tears moistened her eyes. The latter nodded approvingly then smiled wide enough to show fangs as her gaze fell on my shoulder.

"I'm taking credit for awakening you to your biting kink. Troy owes me big time," the vampire said.

I flushed. "Look who's talking! I refuse to believe Allegra isn't getting hers in."

"Don't!" Noah slapped at Allegra as she laughed and opened her arms to hug me, then twitched the train again. "You'll ruin everything."

Allegra stuck her tongue out but crossed her arms over the front of her tux and kept her hugs to herself. "You look gorgeous, sister. And I'm just... This is better than I ever dared dream of for Troy. He—"

The scent of lemon zest cut her off as Duke materialized, wearing the lithe, young Black man that was his favorite shape but nothing near what Noah had dictated for wedding apparel.

Noah sighed irritably. "Black, gold, or crimson, djinni. Even you can remember that much, I don't care how old you are."

A shimmer rippled over Duke as his clothes changed to a trim red suit with a black shirt and gold accents, but he didn't otherwise acknowledge Noah as he looked me over with a keen eye. "You're even more beautiful than your mother," he finally said. "I don't know how, but you are. You're sure you want the elf bastard?"

"Be nice," I said, gentler than I would have if I hadn't caught the emotion in the pitch of his voice and the glimmer in his carnelian eyes.

He offered his arm. "Fine. But I will still say Quinlan would probably have tried thrashing me for handing his daughter to a Monteague. *Tried*, mind you."

That made tears swell in my own eyes. "Nah. He'd be okay with it, this once."

Silence fell as everyone gave me a moment to swallow down the memory of meeting my parents in a dream. My dad had been pleased about Troy.

This was a good thing.

A happy thing, even if they couldn't be here to see it.

"Let's go," I said when I'd blinked back the tears enough that I wouldn't ruin my makeup. "I want my elf."

"Of course you do," Duke grumbled as he made a shooing motion to the rest.

They hurried out to take their places, with Allegra splitting off to find Troy. Unlike mundane weddings, elven weddings had the bride at the altar waiting to receive the groom. As the last ranking female member of Troy's birth House, Allegra would be handing him over and signing the amendment to the claim paperwork, making him a husband and not just a consort and giving him more formalized power in the House.

I found the whole situation extremely uncomfortable—the contract still laid out the terms of my *ownership* of Troy, not just the terms of his service to me as queen as I'd been led to believe—but they both insisted it would keep him safe and give him room to move in elven society. He needed to do things his way to heal and enact reform, so all I could do was get out of the way and be a safety net if he needed one.

Those thoughts fled as Duke and I reached the front of the assembly in the gardens.

I approached barefoot, in the elven custom, and the grass was cool as I approached a vine- and flower-wreathed arch where Janae stood as officiant. The sun had just set, and the moon was on its way to following, leaving us in the gloaming surrounded by sparkling fairy lights and the scent of jasmine. A small fae ensemble played hauntingly beautiful music that ached with both power and yearning.

Members from every local faction were present, plus representatives from factions across the country and even a smattering of mundanes. Jo, now permanently assigned as senior Otherside reporter, snapped away from the side. She was the only press Troy and I had agreed to allow, and having exclusive rights to the wedding of the century was further solidifying her reputation and proving her range. We trusted her to paint the event in the right light—a moment for healing and peace, rather than frivolity while others suffered—so it worked out.

Janae offered me a reassuring smile as I reached my spot, and I tried to give her one back.

I wanted this. I just had never thought it would be mine, and it was hard to encompass the idea that I could destroy whole buildings and government agencies and then be in a beautiful wedding awaiting the appearance of the love of my life a month later.

Fortunately, there wasn't a long wait before the music shifted to something far more sultry.

Troy had warned me about it—that elven weddings were as much fertility rite as power brokering—but it still threw me for a heartbeat. This ceremony wasn't about romance for Otherside. It was solidifying dynasties, in every way. As long as Troy got what he wanted, it could be whatever it needed to be, as far as I was concerned. He'd more than earned it.

Allegra stepped forth and surveyed the gathering with a critical eye before turning to gesture Troy through the gauze draped at the end of the aisle.

My breath caught as he stepped forward. Not because he was dressed in an exquisite black tux with gold accents and looked as good as he ever had but because when his gaze found me, the bond stuttered, and he cast his eyes downward before flicking them back up to steal another look at me. From Allegra's tight expression, he was being bold, but that just made me grin.

There'd been a lot I hadn't been sure of in the last few months. Or hell, years.

This? Troy?

I was sure of him.

Everything passed in a blur from there, feeling not unlike the haze I usually experienced when we had really good sex. Aether wasn't in play, or at least not more than Troy's usual passive power, but I still felt kind of hypnotized. Like something was happening on a deeper level. I was surrounded by love and joy after a lifetime of isolation and fear. None of this felt real.

Another twinge tightened my guts. I brushed it off as nerves, too focused on Troy now standing opposite with an expression of hunger.

Words were spoken, the legal ones by Janae and then some ceremonial ones in elvish. I responded carefully but firmly with the words I'd practiced when it was my turn to do so. Slid a ring over Troy's finger, to a burst of relief and joy in the bond. Kissed him deeply enough that Janae cleared her throat. And then stood side by side with him, holding his beringed hand up high.

"This elf is mine, by the laws of gods and mortals," I said, scrambling to find the rest of the words I'd practiced. "He is sheltered by me. He is protected by me. And together, we build House Solari in blood and deed."

An oath not only to act in the House's name but to bring forth heirs in it...if I could cycle.

I'd wanted to give Troy his claim papers as a public gesture of where the House was headed, but he'd fought me on it. He still wanted the shield they represented a little while longer. So with those words spoken, I just smiled. "Let the celebration commence!"

Cheers rang out, echoing through the night.

Music and magic rose, all of it in good and fruitful spirits, and everyone moved out onto the grassy lawn to dance beneath the starry sky.

Terrence and Ximena laughed as they spun to the music. To my surprise, so did Val and Rio, the latter looking more than a little smitten, as Laurel, Sofi, and Naz watched them with wide eyes. Vikki and Ana had lightened up, their somber mood at seeing me again for the first time since they'd gone back to Asheville dissipating with the festivities. Mason was avoiding them both by sticking close to a mischievous-looking Lya, who was bantering with Duke and Iaret. Cade bent over laughing at something Mami Wata said, and the water fae hid her own amusement behind a glass of wine. Doc Mike stood with Noah on the edge of the crowd, out together in public for the first time, which was probably why Noah was grinning wide enough to show fangs.

So many people had come to see me and Troy happy. My heart was full.

I got my answer to why Darius wanted to leave the Darkwatch when he approached me and Troy when we took our first break in dancing, towing a dark-skinned woman with her hair in braids behind him.

"Brother, Sister...this is Rip," he said. "She's—"

"An undine?" I blurted out as I caught the shape of her magic.

Darius cleared his throat. "I was going to say she's agreed to be my girlfriend, but yes."

"A pleasure to finally meet you, Arbiter, King Troy," Rip said. Pleasure or not, she looked wary as hell, holding tightly to Darius's hand.

"The pleasure is mine." I smiled as Troy echoed me. "Welcome to the Triangle. You two should come for lunch soon."

She perked up. "I'd like that. I have a few things I hope we can discuss."

"Of course," I said.

They excused themselves, and Troy nodded. "I was right then."

"About what?"

"Just something he came to talk to me about. Alli sent him to an elemental collective when he was exiled. My guess is this Rip probably saved his life."

Before I could comment on that, Troy and I were mobbed by a crowd of happy witches led by Sarah, Will, and Cam, who were, from the look of things, already well into their cups. After them came a group of fae, led by Zanna, who pronounced a range of blessings upon us—some of which made me blush something fierce and had Troy struggling to keep a solemn expression as he expressed his gratitude.

Troy and I were just starting another dance when I finally figured out why I kept having those cramping twinges in my lower belly.

It wasn't nerves.

I'd had this once before, so long ago that I'd forgotten what it felt like until now.

"Oh fuck," I whispered.

Troy stiffened. "What?"

"I need the bathroom. Right now."

With a smoothness belying the sudden alarm in the bond, Troy spun us to the edge of the crowd. An Aetheric nudge from him limited interference to quick well-wishes, until Allegra caught up.

"What's wrong?" she hissed in a low voice.

"I don't know," Troy replied. "She—"

I didn't bother trying to explain, just hurried into the bathroom and into a stall. When I got the dress out of the way, I wiped and stared in shock at what I found on the paper.

I was cycling.

If I was human, this wouldn't have been as big a deal, other than it being my fucking wedding night. But I wasn't human, and this had only happened once in my life, a red flag of puberty that had never unfurled again.

Until now.

"Shit," I muttered. This explained why I'd woken up with a twisting, cramping pain in my lower abdomen and a splitting headache that I'd had to hurry and mute before Troy woke up and started worrying.

He'd been a little...*extra*...the last few days. Even more attentive and protective than usual. I'd snapped at him, and he hadn't been able to explain himself but had reined it in with a visible effort. And then there'd been the hunt yesterday, with both of us going beyond even our usual level of enthusiasm both in the hunt part and the fucking afterward.

I'd thought it was just wedding stress compounding everything else we were dealing with or another physical adjustment to my magical power increase.

Apparently, neither of us knew what an imminently cycling elemental acted or smelled like.

Troy, can you send Allegra in please? I sent.

The door banged open almost immediately.

"Arden," Allegra said, "what the hell—"

"I need a tampon or something." The words came out in a squeak, and I cleared my throat, still staring at the paper in my shaking hand. "Quickly. Please."

Silence met me.

"Allegra?" I hoped I didn't sound as desperate as I felt.

Her whoop brought Troy charging in, from the second bang of the door.

"What?" he demanded with a growl. "And why do I smell blood?"

"The Goddess is blessing your union, brother," Allegra said. Pure joy blended with high amusement to make her practically sing the words. "Stay with her. I need to go find—"

"Allegra!" I hissed. "Goddess fucking sake, can you just go?"

The bond went very tight then the walls went up as Troy's feet got closer under the divider. "Arden, is it true? Are you—"

"I'm cycling." I flared hot in embarrassment, not knowing what the fuck to do with this.

At that, he took a shuddering inhale. "You're cycling. Holy Goddess, you're cycling. On our wedding night."

Before I could figure out what to say to that, he laughed breathily and switched to elvish. Prayers of thanks, I could tell that much. From the sound of it, he was choking up as the words spilled from him.

I might have been flustered, but Troy seemed to be taking all of this as a dramatically good thing, not reacting with the embarrassment or disgust human men often affected when the topic came up. That was nice. That was fucking great. I relaxed as much as I could, given I was trying to make sure I'd caught it before it stained my dress. Ishtar preserve me, I hadn't ruined the damn thing.

Okay. I could deal with this.

I hoped.

What the hell did one do when, rather than handing shit, the Universe and the gods delivered a stream of good things all at once? All paid for in advance but all delivered?

"Troy?" I whispered.

"Je, cariñamí?"

"What did Allegra mean by the Goddess blessing us?"

"An elfess, especially a queen, who unexpectedly cycles or becomes fertile during the wedding days is traditionally seen as being blessed. The union with her elf in general but her in particular." He took what sounded like a calming breath. "It's taken as a sign that not only is the match correct but that the queen and her policies are divinely sanctioned and will bring abundance for her House."

"Oh."

Before I could figure out what else to say, the bathroom door swung open again, bringing a wave of party noises from beyond it.

"Got something!" Etain sang. Her pale hand and arm shot under the stall door, offering a small basket with an assortment of sanitary products. "Allegra assumed sharing the word of the blessing would be a good thing, so we had plenty of offerings. Fortunately, there are enough elves present with both good wishes and devout inclinations that they'd brought some of these as, like, a just-in-case or good-luck measure."

"Ishtar preserve me," I muttered, grabbing a tampon. Sanitary items as votives. Of course the fucking elves would think like that. Once I'd gotten myself sorted out, I emerged to find a small crowd gathered outside the bathroom door propped open by a pleased-looking Allegra flanked by a grinning Maria.

Every member of said crowd cheered at the top of their lungs.

I flushed so hot I thought I'd catch fire.

"All right," Troy hollered with a push of Aether. "We appreciate your enthusiasm. Go drink a toast to our queen and Arbiter."

The crowd dispersed slowly, with Maria and a few of the elves making loud and, from what I could tell, beneficently ribald comments in elvish as the door shut again.

Troy gathered me in close and pressed his forehead to mine. "I'm sorry for all that. It's just such a rare occurrence, and for it to be you and me... It's something truly special, Arden. Even if I can see now how it might be bizarre and uncomfortable to focus on a bodily function like that."

I squirmed a little, equal parts physical and mental discomfort, and Troy soothed the physical part with a wash of Aether through my nerves.

We stood in silence for a few more moments.

"You still wanna be a dad?" I asked when I'd found my courage.

In response, he dropped the walls in the bond.

Hope raged in him. Love. Desire. Gratitude. Everything I'd gotten a flash of when we were negotiating the new Houses and he'd said that having children with me would be a gift he'd be overjoyed to receive, pushed to infinitely higher levels.

"Yes," he said. "But only if you still want me to father those children. It's you, Arden. Only you that I'd consent to getting pregnant. That's not to put pressure on you at all. If you change your mind, then the matter is closed. I'm just saying... In brutal honesty, my entire life, I could never trust that the women who wanted me or the Houses they belonged to would allow me to co-parent. Or that they would protect a wildcard like me the way my mom protected me from Keithia. I want to be a father so much that I decided I'd rather not be one if it meant I couldn't be there to raise and protect my own child, whether potential oyëori or elemental."

"You want it even with the world on the knife's edge of tipping into hell?"

"The world is always on the knife's edge of hell for somebody. We just happen to have enough money and privilege to decide how much hell is too much and what resources we want to deploy toward dealing with it."

That hit me hard.

Troy leaned back and cupped my jaw to tilt my head up. "You are the most powerful being on this plane. You could protect them—protect our family—in a way that nobody did for you. If that's what you decide you want, we'll do it together. If it's not, this marriage still stands. I will be at your side until someone figures out how to kill us, and may the Goddess foil them in their efforts. All I ask is that you want this as much as I do or you tell me no."

I still had my doubts and worries, my fears and concerns about the whole thing. I was still afraid of being *that* responsible for another life, and I knew we were doing it for selfish reasons.

But as I searched in myself for the answer, the Sight, for once, didn't kick me.

It soothed me.

This was mine. This was for me. And all would work out as it should. In regrowing the forest at Eno, in making amends for the destruction I'd caused in word, deed, and money, I'd demonstrated that I was at least working toward balance. I was allowed to claim what I'd been denied: a family of my own.

Once upon a time I'd wanted the strength and power to stand alone. Now I had it and would use it to reclaim and protect what had been taken from me.

"Troy Solari, with your consent, I'd like to have your children."

From the fireworks in the bond and the way Troy swayed on his feet, all of the blood had left his head and shot considerably lower down in his body. He tried and failed to find words but finally managed to clear his throat and say, "My queen, it would be my great honor and pleasure."

We gave ourselves another minute to bask in how good that made us both feel before returning to our own reception, greeted by even more cheers, raised glasses, and saucy comments than before.

It looked like my new beginning was off to an unbelievably smashing start.

Buoyed by the elven reaction to my unexpected cycle into fertility and the hope I could sense in every corner of the venue, I made my way to the DJ stand and raised the glass of champagne I'd snagged on the way over.

"A toast to all of you. For sharing in this night and for believing the future can be better than the past. Not to mention for helping me create a future where I—and hopefully others—can start feeling safe enough to engender that future." I drained my glass, coughing at the bubbles. "And if you're still here in the next hour or so, I'll assume you also want to start a family. Or at least want to celebrate the way I will be, maenad magic and all."

I flushed as I said it. All of that was shameless in a way that I had never quite been on board with. But I was fertile for the first time in my adult life, and between my maenad magic and Troy's passive powers, it wasn't just me who would end the night in someone's bed.

The elves roared their approval. The vampires and fae weren't far behind, even as they scanned the room for blood donors and oath dealers. Even the weres looked hungry—not for death, but for candidates to turn, given I'd lifted that part of the Détente locally after consulting with Terrence and Ximena.

My bounty would be Otherside's. And that was exactly the energy I needed going into my happily ever after.

Chapter 34

The celebration lasted until almost dawn.

I was surprised that we weren't harassed by anyone, whether Otherside or mundane. If it weren't for the massive amounts of politicking, magic, and security involved in getting the event and the coming peace talks together, I would have been more concerned. But our remaining mundane enemies were still in a shambles and Otherside had been more or less appeased—or appropriately warned—by the magnitude of my actions.

Whatever the case, Troy was gently helping me out of my dress as the sun rose.

"Go to sleep," he murmured before kissing me. "An elven wedding is a lot even when there aren't a million other things going on. We can worry about the fun part in a couple of days."

When, presumably, I'd be out of the cycling part and into the part we were both more focused on. Otherside biology worked differently, even if we looked humanoid, and we were guessing we'd have a week, maybe two, for our first try. With the Twilight Covenant signed and no imminent threats, we'd be able to relax and make the most of it.

"I should shower," I mumbled, weaving on my feet and very much the opposite of sober.

Elven weddings were *wild*, and I'd swear that people *wanted* my maenad side to come out. My glass had never been empty and the magic had been so heavy my skin still tingled with it. Between elf and fae magic, we'd managed not to scandalize any of the humans trying to get photos from outside the event, but the ceremony had devolved into something half a step away from an orgy—and the human participants had been as caught up in it as the Othersiders.

I'd been alarmed when I'd noticed, but Allegra had pushed me back into Troy's waiting arms, saying something about needing a baby boom, and he'd spun me into another dance that had me laughing with a soaring heart.

"Cariñamí, you can barely stand." Troy brushed a curl from my forehead as I blinked up at him, tilting his head and smiling in the way he did when he thought I was adorable. "You can shower in the morning."

"Are they going to hate me?" I slurred.

A frown creased his brow. "For what?"

"Pulling them all into my magic."

"No, my love. As you were blessed by the Goddess, you blessed them in turn. It's a good thing. The correct thing. Especially since you warned them." He shrugged out of his jacket, his grin widening at the sharpening of my attention on him before he sobered. "A lot of elves have been worried about the lengthening gaps between cycles. If this—the pheromones and magic—jumpstarts even a handful of others, it'll be another lever I have to lift our agenda and keep you safe."

Elves were weird. All of them. Absolutely batshit.

But if that meant they wouldn't hate me for going maenad on them as guests, I'd deal with it.

"Love you," I said as I sat on the bed and then kept going, my head hitting the soft pillow with a light thump. "More than anything. And I'm glad you're my husband."

The thrill of pleasure at the word "husband" was almost enough to wake me up, but I fell asleep to him saying, "I'm honored you're my wife."

△▽△▽

A few mornings later, I woke feeling hungry. Not for food but for Troy. I was vaguely aware that it was earlier than I was usually waking up these days but that the moon had just risen, from a newly expanded sense of the world that I was still working to dampen to background noise again. Beyond everything else though, was the intense need for the man lying next to me, sleeping on with apparent ignorance that I was barely restraining myself from an aggressive wake-up.

That wasn't right. If he was sleeping, he couldn't confirm he was still consenting.

After a quick trip to the bathroom to confirm I was done cycling and splash my face in a futile effort to cool down, I stalked back to bed, still trying to stop myself from pouncing on him—only to find him wide awake and waiting for me, lying on his side propped on an elbow.

His nostrils flared as he took the scent in the room, probably not for the first time, looking me up and down as he did. "Given you look like you're hunting, is it... Are you—"

I gave in to my instincts and leapt for the bed, landing beside him and barely holding myself back from grabbing him. Yes, he had a breeding kink that I'd learned about in this very bed, but he'd also been used and abused by princesses and queens who wanted him to sire children on them. I couldn't—

"Arden."

I opened my eyes, not even realizing that I'd closed them and was practically panting.

Troy was on his back, one hand in a hesitant reach for me. "Do you still want this?"

"Yes. I just— I feel like I'm losing my mind. And I don't want to push you into a bad memory."

"You won't. I want this, with you. Come here."

My control snapped, and I practically threw myself on top of him, yanking the sheet from him.

He'd consented. He was *mine.*

I fell on him, unable to hold back my eagerness. Inhaling to take in his scent and intoxicate myself with it as I nipped at his throat and ground against him.

"Arden. Arden!"

I froze. Was this too much?

"You're not too much." Shame flared in the bond. "I just—I'm not going to last long, my love. I'm sorry."

I blinked, trying to figure out why that was a cause for shame.

Oh. Because he was supposed to serve me.

I didn't care. I just wanted him. Right now.

"Follow your instincts," I breathed in his ear. "And listen to your body."

"My body is about to explode."

I reached down and slid him into me, taking him deep.

Troy rewarded me by tilting his head back and squeezing his eyes shut. A growl-whine I'd never heard before escaped him, cut off abruptly with another burst of embarrassment.

Ooh. His control was even worse than mine just now.

This was absolutely delicious. It was always me pushed to the edge of control by him. Now something about me or the hormones or both was shattering the iron grip he held on himself.

I rocked on him, pinning him to the bed with a hand around his throat as he'd done so many times to me. "You want to please me?"

"Yes." He gasped the word between pants that grew shorter with each rock of my hips against his. "But I—"

"Then breed me," I whispered into his ear.

Troy swore in elvish and gripped my hips, holding me tight against him as the bond exploded with lust and he emptied into me. When he finished, he rolled us, keeping himself tightly sealed to me, and thrust a few times before stopping and burying his face in the pillow.

I have never been that fast. Not even when I was fifteen. The bond was a riot with his feelings about that: the ongoing embarrassment at his lack of control but also a wild disbelief that he'd just bred me while I was fertile and an instinctual thrill of triumph at doing so.

"I'll make you a deal," I said, still whispering. I didn't know why, but it seemed to work for him so I kept doing it.

What deal?

"If you promise to follow your instincts on how and when, you can have me however and whenever you want."

Elven stamina roared into play as he started hardening again at that level of consent and trust.

"Because Troy? I have a theory."

He pulled away just enough to see my face. "What's that?"

"I think part of the reason elven fertility is dropping is because y'all have too many rules about who can do what and when and how. I think the moon is more tied to it than you realize, given it's just risen, and I think bites—blood exchanges—might help."

Troy's mind spun dizzyingly in the bond at the thoughts that'd come to me with the combination of moonrise and the intensity and swiftness of what'd just happened, combined with his culturally frowned-upon habit of biting me any time I'd allow it in a moment of passion.

The bond was wide open, so he read the direction of my thoughts as quickly as I thought them.

I didn't expect him to laugh.

"If an elemental has figured out why elves struggle to breed—" Troy cut off in chuckles that made him jerk inside me in a way that set me on fire again.

With an approximation of one of his growls, I rolled my hips. "Shut up and fuck me."

"As my queen commands." Pure pleasure rolled through the bond and reverberated through us both as he suited action to words and moved.

Blood. Blood was part of this. I didn't know how or why, but it was.

Troy, twined into my mind as deeply as he was, caught the stray thought. Without stopping in his relentless motion, he dropped the sharp teeth and nipped the meat of his own palm then offered me that hand.

I took it and pulled. The wound wasn't very deep, but as a splash of rosemary and sage hit my tongue, magic flared.

"Bite me, Troy," I panted. "Now."

He didn't need a second invitation. Aether and his teeth sank into me, and magic spiraled again, so tight and hot that I came from the waves of pleasure it sent crashing through me. From his groan and the faster pace of his thrusts, it was hitting him as well.

Troy was always impossibly good in bed, but it was like the combination of pheromones and his own personal desires not only being set free but having a chance to bear fruit inspired him to new, almost frantic heights. He lasted slightly longer this time, and longer still the third, like he was having to relearn his body and mine on the fly. It was almost like the one time we'd slept together after losing the bond, right before the Wild Hunt, when Roman had abdicated and Troy and I were still new enough to each other that he was gonna try sleeping on the couch rather than with me.

Something about it made me even hotter for him than usual. I didn't give a shit for skill or anything. I just needed him.

Finally, both of us wore out. We stayed close to each other, falling into a jumble of limbs even as breath slowed and we fell asleep again.

△▽△▽

Twilight Covenant or not, there were still a last few skirmishes to end and some rogue individuals to bring to heel.

It was too soon to tell if Troy and I would be starting our family, but either way, it fell to me as High Arbiter to bring everyone in the jurisdictions that'd signed the Covenant into line.

The necessity of my direct involvement brought out a new level of uncompromising savagery in Troy; he wasn't about to allow even the possibility of his new dynasty to come under threat. Fortunately, nobody dared accuse him of ferality, not when I was directly threatened by some of the more powerful Othersiders on a few occasions.

Other than that, our diplomatic efforts had been so unexpectedly successful that I didn't even need to be present personally to bring an end to all the flashpoints. The elves, working under my authority, carried out political ops on both coasts, smoothing the path to functional and collaborative government between mundanes and supernaturals of all kinds. Vampires seized key placements in the financial systems and ensured the correct funds reached the right people—even when those people were mundane and especially if those people had been historically disadvantaged. The werewolves took responsibility for the military and police, while the smaller wereclans focused on community support. The fae and djinn provided cover with their illusions and binding deals, the witches provided shelter and healing where it was needed, and the elementals stepped forth for the first time since Atlantis and took an active hand in rebalancing environmental harms.

Tensions eased, money reached the people who needed it despite the absence of federal leadership, forces of order actually protected communities for once, those who needed healing received it, and those who deserved a comeuppance got that too. That wasn't to say there was some kind of utopia or that we'd achieved world peace or some nonsense. Both in the US and abroad, we still fought battles with those who wanted us or any humans who didn't meet some bullshit standard dead.

Rebuilding everything that'd been destroyed in the Twilight War would take time. Goodwill was still in short supply in many quarters, as was trust.

The Court of Nightmares had words for me as well, and I wasn't ashamed to live up to the role I'd inherited as I fought them off and told them to mind their own fucking business for a time while I fought for the plane I still belonged to.

But we had a tentative, fragile peace.

Which was how Otherside and mundane humanity managed to reach something resembling an equilibrium just in time for the July new moon.

The peace was still too new for me to trust that it would last, but Troy had mentioned that the first new moon after a wedding was special—and for us, it was, for more reasons than just the peace.

Having approved the architectural plans for our new home on the grounds of the old one, Troy and I stood at the spot at the center of the building space Ximena's people had marked out. My best guess was that it was where my old living room had been. The place that, while not what I'd consider the heart—that was the bedroom—was where Troy had kept me alive after Neith's test and formally thrown his lot in with mine. The place where we'd really become a couple, our goals aligning and our priorities shifting.

Where he'd chosen me over his birth House and unlocked the first step to a new future.

Yeah, my dad had been right in the Duat. I could have done it alone. I was a primordial elemental. A Nightmare.

I was Arden fucking Finch of House Solari.

But that new future could have taken many forms. From what Duke had said, my mom had seen that. From the prophetic dream Despair had sent, I could have achieved a future where I lived, all on my own—in every sense of the word.

This was the future I wanted.

My fingers twined in Troy's, our bare feet in the dirt that would soon support our new home. The wild possibility of new life sang between us. The open potential of the future stretched before us.

I bowed my head and squeezed my eyes shut, letting the salt of my tears drop from my cheeks to mingle with the earth.

At my side, Troy did the same before clearing his throat. "We should make an offering."

In wordless agreement, I drew the godblade I'd taken to carrying again from the sheath at my back and made a quick cut in the heel of my palm before passing it to Troy. He mimicked my cut and we clasped hands, squeezing to let our mingled blood drip to the earth.

"May the Goddess bless and protect this place," Troy murmured. "May She bless and protect us and our House."

"May we be blessed and protected," I said.

We stood facing each other with clasped hands until the wounds stopped bleeding.

Then I darted in and stole a kiss.

"Hunt me," I said.

The bond flared with heat. "Run."

As I did, the land seemed to come alive. It recognized this dynamic, the heat in it, the desire, the love.

So I ran—until I decided to turn the tables on Troy and chase him instead.

The bond stuttered with surprise as he caught my intention and skidded to a stop then immediately threw himself in a pivot and took off.

Elementals might be natural prey for elves. But sometimes even prey could get the upper hand.

Our hunt changed directions a few more times. We ended up facing each other in the clearing where our new house would stand, out of breath and wild.

This time, when Troy launched himself at me, I stood firm.

He tackled me to the ground and we rolled, wrestling until I was on top.

I snarled as I pinned him, daring him to keep fighting.

"You win, my queen," he gasped, equal parts laughter from the joy of fighting me and arousal from what might come next. "Claim your forfeit."

"All I want is you," I said.

"Then take me."

With a thought, I smoothed the ground under us. Then I rose and stripped, standing naked under the night sky on my land and feeling powerful in it.

That feeling reverberated down the bond, making Troy's breath catch. "You're a goddess."

"Not yet." I grinned. "But you'll be the first to know if that does happen."

Rather than making him feel insecure, all that did was make Troy even hotter for me. He sat up and stripped out of his shirt and pants before running his hands up my legs. "May I?"

I moved closer. "You may."

He shifted to his knees and buried his face between my thighs, steadying my hips with a tight grip as he worshipped me with his mouth. His tongue moved cleverly between my folds to circle my clit.

I tilted my head back to the sky, accepting what he wanted to give and I wanted to receive: pleasure and reassurance. Every moment of intimacy that'd passed during my fertility window had passed in a haze, a biological imperative as much as it was a choice.

This was a reconnection, and in it, I found the specialness Troy had spoken about. After doing so much for others and then losing ourselves completely in the cloud of hormones, this was *us*.

My climax rose.

Troy slipped two fingers into me, curling them against the tender spot inside me, driving me closer and closer to orgasm until—

I gasped then cried out as it rolled over me, letting my knees buckle as his hands shifted to indicate he could steady me before sliding down between them to straddle him.

"I love you," I said, kissing him and tasting myself.

Rather than answering, he nudged me up just enough to slide his cock into me in a single smooth motion that had me throwing my head back in pleasure. He rocked, thrusting upward, until I found enough presence of mind to match him.

"I love you too," he whispered. "Always and forever."

We moved together under the stars as orgasms rose in both of us. Then he dropped his teeth and reopened the cut in his palm. "Have me."

I took the offered blood, flashing back to the first day we'd fucked after I'd finished cycling, sensing that he was telling me something with this.

Whether we were successful this round or not, he was mine.

I pulled his head to the juncture of my shoulder and neck. "I'm yours."

Aether flared, sending us both into a feedback loop of pleasure as his teeth sank deep.

When we finally came back to ourselves, we lay side-by-side on the ground that'd eventually be our new home.

It would take almost a year to build, but I was okay with that. We had a place to stay and work to do in the meantime.

It was finally my turn, *our* turn, to have some peace—because instead of waiting for the world or anyone in it to give it to me, I was claiming it for myself.

For both of us.

Rage chained in love. Love building peace.

After spending most of my life in hiding, afraid of my true power and unwilling to do what was necessary to create space and safety for myself, I'd stepped up and into my gifts and forced the world to play my game.

And I'd won.

Now everything was mine for the taking, and I was going to enjoy it all to the fullest.

Starting right here, right now—and never stopping.

Want more?

This is the end of the main Shadows of Otherside series, but there's more to the world of Otherside.

You can get more Shadows of Otherside content in a few different ways:

- Read the spicy spin-off paranormal romance series, Otherside Heat (featuring Lya and Cade): whwrites.com/otherside-heat

- Read *Shadows and Honor*, a novella from Troy's point of view set between the Huntress Cycle and the Trickster Cycle: whwrites.com/shadows-honor

- Read *Deeper into the Shadows*, a novel-length compilation of bonus content from the perspectives of multiple characters: whwrites.com/deeper-shadows

Lastly, if you enjoyed this book, **please consider posting a review**, recommending it on Goodreads or BookBub, or telling a friend who might also enjoy it. As always, thank you for reading, and for your support!

Acknowledgments

When I published *Eternal Huntress* back in 2021, I thought that was going to be the last book in the world of Otherside. Three years and ten more books later, that was clearly not the case. But this time, I think I've gotten Arden and Troy to their happy ending. (Of course, there's the little post-series drabbles I jot down when they come to mind, but those are nothing resembling a book. The standalone I'm drafting now might be another story, but it won't be Arden and Troy.)

For everyone who has stuck around to the end, especially those who have read the spin-offs, left reviews, and recommended this series for others to find, you have my deepest and most sincere thanks. All of this started as an idea during the worst time of my life back in January 2016, and it's been wild to see that idea grow and transform into this series. That others have enjoyed it as well is something I'll always be grateful for.

To Cal and Stephanie, my beta readers, thank you for all your reactions and recommendations. To Jeni Chappelle, my editor, thank you for asking the questions that kept me thinking about how to push the books into a bigger and better story. To Pintado, my cover designer, thank you for the stellar covers that caught readers' attention. And to the friends and family who encouraged me behind the scenes, thank you for being my champions. For this book in particular, a special thank you to Dr. Lauren Anderson, who helped me figure out some of the nuances of the biggest scenes.

Also by Whitney Hill

The Shadows of Otherside series
Elemental
Eldritch Sparks
Ethereal Secrets
Ebon Rebellion
Eternal Huntress
Shadows and Honor
Tempered Illusions
Talion Rule
Temporal Gifts
Trickster Magic
Deeper into the Shadows
Twilight Covenant

The Otherside Heat series
Secrets and Truths
Curses and Faith
Menace and Memory

The Flesh and Blood series (as Remy Harmon)
Bluebloods

About the Author

Whitney Hill is an author and speaker. The bestselling first book in her Shadows of Otherside series, *Elemental*, was the grand prize winner of the 8th Annual Writer's Digest Self-Published E-Book Awards and a Finalist in the Next Generation Indie Book Awards. Her second book, *Eldritch Sparks*, was named one of the Top 100 Indie Books of 2021 by Kirkus Reviews.

When she's not writing, Whitney enjoys hiking in North Carolina's beautiful state parks and playing video games.

- Learn more, get in touch, or buy books directly from the author: whitneyhillwrites.com

- Get email updates: whwrites.com/newsletter

- Instagram: instagram.com/write_wherever